Maggie Craig was brought up in Clydebank and Glasgow, the youngest of four children of a railwayman father and a mother who worked in the typing pool of John Brown Land Boilers. Maggie was working as a medical secretary when she met her Welsh husband, Will, when he was doing part of his apprenticeship in a Clydeside shipyard, and she and Will subsequently sailed the world on oil tankers before settling in Glasgow and starting a family.

Maggie now lives in an old blacksmith's house in rural Aberdeenshire with Will and their two children. She is the author of DAMN' REBEL BITCHES, which tells the story of the women of the Jacobite rebellion. Her five previous novels, THE RIVER FLOWS ON, WHEN THE LIGHTS COME ON AGAIN, THE STATIONMASTER'S DAUGHTER, THE BIRD FLIES HIGH and A STAR TO STEER BY, are all available from Headline.

Praise for Maggie Craig:

'With this enthralling, entertaining saga, Maggie Craig shows once again she's on her way to becoming Scotland's queen of romantic fiction.' *Daily Record*

'A gripping and moving family story' *Scottish Sunday Post*

For more information about Maggie and her novels, please visit www.maggiecrai

MAGGIE CRAIG

The Dancing Days

headline

First published in Great Britain in 2004
by HEADLINE BOOK PUBLISHING

First published in paperback in 2005
by HEADLINE BOOK PUBLISHING

2

ISBN 0 7472 6527 5

Typeset in Bembo by Avon DataSet Ltd,
Bidford-on-Avon, Warwickshire

Printed and bound in Great Britain by
Mackays of Chatham plc, Chatham, Kent

HEADLINE BOOK PUBLISHING
A division of Hodder Headline
338 Euston Road
London NW1 3BH

www.headline.co.uk
www.hodderheadline.com

To everyone who loves to dance

and to my mother, Molly,
who loved Helensburgh

and remembering always
the warm and wonderful
Fiona McLaughlin,
who gave off light.

Acknowledgements

I SHOULD LIKE to express my gratitude to the following people:

Nicky Killen of the Mitchell Library, Glasgow, for working the scary microfilm copying machine for me.

May Mitchell of Strathclyde Police Museum in Glasgow, for giving me a comprehensive tour of the fascinating exhibits and answering my many questions on one in particular.

Sandro Nunziata of Buenos Aires and Clea Wallace and Paul Rous of Dudendance, for introducing my better half and me to the passion and mystery of the Argentinian Tango.

Elizabeth Casciani for writing her informative and inspirational *Oh, How We Danced! The History of Ballroom Dancing in Scotland*.

Mrs Janet McKie, née Craig (a.k.a. Auntie Jenny), for telling me of her days as a lady soldier in the ATS.

Ailie Scullion, Catriona Malan and Elspeth Beaton, for not minding at all about being accosted in a car park and saving me from geographical embarrassment as to what you can and cannot see from Helensburgh.

Elizabeth Sutherland for putting me right on some points of clerical and ecclesiastical terminology.

My fellow members of the Scottish Association of Writers, for a decade's worth and more of friendship, fellowship, mutual encouragement and laughter, and the SAW itself for allowing me to finish the first draft of this novel with the Clyde outside my window.

Harriet Evans, for her incisive and challenging editing.

Yvonne Holland, for her skilful and sensitive copy-editing.

Will, as usual, for everything. Especially this time.

Prologue

T HE WHOLE city was dancing. Or so it seemed. Everywhere you looked you saw people finding it impossible to keep their feet still and their toes from tapping. They weren't doing that only in the glittering *palais de danse*, which studded Glasgow like twinkling stars in the night sky.

In students' unions, clever, disillusioned young people kicked up their heels and kicked over the traces, cocking a snook at their elders and the horrors of the world those elders had made. Stamping their feet and shimmying, they laughed in delight when outraged parents and scandalised ministers condemned all dancing as lewd, immoral and shameless.

In spacious Victorian villas, Bright Young Things took equal pleasure in shocking the old, the religious and the staid. Then they lit up another cigarette and called for another cocktail.

In lavish art deco tea-rooms in Sauchiehall Street, middle-aged women, disappointed by their husbands, surrendered themselves to the smouldering passion of the tango: and made fools of themselves over the young men hired to dance it with them.

In tennis clubs in garden suburbs, couples who'd made it out of the slums before the Crash perfected the intricate steps of the foxtrot and the smooth glide of the waltz.

The people they'd left behind in the tenements danced

too. How they danced. At street corners and in tram queues, shipyard apprentices, office clerks, factory lassies and the thousands who had nothing to do all day but collect their dole gave themselves over to the exuberance of the charleston. They supplied the accompaniment themselves, belting out the irresistible and compulsive beat – pah-pah, pah-pah, pah-pah-pah-pah, pah-pah – as they went along.

Once the drudgery of the working day was behind them, young men and women spruced themselves up, polished their dancing shoes, put on their best clothes and took to the floor in search of fun, relaxation and romance.

Countless marriages started at the dancing.

People whose paths might otherwise never have crossed met at the dancing.

PART I

PART I

Chapter 1

December 1932

COULD THIS be what it felt like to drink champagne? Favoured, if the newsreels were to be believed, by Bright Young Things and dashing royal princes alike, that exotic and expensive drink had never passed Jean Dunlop's lips. Bubbles of excitement were coursing through her veins all the same, plunging from the top of her head to the soles of her feet before shooting all the way back up again.

She was here at last: at a real live dance in a real live dance hall. She was so excited she could hardly breathe. That tonight was Christmas Eve made it all the more special.

Most of the people milling around waiting for the dance to begin would be off work tomorrow only because of the happy accident of Christmas Day falling on a Sunday this year. The big Scottish festival was next weekend: Hogmanay. But Jean's mother had always liked to keep Christmas too.

Fighting the urge to glance just one more time across what seemed like the miles of gleaming wooden floorboards that separated the two genders, instinct told Jean to at least stop fidgeting. She settled for standing with her arms by her sides, her nervous fingers concealed by the generously cut folds of her frock.

She became aware that she was under scrutiny from her own side of the great divide. The peroxide blonde in the low-necked and sleeveless glittery silver dress and matching evening shoes was giving her the top-to-toe treatment. The young woman's eyes lingered first on Jean's long fall of fair hair before passing down over her dress to her shoes.

She murmured something to her friends, standing next to her on the edge of the dance floor. One by one, with that surreptitious glance that inevitably follows the instruction: 'don't look now but there's a girl over there . . .', each of them did exactly what she had done.

None of them tried too hard to conceal their amusement at what they saw. Once they'd had their fun they resumed their unabashed scrutiny of what talent there might be among the young men shuffling their feet on the opposite side of the hall.

Jean knew fine well what they'd been laughing at. She wasn't exactly dressed for dancing. Her sensible black leather lace-ups were much too sturdy, she wore no make-up, her hair was unfashionably long and her dress was an unmitigated disaster.

That started with its shade, a quite disgusting green, which did absolutely nothing for a girl with Jean's colouring. Its sludge-like hue neither complemented her blonde hair nor contrasted with it. The sickly coldness of the shade failed to highlight the warm peach of her complexion. To add insult to injury, the shapeless garment was a good two sizes too big for her and, with its demurely high neckline and wrist-length sleeves, unquestionably an afternoon frock rather than one you would wear to go out in the evening.

Jean squared her shoulders. She had known all of that long before she had summoned up the courage to come here tonight. That had taken her some time to do, even after the onset of winter and the certainty of short days and long dark nights. She'd had plenty of time to consider the possibility of wearing the brown skirt and cream blouse that suited her so much better, but after much deliberation she had rejected that idea. She might not know much but she knew you didn't put on a skirt and a blouse to go to the dancing.

You wore a dress. She was wearing the only one she possessed. Her shoes were well polished and her hair well brushed. Before she had come out, carefully and making sure both sides were exactly equal, she had scooped some of those bright waves back from her face. A pretty clasp secured them high up on the back of her head. She was neat, clean and presentable, and she wasn't going to allow some nasty little madams to put her off.

Jean cast a defiant glance in their direction. One day she was going to have dozens of pretty dancing slippers and scores of beautiful evening dresses. And, in the same way that her hair colour hadn't come out of a bottle, neither would her future wardrobe be made of tawdry and garish materials like the artificial silks those girls were wearing. Miss Jean Dunlop's clothes would be fashioned from the finest fabrics money could buy.

Quite how she was going to achieve this particular ambition was something about which she remained a little hazy. When it came to visualising those luxurious materials, her imagination was more than equal to the task. Lying on a dressmaker's table, ready to be turned into beautiful clothes, she could see those huge bolts of cloth so clearly she felt she could almost reach out and take them between her fingertips. There were heavy satins and crêpe de Chines in gleaming yellow and glowing red, ornate brocades in pink and purple and gold, soft-to-the-touch velvets in midnight blue and emerald green . . .

The band struck up. Head snapping round towards the drum rolls and crashing chords, Jean saw a man in a dark evening suit walk forward to the microphone, which rose like a black sunflower at the front of the stage. His fair hair was slicked back, a neatly trimmed moustache crowned his top lip and his clothes had obviously been cut by a tailor who knew his trade.

'Ladies and gentlemen,' said the bandleader, his smile a mile wide and his arms opening to the full extent of their reach, 'welcome! Before we ask you to take your partners for the first dance, we'd like to play a little number to get us all in the mood.'

Entranced, Jean gazed up at him and the musicians who sat behind him. There was a saxophonist, a trumpet player, a pianist, a banjo player and a drummer. Och, but was this not wonderfully, unimaginably better than straining her ears to hear snatches of music floating out through someone's open window?

She recognised the tune immediately: 'Button Up Your Overcoat'. A big hit when it first came out, it was still hugely popular. Lots of people played it on their gramophones.

Her foot was tapping well before the man in the beautiful evening clothes began to sing the words. It was impossible not to join in, impossible not to move along to the bouncy, devil-may-care rhythm. Experiencing for the first time the pleasure of watching and listening to real musicians, Jean wanted to laugh out loud with joy. There couldn't be anything wrong or sinful about this. There simply couldn't.

The first number came to an end and the announcement was made that the gentlemen should now choose their partners. A bolt of sheer holy terror struck Jean. What if nobody asked her to dance? What if her dowdy dress and old-fashioned hairstyle made her look like a schoolgirl and not the poised young woman of nearly eighteen she tried so hard to be?

The girls who had laughed at her clumpy footwear and unshingled hair would laugh even harder as they whirled past her, shod in their dainty little shoes and clasped in the arms of the boys who would undoubtedly ask them up on to the floor.

Bracing herself for the humiliation and the disappointment, Jean dropped her eyes to the wooden boards at her feet. Feeling the vibration as one half of the hall moved towards the other half with all the determination of an advancing army, she thought wildly about the bible stories with which she was so familiar. Perhaps the floor might open up in front of her like the Red Sea parting to allow the safe passage of the Israelites, and she could make good her escape. Maybe she should simply put one foot in front of the other, thread her way through the advancing hordes, and head for the exit . . .

'Are ye dancing, hen?'

She raised her head and found herself looking into warm and laughing eyes. They were blue, but not at all like the colour of the sky. These eyes were the same deep shade as the ink she remembered using at school.

Somehow she succeeded in stuttering out what even she knew was the traditional reply to the question the young man had put to her. 'Are y-you a-asking?'

His wide mouth curving, he cocked his head to one side. His black hair was thick and wavy and his teeth were very white. 'I'm asking.'

Jean took a quick breath. 'Then I'm dancing.'

'Good,' he said, 'I'd feel a right eejit staunin' here if you were gonnae turn me doon.' He extended his right arm towards her, inviting her to put her hand in his. His speech was rough and although his charcoal-grey suit was well brushed and pressed, it was also worn and shiny. Yet the gesture was both confident and graceful. He had a really nice smile too, open and friendly and a wee bit mischievous all at the same time. Spirits soaring, Jean allowed him to lead her out on to the dance floor.

The first dance was announced. 'A foxtrot,' her partner murmured, repeating what the band leader had said. 'You all right wi' one o' those? The footwork can be a wee bit tricky. If ye dae it properly, like.'

'I'm f-fine with a foxtrot.' She was nervous, but secure in the knowledge that she'd been practising the most popular dances for months: the foxtrot, the waltz, the quickstep and the tango – she knew them all. She transferred her right hand to his left and laid her own left hand on his shoulder.

With a little shiver of excitement and anticipation, she felt his fingers close about her own and his right hand come to rest halfway up her back. She was getting the champagne feeling again. She only hoped her palms weren't going to start sweating.

'I havenae noticed you in here before.'

Once again, she had to draw in a swift little breath before she could answer him. 'It's the first time I've been here.'

'Ah,' he said, 'that'll explain it, then.'

The band struck up again. Jean and the young man glided off, him leading her confidently away from the edges of the room. Within seconds Jean had tripped over his feet and her own.

'Sorry!' Horrified by her clumsiness, she snatched her hands out of his and sprang back: straight into the couple behind them.

'In the name o' God!' came an outraged young male voice. 'Would you mind looking where you're going?'

'Aye,' his partner snapped. 'If folk cannae dance properly they've nae right to be on the floor!'

Apologies tumbling out of her mouth, Jean turned round. The girl whose pretty face was made ugly by the scowl now contorting it was one of those who had laughed at her earlier. A deep and level voice cut through both Jean's apologies and the other girl's recriminations. 'Och, stow it,' said her own partner. 'We all had to learn sometime. Come here, hen.'

His hands were on her shoulders, bringing her back round to face him. 'Start again,' he said. 'Wait for the right beat, now.' He began counting them out, to help her.

For a few bars everything went like a dream. Jean might have known it was too good to last. This time he was ready for her, his hands tightening their grip even as she tried to loosen hers. 'The gentleman's supposed to lead, you know. No' the lady.'

The rebuke had been issued in a mild enough tone of voice. Jean bit her lip in embarrassment all the same. 'I know that!' she blurted out. 'I do know that!'

'It's no' a matter o' life and death, lassie,' he said calmly. 'Just remember to let me take the lead.'

She did her best. Her dancing only went from bad to worse. It all came to a nightmarish end when Jean somehow managed to achieve what shouldn't even have been physically possible. She trod on his right foot with her right foot.

'Ow!' he yelled, abruptly releasing her. 'Mammy, Daddy!' he exclaimed, peering down at her shoes. 'Are those pit boots you're wearing or what?'

Completely forgetting that she ought to look over her shoulder to check if there was anyone behind her, Jean stepped back. Only luck saved her from another bad-tempered collision. 'Sorry!' she said, her hazel eyes huge as she gazed up at him. 'I'm so sorry! Thank you for asking me to dance, but

I think I'd better go now. I'm really so very sorry!' Spinning round in a swirl of green frock and rippling blonde waves, she fled.

When she reached the ladies' room she allowed herself the luxury of a few tears. Then she splashed her face with cold water and surveyed herself in the mirrors set above the washbasins.

'Stupid, stupid, stupid,' she muttered. 'How could you possibly think you could learn to dance without a partner? You've made a complete fool of yourself, Jean Dunlop. You'll never be able to show your face in here again.'

She sighed and studied her reflection. Weeks and months of getting her courage up to come, and now she had fallen at the first hurdle. Quite literally. Wild horses couldn't have dragged her back out on to that dance floor.

A flash of grim humour bobbed to the surface. The Four Horsemen of the Apocalypse and their mighty steeds combined couldn't have dragged her back out on to that dance floor. Jean pulled open the door of the ladies' room, ready to scuttle to the cloakroom, fetch her coat and bag and get out of here as fast as her legs could carry her.

Smoking a cigarette, the young man with the inky-blue eyes was standing with one shoulder propped against the wall of the foyer.

Chapter 2

WHEN HE saw Jean he straightened up and took the cigarette from his lips. 'You a' right, lassie?'

Jean gazed at him in bewilderment. 'What are you doing here?'

'I'm waiting on you,' he replied. 'I thought we might have another dance.'

'Don't make fun of me,' she said quietly. She headed for the cloakroom, lowering her head in horror when she realised that there were more tears prickling behind her eyes.

Her erstwhile partner caught her before she was halfway there. 'Hey!' he said, wrapping strong fingers around her forearm. He moved his other hand so that the hazy blue smoke of his cigarette wasn't drifting past her face. 'I'm no' making fun o' you. Honest to God, hen. I wouldnae do that.'

There was something in his voice, some note of sincerity that made Jean lift her head and look him in the eye. Standing even more closely together than when they had been dancing – or, in her case, stumbling about the floor and tramping on his feet – she registered that he wasn't hugely taller than she was. Put her in high heels and the two of them would match up very well.

'Dance wi' me?' He might be rough-spoken, his fingers

hard and ridged and his palm callused, but his voice was very soft as he made the request. 'Please?'

Jean flexed her arm under his restraining hand. He loosened his hold immediately, and she took a step back. 'Why would you want to dance with a girl who practically crippled you?'

He laughed. 'I'll survive. And d'ye never look in the mirror, lassie?'

She stared at him. She wasn't used to compliments. 'You think I'm pretty?'

He cocked his dark head to one side, studying her. The gesture reminded Jean of someone, although she couldn't quite put her finger on who it was.

'Pretty's no' the right word for you. Your face is far too interesting to be called pretty.'

While Jean was wondering if 'interesting' might be a kind way of saying 'plain', he came out with another breathtaking observation. 'I'd say "lovely" was mair the right word. "Attractive", too. Definitely attractive. Especially when you relax a wee bit and smile. Instead o' looking as if you're going to your execution.'

Jean stared even harder at him, watching as he stepped over to one of the tall, free-standing chrome ashtrays, which stood like a regiment of soldiers around the wall of the foyer, and leaned down to stub out his cigarette. 'Well,' he queried, as he came back upright, 'are ye gonnae dance wi' me again?'

Jean pulled a face, mocking herself. 'I've got two left feet. Did you not notice?'

'I noticed.' Twisting the smoked end of the cigarette and inserting it into the packet that he had taken from the inside pocket of his jacket, his grin was as dazzling as his white shirt. 'Though I think it was the two *right* feet that did for me in the end. I'll likely bear the scars for life.' Putting the cigarettes away, he pointed one finger at her. 'But I don't think you've

14

really got two left feet. Your problem is that you've never danced wi' a partner afore. Or to music. You've been learning from some o' those wee charts you get in the newspaper and the magazines. The ones wi' black footprints on them that show you where to put your feet. Am I no' right?'

'I bought a book,' she admitted. '*Modern Ballroom Dancing*.'

'By Victor Silvester? It's a good book. It helped me when I was learning. Although I took a course of lessons too. A couple of years ago, when there was plenty of overtime and I had some spare cash.'

'The book's all set out very clearly,' Jean said, 'but it's still not easy trying to do it on your own.'

'Cannae be,' he said blithely. 'It is an activity made for two, after all. So why don't you try it again wi' me? Right now and right here.' He held his hand out in invitation.

'Och,' Jean said, shaking her head, 'it's very nice of you to bother, but I don't think—'

'Be a devil,' he said softly.

Jean looked into his eyes and realised that those wild horses wouldn't be necessary. She was desperate to try again. Once more, she put her hands in his. 'You're sure you don't mind dancing with a beginner?'

'I don't mind. We'll stay in the lobby for now,' he said as he took hold of her. 'We can hear the music fine. That's the important thing, ye know, to hear the music.' He corrected himself. 'To really *feel* the music.' He lifted his right hand off her back long enough to slap himself on the chest. 'In here. The heart and the guts as well as the feet. Do that now,' he instructed. 'Forget about the steps for the moment. Just feel the music. I know fine well ye can that, because I saw you doing it earlier. Before the dancing started.'

'It made me want to move,' Jean agreed, an odd little shiver running through her body at the knowledge that he had noticed her well before he had asked her to dance. 'Sort of instinctively. Not really thinking about it.'

He nodded his dark head. 'That's the best way. Allow the music to take you. Let it do the real leading, like. Relax into it. We'll no' go anywhere until we've done that. There's no hurry. We havenae got a train to catch. Just feel the music,' he said again.

All at once uncomfortably hot, Jean blurted out a question. 'Why are you being so nice to me?'

The only answer she got to that was yet another smile. It spread across his face in stages, curving first one side of his mouth and then the other before stealing into his remarkable eyes. Like the sun coming up in the morning, she thought, warming everything that it touches.

'Relax,' he said again. 'Nothing bad's gonnae happen to you. Feel the music.'

Jean did her best to obey that instruction. At first she found it difficult. Her concentration kept straying to what it felt like to be standing here with her fingers enveloped in his and her other hand resting on his shoulder. She was very aware too of his free hand as it rested lightly on her back. How odd it felt to be held in such an intimate embrace by someone you'd only just met, a virtual stranger. How nice it felt.

'Slow your breathing right down,' he suggested, his own breath warm against her forehead. 'Take control o' it. Then let the music take control o' you. Go with it.'

Jean's eyes were on his tie. Striped in shades of blue, it was fastened in a stylishly large Windsor knot. She focused her gaze on it, shutting out everything else but the glorious sounds being made by the band.

All at once she was there. Going with the music. Her partner's grip on her relaxed for the merest second before subtly tightening.

16

'That's good,' he murmured. 'Ready to start moving now?'

Jean nodded. 'I'll try and remember to follow your lead this time.'

'Glad to hear it.' There was a rumble of laughter in his voice. 'Pay attention to what my right hand's doing.'

For the next few moments Jean worked hard on learning the code being passed to her through the subtle movements of his fingers on her back: the pressure that meant *move towards me*, or the relaxation of that pressure that meant they were about to change direction and she had to step backwards. Knowing the movement was coming, she even managed to do that without falling over.

'You've got it,' her partner said. 'Without me having to spell it out, either. You're a natural.'

Jean gazed at him out of shining eyes. 'You really think so?'

For a moment he looked quite stern. 'I don't say things I don't mean. Pride myself on that, ye might say. You and me were obviously born to dance together, lassie. The name's Andrew Logan, by the way. Maist folk call me Andy. What d'they call you?'

'Jean.'

'Jean what?' he queried, continuing to propel them both around the lobby under the bemused gaze of the cloakroom attendant.

She hesitated. 'Just Jean. Would you mind if we left it at that for the moment?'

'Mystery woman, eh? Now you've condemned me to lie awake tonight wondering whether you're on the run after committing some heinous crime. Maybe you're wanted for murder. Or maybe you're an international jewel thief. Or possibly the agent of a foreign power plotting the downfall o' the government.'

Jean giggled. 'How about you? Do you have a guilty secret?'

'Me? I'm an open book. Although you are mixing wi' the riffraff o' Partick here, Just Jean. Born and raised on the wrong side o' Dumbarton Road. I bet you live up the hill. Still feeling the music?'

'Yes. And I do live up the hill but only because I'm in service at a house up there.'

'Where they like you to mind your p's and q's?'

'Why d'you say that?'

'Because you're what my mother would call well spoken,' he said, executing another neat change of direction. 'Well done, by the way.' This time Jean had managed to follow him round the corner of the foyer without stumbling and without the resulting need for a stop so she could regain her balance. 'What she would also call a "superior" sort of a girl. No' the kind who usually ends up as a skivvy.'

'How d'you know I'm not a lady's mind?' Jean queried, a little piqued by his all-too-accurate summing up of the position she occupied. If she was well spoken, she had acquired that by herself, maybe from all the reading that she did. The people she worked for barely exchanged the time of day with her.

'Your hands,' he said succinctly. 'They're no' quite as rough as my own. But they belong to somebody who has to work for a living.'

As Jean's instinctive attempt to withdraw those hands met with no success, Andrew Logan gave her another of his stern looks.

'It wasnae a criticism. Merely an observation. I prefer folk who work for a living.' He raised his black eyebrows in an expression of regret. 'Though I don't blame anybody who's out o' work. Especially these days.'

'But you're not idle?'

'No, thank God. I'm a coalman. Slump or no slump, folk still need to keep warm.'

Nodding in agreement, Jean thought that it seemed exactly the right sort of job for him. She could see him doing it: shouldering a bag of coal as though it weighed no more than a bag of feathers; exchanging racy jokes and cheeky banter with the housewives on his regular delivery round, his teeth more white and his eyes more blue against a face smothered in coal dust; standing between two tenement blocks and cupping one hand round his mouth to yell out the price of coal briquettes to the windows above.

'How come a lassie like you ends up in service?'

Jean raised her own eyebrows. 'Maybe my family fell on hard times.'

'Still playing the mystery woman, eh?' He released one of those work-reddened hands of hers, enabling him to strike the back of his forehead with his own in a dramatic gesture.

'I get it,' he said triumphantly. 'You're yon Russian princess who escaped the Bolshevik bullets when they massacred the Tsar and the rest o' the Romanovs.' He used his own temporarily freed hand to sketch her a curlicue of a bow. 'Pray forgive me if I have been too forward, Your Royal Highness.'

'You're aff your heid,' Jean said amiably.

'I dare say my sisters would agree wi' you there.' He took hold of her again.

'How many sisters do you have?'

'A hale coven o' them. Have ye noticed that we've now made several circuits o' this lobby and you havenae stood on my foot once? Ow!' he shrieked.

'Oh,' Jean said, one released hand flying to her mouth in a gesture of dismay. 'I'm sorry. I'm really so very sorry!'

Now he would definitely give up on her. He might well

19

come out with a few choice words too. He'd be entitled to. After that he would stride back into the hall proper and find himself a girl who knew how to dance and who wasn't going to kick her partner black and blue in the process.

Andrew Logan did none of those things. He stayed where he was, threw his head back and laughed. 'I spoke too soon there, eh?' He wagged an admonishing finger at her. 'One very important lesson you have to learn when you start dancing is no' to look at your feet. Nor your partner's feet either. It's a sure-fire way to trip up.'

'Where should I look, then?'

'At me.' His lips twitched. 'If you can stand to study this ugly mug.'

'It's no hardship,' Jean assured him. 'You're very good looking.'

He gave a quick bark of laughter. 'You're one o' a kind, Just Jean.'

'I'm sorry,' she said, wanting to kick herself. 'I don't think I'm very good at talking to boys.'

He reached for her again. 'You're doing just fine as far as this boy's concerned. You're doing just fine at the dancing too. All you need is a wee bit mair practice. When this number's finished we're going back into the hall. All right?'

She was Cinderella, the wave of her fairy godmother's wand transporting her from the drudgery of never-ending housework to the sparkling enchantment of the ball. She was Cinderella, spinning around the room in the arms of her very own Prince Charming. She was Cinderella, and it was as if she were dancing on air rather than the solid wood of the dance floor.

Over the next hour Jean somehow managed – with lots of help from Andrew Logan – neither to fall over nor to trip him up through two foxtrots, two quicksteps, one tango and one waltz. In the course of her voracious reading she had seen somewhere recently that horses sweat, gentlemen perspire and ladies gently glow. By the time the bandleader announced the last dance of the first half, she knew what a lie that was.

Embarrassed that her partner must also be aware that she was doing what only horses were supposed to, Jean blurted out, 'This is good exercise!'

'Mair fun than the Women's League o' Health and Beauty? How are your feet doing?'

'Ready to raise the white flag and surrender—' Hearing the bandleader announce the final dance before the interval, Jean interrupted herself. Clapping her hands together like a delighted child, she turned a beaming face to Andrew Logan. 'I *love* the charleston!'

He laughed. 'Let's do it, then. Take it away, Just Jean!' Holding her left hand firmly in his right, he spun her out into the patch of clear space that had opened up beside them.

A jewellery box. A small, square jewellery box covered in wine-red Moroccan leather. It had stood in the middle of her grandmother's dressing table and sometimes Jean had been allowed to play with it. When you lifted the lid it turned out to be a music box as well, with a little ballerina pirouetting on top of it.

Tonight she was the ballerina. Except that no graceful lady in white net and tulle ever danced anything so exuberant as the charleston. Jean kicked up her heels and threw herself into it. Spreading her fingers and keeping perfect time with the music, she drew little circles in the air. She made the vampish faces at Andrew Logan that the charleston always seemed to demand.

Now she really was glowing, revelling in the music and

exhilarated by the sheer pleasure of moving her body. I'm glad to be alive, she thought. *Och, I'm so glad to be alive!*

As the music crashed to its rousing finale, the dancers stopped dancing, turned towards the stage and gave the band the wild applause, appreciative whistles and foot-stamping their hard work and musicianship had earned them.

'You didnae need me to teach ye anything there, Just Jean!'

'My-mother-and-I-used-to-do-the-charleston,' she responded breathlessly, one hand splaying out over her chest as she recovered from the exertion. She cast him an anxious glance. 'Sorry if I got a bit carried away.'

'Don't apologise. It was fun watching you.'

Jean blushed and looked away, watching as their fellow dancers began to move slowly towards the bank of glass doors that led out into the foyer. Then, turning back to Andrew Logan with a quick, shy dip of the head: 'The skivvy's felt like Cinderella tonight. Thank you for giving me such a wonderful evening.'

He looked nonplussed. 'It's only the interval. We get to do it all again once we've got our breath back. Stand you a lemonade?' He waved one arm in the direction of the foyer. 'There's a refreshment room through there.'

'That's very kind of you but I'm afraid I've got to go now. Otherwise my coach is going to turn back into a pumpkin.'

'You cannae go home now,' he protested. 'You and me are only getting into the swing o' things. Can ye no' feel that yourself, lassie?'

Her eyes were soft with regret. 'I can. I really wish that I could stay. But I'm expected in by ten.'

'On a Saturday night?' His incredulity was obvious.

'I've got work to do when I go back.'

'No' much o' a night off, is it?' He ran his fingers through his hair, transforming it from sleek neatness into a mass of

22

swirling waves that shone under the brilliance of the overhead lights. As black as a raven's wing – wasn't that the expression?

'Would the folk ye work for no' stretch a point? Seeing as how it's Christmas Eve?'

'I very much doubt it,' Jean murmured, fighting an impulse to tell him why her employers stretching a point about her going to the dancing was likely to happen only some considerable time after hell froze over.

'Are they gey strict wi' you?'

Jean gave him a lopsided smile. 'You might say that. I really am sorry I can't stay any longer.'

'It's no' your fault if they're strict. Stop apologising. If there's nothing else for it let's go and get your coat and hat and I'll walk you home.'

'You don't need to do that.'

'I know I don't *need* to,' he responded. 'But I'd like to.'

'I'd much rather you stayed and enjoyed the second half.'

He turned his hands palm upwards and raised them in a questioning gesture. 'How am I supposed to do that if you're no' here?'

He was only being gallant. She knew that. A boy like him would hardly be interested in someone like her. Probably he'd recently broken up with one girlfriend and hadn't yet found another. She couldn't imagine it would be long before he did. She hadn't missed all the flirtatious glances being sent his way this evening, nor all of the girls who'd made a point of saying hello to him between dances.

As Jean opened her mouth to insist once more that she would walk home on her own the decision was taken out of her hands.

'Look out.' Andrew's gaze drifted over Jean's shoulder, his body stiffening into alertness. 'Trouble just walked through the door.'

23

Chapter 3

'DON'T LOOK round,' Andrew murmured. 'It never does to draw attention to yourself when half a battalion o' the Bruce Street Boys decide to grace us wi' their presence.'

'The Bruce Street Boys?' Taking her cue from him, Jean kept her voice low.

His was grim. 'Aye. Down from Temple and looking for a fight. Which they're undoubtedly gonnae get. There's a fair few o' Partick's own local warriors in here the night. You and me,' he went on, taking her hand and already beginning to pull her across the dance floor, 'will now gravitate towards the exit. Unobtrusively. But *swiftly*.'

She might have laughed at the comically dramatic emphasis he had given that last word, if her attention hadn't been caught at that precise moment by the flash of cold steel.

Jean gasped, and followed the razor's trajectory up from its owner's waistcoat pocket to somewhere not very far away from her face. Behind the vicious and gleaming blade the tall young man who wielded it was gazing down at her, his eyes cool and measuring.

She gasped again, and felt Andrew's fist in the small of her back, edging her towards the glass doors that led out into the foyer. Unfortunately the man with the razor was standing right in front of them. Jean found herself unable to take her

24

eyes off him. Or the vicious weapon he wielded.

'Nae offence, pal. She doesnae know the score.'

The tall young man looked at Andrew. He was smartly dressed, his dark suit and matching waistcoat a dramatic contrast to hair the same colour as boiling toffee. 'I don't fight wi' lassies.' His smile was as wide as it was unexpected, as charming as it was chilling. 'Or non-combatants.' He stood aside to let them pass. 'On your way, youse two.'

'Your cloakroom ticket.' The words were rattled out like rifle shots.

'What?' Jean asked, out of breath after being hustled at speed across the foyer. From the expressions on the faces of the lads who now filled it, none of them had come here to dance. Yet there was a kind of ghastly choreography in the way so many of them moved as one, pushing back the jacket fronts of their suits to expose the ivory-coloured razor handles sticking up from their waistcoat pockets.

Andrew held out his hand. 'In your shoe, is it? Hurry up, Just Jean!'

He'd guessed correctly as to where her ticket was. Catching his urgency at last, Jean hastily retrieved it and shoved her foot back into her shoe without untying the laces.

'What about your coat and hat?'

'Don't you worry about them.' Grabbing her things from the cloakroom girl, he shoved her towards the door out into the street. 'Up Byres Road. Now!'

As they clattered down the three long steps of the dance hall's entrance, he took a firmer grip on her belongings with one hand and extended the other to her. 'Fast as you can, Just Jean!'

They took Partick Cross at a diagonal trajectory, dodging two clanking trams travelling in opposite directions, both of their drivers ringing furious warning bells at this additional hazard they had to cope with on a frosty Christmas Eve.

Reaching the foot of Byres Road offered only temporary relief from danger. By the time Jean and Andrew stepped up over the gutter, the violence behind them had begun to spill out on to the pavement in front of the dance hall. It could only be a matter of seconds before it overflowed into the road. That would give the tram drivers a lot more to worry about than one jay-walking couple.

'Come on!' urged Andrew as Jean paused, clutching the developing stitch in her side.

'Just-a-minute!' she managed, unable to prevent herself from looking back across Dumbarton Road. What was going on over there was developing into a pitched battle, the grunts and groans of its foot soldiers echoing hideously through the darkness of the night. As Jean watched and listened, those grunts and groans were punctuated by the clatter of broken glass.

Shockingly loud, a piercing scream of pain rang out. Someone must have been cut by one of those awful cut-throat razors. Jean's stomach heaved. 'I'm going to be sick!'

'No' here you're no'. Hold on to it for thirty seconds! And run!'

They sped past a school. Heart pounding with fear, the sickness rising in her throat, Jean thought crazily that it looked as if the green-painted iron railings that enclosed its playground were rushing towards them rather than the other way round.

'In here,' ordered Andrew Logan breathlessly, pulling Jean round the curve in which the railings ended. 'Mind your feet, the pavement's a wee bit rough where this big tree's roots have broken through.' He threw the strap of her bag over the green railings and threaded her coat through them.

'Now you can be sick. I'll hold your hair.'

As soon as she was sure she was finished he insisted they keep moving, putting more distance between themselves and the spreading violence. Despite the protection afforded by the old tree, where they had been standing was in Church Street, directly opposite the entrance to the Western Infirmary's casualty department. The walking wounded from the fight were going to reach it sooner rather than later, and the chances of running battles erupting in and around the hospital were high.

'I think we'll be safe enough here,' he said, once they had reached the corner of University Avenue. 'Here, hen. Let me help you on wi' your coat. You're shivering.'

Jean shook her head. 'It's n-not the c-cold.'

He held her coat out for her anyway, and she obediently slipped her arms into its sleeves and began to do up the buttons. Her hands were shaking. She saw his eyes go to them.

'Never seen anything like that afore?'

'I h-have. I was t-terrified then t-too.' She had managed the buttons. Now she thrust her hands in her pockets to retrieve her gloves and knitted tammy. Stupidly, not thinking straight, she pulled the gloves on first. They made her all fingers and thumbs when she tried to put on the hat.

'Here,' Andrew said, taking the soft wool out of her unsteady hands. 'I'll do it.' He swung the hat over her head. Surprising her with the delicacy of his touch, he proceeded to tuck the little tendrils of hair that danced around her face in under the tammy. As though she were a child he was looking after.

'There,' he said. 'That's you. We'll no' bother wi' a jaunty angle the night, eh?'

His eyes narrowed as he stepped back to survey his

handiwork. 'You're looking a bit pale and interesting, Just Jean. Can I no' take ye somewhere for a wee cup o' tea?'

'I'll be all right.' She gave him a wan smile. 'I seem to have stopped stuttering, at least. No need to call an ambulance.' She glanced across the road junction at the large clock that hung above the door of a jeweller's shop. 'It's a quarter-past nine. I'd better take a tram along the road. Is that one coming now?'

Andrew swung round briefly to look up University Avenue. 'It is. I'm coming with you, though. To see ye safe home.'

'Och,' Jean said, backing away from him as she headed for the tram stop, 'please don't do that. If Mrs Fairbairn saw you I'd get into so much trouble.'

'Because someone saw you home on a Saturday night?' He shook his head. 'It's time you got shot o' these folk you work for, Jean.'

The tram was braking now, gliding to a graceful stop. 'I know it is. But it's not that simple, you know?'

'It never is. What age are you?'

She blinked at the sudden change of subject. 'Nearly eighteen.'

Andrew laughed. He had a wonderful laugh, deep and throaty and pitched halfway between a guffaw and a chuckle. 'How near is nearly?'

'My birthday's in April.'

The tram came to a halt. There were some people on the platform, waiting to get off. Jean stood back politely, allowing them the space to do so.

'I'm nearly twenty-two.' He laughed again. 'Although more near to it than you are to eighteen. My birthday's next Saturday. On Hogmanay.'

The last passenger got off and Jean climbed up on to the platform. Soon she'd be clanking up Highburgh Road, and

Andrew Logan would be walking back down Byres Road and she'd probably never see him again.

'Jean?'

She whirled round, wrapping her fingers around the vertical pole that bisected the entrance platform. 'Yes?'

'Look, this is probably no' the best time to ask ye this—' The bell rang and the tram began to move. 'Bloody hell! This is the *only* time I can ask you this! Excuse my French, by the way!' He was running, easily keeping pace with the tram as it trundled cautiously towards the junction with Byres Road. 'Tell me where you live! And when your next evening off is!'

'Clarence Drive,' she called back, 'and next Saturday! Oh, be careful!' For the tram was gathering speed now, sailing through the crossroads. Andrew Logan was still running alongside it.

'Meet me at the dance hall! There'll no' be any trouble there next week! That lot'll lie low for a while! I'll wait for you outside! Half-past seven!'

'What if I can't make it next week?' He was beginning to fall behind now. Holding on to the pole, Jean swivelled round so she could still see him.

'Then I'll wait every week until you can!' Now, at last, he was out of puff. He stopped and strode up on to the pavement. Bending at the waist, he slid his hands down to grip his knees before coming back upright again, his face alight with laughter.

'Would you wait for a month?' she shouted.

'I'd wait for a year, Just Jean!' He raised a hand in farewell. 'I'd wait for a year! And Merry Christmas!'

'Dead romantic,' came a rough female voice from behind Jean. 'But may I remind you, young lady, that City o' Glasgow regulations designate this mode o' conveyance as a tram caur, no' a balcony in fair Verona.'

The clippie, whose dark green uniform was filled to bursting point by a bosom of quite magnificent proportions, hadn't finished exercising her tongue. Jean could tell that from the expression on her face. Which was quite a feat when that face looked more like a rigid plaster mask than something belonging to a real live human being. The woman had half the cosmetic counter at Boots clarted on to herself.

Typical of her tribe – that's what Jean was thinking as she stood waiting for the punch line. Too much make-up, a sarcastic tongue, a big bust and a liking for decorating said bust with all manner of metal badges, official and otherwise, seemed to be a common trait among conductresses. The woman nodded a head covered in curls in a shade of red entirely unknown to nature. 'And yon eejit back there is no' Romeo, either.'

'How,' Jean asked with some dignity, 'would you know? I'll have a tuppenny one, please.'

Fingers curved around the large diamond-cut brass knob that opened the scullery door, Jean allowed her hand to slide off the chilly metal. As soon as she stepped inside the house it would be over. Out here all of the experiences she had brought back up the hill with her were warming and brightening the darkness of this cold night.

They were warming and brightening Jean's heart too, touching her lonely and hungry spirit. Her long-awaited and long-prepared-for adventure had more than lived up to her expectations. It had lived up to them a thousand times over.

There had been the wonderful music. It was echoing still inside her head. There had been the joy of finding her feet – in the most literal sense of that expression – and the joy of meeting the young man who had helped her do that. Jean smiled in the darkness.

Swinging her handbag bandolier-style across her chest, she walked forward to the edge of the drying-green. Its short blades of grass were turning silver as the frost took hold of them, but they were less slippy than the paving slabs at the back door.

She began to dance, trying out some of the steps she had used tonight. She whispered a name into the misty night. 'Andrew Logan.' She corrected herself. 'Andy.'

Andy of the inky-blue eyes and the dazzling white smile. Andy, whose quick wits had spirited them both away up Byres Road before they could be caught up in the violence. Jean's smile became a frown.

The gang-fight had terrified her. Memories and emotions she'd much rather not have revisited had come flooding back. They dated from the year she and her mother had spent in a damp single-end in a filthy and run-down tenement in Dumbarton. The street had been one of the Clydeside town's roughest.

Trouble from the local gangs on Friday and Saturday nights had been a regular occurrence. Midweek evenings had also seen more than their fair share of drunken brawls. After the first occasion on which the window of their ground-floor flat had been shattered by a badly aimed brick, Alison Dunlop and her daughter had retreated at the first sight or sound of trouble to the box-bed they shared. It was the furthest away they could get from the street outside.

Jean could remember sitting in the innermost corner of the high bed, her knees drawn up and Alison's skinny arms wrapped tightly about her quivering shoulders. It was a horrible memory. Everything about that year had been horrible. Especially its legacy. It must have been then that the tuberculosis had crept into her country-bred mother's lungs.

Jean took a deep breath and gave herself a moment. Young

31

though she was, she had already learned how dangerous it was to dwell on bad memories. Doing so was like knowingly walking deeper and deeper into boggy ground. In no time at all you could find yourself stuck fast in the quagmire, mired for days in old sorrows and old unhappiness.

Much better to acknowledge the treacherous marsh was there before striking out resolutely for the higher and the drier ground. Especially when that higher ground held a new set of memories. Happy ones. Exciting ones . . .

Jean shut her eyes, the better to view her mental picture of Andrew Logan. She could imagine she felt his hand, solid and strong on her back, its warmth once more penetrating the thin material of her frock. She could imagine she felt his fingers. Strong and confident, they curled themselves firmly around her own. She could imagine she heard his voice, shouting after her as she stood on the platform of the tram car: *Meet me at the dance hall! I'll wait for you outside! Half-past seven! . . . And Merry Christmas!*

Somewhere behind Jean and off to her left, in the big old trees that surrounded nearby St Martin's church, an owl hooted. Her eyes snapped open.

Startled, she gazed for a few confused seconds at the dark and looming shape of the large Victorian house in whose back garden she stood. Then she came down to earth with a bump so forceful she wondered why nobody had flung up a window, stuck their head out and demanded to know what the hell the noise was.

Except that no one in this house would ever have used even such a mild swear word as *hell*. She was standing in the back garden of St Martin's Manse. It was home to the Reverend Ronald Fairbairn and his wife, Elizabeth.

The Reverend Mr Fairbairn was famous for three things. Firstly, he was an eloquent and charismatic preacher.

Secondly, he was a staunch upholder of that most rigorous and unbending branch of Christianity: the one that insisted that men and women must live according to God's Law, their lives governed by an unwavering belief in the literal truth of the word of God, as given to mankind through the pages of the Bible.

This belief led naturally to the minister's insistence that all Christians must lead an unshakably moral and upright life. The world was a decadent and degraded place, full of sin and an affront to its Creator. It was every Christian's bounden duty to fight the good fight, resist temptation and speak up against that sin wherever it reared its foul and disgusting head.

The third thing for which the Reverend Mr Fairbairn was famous was his outspoken opposition to what he considered one of the worst sins of all. Dancing. Via the medium of his public speaking and his frequent newspaper articles, his trenchant and outspoken views on the subject were known well beyond the boundaries of his own parish.

They were well known closer to home too. Especially to his young maid-of-all-work, the humblest member of the small staff that saw to the needs of him, his wife and the numerous visitors to the manse. That maid-of-all-work who'd spent this Saturday evening engaged in the activity her employer abhorred above all others.

Jean swallowed hard, and once more gripped the cold metal door knob. Now all she had to do was go in there and hope she hadn't broken the eleventh commandment. *Thou shalt not get found out.*

Chapter 4

'THERE YOU are at last,' the parlour maid said crossly. 'I thought I might have to end up setting the morning-room and dining-room tables myself before I go home.'

Coming into the kitchen from the scullery, Jean glanced at the clock that hung on the kitchen wall next to the door leading through to the rest of the house. She didn't bother to point out that she was back in at exactly the same time she always was on a Saturday evening.

'Get your apron on, Jean,' said the cook. 'There's plenty of work to be done before we get to our beds tonight. Did you have a nice time with the girls?' she added absently.

'I've had a lovely evening, thanks.' Jean lifted her grey overall down from the peg behind the door. Wrapping it about herself and tying its strings around her slim waist, she stepped over to the big deep sink set under the tall window overlooking the garden. She lifted one of the upturned tumblers standing on the thick wooden draining board and stuck it under the swan's neck of the gleaming brass tap.

She was thirsty, but the action also had the benefit of hiding her face from both Cook and the parlour maid. As far as they knew, Jean had spent the evening with a group of housemaids in the area, who had become friendly with each other.

Being economical with the truth rather than telling a downright lie about where she'd really been tonight had salved Jean's conscience, but it hadn't made her any less worried that she might somehow give herself away. She couldn't believe that the excitement simmering away beneath the surface wasn't showing in her face. Anne Reid, the parlour maid, had sharp eyes, a nasty nature and an inclination to gossip. Jean couldn't believe that she wasn't going to notice there was something different about her.

Sipping her water, Jean turned and leaned against the rounded edge of the deep porcelain sink, striving for nonchalance. When she saw that both the cook and Anne were bustling like demented bumblebees around the tea trolley, which stood next to the kitchen table, Jean's small sigh of relief made the water below her lips bubble. Swivelling round to rinse out her glass and place it back on the draining board, she pulled a face at her own reflection, comically elongated in the shining surface of the brass tap. She'd been daft to think that anyone in this house might be interested enough even to notice that there was anything different about her.

'For goodness' sake, Jean,' snapped Cook. 'Get on with your work!'

The older woman was always irritable on a Saturday. Small wonder. The manse kept the Sabbath.

Mr Fairbairn's position on the subject was uncompromising. Since the Lord had toiled for six days and rested on the seventh, that imposed on man the obligation to do likewise. No work could be done on a Sunday, neither a bed made nor a dish washed. Allowed for reasons of economy to die down and go out during the week, the fires were kept in overnight so they didn't need to be relaid and relit on the Sabbath.

As far as possible, the tables were set in advance and no

food could be cooked either. Sunday's meals were always eaten cold, and the fact that tomorrow was Christmas Day was going to make no difference to that. As far as the Reverend Ronald Fairbairn was concerned, Christmas was as much of a pagan celebration as Hogmanay.

The compressing of forty-eight hours worth of chores into the time available within a mere twenty-four wasn't easy. The cook had to prepare two sets of meals on a Saturday, not to mention baking double the amount of both plain bread and the cakes and scones and gingerbread required for two afternoon teas and two suppers. Man might well keep the Sabbath, but woman had to work twice as hard on the days on either side of it to enable him to do so.

Jean's day had also been full. All of her days were, but Saturdays were worse than most. Her three hours off in the evening were a mere interlude.

She'd been downstairs by half-past five this morning, starting as she always did with the fires. After dealing with that messy chore she'd repaired to the kitchen to wash her hands and arms and eat a quick bowl of porridge. The remainder of the morning had been spent sweeping and dusting and beating carpets.

She'd spent the afternoon up to her elbows in water and washing soda, scrubbing away at cups and plates and twice the usual number of greasy roasting tins and sticky baking trays. No wonder her hands were red and rough ... and that observation had sent her thoughts winging straight back to Andrew Logan.

Jean's eyes briefly fluttered closed, a wonderfully warm feeling enveloping her whole body. Who was she trying to kid? Her thoughts hadn't left Andrew Logan since the moment he had first asked her to dance.

He was back in her mind's eye. Andy of the inky-blue eyes

and the dazzling white smile. Andy running alongside the tram car as it crossed Byres Road. Andy asking her to meet him at the dance hall next week—

'The tables, Jean!' The sharp voice jarred like chalk being dragged across a blackboard.

During the week, laying the tables was a task that fell to Anne Reid. So Anne could get off as soon as she'd finished serving supper, Jean was graciously allowed to do it on Saturday nights. The older girl spent Saturday and Sunday nights with her family, returning to the manse on a Monday morning. It was always a relief when she left. A thoroughly unpleasant young woman, she seldom lost any opportunity of reminding Jean of her own lowly position.

As she did now, pushing past the younger girl where she stood loading cutlery from the drawer of the big kitchen dresser on to a wooden tray. Lifting down the huge two-handled teapot, which was a necessity of life in this busy manse, Anne brandished it at her. 'Make sure you do the tables properly. I'll be coming to check on you before I leave.'

'I do know how to set a table,' Jean muttered under her breath.

The parlour maid was already returning to the stove and the boiling kettle. She didn't expect Jean to answer back. No one in this house expected Jean to answer back.

She'd been so young when she'd arrived at the manse. Not long past her fourteenth birthday, she'd also been painfully shy, more than a little lost, extremely unsure of herself and badly missing her mother. Hardly capable of saying boo to the proverbial goose.

That was almost four years ago now. She had grown and she had matured. Lonely and largely ignored unless she was on the receiving end of a telling-off, she'd done most of that growing-up on her own. No one in this household had noticed the changes. They were there all the same: growing stronger every day.

It was five minutes to midnight and Jean was drooping with tiredness. Tiptoeing through the draughty corridors of the manse, she closed the door of her room behind her and sank down on to the edge of her bed. A heartfelt groan of thankfulness escaped her lips. Halfway through, it transformed itself into a huge yawn.

Her last job of the day had been tending to the fires in the morning room, drawing room and dining room. She had raked the coals and gingerly carried all three of the hot ash-pans in turn outside to empty them. After replacing them under the grates, she'd made several more trips to the chilly outside world for coal, replenishing the fires and the brass coal scuttles that stood next to each of them. The job wasn't over until she'd swept and washed the tiles of the hearth and polished the scuttles back to their normal gleaming state.

Tomorrow she could look forward to listening to not one but two of the Reverend's interminable sermons. Her attendance at both morning and evening service at St Martin's had never been a matter of choice. Oh, goody.

All those trips to the dustbin and the coal bunker had made Jean's arms ache almost as much as her feet. For the past two hours the latter in particular had been exacting their revenge on her for what she had put them through today. The pain was so intense she delayed removing her shoes for a moment merely to prolong the wonderful anticipation of the exquisite pleasure she would get when she did.

She undressed most of the way, took her nightie out from under her pillow and pulled it on over her head. Standing up and smoothing it down over her hips, she put the light out and opened the curtains before she took off her shoes and stockings. She tugged open the laces of the heavy black shoes, eased her feet out of them and let out a sigh of sheer bliss.

After that she rolled down her stockings and plucked them from her toes, unhooked her suspender belt and threw the whole lot on to the upright chair that stood in the corner of her room.

She climbed into bed and sat gazing out of the window. The moon was waxing, noticeably bigger than it had been on the previous night. She couldn't remember if that was a good or a bad omen. Both her mother and her grandmother had been full of lore about that sort of thing. Jean had soon found out that even the most harmless of superstitions weren't tolerated in this household.

Given that the entire life of the manse and its occupants revolved around the worship of someone you couldn't see or hear and whose existence you couldn't prove, Jean thought that was a bit rich. Wasn't religion itself one big superstition?

'You'd better keep that opinion to yourself, Miss Dunlop,' she murmured, her lips twitching. 'Otherwise you'll be out on the street without a reference.' Her lips settled into a deeper curve. 'Or maybe God Himself will prove His existence to you by smiting you down with a thunderbolt.'

Pulling the covers up to her waist, Jean considered the indisputable fact that if God did exist, He hadn't yet felt the need to administer such a punishment for her blasphemy.

He hadn't done so when she had sat in church Sunday after Sunday nursing rebellious thoughts. Not even when she had silently wondered what sort of a supposedly wonderful and compassionate Being required His people to approach Him in such fear and trembling. Not even when she had struggled to understand why the sin of pride was so awful, yet

God himself had to be praised to the skies by the self-described miserable sinners who worshipped him.

So far God hadn't apparently felt the need to punish her for breaking any of the Fairbairns' rules either. The minister's wife had made those clear to Jean when she had first arrived at the manse. Those rare moments when Elizabeth Fairbairn spoke to her now usually involved an issuing of reminders about them. Like Moses coming down from the mountainside with the Ten Commandments graven on tablets of stone.

On her regular Tuesday afternoons off Jean might go for a walk or to the Art Galleries at Kelvingrove or to a respectable tea-room to meet girls of her own status and situation. On no account was she to enter an Italian café, a picture house, a dance hall or any other place of 'cheap entertainment'. Those were the words the minister's wife always used. 'Cheap entertainment'. They were always spat out as though Mrs Fairbairn had a bad taste in her mouth.

On Sundays the restrictions were worse. Only the walk was permitted. If Jean wanted to pass the long boring hours by reading, she had to restrict herself to the Bible or the collections of sermons and commentaries on scripture, which lined the walls of the minister's study. So far she'd managed to resist the temptation to ask him if she might borrow one of the weighty tomes.

Last April, unable to resist the spurts of rebellion that had shot to the surface on her seventeenth birthday and refused to go away again, Jean had spent several consecutive days off breaking all of the rules in turn. She'd drunk coffee in an Italian café, seen a matinée at the picture house and joined the local library, smuggling back a selection of books she knew would be disapproved of on weekdays as much as Sundays: romances and detective stories and tales of high adventure. She'd been working her way through the library's stocks ever since.

She'd have to admit that Mr and Mrs Fairbairn were right about one thing, though. As the minister constantly reminded his flock from the pulpit, one small sin definitely did lead on to more and bigger sins. It was watching musical films up on the screen – debonair gentlemen in dark evening clothes swapping witty repartee and sharing romantic moments with lovely women in gloriously frothy dresses – that had really made her want to go dancing.

Jean's stomach lurched. If the minister and his wife ever found out where she'd been tonight she'd be for the high jump. They might very well throw her out on to the street without a reference. Did she dare go again next week, or was she going to have to leave it for a while?

She chewed her lip and thought about it. Sometimes she thought that what she really wanted was to get the sack. At least then she'd be free. Free from having every aspect of her life controlled, from being paid a pittance, worked like a dog and dressed in hand-me-downs Mrs Fairbairn chose for her out of the clothes donated by the congregation for redistribution to those in need.

She'd also be without a roof over her head. This house wasn't home – Jean never thought of or referred to it as such – but it was all she had known for the past four years. At the very least she was clothed and well fed and safe. She might choose not to dwell on that year in the rough street but that didn't mean the memory of its horrors went away.

Jean shivered. One of the mental pictures that always came back to her when she did reluctantly think about that place were the rats. Sleek coats. Tails like coiled whips. Bright, cunning and intelligent eyes. The way that they moved. She could visualise them now, fluid as water as they slid round

41

corners and swarmed over rubbish piled up in filthy back courts. She and her mother had often gone hungry during that year. The rats had always managed to find something to feast on.

Jean dreaded ending up somewhere like that again. As she might do if she were dismissed from here. The savings she'd made from her paltry wages wouldn't exactly pay for palatial lodgings while she looked for another job. What luck would she have finding another job without a reference, anyway? The economic slump meant that there were hundreds of people looking for work. Employers could pick and choose.

Nor did Jean have any relatives who might take her in. Orphaned young himself, her father had been killed in the war. The grandparents she'd known and loved were also dead.

Her grandfather had been a shepherd on a big farm in the hills between Helensburgh and the western shore of Loch Lomond. His death a few months after that of his beloved wife had inevitably meant Alison Dunlop and her daughter leaving the tied cottage to which Jamie Colquhoun's job had entitled him.

'I'm all alone in the world,' Jean said out loud, half serious and half making fun of herself.

No, you're not. Not now.

The little voice was inside her head. It made her jump all the same. Startled, she gazed up once more at the moon.

'He just fancies you,' she told herself. 'Probably fancies loads of girls. All he's looking for is a bit of fun.'

Fun. She could be doing with some of that herself. She was seventeen years old and she wanted bright lights and pretty clothes and to go to the dancing with a handsome boy with flashing eyes and a ready smile. Pulling the sheet and blankets up over herself, Jean slid down the bed. She took one last look at the moon before she closed her eyes.

'Wait for me next week, Andrew Logan,' she murmured. 'I'll be there.'

Her last thought before sleep claimed her was that on Tuesday afternoon, when she went to Byres Road, she would buy herself some nice scented hand cream.

As Jean gazed out at the moon, Andrew Logan – who had taken the *very* long way home – was extracting his key from the lock of the two-apartment tenement flat he and his family called home.

'Is that you, son?' called a voice from the front room.

He curled his fingers round the edge of the door and spoke softly into the darkness. 'Aye, Ma. Ye can go to sleep now.'

'Did you have a nice time at the dancing?'

'Grand. I'll tell ye all about it in the morning.'

'There wasnae any trouble?'

'No,' he lied. Time enough for her to worry about the gang-fight if and when some old biddy told her about it tomorrow morning when she went to the kirk. 'Good night, Ma.'

He walked through to the kitchen, standing for a moment in the doorway to allow his eyes to adjust to the gloom. That way he might manage to pick a course through those of his sisters who shared this room with him without tripping over any of them and earning himself a sleepy curse.

Screened by the big old clothes-horse, which was never free of drying laundry, he slept in front of the window. The shirts and vests, and the skirts, blouses and dresses that vastly outnumbered them, gave him, the only boy in the family, a modicum of privacy.

That precious asset was often invaded by his youngest sister, Chrissie, reading a book by the torch he had given her for her birthday two years before. Sneaking behind the clothes-horse was her way of avoiding her big sisters' complaints that they needed their beauty sleep, not to mention the blood-curdling threats that if that wee swot didn't switch off that bloody torch pronto, she was going to get well and truly thumped.

She was there again tonight, fast asleep with an open book clutched to her skinny, little girl's chest. Andrew plucked it from her relaxed grasp and held it closer to the moonlight spilling in through the window. *German Irregular Verbs*.

He bestowed a fond smile on his sleeping sister. Only Chrissie would think a topic like that made for entertaining bedtime reading. He found the folded sheet of paper she always used to mark her place, closed the book over it, laid it on the floor and scooped her up into his arms.

'Back to your own bed, pet,' he murmured.

She barely stirred during the transfer. As he pulled the covers of the pull-out bed up over her, her eyelids fluttered open and she asked the same question their mother had posed. 'Did you have a nice time at the dancing, Andy?'

'A great time. As a matter of fact, Chrissie,' he whispered, knowing from past experience that she wouldn't recall this conversation come the morning, 'I think I might be in love.'

He went behind the clothes-horse screen, stripped down to the vest and underpants in which he slept and lay down on his own shakedown. His wee sister had warmed it up nicely for him. He could see the moon through the window, a great yellow orb shining down on the slate roof of the wash house and the outdoor lavvies. He thought about Jean Dunlop and his hand drifted down his body. He was already hardening.

What the hell did he think he was doing? Chrissie and his

other sisters were only feet away from him. With a soft moan of frustration, Andrew brought his hand back up to his chest.

Served him right. He shouldn't be thinking about a girl like Jean that way anyway. That she was as fresh and innocent as an April morning was obvious. It shone out of her.

Sometimes he felt as dirty as the bags of coal he delivered. Not because of the two serious love affairs that he'd had. Both of those had run their courses – fires that had burned fiercely and then guttered out, ending by mutual agreement and in sadness, not bitterness. The memories of trysts in the back row of the pictures when hands and mouths had roamed free were still sweet.

Reflecting on his dealings with those local girls, who were very accommodating, if not exactly discerning or exclusive, was a lot less comfortable. The lassies were always more than willing but the sweaty and fumbling encounters he'd had with them had always bothered him afterwards.

Of course *afterwards*, Andrew thought, putting his hands behind his head. You don't give a damn about the morality of it at the time. Not in the heat of the moment. He knew what Robert Burns had said: 'A standing prick has nae conscience.'

If he'd been taking a short cut home through some shadowy close or back court and stumbled across any lad doing with his sisters what he'd done with those girls he'd have knocked them into next week. 'Bloody hypocrite,' he murmured. 'That's what you are, Andrew Logan.'

He lay there and wondered if he was too old for Just Jean. *Nearly eighteen.* He could hear her voice in his head, see her earnest little face as she tried to convince him that she was all grown-up. He smiled at the memory.

Och, but she was so lovely . . . That glorious hair, the soft hazel eyes, the bloom of her skin. Lovely lips too. How would you describe their colour? He thought about that for a moment and came up with dark sugar pink. Beautifully soft. Crying out to be kissed.

When he caught himself mentally undressing her, peeling off that shapeless sack of a dress she'd been wearing and wondering what else about her might be a dark sugar pink, he groaned again and did his best to elevate his thoughts.

It was a struggle, but he managed it by dint of the adaptation of a favourite daydream. That was the one where he won a fortune on the football pools and bought a huge house – somewhere out in the country or maybe by the sea – where every member of the Logan family could have a room to her- or himself. He longed to give his mother the respectability she craved. He longed to give her so much more.

Now and again he poked gentle fun at Bella Logan for how much she worried about winning and retaining the good opinion of their neighbours. In reality, knowing only too well what his late father had put her through, he understood exactly why those good opinions mattered so much to his mother.

Lying there indulging in the familiar fantasy of buying that lovely big house, he realised that tonight the dream had altered slightly. Now his castle in the air had a room in it for Jean too.

Just Jean. He didn't even know her second name. If she didn't come to the dancing on Hogmanay he'd go up one side of Clarence Drive and down the other, searching for every bell with the name Fairbairn beneath it. Once he found it he'd take himself round to the kitchen door and think up some excuse for needing to see the housemaid. Then they would take it from there.

A girl like her would have to be wooed and courted. Walks in the park. Wee silly presents. A train ride to Balloch and a picnic by Loch Lomond. A little hand-holding. A few stolen kisses. She would blush, and pretend to be angry with him; but she wouldn't really be angry. . .

She was such an intriguing mixture, bold one moment and blushing in shy confusion the next. Hidden depths, he thought dreamily. Definitely hidden depths.

He fell asleep dreaming of planting gentle little kisses on her beautiful mouth.

Chapter 5

JEAN GLANCED for the umpteenth time at the little wristwatch she'd bought herself for her seventeenth birthday back in April. Twenty-five to eight. Andrew Logan was late.

Standing on the very end of the three long steps outside the wide entrance doors of the *palais*, she transferred her gaze to the broad expanse of pavement that lay between those steps and Dumbarton Road. Both it and the street beyond it were glistening with frost.

Struck by the beams of light radiating down from the tall lampposts that edged the pavement, tiny gleaming points of light dotted both surfaces. They looked like sparks glowing and crackling in a log fire.

Not a great description, Jean thought, narrowing her eyes and thinking about it. The sparks thrown off by log fires were warm and welcoming. The frost gleaming on the pavement and the road was as cold as charity, a visual manifestation of the merciless December chill. Like a stealthy army creeping up on a sleeping enemy, it was silently but swiftly seizing control of the night air.

Well shod and warmly clad though she was, the bitter frost was also mounting an assault on Jean's feet. She didn't need to be able to see her toes to know that they had turned white. She had been standing still for fifteen minutes, of course. That was asking for trouble on a night as cold as this one.

She'd arrived at twenty past seven, knowing fine well she'd be too early but unable to contain her excitement any longer. Simmering inside her throughout the whole of this long week, it had reached boiling point well before Saturday afternoon.

She looked at her watch again. Twenty to eight. Now he was ten minutes late. Her head snapped up, responding to the sound of rapidly approaching male footsteps.

'Rotten swine given ye a dizzy, hen?' The man who'd made the comment chortled, and went on his way.

'Very amusing,' Jean mouthed after him. *A dizzy*. Short for disappointment. What people called it when someone didn't turn up for a date. Ten minutes later, she came to the reluctant conclusion that the horrible man had been right. Andrew Logan had stood her up. Numb with disappointment, she flexed her stiff toes, moved her feet, which now felt like the blocks of ice you saw on a fishmonger's marble slab, and headed for the edge of the pavement.

As she crossed Dumbarton Road she was thinking that she'd been dizzy: in the sense of being daft and naïve. Probably Andrew Logan had gone home last week and had a good laugh about her. She would have been a funny story to tell his workmates when he'd arrived at the coal-yard on Monday.

She could hear him, making a joke of it. Making a joke of her. 'Aye, the lassie couldnae dance for toffee. Kept stepping on my feet wi' her big tackety boots. *And* she was practically sick all over me!'

Jean bit back a sob and quickened her step. Feet beating out an angry tattoo on the pavement, she turned into

Hyndland Street. She hadn't thought Andrew Logan was like that. She really hadn't—

'Just Jean! Hang on!'

She whirled round so fast she almost lost her balance on the increasingly slippy pavement. As she hastily shifted her weight from one foot to the other to regain it, she saw that Andrew appeared to be in much the same predicament. He was doubled up and hanging on to a lamppost. He must have hurtled round the corner of Hyndland Street at a rate of knots.

Despite the cold he wasn't wearing an overcoat or a hat, only a mustard-coloured muffler knotted at his throat, the lapels of his suit jacket turned up around it. Straightening up, he unhooked his arm from the lamppost, gave himself a little shake and came running up to her where she stood under another streetlight.

He took the last few yards at a glide, sliding along a lengthy frozen puddle with his arms outstretched to keep his balance. 'I doubt the weans have been polishing this one well today!'

'You'll fall!' Jean shrieked.

'No, I'll no'. Have ye no faith in me, woman?' He flexed his knees, directed his body in a graceful arc and came to a halt in front of her in exactly the style of one of the glamorous ice skaters you saw in the newsreels.

'You're a veritable Sonja Henie.'

He acknowledged the compliment with a swift inclination of his dark head before coming out with succession of tumbling apologies. 'I'm sorry I'm late. Very, very sorry.' He sounded a little breathless. Or maybe nervous. 'Can you forgive me for it, Just Jean?'

'Only if you've got an awfully good excuse.' She had folded her arms and her lips were pursed but her heart was singing at the sight of him. Like his own, her words were as visible as

50

they were audible. The breath on which they were expelled rose like wisps of white smoke into the freezing chill of the night air.

'I've got a *bloody* good excuse.' He raised his dark eyebrows at her, then pulled an apologetic face. 'Sorry for swearing in front o' ye, lassie. I havenae had a very good day.'

Jean frowned. 'What's happened?'

'I've lost my job. I was paid off this morning.'

'Och, Andy,' she cried, laying a gloved hand on the sleeve of his jacket, 'I'm so sorry! Would you like to go somewhere and talk about it?'

All at once his deep voice was savage. 'No. I got my cards at midday and I've done nothing *but* talk about it ever since. That's why I'm late meeting you. Family conference.'

'What *would* you like to do now?'

'Take you dancing.' There was something in his eyes, a mixture of emotions she couldn't quite decipher.

Don't make a fuss about his bad news. Obeying the instruction her brain flashed her, Jean posed a matter-of-fact question. 'Why don't we do that, then? We'll both catch our deaths of cold if we stand around here for much longer.'

Andrew Logan looked at her. 'Why would a girl o' your calibre want to go dancing wi' someone who's just joined the ranks o' the unemployed, Just Jean?'

She gazed into his eyes. As blue as the sea, she thought, and as deep. Yet now he was allowing her to see exactly what those emotions were that buffeted him. She should have recognised them. You saw them everywhere. They were in the eyes of so many men: the ones who loitered on street corners all day for want of something better to do; the ones who tramped for miles in search of jobs that simply weren't there; the ones who built bonfires on patches of waste ground and stood for hours staring sightlessly into the flames.

51

Even in more affluent areas like Hyndland, men were losing their jobs. From time to time you saw families moving out of their pleasant red sandstone homes, heading off for some place where the rent was cheaper. The children were confused, the mothers pale and anxious and the fathers had that same wounded look in their eyes.

'My name's Jean Dunlop,' she said briskly. 'I was secretive about my surname because I work for the Reverend Ronald Fairbairn and his wife, and I was scared they might find out that I'd been to the dancing. He's the minister of St Martin's kirk up on Clarence Drive.'

'The Reverend Ronald Fairbairn,' Andrew repeated, his eyes widening as realisation dawned. 'Him who's aye standing up on his soapbox at Stewartfield Street on a Saturday afternoon going on about "the evils inherent in this vile dance craze"?' He had imitated the minister's sonorous tones exactly.

'You've heard him speak?'

'I've answered him back. As a matter of fact, I've even taken him on. A couple of weeks ago.'

Jean's jaw dropped. 'No! What did you say to him?'

'Asked him how he could be so agin dancing when it's mentioned in the Bible.' His face once more bright and alive, Andrew stuck his hands in his pockets and rocked back on his heels, clearly savouring the memory. 'I specifically quoted that passage about there being a time to mourn and a time to dance. Asked him to explain that one to us miserable sinners he was so busy castigating.'

Jean cast him a wry glance. 'And he told you that even the Devil can quote Scripture to suit his own ends and then proceeded to bamboozle you with ancient languages and words being wrongly translated into English.' Her voice acquired a sarcastic tinge. ' "Dancing" doesn't actually mean *dancing*. Or it means something different in the Bible from what we mean by it now— What are you doing?'

For Andrew had reeled back and was subjecting Jean's slight frame to an exaggerated visual scrutiny. 'Looking for your crystal ball. Where d'ye keep it?'

'Och, you!' she said, and struck him a playful blow on the shoulder.

Andrew pretended to flinch, drawing his hands from his pockets as he did so. 'Seriously, though. How did you know that's what he said to me?'

'Because that's what he *always* says.'

Andrew grinned at her world-weary tones. 'So he believes in the literal truth o' the Bible but only as he personally interprets it?'

'You've got it exactly.'

'Which doesnae alter the fact that he wouldnae exactly be over the moon if he knew that his housemaid was engaging in "the vile dance craze"?'

'You might say that.' Jean had been trying to maintain a nonchalant attitude. That she hadn't succeeded was obvious from the sombre expression that now crossed Andrew's face.

'Would you get your marching orders if they found out?' Jean's stomach lurched. 'Probably.'

'But you could go back to your folks?'

'I haven't got any folks. As far as I know I don't have a relative in the world.'

'Och, Jean!' he exclaimed. 'You poor wee soul!'

'Don't worry about it,' she said, amused and touched by his reaction. 'I've got used to it.'

'Both your parents are dead?'

'My father was killed in the war.'

'And your ma?'

Jean hesitated. She never volunteered this information to anybody. 'She had tuberculosis. She got me the job at the manse and died in the sanatorium two months later. It's almost four years now since she died.'

Andrew's response was immediate. 'I'm sorry, Jean. It's a horrible disease. "The captain of all the men of death." That's what they call it, isn't it?'

She looked anxiously up at him. 'You don't think the worse of me?'

'Because your ma died o' consumption? Why on earth would I?'

'People do.' Jean's voice was flat. 'Think I might contaminate them or something.'

'Aye,' Andrew said grimly. 'I know what you mean. Folk who think like that arenae worth bothering with. You'd have done the march past at the time, though. Did ye no'?'

Jean nodded. 'The march past' – the name given to the legally required examination of all the relatives, workmates and any other contacts of a TB sufferer. 'I still go to the doctor every year for a check-up. My lungs are really healthy. Sound as a bell.'

'I'm very glad to hear it,' Andrew Logan said, responding to her earnestness with grave and solemn courtesy. 'You've obviously got the heart o' Bruce too.'

Jean expelled a breath of disbelief. 'Me? I'm scared of lots of things.'

'But you're here tonight,' he pointed out. 'Even though you think your minister and his wife might sack you if they found out what you were up to.'

'I want to dance,' Jean said simply. 'I really, really want to dance.'

His mouth curved into the deepest of smiles. 'Nothing like it, is there?'

'Nothing in the world,' Jean agreed, her eyes shining.

'So you still want to go dancing wi' me?'

'I still want to go dancing with you. Happy birthday, by the way. I'm sorry I haven't got a present for you.'

He was smiling down at her. 'You just gave me one, Jean.'

'Don't you want to get home to your family? Seeing as how it's Hogmanay?'

It was twenty to ten and they were back in Hyndland Street. Jean had given in to Andrew's plea that she should let him see her at least some of the way back to Clarence Drive. He'd managed to convince her that nobody was going to notice a boy and girl walking together at this time on a cold winter's night. The first-footers wouldn't venture forth until after the bells, and anyone about earlier than midnight would likely be in too much of a hurry to get in out of the cold to pay much attention to anyone else.

Jean had decided that he was very probably right. Besides, Mr Fairbairn's flock tended to be the sort of sedate folk who spent Saturday evenings by their own firesides. Even if this particular Saturday evening was Hogmanay. Or maybe especially because it was.

'Nope,' Andrew said in response to her question. 'This is a day when any sane man prefers to be out o' the house for as long as possible. There's six women in there washing and cleaning and dusting and polishing everything that doesnae move. And some things that do.' He raised his black eyebrows at her. 'Including me.'

Jean laughed. 'Won't you be forced to submit when you get back anyway?'

'Nae doubt about it. I'm putty in their hands. How about you? Did you have to take part in the big clean-up today?'

'Only the normal Saturday big clean-up. We don't stay up to see the New Year in either.'

Andrew looked shocked. 'I've never heard o' folk who don't stay up at least until the bells.'

'That would be celebrating a heathen festival. I stay up, though. My mother and my grandparents always did. So I open my window and I listen to the ships on the river sounding their foghorns and I toast the New Year with a glass of lemonade.'

'All on your own? Och, Jean!' He sounded so dismayed on her behalf that she laughed again.

'I'll be fine. Especially after the lovely evening I've had.'

'I'll raise my own glass o' lemonade to you at midnight. You any relation to the folk who make the tyres?'

'I doubt very much that my father was one of those Dunlops. Although I keep hoping that some sunny day I'll get a letter from a lawyer telling me that my long-lost Great-Aunt Jemima has died and left me a fortune. But I don't think I'll hold my breath while I wait for that to happen.'

They followed the road as it split to go round the church, which sat at the top of Hyndland Street, where it veered off to the left and began to slope upwards towards Highburgh Road. Jean stopped, making Andrew stop too. For a moment, they simply stood and looked at one another.

She thought she knew what was coming. She was a little breathless all the same. He was four years older than her. He would expect . . . certain things. The sort of things young and handsome men like him did expect from their girlfriends. The sort of things that Jean knew about only in theory, from reading descriptions of them in romantic novels.

At the very least he would want to kiss her good night. The thought of what it would feel like to have his mouth on hers was enough to send shivers of trepidation running up and down her spine. It wasn't that she didn't want him to kiss her. She'd spent a large part of last week dreaming about exactly that. She was worried about kissing him back.

The romantic novels were long on lyrical descriptions but a bit short on step-by-step instructions. How would she know if she was doing it properly? What did you do with your nose? Didn't your teeth bash together? She couldn't bear it if her lack of experience was going to show so much it would make him laugh at her.

The tension was rising. One of them had to say something. 'Well,' Jean said brightly, when it became obvious that it was going to have to be her. 'Happy New Year when it comes.'

'Same to you,' he said.

'I hope I didn't tramp on your feet too many times tonight.'

'I'm counting my bruises in dozens rather than hundreds. That has to be a bit o' an improvement.'

'*Very* funny.'

She waited for him to say something else. Her spirits plummeted when he didn't. She'd got this wrong. Here she was worrying about what she was going to do when he kissed her and he wasn't even going to ask her to meet him again. Yet he was making jokes and smiling at her. Perplexed and embarrassed, and wondering if she'd made an almighty fool of herself, Jean mumbled a 'Good night' and turned away from him to walk up the brae.

'Don't go yet.' He smiled faintly when she swung back round to face him. 'You look as scared as I feel.'

'What have you got to be scared of?' she asked, surprised.

'Not seeing you again.'

'Do you want to see me again?'

'Aye,' he said softly, 'I want that very much.'

Jean frowned, her puzzlement deepening. 'Then why don't you ask me? Like you did last Saturday?'

'Things have changed since last Saturday.'

'Because you're out of work?'

'Exactly. I'll no' court any lassie when I'm idle.'

Relief flooded through Jean. 'Is that all that's wrong?'

His voice was a lot more than rueful. 'From where I'm standing that feels like quite a lot to be wrong.'

'Och, Andy! Of course it's a lot to be wrong. But do you think it really matters to me that you're out of work?'

'It matters to me. I might no' even have the money to take myself to the dancing next week, let alone pay you in.'

'You didn't need to pay us both in tonight,' she said severely, recalling the verbal tussle they'd had about that. 'And I could pay us both in next week.'

'No, you could not. Any man who lets a woman pay his way is a gigolo, no' a gentleman.' For a moment he looked quite stern.

'You don't think it'll be easy to find another job?'

'There are no jobs, Jean. We both know that.'

'But you'll look all the same?'

'Of course I will. Once the New Year's past. I'm going round every coal-yard I know.' He pulled a face. 'As of now, I've got loads o' spare time.'

Loads of spare time. Jean digested that piece of information and took a deep breath. It was now or never. 'Would you be free next Tuesday afternoon?'

'Why?'

She rattled the question out before her courage could fail her. 'I thought you might like to meet up for coffee. Just as friends,' she explained hastily. 'There would be nothing wrong with that, would there?'

Her bravado deserted her when she saw the look on his face. It was a mixture of surprise and amusement.

'Don't tell me. Girls aren't supposed to ask boys out.'

'It's no' the way things ordinarily happen,' Andrew conceded. 'Then again, I'm beginning to realise that Miss Jean Dunlop is no ordinary girl. Just as friends?'

She nodded. Andrew smiled.

'Tell me the time and the place and I'll be there.'

Chapter 6

'SO MUCH for me thinking folk would always need coal-men,' Andrew said as he slid into the booth opposite Jean. It was Tuesday afternoon and they were meeting, as arranged, in the Italian café at the top of Byres Road, near Hillhead subway station.

Since Jean had first broken the Fairbairns' rules and gone there, it had become one of her favourite bolt holes. Her employers' objection to such establishments was that they were run by people who had committed the twin and unforgivable sins of being both foreigners and Roman Catholics. Jean had soon found out for herself that foreigners and Roman Catholics were people just like everyone else.

Some of them were very nice people indeed: like Mr Rossi, who owned this particular café. Deeply grooved with the lines that life had put there, his olive-skinned face was wreathed in smiles as he came over to take Jean and Andrew's order. Once he and Jean had exchanged the time of day and he had gone back behind his tall glass counter to make their coffee, she tugged off her knitted gloves and gazed sympathetically at Andrew across the narrow white marble table.

'None of the coal-yards taking anybody on?'

He shook his head. 'Seems that everyone's customers are

cutting back on their orders. Every coal merchant I went to yesterday and everyone I saw this morning is singing the same tune.' He unfastened his yellow muffler and tugged it free of the neck of his jacket. 'I'll need to try further afield the morn.'

'People must be really struggling if they can't even afford to buy enough coal in the depths of winter,' Jean said, shaking her head in dismay. 'This slump's getting worse and worse. It's well over two years since the Crash. Should things not be starting to get better by now?'

'Dunno.' Andrew rubbed his hands over his face. He'd been waiting for her this time, taking some shelter from the cold in the entrance to the underground, and his fingers were still white with the cold. 'You'd have to consult a student o' economics about that. The only thing I know is that most folk are in the same boat as me. No' that it's much consolation.'

He grimaced. 'That's the wrong thingummy. Absolutely the wrong thingummy. There's no boat to *be* in, no' the whole length o' the Clyde. Once they stopped work on the Cunarder down at Clydebank it was only a matter o' time before everyone else closed their gates. And once the shipyards stop working so do the rest o' us. We're a' dependent on each other.' He gave Jean another rueful smile. 'I suppose I hadnae properly realised that until now. The wrong thingummy,' he mused. 'What is the right word?'

'The wrong metaphor.' Beginning to warm up after her half-hour walk from Clarence Drive, Jean undid her coat, shrugged her shoulders out of it and allowed it to slide down behind her. Plucking her tammy from her head, she shook her hair free and placed the little hat next to the gloves she'd already laid on the bench seat beside her.

'Aye. The wrong metaphor. I knew you'd know. You're one o' the brainy ones. Like my wee sister Christine.'

'I'm not that clever.'

'Aye you are.' Taking his eyes off Jean's hair, Andrew unbuttoned his jacket and slipped a hand inside it, bringing out a packet of cigarettes. He flipped open the lid and offered them to her across the table.

'No, thanks,' she said regretfully. 'They'd smell them on me. Couldn't you look for a different sort of job?'

'Like what?' he demanded, one sceptical eyebrow cocked. 'What else could someone like me do?'

Jean slid her own scarf off, tossed it on to her hat and gloves and propped her chin on her fists. 'You could always set yourself up as a dancing master.'

He let out a snort of derision. 'Who would come to me? Besides, I'd need smart threads and the money to hire a hall and a pianist. Or, at the very least, a gramophone.' He grimaced. 'I've got one o' those – won it in a dancing competition – but I'm pretty sure I'm gonnae have to put it in the pawn before long.' He contemplated the cigarette he'd taken out for himself. With a sigh, he replaced it and returned the packet to his inside pocket. 'Better start rationing myself on these things too.'

'Don't some of the big halls up in the town employ instructors?' Jean asked, remembering something she had read in the minister's *Glasgow Herald*.

'Dancing partners? Aye. Most o' them do.'

'Dancing partners?' she queried, unfamiliar with the term. 'They do more than teach?'

The two of them leaned back to allow Mr Rossi to put two glass cups of frothy coffee in front of them, smiling their thanks up at him before he moved on to deal with the customers at the next table.

'They're paid to dance with folk who go along without partners o' their own,' Andrew said in response to Jean's

62

question. 'That's their main job, really. More than the teaching.'

Jean frowned. 'But why don't those folk just ask someone else who's gone along on their own?'

'Lots o' reasons. Because they're shy. Or because they're only in Glasgow for the evening and it's simpler to pay someone to give them a couple o' dances. Or because they're good dancers themselves and they want to dance wi' other good dancers. Or because they're married but their husbands or wives don't like to dance.'

Jean watched as he took an exploratory sip of coffee, digesting what he had said. 'How do the dancing partners get paid?'

Andrew set his cup back in its saucer. 'I think they get a weekly retainer. That's on top o' so much per dance.'

'How does that work?'

'There's usually a kiosk. It sells tickets to the punters for a sixpence. The punters give those to the dancing partners they've chosen and the partners hand all their tickets in at the end o' the evening and get about half the face value o' them.'

'All of those tuppence-halfpennies or threepences would soon mount up,' Jean said eagerly. 'Would being a dancing partner not be an ideal job for you?'

'Even if I wanted to turn myself into a lounge lizard and dance wi' fat old wifies, those jobs are like gold dust. Ye have to audition and have those smart clothes and a' that sort o' thing.'

Jean looked thoughtfully at him. Her question had provoked both a rather emphatic no and a rather wistful yes. She filed that information away for future reference.

'What do your parents say about you losing your job? Is your father still working?'

'My father's dead,' he said flatly. 'My mother and my sisters had plenty to say about it. First we had to listen while

63

Alice cried down all sorts o' curses on international financiers and the government and filthy capitalists. Bit o' a political firebrand, our Alice,' he added ruminatively. 'After which Chrissie got the job o' calming both Ma and Alice doon. She's the youngest but she's aye been the peacemaker. Unlike Agnes.'

'What's she like?'

'She's the nippy sweetie o' the family. She started going her dinger about how the hell I thought I was going out tae the dancing when we had to save all the money we had, because that rainy day we've a' been worried about has arrived. Then Ma told Agnes to save her breath to cool her porridge. Hadn't I been working like a dog, and out in all weathers, ever since I'd left the school and wasn't it obvious that I was itching to go out and couldn't any fool tell there was some lassie waiting for me? That poor lassie was gonnae be black-affronted if I didnae turn up and Ma hadnae raised a son who would treat a young lady like that. Then one o' the twins came in on my side and the other on Agnes's side—' He broke off. 'I live in the crazy house. As you can maybe guess.'

Jean gazed at him in amazement. 'The house you live in sounds wonderful.'

'You wouldnae say that if you'd ever been on the receiving end o' a clip round the lug from Mrs Bella Logan. No' that it ever has much impact but I let her think it does.'

Jean shook her head in bemused astonishment at his tolerant tone.

'Are your sisters working?'

'Two are, two arenae. The wee one's still at school.'

'Money's going to be tight?'

'As a drum. I'll get dole, I suppose,' Andrew said, looking less than enchanted by the prospect, 'but it'll no' be very much.' He wrapped his hands around the big glass coffee cup, and momentarily closed his eyes. 'Och, but that feels lovely and warm!'

Jean glanced down at his interwoven fingers. They were still white. 'You should be wearing gloves on a day like this,' she scolded. 'Not to mention an overcoat.'

He opened his eyes and looked straight at her. 'Aye. So I should.'

'Oh,' Jean said in a very small voice, realising too late that his lack of an overcoat wasn't a matter of choice. Embarrassed by her tactlessness, she bit her lip. If he and his family had been struggling to survive when he was in work, how much worse was it going to be now that he had lost his job?

'Forget it and move on. Let's talk about something else.'

'Tell me about your wee sister Christine, then. She's the clever one?'

His face lit up. 'Chrissie *eats* books. About anything and everything. Her teacher says she's got a particular aptitude for French and German. Gives her extra classes in those for free,' he added proudly.

'Are you hoping she can stay on at school?'

'Aye.' He shot Jean an anxious look across the table. 'A wee touch ambitious, d'ye think?'

'There's nothing wrong with ambition.'

'No,' he agreed. 'I think I'm gonnae have that fag after all. D'ye mind?'

'On you go,' Jean said, watching as he brought out cigarettes and matches. She lifted the square black marble ashtray from the end of the table nearest the wall and placed it in front of him. He lit up, narrowing his blue eyes against the smoke.

'Ah,' he sighed a few seconds later, 'that's better.' Dropping his hand from his mouth he transferred the cigarette to his left hand and rested his wrist on the edge of the table so that the smoke wasn't drifting in Jean's direction. It was his eyes that drifted, back to her head. 'You've the bonniest hair.'

'Och,' she said shyly, one hand going to the thick golden waves. 'I think it would look a lot nicer if I got it cut.'

'I'd have to disagree wi' you there, Just Jean.' He took another sip of coffee. Once he'd set the cup down again, he laid his right hand flat beside it. At the same moment Jean took her own left hand from her hair and curled her fingers around the edge of the table.

'But why no' get it cut if that's what ye really want?'

'Not allowed to. Mrs Fairbairn says I'm too young.'

'These folk seem to want to run your life for you.'

'You don't know the half of it. She even chooses my clothes for me. And my shoes.'

Andrew gave her a lazy smile. 'So she's the guilty party. One o' these fine days I'll have to come up the hill and put a half-brick through one o' her windaes.' The hand that was lying on the table inched forward. Now it was no distance from Jean's own fingers. 'Could ye no' leave and get a job somewhere else?'

'I don't think I'd get much of a reference,' Jean said. 'That's the problem.'

The hand that had been straying across the table retreated. 'That is a problem. Even wi' a good one, it's hard to find another job.' He sighed. 'Back to the same old subject, eh?'

At least the church was warm. That was something, especially on such a chilly Sunday morning as this one. Still half-asleep, Jean followed Mrs Fairbairn and the housekeeper down the aisle. Both of them stood back so she could enter the pew first. They always did that, and it always made her feel like an animal being herded into a pen.

Sliding along the smooth dark wood, polished to a mirror-like sheen by who knows how many coated bottoms over the years since St Martin's had been built, Jean took her usual place next to the wall.

She undid the top buttons of her coat and surreptitiously raised her right foot to place it on top of one of the chunky little radiators that stood at intervals around the interior of the building. Although the buildings belonging to St Martin's sprawled over a surprisingly large area, the walk from the manse to the church was hardly a long one. Jean's feet were freezing all the same.

She was going to be here for the next hour and a half at least, and far too much of that was going to be occupied by Mr Fairbairn's sermon. She might as well make herself warm and comfortable. Jean lifted her eyes to the stained-glass window behind the communion table, which depicted St Martin and the beggar, the former in the act of tearing his cloak in half to share with the latter. Its colours were glorious: wine reds, cobalt blues and deep, shimmering greens.

The Reverend Mr Fairbairn found it too rich for his taste and was never loath to express his opinion on the matter. If he'd had his way he'd have had it replaced with plain glass. But the window had been here from when St Martin's had been built in the 1880s and many of the parishioners were deeply attached to it.

Jean loved it too. Its richness called to something in her soul that had long been neglected and unfulfilled. The window also gave her something on which to seem to fix her attention while she practised an art at which she had become an expert. Gazing piously up at St Martin she might look as if she were listening attentively to the minister and the bible readings but her thoughts could be flying free.

She'd had some real good thinks while she'd been sitting here in this pew: privately setting the world to rights, working out what she felt about lots of other things, dreaming about her own personal future. This morning, like an arrow flying true to the target, her thoughts had only one focus: Andrew Logan.

As she stood up with the rest of the congregation to sing the first hymn and sat down again and bowed her head for the first prayer, Jean was mentally wrestling with one question. Was there any way she could help him find another job?

That question ran round her head all through the second hymn too, and while the minister read out the intimations. Part of her brain registered the familiar details of Boys' Brigade, Women's Guild, Sunday school and communion classes and committee meetings to be held in the church hall, the vestry or the manse respectively but most of it was concentrating on Andrew's problem.

She was sure he would make an excellent professional dancing partner. She mentally ticked off all of the attributes he would bring to the job. He was a wonderful dancer. He also had the gift of being able to teach it – she could testify to that. He was handsome and debonair, a graceful mover even when he wasn't dancing. He was tall enough, but not too tall. He'd be able to comfortably partner women of most heights. He was a good conversationalist, quick-witted and possessed of a terrific sense of humour. He was absolutely ideal for the job.

Apart from the fact that he had absolutely no confidence in his own ability to do it. Jean thought about that for a while. Looking the part was important. Of course it was. Andrew didn't really have what he'd referred to as 'smart threads'. Surely any *palais* manager worth his salt who saw him dance would advance him the funds to buy those? Assuming that same *palais* manager watched a confident Andrew dance.

How did people gain confidence? Jean thought some more and came up with an answer that satisfied her. By doing things they were good at and having other people tell them that they were good at them.

An outbreak of genteel coughing rippled through the congregation. The minister was climbing the steps to his pulpit. He always did a reading before he began his sermon. The big heavy Bible had been placed there in readiness, open on the old wooden lectern, which was fixed to the front edge of the pulpit.

The Reverend had a beautiful voice, deep and rounded. It could be terrifyingly harsh when he raged against sin but it was as warm and as mellow as an autumn day when he spoke of his Saviour or read from the Bible. Jean caught up with the actual words halfway through.

' ". . . and a time to pluck up that which is planted; A time to kill, and a time to heal; a time to break down, and a time to build up; A time to weep, and a time to laugh; a time to mourn, and a time to dance . . ." '

Jean blinked. How odd that he should choose to read those verses today.

' ". . . A time to love, and a time to hate; a time of war, and a time of peace".' With a decisive thump, the minister closed the big Bible. Jean jumped, earning herself a steely look of reproach along the pew from Elizabeth Fairbairn.

'Amen,' said the Reverend, 'and may God bless unto us this reading from his Holy Word, and to His name be all the glory and all the praise.'

Gripping the edge of the pulpit with one hand, Mr Fairbairn leaned forward and launched into his sermon. 'Two weeks ago,' he boomed, 'when I took the Word of God on to the streets of this latter-day Sodom and Gomorrah which surrounds us, one of those sinners who has allowed the Devil to enter his life dared to quote the Good Book to me in defence of his sin.'

Jean took her foot off the radiator and suddenly noticed how hard the pew was. It couldn't be. Could it? The minister struck the Bible in front of him with the flat of his free hand.

'This is the passage which he *dared* to quote to me,' the Reverend thundered, leaning forward so far that a horrified yet fascinated Jean wondered if there might be a real danger of him quite literally launching himself right into the middle of the congregation.

'That which contains these words: "a time to mourn, and a time to dance;" thinking thereby that he had found justification for his sin which I would be unable to gainsay. "It's in the Bible," this young man said to me. "There are other places where the Bible mentions dancing. How can you be so against it when it's in the Bible?" '

It *was* Andrew he was talking about. Jean had to convert a giggle into a cough.

The Reverend released his hold on the pulpit, rocked back on his heels and puffed out his chest in its black Geneva gown. 'He was wrong! A sinner is always wrong! And now I'm going to say to you what I said to him!'

Pin back your lugs, Jean thought cynically, remembering one of her grandmother's favourite expressions. It's only going to take him half an hour to tell us that he's right and Andy's wrong.

She was correct. Within a few sentences, the minister was off into those ancient languages. How Andrew was going to laugh when she told him that he'd been quoted from the pulpit. He would throw back his wavy head and laugh that lovely deep laugh of his, his inky-blue eyes glinting with distinctly unholy glee. Jean felt herself begin to melt. The warmth suffusing her body was nothing to do with the radiator next to her leg.

She had to think of some way to help him find a new job. She simply had to. Not only for him but for herself too, so that the two of them could walk out together.

Jean fixed her eyes once more on the stained-glass picture of St Martin. Would it be blasphemous to pray to him for help? She might have her doubts about God Himself but she'd always had an affection for the saint after whom the church was named. He must have been a kind man, tearing his cloak in half to share with someone most other people considered to be the lowest of the low.

Christians ought to be kind. Jean's experiences at St Martin's had failed to convince her that enough of them were. Take the minister's wife as an example. She wasn't kind at all. She and the ladies of the congregation did make regular collections of clothes discarded by the better-off for redistribution to the needy. It was obvious that Mrs Fairbairn took no pleasure at all in the task.

Jean had heard her talking about it. Elizabeth Fairbairn worried that giving people something for nothing would only make them lazy and work-shy. She was adamant the clothes should go only to the 'deserving poor'. More than once, when she heard that a man had been seen drunk in the street or had heard some other bad story about him, she had refused to allow any clothes to go to his family.

There was a collection going on at the moment, the coats and shoes and hats beginning to pile up in and under trestle tables in the church hall. Jean was helping sort them out on a couple of afternoons next week. The actual redistribution was scheduled to take place the following Saturday.

Jean would put away the empty trestle tables on Monday or Tuesday. The church hall wasn't used on either of those days.

It wasn't used a great deal during most days, as a matter of fact. There were always mutterings about the expense of heating it when most of the activity that took place in it happened in the evenings, but the church officer wouldn't be budged on that point. Two years before, a burst pipe in there had caused no end of damage. Fearful that the risk of such a disaster occurring again was high, he insisted that the new heating system installed after the flood was kept on throughout the winter. Behind the church itself and not directly connected to it, none of the hall's four sides was protected from the ravages of the weather by any other building.

I wish I could protect Andrew Logan from the ravages of the weather. He always looks so cold.

Jean only just managed not to slap her hand against her forehead. What sort of an idiot was she? All of those clothes were piled up in the church hall and she was going to be helping sort them out.

She remembered what he had said when she'd suggested he set himself up as a dancing master: *Besides, I'd need smart threads and the money to hire a hall and a pianist. Or, at the very least, a gramophone.*

She couldn't guarantee that she could find him smart threads but she could at least find him warm ones. That was one thing she could do for him. Getting him to accept such a gift was another matter entirely. She'd have to cross that bridge when she came to it.

A nice warm coat, she thought happily. There must be several of those in the collection. All she had to do was pick one out, wait until everyone else was busy and then hide it somewhere until she could get it to Andy. The church hall was full of cupboards, half of them more or less empty. Like the hall itself so much of the time.

The idea that came to her then was so audacious it made

her gasp. That earned her another glare from Elizabeth Fairbairn.

Jean couldn't have cared less. She knew where the spare key to the church hall was.

Chapter 7

'YOU ABSOLUTELY sure about this, Jean? No' worried someone's gonnae see us?'

'I'm sure.' She pulled the door wider open, ready to usher him in through the porch set against the back wall of the church hall. So she could be certain it was him, Andrew had given the signal on which they had agreed: two knocks, a short pause, then three more knocks.

'We're as far away from the manse as you can get here. As long as no one noticed you coming up the path from Clarence Drive we'll be fine.'

'I came the back way to make sure nobody did. Plus I decided to wear my working clothes. If anybody did notice me, they'll just think I was coming in to mend something.'

'There's not a back way,' Jean said, puzzled. 'It's all people's gardens.'

He flashed her a roguish grin. 'That's why it's as well I'm in my working clothes. I climbed a few walls to get here. Including that one.' He raised a hand above his shoulder and indicated where he meant with his thumb. 'How about the folk who live over there? Do their windaes no' overlook this door?'

'The trees are in the way.'

He swivelled round, lifting his head towards the trees and

the cawing rooks swooping and diving in and through their branches. He had to adjust his gaze upwards to do it. The row of trees, which stood against the long wall that delineated the backs of the gardens of the houses behind the church, were massively tall. Bare of foliage though they were at this time of year, the intricate network of their branches still provided lots of cover.

'I see what you mean. Those trees must have been here long before the hooses were. The birds' nests look gey precarious, don't they?'

'Seem to suit them all right,' Jean said. 'Come on in.'

As he stepped into the kitchen housed in the large wooden porch, she slipped round behind him. One hand on the knob and the other flat against the door, she pushed it to, shutting out both the chill of the January day and the harsh cries of the rooks. She turned and stood for a moment, leaning against the door with her hands behind her.

The young man standing there looking back at her wore a navy-blue knitted hat and a jacket in a coarse tweed whose colour might once have been brown. The cloth was so faded it was hard to tell. The jacket had black leather patches at the elbows and the sleeves were frayed at the cuffs. Over one shoulder of it was slung a drawstring bag made out of a dark and heavy cotton. Judging by the bulges that distorted its shape, it held a pair of shoes and several records.

Bagged at the knees, Andrew's trousers were corduroys, although the cording was worn away in several places to a smooth shine. When his jacket rode up while he untied his muffler and slid that off, Jean could see the thick black belt at his waist and the blue and white striped shirt above it. It was buttoned up to the neck but had no collar.

His working clothes. He looked different in them. Stronger. More solid. More male.

He tugged off the little knitted hat and tossed it and the yellow muffler on to one of the waist-high cupboards that ran along one wall of the kitchen. 'Hello, Just Jean.'

'Hello.'

'You look a wee touch wary,' he observed.

'Do I?' Her voice came out high and squeaky.

'Aye.' He took a step towards her. She jumped. 'Och, Jean,' he said softly, 'you don't need to be scared of me. There's no way I'd ever try to take advantage of you.'

Her cheeks flamed red. 'I know that,' she managed, her voice still not quite her own.

Andrew tactfully changed the subject. 'You don't mind that I'm no' wearing my suit? My clothes are perfectly clean. Ma's been going at them like a fury, determined to get every last ounce o' coal dust out o' them or die in the attempt. Raised enough out o' my jacket alone to keep a fire going for a week.'

'I don't mind,' replied a still rather rosy-faced Jean. 'I'm only wearing my ordinary clothes today. Not that I was exactly wearing a ball gown when we first met at the *palais*.'

He looked her over, taking in the brown woollen skirt, cream blouse with the little collar and the fawn cardigan with the Fair Isle yoke.

'You look very nice. Those colours really suit you. More than—' He stopped himself but she knew what words had been on the tip of his tongue.

'It's all right. You can say it. I know that green dress does nothing for me. I'm afraid all of my clothes are hand-me-downs. Some fit me better than others. Sometimes I think Mrs Fairbairn deliberately picks out the most unflattering ones she can find.'

'Mair than likely. I expect the old witch is jealous o' your youth and beauty.'

Jean blushed again but the questions he put next successfully took her mind off the embarrassment of being here alone with him.

'Are you *certain* sure that you want to do this? The Reverend and his wife would hit the roof if they knew there was dancing going on in their own church hall, would they no'?'

Jean had been through all of this in her own mind. It was over a week since she'd had her brainwave in church and she'd had plenty of time to think about it. She answered Andrew quite calmly. 'This is the only way for you to practise teaching and for me to learn how to dance properly. I'm fed up living by their rules, anyway. Shall we get started with the lessons?'

He studied her for a moment, then issued a cheerful instruction. 'Lead on, Macduff.'

She walked out into the corridor, past storerooms, cupboards and two small meeting rooms. Catching sight of their reflections in the full-length mirror on the wall between the ladies' and gents' toilets, she saw that Andrew was looking at her feet.

'New shoes, Cinderella?'

'Bought them after I left you last Tuesday,' she responded, holding open one of the double doors that led into the hall proper. She had thought he would immediately turn his attention to an assessment of that but for the moment he seemed more interested in her shoes.

She walked out into the hall, stopped, and glanced down. She'd had them for a week now but the warm glow of satisfaction was still there. Neat, light and dainty, they were dark brown with a narrow strap across the instep secured by a little imitation pearl. The most exciting thing of all was that her new shoes had high heels.

Andrew was pacing around her, describing a perfect circle. He stopped, cocking his head to one side in that gesture she was coming to realise was characteristic of him. 'Sure you'll no' get dizzy up there?'

'They're not *that* high.'

'Will ye no' go to hell for wearing such frivolous footwear?'

'No. I'll go to heaven for sparing your poor feet and shins any more unnecessary suffering.'

'That's a rash statement. Let's put it to the test, Miss Dunlop. Did ye bring something in case we need to muffle the gramophone?'

'A scarf,' she said, walking forward to the small stage at the end of the hall where the gramophone stood. 'I've got it here. Do we put it over the horn or in it?'

'Probably in it,' he said, following her down the room, 'but we'll experiment and see what works best. Considering how the Reverend feels about the whole matter, I was a bit surprised to hear that the church hall had a gramophone.'

'The Boys' Brigade practise their marching to music. That's why it's here.'

Moving over to one of the chairs ranged around the wall, Andrew sat down and began rummaging in his drawstring bag. Producing a pair of black shoes and a handful of records in brightly coloured paper sleeves, he handed the latter to Jean. 'Here. See what you think o' these. Who are your favourite bands?'

Looking excitedly through the half-dozen or so records, Jean threw an apologetic smile over her shoulder at him. He had taken his jacket off and draped it over the back of the chair. Now he was easing his feet out of heavy working boots.

'I'm not sure I even know the names of any bands.'

Andrew slid his feet into his dancing shoes, did up their laces and extracted a soft cloth from his bag. He proceeded to draw it across the shoes to buff them up, raising first one knee and then the other to bring them closer to his hands. 'So you've never heard of Ambrose and his Orchestra or the Savoy Orpheans or Jack Hylton and his Orchestra? There's all o' the Yanks too. Folk like Duke Ellington and Louis Armstrong. They make a rare sound.'

'None of them,' Jean confessed.

Shoes now apparently shined to his satisfaction, Andrew rose to his feet. 'I see I shall have to take your musical education in hand, Miss Dunlop. Good dancers have to have a wide knowledge o' music. It's expected.'

'So,' she asked eagerly, 'what's the first record we're going to dance to?'

'None o' them. We're gonnae start off by teaching you how to walk.'

'How to *walk*?' she repeated, puzzled.

'Aye.' He walked out into the centre of the hall, then stopped. Bunching his hands into fists at his waist, he swivelled round on the balls of his feet. 'This is perfect. Nice and warm too. I thought it might be the opposite. I never think o' churches as being warm places.'

She explained about the burst pipes and the church officer's determination that a similar accident shouldn't happen again. Andrew's eyes dropped to the floor as he listened to her. 'The Boys' Brigade doesn't seem to have done too much damage to the floor.'

'The church officer again. He makes sure it gets looked after.'

'But there's never any dances held here?'

'None.'

'Some churches hold dances though, don't they? It's no' every minister who thinks dancing's the work o' the Devil. After all,' he said, putting on the pan loaf, 'am I not right in thinking that the Bible does include various texts which mention dancing?'

Jean laughed. She'd been right. He had been mightily amused to hear that Mr Fairbairn had quoted his conversation with him. 'How come you know your Bible so well?'

'Put the blame on my dear departed father. When he wasnae hitting the bottle or his weans he was hitting the Bible. On one memorable occasion he gave me six o' the best *with* the Bible. I couldnae sit down for a week. Bible thumping at its maist literal.'

'Did he often hit you?' Jean asked, her eyes soft with sympathy.

'No' once I got big enough to hit back,' Andrew answered drily. 'Or to do something about it when he decided in his infinite wisdom that my mother or one o' the girls had earned a doing. Right. Let's get started.' He extended his left arm to her and she came forward a little shyly to join him.

'Put your hand in mine. No, stay where you are. We're going to walk down the hall together. Side by side.'

'You really think I need to practise how to walk?'

'Everybody does. When we do it in real life there's a' sorts o' other things going on. Like putting your heid doon against the wind or the rain, for instance, or waving to someone ye know on the other side o' the road. When you're dancing, walking becomes something different. It's the first step o' every dance you're ever gonnae learn, so you have to do it properly. Don't frown.'

'I'm concentrating.'

'Fine. But you're supposed to look as if you're enjoying yourself when you're dancing. That's important too. Don't forget it.'

He's quite strict, she thought, a funny little thrill of excitement running through her at the revelation of this hitherto unseen facet of his character. Teaching her to dance was obviously something to be taken seriously. That would surely make him an excellent instructor and dancing partner.

'Right,' he said again. 'Gracefully and lightly. But definitely and confidently too. Make sure you put your heels down first, then your toes. Imagine we've both got a straight line in front of us, marked on the floor. We're gonnae follow that line, and we're gonnae count out this beat while we do it. One, two, three, four. One, two, three, four. Got that?'

'Each step's a beat?'

'Aye. You lead off on your left foot, me on my right. Go.'

They proceeded down the length of the hall, counting out the beat together and stopping a few feet before they came up against the stage. 'Again?' Jean asked, already beginning to turn.

'Did I tell you to turn?' He was glowering at her. 'I don't think so.'

'S-sorry!' Jean stuttered, caught between the feelings she remembered having at school when she'd incurred the wrath of a strict teacher, and amusement at how fierce Andrew sounded. 'We're not turning?'

He spoke with exaggerated patience, once more putting on the pan loaf. Each and every word was carefully enunciated. 'If you will give me the chance, I shall tell you what we are going to do.'

'Right,' Jean said, raising her hand to hide her quivering mouth. 'Sorry.'

'Stop apologising and listen. We're not turning because we are now going to walk backwards. It's a skill you in particular are going to have to perfect – given that everything the gentleman does, the lady has to do too. Usually backwards.' The ferocious glower relaxed. 'No' to mention wearing that form of torture only women have to put up with: high heels.

81

Since you're not used to wearing them I suspect you're gonnae find this quite tricky at first. This time the toe goes down before the heel.'

He had the gift of prophecy. Jean found walking backwards a little more than quite tricky. She stumbled almost immediately. Her hand had been lightly resting in his. Now she was grabbing on to it for dear life as she fought not to fall over. Andrew bore it manfully until she was upright again. The ticking-off came only after she had safely regained her balance.

'You must *never* use your partner to help maintain your own balance. At the very worst you could bring both o' you down. At the very least you'll make both o' you look ungainly. You're responsible for keeping your own balance.'

Jean pushed back the thick strand of golden waves that had fallen forward over her face. 'I thought that was why we were holding hands.'

'We're holding hands because I like holding your hand.' That was the only remotely flirtatious comment she got out of him over the next hard-working hour and a half.

'What about Saturday?'

'What about it?' She was sitting opposite him at the small square table in the hall's kitchen, watching him consume a second piece of iced gingerbread. It was part of a small hoard of home-baking she'd smuggled across from the manse's kitchen. Since he had refused point-blank to accept any payment for the lessons, Jean had decided the least she could do was provide him with his afternoon tea.

'Would you like me to give you another lesson on Saturday evening?' he asked.

'I'd love you to.'

'What about anybody seeing lights on in the hall?'

'There's wooden shutters,' she said. 'We can close them.'

'You've got it all worked out,' he said admiringly.

'I like to plan ahead. Would you like some more tea?'

'I'm grand, thanks.' He pushed his chair back and rose to his feet. 'You'd probably better be getting back to work before anyone misses you. Can I help you clear up these things afore I go?'

'Would you know where to start?' Jean teased, gazing up at him. 'I expect your mother and sisters do everything for you.'

He grinned down at her. 'They'd probably agree wi' you there. But I thought I'd better make the offer. If you're sure you can manage, I should maybe push off now.'

'Don't go yet,' Jean said lightly. 'I've got something for you. Will you wait here for a wee minute?'

She was back in thirty seconds. When he saw what she had draped across her outstretched arms Andrew went very still. 'What's that?'

'What it looks like.' She thrust the coat towards him. 'It's for you.'

The look he sent her was as black as his brows. 'I told you I didn't want you to pay me for the lessons.'

'I'm not paying you. Call it a late birthday present. One that didn't cost me anything.'

'You stole it?'

'Of course I didn't steal it.' Jean rolled her eyes and told him where it had come from.

'It's charity, then,' he said flatly.

Say something funny, Jean thought: something to make him laugh and relax and accept the bloody thing. 'These collections the Church makes are where all my own clothes come from, you know. I'm not sure if either of us are the *deserving* poor, though. Isn't that the most awful expression?'

She realised her mistake the moment the words were out

of her mouth. Andrew's eyes were suddenly glittering like gemstones. ' "The deserving poor"? I don't think I'm one o' them, do you?' His voice was as bitter as vinegar. 'I'm the feckless kind o' poor. The sort who'd rather spend time dancing wi' a beautiful girl than going off on the tramp looking for work.'

Jean thought about reminding him that the dancing session they'd just had was all about him looking for work but the reference to 'a beautiful girl' threw her. She decided it was safer to ignore everything he had said.

'Just try the coat on and see if it fits you.' She strove to make her voice light. 'I risked life and limb to get this, you know. Nearly got caught when I was hiding it away at the back of the cupboard.'

'Jean . . .'

'Turn around,' she coaxed. 'I'll help you on with it.'

He gave her one last despairing look and did as he was bid.

'It might have been made for you,' she breathed as she looked him over. 'Come out and see for yourself in the mirror in the corridor.'

He stopped dead when he caught sight of his own reflection. Jean was sure the comment that rose to his lips and was immediately stifled was a favourable one. She pressed her advantage shamelessly.

'See? You look great in it. The colour matches your eyes and the length's perfect. I always think men look dashing in long coats, don't you? As if they're wearing a cloak from days of old.'

The temptation to blether on, if only to fill the silence, was strong. Jean was wise enough to resist it. Andrew's voice was flat, apparently devoid of expression. 'Ma's been so worried about me being cold.'

'I've been worried about you being cold too.' In the mirror, their eyes met and held, and Jean saw the emotion that the carefully expressionless voice had been trying so hard not to betray. 'Andy,' she said gently, 'I'm really sorry if I've offended you or hurt your pride. I'm really so sorry if I've done that.'

The heavy wool of the navy coat flared out as he swung round to face her. 'Sorry for what?' he demanded, a catch in his voice. 'Caring about me being cold? Wanting to keep me warm? It's me who needs to be apologising, Jean. No' you.'

'You'll take it, then?'

'Wi' heartfelt thanks.' He stretched out a hand to her face and drew the tips of his fingers along her cheek, his touch as light as thistledown. 'You're one in a million, Jean Dunlop.'

'I'm glad you realise that,' she said lightly.

He swung back round to survey his reflection. 'Dashing?'

'No doubt about it.'

In the mirror, his eyes once more met hers. This time they smiled at one another.

Chapter 8

'KEEP YOUR shoulders down.'

'I thought I was supposed to be doing my rise and fall,' Jean countered.

'Aye, but wi' the whole o' your body. No' just bits o' it. You're supposed to move across the floor like a swan gliding across a pond, no' bounce like a rubber ball some wee lassie's sent stoating through a close.'

As Jean had quickly discovered, Andrew's criticisms of her dancing were often couched in cheerfully sarcastic terms. Yet they were delivered with such an abundance of good humour that it was impossible to take offence. Hard taskmaster though he was, he was also quick to offer praise whenever he judged Jean to have earned it.

Guiding her through all of the popular dances, his approach was both systematic and thorough. Only once they were both convinced that she had a complete grasp of one did he allow her to move on to another. Part of each session was then devoted to more practice on those she had already learned.

Young Mr Logan also knew when to push his pupil hard and when to recognise that she'd had enough. As a cold January gave way to an equally chilly February there were afternoons when the high standards he set for her found Jean on the verge of tears and wailing that she was *never* going to be able to dance properly. Today was one of those afternoons.

With an exclamation of disgust at her own ineptitude, she dropped her hands and stepped out of his embrace. 'I'm clumsy and I'm stupid and I do have two left feet. That's all there is to it. We might as well give this up now.'

'You're no' clumsy and you're no' stupid.' Andrew folded his freed arms over his blue and white striped chest and fixed her with a stern look. 'You also have one perfectly good left foot and one perfectly good right one. You're doing fine, Jean. Really beginning to get the hang of it.'

She looked at him out of eyes that glittered with tears of frustration. 'Am I?'

'Of course you are. It's all starting to come together. One day very soon you'll no' even have to think about where you put your feet or keep reminding yourself about your carriage and deportment. It'll all come naturally. You'll soon be gliding across the floor as gracefully as that swan I keep going on about.'

Jean dashed away her tears. 'D'you really think so, Andy?'

'I know so,' he said firmly. 'I wasnae trying to soft-soap you when I said you were a natural. I don't say things I don't mean.' Uncrossing his arms, he swivelled round on the balls of his feet and walked over to the stage to lift the gramophone needle off the record, which had been playing to itself for the last minute. A still rather forlorn Jean gazed after him.

'I thought I did have some natural aptitude but I seem to have lost it.'

'You'll get it back,' he promised. 'It's got pushed to the edges because you're concentrating on mastering technique. Which you're doing extremely well,' he added encouragingly. 'Right, then. D'you want to stop now, or will we finish practising our foxtrot and run through the tango one last time?'

He had lifted the solid black disc from the turntable and was standing there holding it in one hand and its coloured paper sleeve in the other. His question might have sounded casual but Jean Dunlop recognised a challenge when she heard one. She lifted her chin and squared her shoulders. 'Put that record back on.'

'No' wanting to give up after all, then?' The warm, slow smile was spreading across his face.

'No,' Jean said, 'I want to keep dancing.'

So they kept dancing. They also kept talking. As Jean progressed and improved, needing only an occasional reminder or correction from Andrew, he even began to allow her to do the two things at the same time. They talked about anything and everything.

He took great pleasure in introducing her to the music he loved. Sometimes Jean's head buzzed like a swarm of bees with the names of all of the trombonists and saxophonists and drummers and vocalists and band leaders, not to mention all of their respective musical family trees. Andrew seemed to know the history of each and every orchestra, and each and every individual who'd ever played in them.

Sometimes he teased her by pretending he'd forgotten to bring the records with the tunes on them that had become her favourites: 'Button Up Your Overcoat', of course, 'I Guess I'll Have to Change my Plan'; 'Spread a Little Happiness'; 'Let's Do It'.

They also spent time setting the world to rights. Jean the avid reader was more than a match for Andrew here, although he held his own in what often became hotly argued debates. Such exchanges usually ended with a shared admission that they were glad they weren't in charge of things. Who would want to run a world that had so many terrible problems in it?

She learned about his family, getting to know his mother and his sisters through his affectionate tales of them. They talked about her own lack of family, a topic that clearly fascinated Andrew. Although he cheerfully admitted that living in a house full of women frequently drove him nuts, he couldn't imagine being without his mother and sisters.

'What about your father?' he asked one day. 'Did he no' have any relatives either?'

'Not as far as I know. He was his parents' only child and I think they were both quite young when they died.'

Andrew moved the fingers of his right hand against Jean's back. Her footwork now neatly marrying up with his, she obeyed the silent instruction to back into the turn that would lead them away from the stage.

'You knew your mother's parents, though?'

'Aye.' Her eyes went a little dreamy as the part of her brain that wasn't thinking about where she was putting her feet drifted back to her childhood.

'Mind and keep your body weight forward,' Andrew murmured. 'Almost as though I'm trying to push you over and you're resisting. Tell me about your grandparents.'

'I remember going out picking raspberries with my grannie. Brambles too. She knew exactly where to go to find them. Like she knew the name of every flower and plant and every herb that ever grew.'

'Did she make jam?'

'Jars and jars of it. They were both real country people. Knew all these wee rhymes about the weather and the signs which foretell snow or gales or whatever.'

'How do you tell if it's gonnae snow?'

'It might be because the geese are flying in a particular direction.' Jean adopted a mysterious voice. 'Or that there's a blue flame flickering on the fire.'

'Handy to know that,' Andrew observed.

'Particularly if you're looking after sheep that are lambing.'

'Your grandfather was a shepherd?'

'Throw the boy a peanut. Ten out of ten for deduction, Sherlock.'

'Cheeky wee bisom,' he said amiably. 'Where did he tend his flocks?'

'Near Helensburgh. Up the hill behind it. Off the road that goes across to Loch Lomond.'

'I've hiked over that road. Lovely scenery. We're coming up to the end of the record. Shall we concentrate on our finish?'

They completed their foxtrot with a flourish and he suggested a breather. 'I'll go and get us some water,' he added easily, and took himself off to the kitchen. He was quite at home here now.

When he came back into the hall with a jug and two tumblers on a tray, Jean was sitting on the floor under one of the hall's windows with her legs outstretched. Andrew set the tray on the floor next to her.

'Thirsty work,' he commented, pouring out water for both of them before sinking down on to the floor himself.

Jean agreed with him and gratefully swallowed a mouthful of the cold, clear water before tilting her head back against the wooden panelling that lined the walls of the church hall.

'So when your grandfather died you and your ma were turfed out o' his cottage?'

'It wasn't as bad as that. They gave us a month or so to get organised, but they did need the house for the new shepherd and his family.'

'What happened to your grandfather's dog?' Andrew asked curiously. 'Are shepherds and their dogs no' really close?'

'They are. So close that Fly pined away. He died the day before we moved out.'

'Almost as if he knew?'

'He *did* know,' Jean said. 'I'm convinced of that. He wasn't an old dog, either. Only about six . . . Oh!'

'What?' Andrew asked, jerking back in exaggerated and comic response.

Jean laughed. 'I've just remembered something. You could always tell when Fly was thinking about something or waiting for an instruction from his master because he would stand with his head cocked to one side. You do it too,' she said triumphantly, 'and I've been trying to remember who you reminded me of. Now I know.'

'I remind you o' a dug,' he murmured. 'Thanks very much.'

She patted his arm and laughed again. 'Och, but he was such an intelligent dog! It's a compliment to be compared to a collie.'

'Aye,' Andrew said drily. 'Right. Let me know if you want any sheep rounded up. Do you look like your ma?'

'A bit. But she was beautiful. Inside and out.'

Andrew looked at her thoughtfully. 'Some folk might think that describes her daughter too.'

Jean gave him an uncertain little smile. 'She was a much better person than I'll ever be. "The world is full of possibilities." That was one of the things she always said to me. It was one of the last things she said to me when she left me at the manse.' Her voice shook.

Andrew took her hand in his and gave it a comforting squeeze. 'What else did she say to you?'

'That I probably wasn't going to like it there very much but the important thing was that I'd have a roof over my head and be safe. She knew it might be difficult for me but I had to stick it out for as long as I could. Until I'd saved up enough money to be able to go out into the world and do whatever it was that I was destined to do.' She smiled at him.

'For some reason she always thought I was destined to do something.'

'I'm sure you are,' Andrew said.

'And what would that be?'

He rose to his feet, pulling her up with him. 'Right now your destiny is to dance wi' me. Aren't you the lucky girl?'

PART II

PART II

Chapter 9

April 1933

'CAN I have the last scone?'

Jean pushed the plate towards him. 'Help yourself.' She was glad that she'd established the precedent of giving him afternoon tea in the kitchen of the church hall after the very first dancing lesson. He had lost weight over the weeks of his unemployment, those weeks that were now beginning to turn into months. Even his face had grown thinner.

Realising how tough life must be in the Logan household these days, Jean was continually having to stifle an impulse not only to feed him while he was here but also to send him home each time with a package of home-baking under his arm.

He was happy enough to sit here taking tea with her, one friend giving hospitality to another. She knew he would reject outright the offer of anything more than that. If she had learned one thing about Andrew Logan, it was that he hated the idea of being the object of anybody's charity.

She also knew that he loathed having to join the queue at the Labour Exchange each week. Jean suspected that if it hadn't been for the need to bring something in to give to his mother, he would rather have starved than accept the meagre dole.

Pressing her fingertips together, she made a steeple of her hands and watched him splitting and buttering his third scone. He was in an unusually spiky mood today, irritable throughout the lesson, his acerbic criticisms noticeably less good-natured. They had finished a good fifteen minutes earlier than usual. She wasn't in the best of moods herself.

The idea of these sessions had been to build up Andrew's confidence as a teacher, giving him the impetus to apply for a position as a dancing partner. So far as Jean knew, he hadn't yet been to one single *palais de danse*. She couldn't understand why he didn't make a start: especially when he hated being on the dole; especially when he must know what a risk she herself was running by meeting him in the church hall twice a week.

That risk was increasing as the weeks wore on. The more often she and Andrew met here, the more likely it was that they would get found out. Initially fired up with enthusiasm, Jean had found it easy to discount the possibility of anyone connected with St Martin's unexpectedly feeling the need to visit the hall on a Tuesday afternoon or a Saturday evening. Now her imagination kept coming up with all sorts of reasons why they might well do precisely that.

Like one of those films that had your heart leaping into your mouth each time danger threatened the hero and heroine, a series of mental pictures had begun to form in Jean's head. First she and Andrew were birling around the hall, completely absorbed in their dancing. The second scene shifted the action to the path that led round the back of the church. Both the minister and his wife were marching along it, leading a phalanx that included the church officer and several of the grimmer-faced elders.

The third scene cut back to the inside of the hall where the two young dancers were still circling the hall, blissfully unaware of what was heading their way, too caught up in what they were doing even to hear the opening of doors. It wasn't until Jean followed Andrew round in a graceful turn that they found themselves face-to-face with the firing squad.

Jean's self-directed film stopped dead at that point. She couldn't get beyond the stunned silence and the looks of frozen horror on the faces of all parties. She wasn't sure that she wanted to. She certainly didn't ever want to encounter the situation in real life.

She worried too that she might let the cat out of the bag by something she said or did. Last Saturday night, when she went back into the manse, she had caught herself dancing through the scullery, still practising her steps. The realisation of what she was unconsciously doing had made her laugh. Maybe Andrew's promise that soon she would begin to find dancing as natural as breathing was coming true.

That happy thought had sent her into the kitchen smiling and with a sparkle in her eyes. The parlour maid had given her a very sharp look indeed. Anne Reid wasn't clever exactly, but she had a native shrewdness and she was also extremely nosy. It wasn't a comfortable combination to be contemplated by someone who had a secret to keep.

At the beginning, when Jean had first suggested the idea of them using the church hall, Andrew had seemed fully aware of the risk she was running and appreciative of her for taking it. He seemed to have forgotten about that now. And today was her birthday and he had obviously forgotten all about that too.

The previous week he'd made a carefully casual comment about her soon turning eighteen. She'd assumed he was checking to make sure he'd got the date right.

She hadn't been expecting a present. The amount of spare cash he had was minute. She had been hoping for a card and she wouldn't have minded a bit if it had been a home-made one. At the very least she had thought he would wish her Happy Birthday as soon as he came through the door. It looked as if she'd been wrong on both counts.

He looked up and found her watching him. 'If you want half o' this scone, why don't you say so?'

'Because I don't,' she retorted, her voice sharpening in response to his own challenging tone.

'You can have it if you want.' He pushed the plate towards her. She pushed it back.

'I've already told you I don't want it.' Jean's temper flared, boiling over into an aggressively put question. 'Have you applied for any positions as a dancing partner yet?'

'Is that no' my business?' He lifted one half of the scone and sank his lovely white teeth into it.

Jean drew her breath in at that response. If he thought that was the conversation over, he had another think coming. Leaning over the table, she whipped the second half of the scone out of his reach.

'Hey!' he protested. 'I'm no' finished yet!'

'Neither am I,' she snapped. 'And don't speak with your mouth full. I think it's my business too. Is that not why we're meeting here twice a week?'

Andrew swallowed what was in his mouth. It gave Jean considerable satisfaction to observe that he had to force it down. 'Is it?' he demanded.

'I thought that was the general idea.'

'I think that was *your* idea,' he retorted. 'No' mine.'

The sheer ingratitude of that response fanned the flames of Jean's anger. 'Are you not going to apply for any jobs?'

He cast her a baleful look from under knitted black brows. 'I've applied for hundreds o' jobs.'

'As a coalman,' she said, 'or a navvy.'

'That's what I am. An unskilled labourer.'

'You could be a highly skilled dancing partner.'

'Could I?'

There was considerable belligerence in those two little words. Underneath them, Jean could hear something else: uncertainty. The realisation that his self-esteem continued to be so shaky gentled her voice.

'Have some faith in yourself, Andy,' she urged. 'You dance beautifully. You're good-looking. Hard though it is to believe at the moment,' she teased, trying to coax a smile out of him, 'when you put your mind to it you can be quite charming.'

'Being a professional partner takes a lot more than being a good dancer,' he said, still fixing her with the steely glare. 'Or even a good teacher. You have to be . . .' he paused, searching for the right word, '. . . *smooth*. I'm rough as hell. Give me my scone back.'

'Tell me what you mean by "smooth" and I will.'

For a moment he said nothing. When Jean determinedly held his gaze, he came out with a few definitions. 'The gift o' the gab. Well spoken. Well groomed. Well dressed. Bags o' self-confidence.'

Jean placed the plate in front of him, lifted her hands and began ticking points off on her fingers. '*You've* got the gift of the gab. You can be well spoken when you want to be. You wear what clothes you do have well and once any dance hall manager sees what a good dancer and teacher you are, he'd likely be more than happy to advance you the money to buy some really nice ones. You've got loads of confidence when you're teaching me. Why shouldn't you have that with other people?'

When he didn't answer her, Jean tried again. 'Don't you think you've made up your mind to be beaten before you've even tried? Don't you think you're being a bit defeatist?'

'De-fea-tist,' he repeated, stretching out the syllables of the word. 'Is that what you think I am?'

'You're throwing all sorts of obstacles into your own path. Are there not enough there already?'

He rose abruptly to his feet. 'I'm off. Thanks for the tea and scones.'

Caught between anger and dismay, Jean stood up too. He was already lifting the navy-blue coat down from the pegs beside the back door. It might be April according to the calendar but nobody seemed to have told the weather that spring had arrived.

'What about Saturday?' He had put that question with his back to her, apparently more concerned with putting his coat on than worrying whether she might be upset.

'Maybe you shouldn't bother coming on Saturday,' she snapped. 'There doesn't seem to be much point.'

'Please yourself.' Andrew turned, thrusting his hand deep into the coat's inside pocket. 'Here,' he said roughly. 'Happy Birthday.'

Jean walked forward and took the small parcel from him. It was neatly wrapped in newspaper and tied up in string. She held it between her two hands and gazed down at it. From its weight and its size it had to be a book.

'Oh,' she said, 'I thought you'd forgotten.'

'You thought wrong.'

Jean raised her eyes from the parcel to his face. 'Will you stay while I open it?'

'No.' His fingers were already wrapped around the doorknob. 'It's no' much o' a present anyway. Only cost me a shilling.'

'That isn't how you measure a present,' she said, her eyes still on his face.

'Isn't it?'

'You know it isn't. Please stay while I open it.'

He drew in a long breath. 'All right.'

'Come back to the table and finish your scone?'

'No. Open your present and then I'm going.'

Jean returned to the table, laid the parcel on it and carefully undid the string. The newspaper that wrapped it had been meticulously creased and folded over at each end. When she pushed it open, she saw that her surmise had been correct. It was a book.

There was nothing printed on the front cover, so she turned it spine upwards. *Poems and Songs of Robert Tannahill.* She looked up and across at Andrew where he stood watching her, his back to the door. 'This is a lovely present. Thank you.'

'It's no' new,' he said tersely. 'I bought it in a second-hand bookshop.'

'Owned and loved by someone else before you found it and picked it out for me,' Jean said, her eyes on his face. 'When I've got a house of my own I'm going to fill it with second-hand books.'

He slanted her a look from under his black brows. 'That's what Chrissie says.'

'Chrissie must be a very sensible person. I'd like to meet her one of these days.'

Andrew hesitated, as though he were on the brink of saying something. Jean had been hoping for a while now that an invitation to meet his mother and sisters might be forthcoming. So far the prospect hadn't even been mentioned. It wasn't mentioned now.

'I'm going,' he said again.

'Could you not stay a wee bit longer?' Jean asked. 'I've got nearly half an hour before I have to be back over at the manse. And it is my birthday.' She turned down the corners of her mouth, doing her best to look as if she were making fun of herself.

'You didnae get a present or a card from anyone over there?' Andrew inclined his dark head, indicating the general direction of the manse.

Jean shook her own head, aware that her eyes were prickling with tears. 'They've all forgotten. Up until five minutes ago I thought you'd forgotten too.' Her voice shook. 'That I was going to go through the whole day without one single person even wishing me Happy Birthday.'

His hand slid off the doorknob. 'Och, Jean . . .'

The blue eyes and the hazel ones met. A second later Andrew Logan and Jean Dunlop were in each other's arms.

Chapter 10

NEITHER THE hours she'd spent dancing with him nor any love story she'd ever read had prepared Jean for the physical and emotional shock of the intimacy of this mouth-to-mouth contact. Hands thrown up on either side of her head in startled reflex, she found time to wonder how merely touching lips together could provoke these strange and unfamiliar feelings that were all at once and so overwhelmingly surging through her body.

The champagne feeling was back. Only this must be the best and most expensive champagne in the world. Jean's fingers and toes were tingling and her legs felt odd: warm and heavy, as though she might never be able to move them again. It was an odd combination. Heat, excitement and . . . She reached for the appropriate word. Languor. That was it. Heat and excitement and languor, she thought. Then she stopped thinking at all.

Pure instinct brought her hands fluttering down on to Andrew's shoulders. Pure instinct sent them in under the heavy coat, craving the feel of his warm skin beneath the thin cotton of his striped shirt. Tentatively, not very sure what she was about, Jean began not only to surrender to his kiss but also to return it.

He withdrew momentarily: only by a hair's-breadth and

only for long enough to let out a low moan of pleasure. The effect of that strange little sound electrified Jean. Her lips dared to grow bolder. So did Andrew's hands, rising from the grip they had on her waist to roam over her back. One of those hands began to inch its way forward. Once more, he snatched his mouth away from hers.

'Will you let me?' he whispered. 'Say you'll let me touch you, Jean. Please.'

'I'd let you do anything,' she murmured, arching her back to meet those questing fingers. They found their goal, firmly cupping its soft roundness. Jean let out a ragged gasp of pleasure. The fingers twitched. Then they were gone.

When she opened the eyes she had closed she realised that he had transferred both of his hands to her shoulders. He was pushing her away. He stepped back, putting more distance between them. As cold and shocked as if someone had suddenly thrown a bucket of cold water over her, Jean gasped out a question. 'What's wrong?'

Andrew's breathing was both rapid and shallow. 'You're no' supposed to react like that.'

'How am I supposed to react?'

He took one more step back and fetched up against the door for the second time this afternoon. 'You should slap my face or something.'

'I don't want to slap your face.' Jean's voice was filled with the perplexity she felt. 'Tell me what I've done wrong, Andy.'

'You haven't done anything wrong.' He coughed to clear his throat. 'It's me who has. I took advantage of you.'

'You didn't take advantage of me. I wanted you to do it. I liked it when you touched me.'

Andrew's eyelids fluttered briefly shut. 'Don't say things like that.' Slumped against the door, his pocketed hands gathered the navy-blue coat about his slim figure.

Jean looked at him, trying to disentangle the emotions she saw chasing themselves across his face. She felt sick when she thought she had picked out one of them. 'You think I'm cheap,' she said flatly.

'No!' He snapped upright, the denial bursting out of him. 'How could I think that about a girl like you?' Arms falling open, he strode forward and gripped her by her shoulders. The gesture wasn't that of a lover. It was that of a young man at the end of his tether. 'I love you, Jean Dunlop! Don't you know that?'

Struck dumb by his words, she could do nothing but gaze up into his troubled face.

He shook her. 'What d'you think it's been like for me these past weeks? Eh?' he demanded, shaking her again. 'Holding you in my arms and being so close to you and no' being able to allow myself even to kiss you? What *do* you think that's been like?'

'I d–don't kn–know,' Jean stuttered. 'Not unless you t–tell me.'

'Sheer bloody torture!' He shook her for the third time, making his point. 'Absolutely hellish!'

'D'you think you could stop shaking me? It hurts a bit.'

The punishing grip relaxed. 'I'm sorry,' he said as he let go of her. 'I didnae realise what I was doing.'

'Did you realise what you were saying?'

'What?'

'You just told me that you loved me.'

'I do love you.' He folded his arms across his chest and dropped his eyes, apparently fascinated by the speckled yellow oilcloth that covered the floor. He drew the toe of his boot along it.

'Did you mean it?'

That question brought his head snapping back up. 'Of course I meant it. I don't—'

'– say things you don't mean,' Jean supplied.

'No,' he agreed. 'I don't—'

'I love you too,' she interrupted. 'And don't tell me not to say things like that. I'll say what I bloody well want to say.'

He winced. 'Don't swear.'

'You'd drive a saint to swear.'

'Maybe I would. But words like yon still dinnae sound right coming from you.'

'You think I'm so superior, do you?'

'Why d'ye think I've never invited you home to meet Ma and the girls?'

'I don't know. I've been wondering that for some time now.'

'I'm ashamed. Ashamed to show a girl like you where I live.'

'A girl like me? I'm a skivvy, Andy. A maid-of-all-work. I clean out fires and wash dishes and empty chamber pots. That's how superior I am.'

'You're special,' he said stubbornly. 'And what right have I got to spend time wi' someone like you when I've neither a job nor any prospect o' one?'

'You must know you'd at least be in with a chance of getting a job as a dancing partner.'

'I *dream* of getting one o' those jobs. D'you really think I don't?'

'Then why don't you apply for one?' she howled, exasperated with him.

He yelled his answer back at her. 'Because I'm scared of trying and finding that nobody'll take me on! Then I'll have got everybody's hopes up for nothing! Including my own! Besides, I'd never see you if I was doing work like that!'

'Why wouldn't you see me?'

'Because the hours we were both off would never match up. Most o' the big halls do tea-dances as well as afternoon sessions. The best we could hope for would be to see each other for a couple of hours on a Sunday. That's no' enough for me, Jean.'

'It's not enough for me either, Andy. But we'd see each other plenty if we both became dancing partners.'

'What did you say?'

She stared at him, as amazed as he was by the words she had just uttered.

'Are you serious?' he asked.

'I think I am. But do you think I could be good enough?'

'You'd need more practice,' he said slowly, 'but aye, I do think you'd be good enough. But, Jean,' he protested, 'I know you're no' very happy here at the manse but at least you've got security. A roof over your head and a steady wage.'

'I'm suffocating here. Dying for lack of oxygen. I need to get out. Not to mention the fact,' she went on, her eyes still on his sombre face, 'that a life without seeing you would be a life not worth living.'

For a moment, neither of them spoke. Not until Andrew summoned up the courage to ask the question to which he so clearly wanted an answer. 'You really do love me, Jean?'

'I don't say things I don't mean either. Not to you, anyway. Yes,' she said, 'I really do love you.' She smiled at him and then glanced down at the table and the gift he had given her. 'Why did you choose this particular book?'

He walked forward, picked it up and held it out to her. 'Because when I did this in the bookshop it fell open at page 237. Open it and read the poem that's on that page. Out loud, I mean.'

Jean took the book from him and did as he had asked.

'Let us go, lassie, go,
Tae the braes o' Balquihither,
Whar the blaeberries grow
'Mang the bonnie Hielan heather;'

'Balquihither?' she queried, glancing up at him.

'I presume it's the old spelling for Balquhidder. In the Trossachs, isn't it?'

Jean nodded. 'The poem sounds like something I know. Only a wee bit different.'

'This?' he suggested, and began to sing.

'Oh, the summer time is come,
And the trees are sweetly bloomin',
And the wild mountain thyme,
Grows around the bloomin' heather,
Will ye go, lassie, go?'

When he started the chorus, Jean joined in with him.

'And we'll all go together,
To pull wild mountain thyme,
All around the bloomin' heather,
Will ye go, lassie, go?

'You know it?' he asked.

'My grandfather used to sing it to me. It's a beautiful song. Which d'you think came first, the song or the poem?'

'I'd guess it's sometimes hard to tell. All o' these poets collected old folk songs and wrote new ones. It's all mixed up together. Read out the last verse o' the poem.'

Jean bent her head once more over the book.

'Now the simmer is in prime,
  Wi' the flowers richly bloomin',
  Wi' the wild mountain thyme
  A' the moorlan's perfumin';
  Tae our dear native scenes
  Let us journey taegither,
  Whar glad innocence reigns
    'Mang the braes o' Balquither.'

'It's lovely. It made you think of me?' she asked as she closed the book.

'It did. Especially that bit about *glad innocence*. Would I be right in thinking that I'm your first boyfriend?'

Jean blushed. 'Yes. That was my first kiss too. Was I doing it right?'

An imp of mischief danced its way into Andrew's inky-blue eyes. 'I'm no' sure that you were. I think ye need to put in a lot o' practice there too as well as in your dancing. I'm mair than happy to help you perfect your technique in both areas.'

He clasped her loosely by the waist and laughed when her blush deepened. 'Such a bold girl sometimes,' he murmured, dropping a kiss on the end of her nose, 'and such a shy wee lassie at others. I like that.'

'I might be shy,' Jean said, clutching the book of poetry to her chest, 'but I got a bit carried away, didn't I?' She frowned up at him. 'And girls who get carried away can get themselves into trouble.'

'I know,' he said solemnly. 'We'll make some rules for ourselves. So that we don't get too carried away.'

'We could do that?'

'We *will* do that. As long as you pacify me with enough kisses. Let's lose the book for the moment,' he murmured, briefly sparing one hand to pluck it out of her arms and lay it on the table. 'Now, where were we?'

'You were telling me you were going to need a lot of kisses.'

'You owe me loads of 'em. For all those times I wanted to kiss you but didn't.' The imp leaped from his eyes to Jean's.

'Hellish, was it?' she asked, her mouth curving. 'Sheer bloody torture?'

'Both o' those. That's probably why I've been a wee touch short-tempered lately.'

'A wee touch short-tempered?' She gave him a look of exaggerated disbelief. 'Bear with a sore head, more like.'

'Then kiss my sore head better, Just Jean,' he murmured. 'It's my mouth that hurts the most.'

Chapter 11

'PUT YOUR hand out,' Jean said awkwardly, opening her purse and placing half a crown into his palm.

Andrew was sitting beside her on the tram, which was currently taking them past the Art Galleries and on into Sauchiehall Street. He cupped his hand to receive the money but didn't make any move to put it into his pocket. Instead, he bent his dark head and peered at the silver coin. 'What's this?'

'We agreed,' Jean moistened her lips, 'that I would pay for the dancing partners.'

They were on their way to the Waldorf. Situated on the corner of Sauchiehall Street and Scott Street, it was Glasgow's newest *palais de danse*, a lavish conversion of the building that had, until a few years before, been home to the animals of Hengler's Circus and Menagerie. Jean had spotted a newspaper article about the new dance hall, which had been illustrated by a photograph of its '24 expert dance partners', twelve male and twelve female. The article had also mentioned that the Waldorf's tea-dances were to be held on Tuesday and Thursday afternoons.

Andrew raised his head and gave Jean one of his stern looks. 'What we agreed was that we dance three dances each with them. We know it costs sixpence a dance. Ye cannae count, Jean. Take this back and give me one and six.'

'I can count perfectly well, Andrew Logan. The extra's in case you want to buy a lemonade or something. Maybe it's the done thing to buy a drink for the dancing partner.'

'My one will have to go thirsty. The same as I will. Take this back, Jean.'

She tried staring him out. She should have known better than to think she had any hope of forcing him to back down. Sighing, she opened her purse again and exchanged the half-crown for one and sixpence. 'You're as stubborn as a mule.'

'Only just found that out?' he enquired airily. 'You're no' paying my tram fare either. I'm paying yours.'

The clippie was right beside him. He'd bought their tickets before Jean could utter a protest.

'Stubborn as a mule,' she repeated once the conductress was out of earshot.

He leaned away from her, making room between them so he could slide the tram tickets and the one and six into his jacket pocket. 'But you love me for it, don't you, Just Jean?'

'You think so?' Jean raised her eyebrows in what was intended to be an expression of scorn. He pulled a daft face and made her laugh instead before straightening up again and taking her hand in his. 'What's the plan, then?'

'You know what it is.'

'Aye, but I like to hear you talk. Tell me again.'

'Well,' Jean began, 'from what you've told me, there'll probably be a kiosk where we buy the sixpenny tickets. We buy three of those each and we choose a partner. We have one dance with them and then ask if they'll sit the next two out with both of us. At which point we pick their brains.'

'Yeuch. Sounds messy.'

'Especially if they then spill the beans,' Jean said with a

112

quick smile. 'I hope we'll choose partners who're friendly and prepared to do that.'

'It's their job to be friendly, Jean.'

'I suppose. Remind me why we need to dance with them as well as talk to them?'

'To see how they go about it,' he said. 'What their patter is. How they approach the customers. All that sort o' stuff.'

'Aye,' Jean said. She cast him a nervous glance. 'I'm a bit worried about dancing with someone who's not you.'

'You'll be fine. And,' he reminded her as the tram shoogled past the Grand Hotel and through the meeting of all the thoroughfares that fed into the noisy and bustling junction of Charing Cross, 'you're going to have to dance with lots o' different folk if we do get jobs as professional partners.'

'That's true.' She batted her eyelashes at him. 'Will you be jealous when you see me dancing with other men?'

'Stop fishing for compliments, you.' He edged himself towards the aisle. 'Come on. The next stop's ours.'

'Oh,' Jean breathed as they walked into the Waldorf a moment or two later, 'isn't this lovely?'

'It certainly is,' Andrew said admiringly, spinning round with her as the two of them took in the opulence of their surroundings. Jean's eyes opened even wider. 'There's a fountain in the middle of the floor!'

Andrew laughed in delight. 'So there is. We'd better watch we don't dance too close to it and get soaked.'

'Och, but it's lovely, though,' Jean said. 'Is it made of panes of coloured glass?'

'Looks like it. All geometric shapes too.'

'Like the rest of the décor,' Jean said, raising her eyes from the fountain to the high ceiling. The lights up there were enclosed in dramatically angled glass shades whose intricate patchwork of colours echoed those of the fountain: dark green, dark blue and a rich burgundy red.

'It's so stylish,' she breathed, her eyes dropping again to the floor. Polished to a high sheen, the light-coloured wood from which it was made was a wonderful contrast with the dark colours of the fountain and the light shades.

'Aye,' Andrew agreed. 'Even the lassies' dresses fit in.'

Jean followed his gaze to the raised platform beside the stage where the orchestra sat. Corralled off by thick white rope suspended from tall chrome pillars, the girls who were obviously the female dancing partners wore dark blue dresses with one patch pocket bearing a monogrammed *W* picked out in burgundy red. Their male counterparts were suave and elegant in black lounge suits.

'Andy,' Jean said with sudden determination, 'I want to be part of something like this. I really want that.'

'Then let's take the first step,' he said lightly. 'There's the kiosk where you buy the tickets. See you after the first dance, Jean.'

The young man with the neat fair hair and equally neat moustache to whom Jean shyly presented her three tickets did indeed turn out to be friendly. Despite that, the plan encountered its first hitch when she put her proposal to him that they should first have a dance and subsequently sit the next two out together.

'I'm awfully sorry,' he said. 'We're not allowed to sit dances out with patrons. It's against the rules.'

'Are there lots of rules about dancing partners?'

'You'd better believe it,' he said warmly. 'The Ten Commandments and more. You dance very well, by the way.'

Jean had been mightily relieved to discover that she could indeed dance with someone other than Andrew. Observing the varying standard of the other dancers currently circling

114

the floor of the Waldorf, she was even daring to think that under his tutelage she was shaping up quite well. She cast the fair-haired young man a doubtful look all the same. 'I suppose you have to say that to everybody.'

He grinned, and the pan loaf accent relaxed a little. 'Aye. But sometimes I mean it. Keep asking your questions.'

'You don't mind?'

'No' in the slightest,' he said. 'Ask away.'

The parlour maid had been sent into Glasgow to deliver one of Mr Fairbairn's articles to the offices of the *Glasgow Evening Dispatch* in Buchanan Street. Getting away from the manse on a Tuesday was an unexpected pleasure. This was the wee skivvy's afternoon off.

Despite her enjoyment of the outing, Anne Reid frowned as she boarded the tram that would take her back to Hyndland. Something had happened to Jean Dunlop, something that was putting a sparkle in her eyes and a smile on her lips.

When the younger girl had first arrived at the manse it had been easy to bully her. Snivelling for her mother every night, appearing with red-rimmed eyes every morning, wee Jeannie had been an easy target. She was much less of one nowadays. It was very aggravating that she'd learned not to rise to the bait.

There were other things about the maid-of-all-work that bothered Anne. She was too brainy, for a start. It didn't seem right for a skivvy to have brains. It seemed downright unfair that she also had good looks. Although she herself was obviously still unaware of it, Jean Dunlop was growing up into the sort of girl boys were drawn to. Like moths to a flame.

It wasn't only her looks. Though she hated to admit it, Anne recognised that there was something special about Jean.

Even the cheeky delivery boy from the local grocer's came over all tongue-tied and bashful when she spoke to him. No boy had ever reacted like that to Anne.

To make matters worse, recently the skivvy had seemed far too happy with herself into the bargain. Anne was beginning to suspect that wee Jeannie had found herself a boyfriend.

There might be some fun to be had in getting her into trouble with the Fairbairns over that. That would remind her that she really was the lowest of the low, with no family, no money and no status. Anne Reid sat back in her seat, and her frown lifted.

'Aye,' Andy agreed as he and Jean came out of the Waldorf, 'the lassie I was dancing wi'' mentioned all the rules and regulations too. Said there were some shenanigans at a couple o' places a few years back, so the City decided to tighten up on all o' the halls.'

'Shenanigans?'

'Apparently you used to be allowed to book professional partners out.'

'For private dancing lessons?' Jean asked. 'What was wrong with that?'

Andrew ran one finger around the inside of his collar. 'A lot o' the private dancing was o' the horizontal variety, no' the vertical.'

Jean looked at him. When the penny dropped, her mouth formed a shocked and silent little 'Oh'.

'You did ask,' he mumbled, his cheeks as rosy as hers. He nodded back in the direction of the Waldorf. 'That girl in there says the *palais* fall over backwards to be respectable now –' he caught himself on – 'which was undoubtedly the wrong metaphor.'

'Ignore it and move on,' Jean said hurriedly. 'What else did she say?'

'That it's more than her job's worth to allow any o' the customers to see her home. Although lots of them ask if they can.'

Jean was gazing along Sauchiehall Street, striving for sophisticated nonchalance. 'Well,' she said, raising her eyes to a sky that was distinctly more grey than blue, 'that's a good rule, isn't it? I suppose all of the rules are designed to protect professional partners. Shall we cross the road and get the tram? Those clouds are looking a bit ominous.'

'You get the tram if you like. I'm walking back.'

Jean lowered her gaze. 'You paid my fare on the way here.'

He was placing a cigarette between his lips. 'Save your breath to cool your porridge, Jean. You're no' paying my fare home and that's that.'

'We'll both have to walk, then. We've still got lots to talk about.'

'All right. We'll go via Woodlands Road. That'll bring you out closer to home.'

She narrowed her eyes at him. 'And you further from home.'

'Woodlands Road,' he said, nipping the incipient argument in the bud by taking a firm hold of her elbow and steering her across the busy junction in that direction.

Jean gave it up as a bad job. 'My partner said customers can be very generous with tips. He gets lots of presents as well. Ties and hankies and cigarette cases.' She laughed. 'He says you have to tactfully dissuade people from getting your initials engraved on the cigarette cases.'

'Because he sells them off and nobody wants ones wi' somebody else's initials on?'

Jean nodded. 'Gets so many of them, apparently. He also

said it's not so glamorous as it looks. Told me some of the women he dances with have "all the grace of an expectant elephant with bunions".'

Andrew laughed. 'The lassie said something very similar. Although some o' the things she talked about sounded glamorous enough. Like her spotlight number.'

'Which is?'

'The dancing partners take it in turns to do demonstration dances. Something a bit special. She suggested we choose a dance and work out a really good routine to do to it. Did your partner tell you how much he earned?'

'He was a wee bit cagey about that. That's the rain on.'

'So put your brolly up. I see you brought it with you, Miss Careful.'

'Just as well for you,' she retorted as she snapped the umbrella open and swung it up to cover both their heads. 'Did your partner say anything about money?'

'She gave me all the gen. Obviously couldnae resist my charm.'

Jean pursed her lips. 'Are you going to give me all the gen before I poke your eyes out with the spokes of this umbrella?'

'Can I no' spin it out until we get past the Dough School?' He took a puff of his cigarette and somehow managed to grin at her at the same time.

'Tell me right now or I'll not be responsible for my actions.'

'Brace yourself, then. I'm no' wanting you to faint in the street.'

'It's that good?'

'It's that good,' he replied solemnly. 'The basic wage is thirty bob a week—'

'Andy, that's almost three times as much as I'm earning now!'

'Hold your horses. It gets better. Thirty bob a week for

both the men *and* the girls, plus tuppence ha'penny from each of the dance tickets. That varies, seemingly,' he said, drawing closer to Jean as a horse-drawn brewer's dray splashed through a large puddle lapping over the gutter on to the wet and shiny pavement. 'Some places give the dancing partners threepence.'

'How many dances are there in a session?'

'Thirty in the evening, twenty-six at the afternoon tea-dances. Do the sums, Jean.'

'Would all of the halls do two tea-dances a week?'

'Take that as an average, anyway. And mind, there's no dancing on a Sunday. Don't count that in.'

Jean nodded and began to calculate, muttering under her breath as she did so. 'Thirty times tuppence equals sixty which equals five shillings, plus fifteen pence which equals one and three which equals six and threepence a night. Times six equals thirty-six shillings. Plus one and six makes it thirty-seven and six. One pound, seventeen and six.'

'I'll hold on to that figure. Do the afternoons now.'

'That's easy. Fifty-two times tuppence is one hundred and four pence. Divide by twelve and you get eight shillings and eightpence. Add twenty-six pence for the ha'pennies and you get ten and tenpence.'

'Add that to the one pound seventeen and six,' Andrew prompted.

'Two pounds eight and fourpence.'

'Plus the thirty bob basic rate.'

'Three pounds eighteen shillings and fourpence.' Jean frowned. The incredible sum she'd come up with was making her doubt her own mental arithmetic. She turned startled eyes on to Andrew. 'Andy, that's a small fortune. Almost as much in a week than I earn in two months at the manse!'

'Don't forget that you'd have clothes and shoes to buy. No' to mention digs.'

'Digs?'

'I don't think the Fairbairns are gonnae keep you on as a lodger, Jean. Especially if you're working in a dance hall.'

'I don't suppose they would. Where would I get digs?'

'Plenty o' those about. Quite a lot near Sauchiehall Street. Up in Gartnethill, for instance. Boarding houses and folk who let out one or two rooms.'

'What would that cost?'

'I'm no' sure. It depends on whether the landlady cooks for you or if you do it yourself.'

'You might get fed at the dance hall.'

'Possibly. Take off a pound a week for digs and food anyway. I think that would be about right.'

'That's two pounds eighteen and fourpence. That's still a lot of money, Andy.'

'You're counting on getting a partner for every dance on every day,' he warned.

Nothing could dampen Jean's enthusiasm. 'I don't think we would struggle. Particularly not you. Not with your matinée idol good looks and magic feet.'

Despite the notes of caution he had sounded, Jean could sense Andy was as excited as she was. 'Some places give dancing lessons too,' he said. 'On the afternoons when there's not tea-dances. You can earn more money doing that.'

'Andy, you'd be able to give your mother money and still have quite a bit left over for yourself!'

He blinked like a particularly solemn owl. 'I know. Chrissie could stay on at school and everything.'

'Och, Andy, do you think we could do it? You're good enough but am I?'

'You need more practice, Jean, that's all. We've got to fit that in somehow.' They passed the Dough School and wound their way along into Gibson Street. 'Up over the hill or along University Avenue?' he asked as they approached Bank Street.

'University Avenue. Then you'll get home quicker too.'

'I don't mind. I like walking with you.'

'Even when it's raining cats and dogs?'

'Is it raining? I hadn't noticed.' He discarded his half-smoked and soggy cigarette and pulled her arm through his as they lengthened their stride to climb the steepening hill. As they passed the tall Greek portico of the Wellington Church a tram passed, whining with the strain of clanking up the brae. Bright against the rainy gloom of the outside world, yellow light blazed out through its steamed-up windows.

'Cross over now? Right then,' he said as they reached the other pavement, 'how can we fit more practice in? I've got plenty o' free time but you havenae.'

'Well,' Jean said, thinking about it, 'I'm off in the evenings from about eight o'clock until I start washing up the supper things at eleven but that's no good to us. The hall's used every weekday evening.'

'You don't fancy first thing in the morning or last thing at night?'

Jean snorted. 'I get up at five o'clock as it is. And I don't usually get to bed until midnight.'

Andrew shook his head in disapproval. The scanty protection offered by Jean's umbrella hadn't been enough to stop the rain transforming his hair into a mass of dark waves. 'That's slave labour, Jean.'

'Look at it this way: I'll have no trouble finding the energy to dance all week— Oh, I've just had an idea. Come over here for a minute. Under that big old tree.'

They were close to the main entrance of Glasgow University now, walking past the gleaming black railings that bounded its lush and verdant grounds. The tree Jean had spotted was a luxuriant maple whose branches spread out over the broad pavement. When they got in under its shelter she lowered her umbrella and looked at Andrew. 'What about Sunday afternoons?'

'When we usually meet at Mr Rossi's? What about the Sunday school?'

'It clears out of the hall at one o'clock. Once the service is over in the church, all the parents come to collect their children.'

'But it's the Sabbath, Jean,' Andrew protested. 'The minister and his wife would think it was bad enough if they knew we were dancing in the church hall. They'd take it as a real affront if we were doing it on a Sunday.'

'I know,' Jean gulped. 'But in the words of the song, let's do it.'

He smiled his long, slow smile. 'You're the bravest lassie in the world, do you know that?'

'I don't feel very brave right at this particular moment.'

'You need a kiss.'

'In public?'

'Who's gonnae notice in this weather? Everybody's got their heids doon. And we're under this tree too. Folk'll only be able to see our legs.' He took her by the lapels of her coat. 'I love you, by the way.'

'I love you too,' she responded, still a little shy about saying the words. For a moment they simply gazed into one another's eyes. Listening to Andrew's breathing and her own, Jean was aware that the noise of the traffic swishing past on University Avenue had faded away into nothingness. She was dimly aware of the sound of a tram braking but it seemed very far away.

But she was very aware of the strong fingers curled under

her lapels. He'd told her that when he'd still been working he'd spent ages getting his hands clean, rubbing away with a nail brush at the ingrained dirt caused by spending all day carrying bags of coal. Now his hands were smooth and white and well kept: exactly the sort of hands a dancing partner needed.

'Those digs you're gonnae get.'

'What about them?'

'I'll be in the room next to yours.'

She flung her arms around his neck. 'Och, Andy, I was really hoping you were going to say that!' Then she frowned. 'But what are your mother and sisters going to say if you move out?'

'They'll not like it,' he said. 'But it's got to happen sometime. Oh, and we're so cramped at home, Jean. Packed in like sardines. Me moving out will give the lassies more space.'

Jean was still frowning. 'But will they and your mother approve of you becoming a dancing partner?'

'They'll approve o' the money.' His mouth twisted wryly. 'Assuming I can get a dancing job.'

'Of course you can,' Jean said. 'It's me who might not.'

'We'll practise every spare moment you can get away,' he said encouragingly.

'Aye,' she agreed.

'Sunday afternoons, then?'

'Sunday afternoons. I think I need that kiss now.'

His voice was a soft murmur. 'You can have as many kisses as you like.'

The windows of the tram were so steamed up you could hardly see the outside world. Anne Reid rubbed at the pane of glass with her gloved finger, making a circle big enough to look through.

All she could see were legs and feet. Legs and feet were enough. She recognised Jean Dunlop's hand-me-down coat and heavy shoes immediately. Whoever she was with, she was standing extremely close to him.

Anne smiled. All she had to do now was keep her eyes open. And after that all she had to do was light the blue touchpaper and retire.

Chapter 12

'THE TANGO?' Jean looked doubtfully down the hall at Andrew. 'You think we should do the tango for our spotlight number?'

'You love the tango. So do I. We also happen to dance it very well together.'

'All of that's true,' she agreed, although the little frown was still creasing her forehead. 'But it's such a . . . such a *passionate* dance. Such a *provocative* dance.'

In front of the stage and the gramophone, which sat on it, Andrew was standing with his hands bunched into fists at his waist and his legs slightly apart, his left foot gracefully extended to one side. Above his old black corduroy trousers he wore a shirt which might once have been as vibrantly blue as the summer sky. It was gey washed-out looking now. It was also spotlessly clean, starched and freshly ironed. His mother looked after him well.

'That's why it would make a rare spotlight number. We need something dead dramatic. Something that'll make folk sit up and take notice.'

Jean chewed her lip and thought about it. 'I know what you mean. But I think I might find it nearly as embarrassing as taking my clothes off in public.'

He laughed. 'You've fairly got a way wi' words, Jean. But I

don't think you would feel like that. The most important thing about the tango is the atmosphere, isn't it? Getting that right?'

'Y-e-s,' she agreed cautiously, wondering what on earth she was about to be cajoled into doing now.

'How d'ye get that atmosphere?' Andrew answered his own question. 'By getting so deep inside the dance you're no' aware o' anything else. No' aware o' *anybody* else. Let's try that out.'

Still not very sure, Jean watched him lower the needle on to the record he'd picked out.

'The hold's much closer, of course,' she observed as they met in the middle of the floor and he took her in his arms. 'That's one of the things that makes the tango more passionate.'

Andrew raised his eyebrows at her. 'That's one of the things that makes it my favourite dance to do wi' you.'

'Then there's those steps you've been trying to persuade me to incorporate into our routine.'

The black eyebrows were still raised. 'The more daring ones?'

'That would be one word for them.'

'You'd prefer *provocative*?'

'Shameless, more like,' Jean said, thinking of the step that involved her placing her right foot and leg between his two open legs. Or the even worse one where he stepped between hers. He'd had to do quite some coaxing to persuade her to even try those. Now he wanted her to go even further. Him hooking his hand under her knee and drawing her leg up around his waist was only one of the flourishes he'd suggested.

She felt him take his weight on to his right foot, the signal to her that he was going to move off on his left. Jean made the corresponding and contrary adjustments. The music started and she stepped back on to the ball of her right foot. 'One dance where you're not supposed to look as if you're enjoying yourself.'

'No,' he agreed as he continued to propel her backwards and she continued to allow him to do so. 'Reverse turn coming up.' They executed that and proceeded into a promenade before he spoke again. 'You're supposed to look like you're nursing a broken heart after an unhappy love affair or something. Think you can manage that?'

'I'll do my best.' The look she gave him completely contradicted what she'd just said about not looking happy when you danced the tango. 'But I'm afraid I don't know what that feels like.'

His voice was a low growl. 'If I have my way you never will. Back corté coming up.'

'Do you know what it feels like?' she asked curiously after they'd completed that manoeuvre and gone off into another promenade. 'An unhappy love affair, I mean?'

'I thought I did. Since I met you I've realised I never really was in love before.'

'Och, Andy, that's a beautiful thing to say . . .'

'Does it persuade you to try some of those steps you think are so shameless?'

'All right. Let's try 'em now.'

'When I'm good and ready,' he teased. 'Don't you know you're no' allowed to have a mind of your own when we're dancing? You have to do what I tell you to do, move as I direct you. The man's in charge.'

Jean snorted. 'Says who?'

'The rules o' dancing. Wheesht now. Don't talk any more. Concentrate on getting the atmosphere right.'

'I think we can safely say we've got the tango atmosphere,' Jean said a few moments later. The record had finished playing and they had stopped dancing but they were still locked in the tango hold.

'I think you're right.' Like her, Andy was a little breathless. 'Let's tango back to the stage. Don't let go of me.'

'Why? Do you want to run through it all again?'

'No,' he said, slanting a glance down at her, 'I just don't want you to let go of me.'

When they reached the stage, he let go of her only long enough to lift the needle off the record. It was some considerable time later before he drew his head back from hers.

'Dancing the tango with you has a very powerful effect on me.' He sighed happily and positioned her in front of him, crooking both of his arms around her neck.

'Dancing the tango makes you want to strangle me?'

'Nope. It makes me want to do this to you.'

Jean yelped when he demonstrated what 'this' was. 'What precisely are you doing?'

Andrew stopped doing it long enough to answer her question with one of his own. 'What does it feel like?'

'It feels like you're sticking your tongue in my ear.'

'That's what I'll be doing, then. D'ye like it?'

'No. Yes. Oh,' she moaned when he started doing it again, 'maybe I do like it . . .'

'Don't worry,' he murmured against her ear. 'I'll keep doing it for a while so you can make up your mind one way or the other.'

'What d'you mean, "stage" it?'

'Well,' Jean replied, 'the tango's a very theatrical dance, isn't it? You could use it to tell a story. Especially if you're dancing it for other people to watch.'

'Aye,' Andy said, gazing thoughtfully across the café table at her. 'Choreograph it, you mean?'

'That a big word for you to use.'

'Cheeky wee bisom,' he murmured. 'Well, we can work out a routine that would tell a story but how would we do the rest of it?'

'Costumes,' she said triumphantly. 'If we wear the right clothes we can really make an impact.'

'Ah,' he said, 'light begins to dawn. Tell me more.'

'It's all to do with how the tango started.' She blushed faintly. 'In Buenos Aires.'

'Specifically where in Buenos Aires, Miss Dunlop?' His lips twitched. 'Would you be knowing that?'

'You *know* where.'

'Houses of ill repute.'

Jean nodded, relieved that he had come out with a rather more high-falutin expression than any of the others he might have chosen. 'Quite rough places,' she went on. 'Quite poor places.'

'I don't think houses of ill repute are necessarily poor places.' Now his mobile face was poker straight. 'I understand a girl can make quite a healthy living at that game.'

'Andy!' Jean protested in a choked voice. 'Are you trying to embarrass me?'

'Aye. I like to see you blush. Tell me about these costumes you want us to wear.'

'You in your oldest and shabbiest clothes.'

'That won't be difficult. My vast wardrobe offers me an extensive range of shabby garments.'

'Your shirt not ironed and with no collar on it. Your sleeves rolled up to your elbows.'

'Wi' a rakish red kerchief knotted at my throat?'

'Now you're getting into the swing of things.'

'What are you gonnae wear?' The hand raising his cigarette to his lips halted in mid-air. 'I'm no' having you dressed like a

129

streetwalker, Jean. If that's your idea you can forget it right now.'

'Not like a streetwalker,' she said, hurrying over the word. 'But quite poor-looking. Me in old and shabby clothes too. With a couple of holes in my stockings.' She turned her mouth down. 'I have quite an extensive range of those particular items in my own vast wardrobe.'

'Maybe,' he said. 'I'll give it some consideration.'

She scowled at him. 'You're making the decision, are you?'

'We've discussed this before, Jean. The man takes the lead in dancing.'

She put her hands on her hips. 'This is *about* dancing, not the dancing itself. I've got a say in the matter.'

'Of course you do. I only said that to annoy you.' He grinned at her. 'You look like a wee angry fairy. Got a story worked out already?'

'Sort of.'

'I thought you might have. Let's hear it.'

'It's not complicated. But it's all about love and passion.'

'Sounds good. Tell me more.'

'I'm your faithless lover. I've deserted you for someone else but realised that I've made a terrible mistake and come back begging your forgiveness.'

'Do I give it?'

'Not at first. The story's not *that* simple.'

'So I get to make you suffer first?'

'Don't sound so enthusiastic when you say that. But yes, you do. Only because you're so hurt by my betrayal, of course. At first you thrust me away from you.'

'But you keep coming back?'

'Aye. Because I love you so much I'm prepared to humiliate myself, go down on my knees to you, until I manage to

130

convince you that it's you I really love. Which I do in the end.'

'Gluttons for punishment, you faithless lovers.' He propped his chin on his fist and gave her the slow-burning smile. 'I like the sound of you going down on your knees to me. Although maybe no' when other folk are watching.'

Jean sent him a dirty look across the table. 'On my knees to you in dancing terms, I meant. Think you can choreograph my wee story?'

The smile grew even wider. 'Is the Pope a Catholic?'

'One more run-through before you go?'

'I suppose we'd better.' Andrew pretended to groan. Over the past fortnight they'd been concentrating exclusively on their tango routine and the story they were telling through it. Once they had the moves planned out they had practised them over and over again, hammering the steps and pauses and figures so strongly into their heads that their feet and bodies would know what to do without their brains having to tell them.

'Atmosphere,' Andrew said now. 'Let's concentrate on the atmosphere.'

Jean nodded in agreement. There would be no conversation between them from now on although plenty of communication. It was all in the dance: the intricate and interlocking patterns made by their legs and feet; the sensuous intertwining of their bodies; their physical and mental energy focused entirely one on the other; the messages and emotions of the story flashing between their eyes.

They really were so far inside the dance that they were unaware of what was happening outside of it. They didn't hear the door of the church hall opening. They didn't hear the two sets of feet making their way through the kitchen and the corridor. They didn't hear the soft whoosh as the brush on the bottom of the opening door swept over the floorboards of the hall.

The first thing they heard was the sharp intake of breath.

Chapter 13

ELIZABETH FAIRBAIRN'S well-bred tones rang out. 'What *on earth* is going on here?'

For the merest few seconds the shock of discovery locked Jean and Andrew into position. They were at the part where the girl in the dance was kneeling to her lover, beseeching him to forgive her. Her right knee between Andrew's legs and bent at an almost ninety-degree angle, her left leg extended behind her to the full extent of its reach, Jean looked almost as if she were lunging forward in a fencing match.

Andrew had one hand on the back of her waist and the other threaded through her hair. Head bent over her upturned face, he had brought his lips to within a hair's-breadth of hers.

When they'd been developing the routine he'd maintained that they shouldn't actually complete the kiss. At this point the man hadn't yet forgiven the girl for her betrayal of him. Besides, Andrew had added, smiling the kind of smile that did strange things to Jean's insides, it would be so much more *provocative* not to complete the kiss.

Judging by the look on Elizabeth Fairbairn's face, provocative was a very inadequate description of the picture they were presenting to her.

Andrew's breath was warm against Jean's mouth. 'The cook or the minister's wife?'

'The minister's wife.'

'Come up.' Retaining his self-possession, he didn't release his hold on Jean until they were both safely upright. Then he walked forward, hand outstretched. 'Good afternoon, Mrs Fairbairn. My name's Andrew Logan.'

Jean knew before the words were even out of his mouth that his valiant attempt to defuse the situation was doomed to failure. Mrs Fairbairn looked as if she was about to burst a blood vessel. Anne Reid looked triumphant.

She's been spying on us, Jean thought, and now I'm going to find out exactly what happens in the next scene of that wee film I've had playing inside my head. She felt as if she were at the cinema, sitting safely in the darkness of the stalls while she watched the action unfold in front of her up on the silver screen.

Ignoring Andrew's hopeful hand, Elizabeth Fairbairn looked past him at Jean. 'We take you in,' she spat out, 'and this is how you repay us? By *cavorting* in this *shameless* manner under our very noses?' She waved a hand in the direction of the gramophone. 'To that vile music?'

Andrew's face clouded. 'I don't think you heard me, Mrs Fairbairn. I was introducing myself to you.'

He was speaking very properly, very correctly. Elizabeth Fairbairn's gaze swept over him as though he were a piece of dirt on the sole of her shoe. 'I'm addressing my housemaid. Not you.'

Andrew stepped towards her. Elizabeth Fairbairn took a couple of steps back. 'Don't you threaten me, young man!'

'I'm not threatening you, Mrs Fairbairn,' he said, sounding puzzled at the very idea that he might be contemplating any such thing. 'I'm trying to explain what Jean and I have been doing here.'

'I can see that for myself,' she snapped.

'We haven't been doing anything wrong.'

'Not doing anything wrong?' she repeated. '*Not doing anything wrong?*' Her voice rose in outraged disbelief.

'We were dancing,' Andrew said. 'Only dancing.'

'*Only dancing?*' howled Mrs Fairbairn.

They can't understand each other. They can't possibly understand each other. As Jean walked forward to join them the comforting illusion that she was in the cinema watching events unfold on the screen vanished as completely as snow sliding from the parapet of a stone bridge into a river. She was in the thick of this.

They were in Mr Fairbairn's study. The minister was sitting behind his big leather-topped desk and he was bending the full force of his powerful gaze and his equally powerful personality upon Jean and Andrew. His wife stood next to him, one hand resting on the back of her husband's chair. The parlour maid, much to her chagrin, had been dismissed. Jean was pretty certain the girl hadn't moved very far away from the other side of the study door.

Like miscreants being tried for some crime, she and Andrew hadn't been offered chairs. Standing side by side in front of the big desk they stood and listened as the minister demanded an explanation from them for their conduct.

'Not that there *can* be any explanation. Mrs Fairbairn has told me what she saw.' He gestured towards the closed door of his study. 'We have another witness too. Even so, I can hardly credit what my own ears are hearing. I'm bitterly disappointed in you, Jean. What have you to say for yourself?'

Anticipating that the dancing lessons wouldn't remain

secret for ever, Jean had built up the imagined moment of their discovery by the Fairbairns into something terrifying. Yet now she felt strangely calm. She glanced round the room, which she had cleaned and dusted so often. She looked at Mrs Fairbairn. She looked at the minister. For four long years the two of them had governed and controlled her life.

She knew Andrew was ready and willing to leap to her defence. At the drop of that proverbial hat he'd be there. At the same time he seemed to know without having to be told that she had to do this by herself. Jean looked the minister in the eye.

'I've been learning to dance,' she told him. 'Andrew's been teaching me. And I don't think we've been doing anything wrong.'

She imagined she must be one of the few people on Earth who had ever rendered the Reverend Ronald Fairbairn incapable of speech – even if it was only for a few seconds. It wasn't long before his voice spluttered into life again. '*Not done anything wrong*? When the two of you have been carrying on in such a lewd, shameless and disgusting manner? Within the very bounds of *my* church?'

Lewd. Shameless. Disgusting. No. What they had been doing was passionate, provocative and daring. Not lewd, shameless and disgusting. Never that.

'Jean,' the minister intoned, 'you have not only broken the rules of this household, you have broken God's rules, His very commandments—'

'Is that right?' broke in a cynical voice. 'In which one o' the Ten Commandments does it say "Thou shalt not dance"? Would that be after the one that says "Thou shalt not enjoy thyself"?'

Mr Fairbairn's eyes went to Andrew. 'I think you and I have met before.'

'Aye. We have. At the corner o' Stewartfield Street at the back end o' last year.'

'The young man who challenged me on the Bible.' The minister looked again at Jean. 'Where did you meet this person?'

She didn't hesitate. 'In a dance hall in Partick.'

'*A dance hall?*' The minister repeated those innocuous words as though they were the vilest obscenities imaginable. 'One of those dens of vice? Have you learned nothing while you've been in this house, Jean?'

'I've learned lots of things while I've been in this house. I've learned about coldness and unkindness.' She cast Mrs Fairbairn a measuring glance. 'Oh, I've learned so much about coldness and unkindness!'

'You ungrateful little bitch,' hissed Elizabeth Fairbairn. 'We took you in. We didn't have to. I never wanted to. Your mother had *tuberculosis*. A disease of the poor and the feckless. Yet out of our Christian charity we took you in. We fed you, we clothed you, we saw to your moral education—'

'And worked her like a dog,' Andrew put in hotly. 'And dressed her in hand-me-downs when ye didnae have to and never gave her a kind word.'

'How dare you speak to me like that?' The minister's wife raised one arm and pointed towards the door. 'Get out of my house!'

'No' without Jean.'

The words were softly spoken. They fell like a bombshell, momentarily silencing everyone in the study. Except Andrew. He turned and held out his hand to her. 'Will ye come wi' me, Jean?' He said some words under his breath that were intended for her ears only. 'Will ye go, lassie, go?'

'Jean,' the minister said, 'think about this! Please! I do feel a certain responsibility towards you. Your mother gave you into our care, after all—'

'A fine job you made o' it,' Andrew said witheringly.

The minister wasn't prepared to be silenced again. 'Jean, I can't pretend that your conduct hasn't shocked me to the core but I'm prepared to give you one last chance. Here are the conditions. You will once again become the dutiful, obedient and modest girl I always thought you to be. You will be respectful towards myself and Mrs Fairbairn. You will give up your *dancing*.' He uttered the word as if being forced to have it in his mouth was like eating poison. 'You will also agree never to see this young man again.'

Jean didn't even look at him. She simply extended her hand to Andrew. He grasped it immediately. As though they were dancing some old-fashioned courtly measure, they turned as one and headed for the door.

'You'll be sorry, my girl. Once he's had his fun with you he'll leave you lying in the gutter. Don't think you can come running back to us for help when that happens.'

Jean felt the quiver run through Andrew's fingers. Once again she turned with him. He looked Elizabeth Fairbairn dead in the eye and pronounced his farewell to her with impeccable precision. 'Fuck off, you damned filthy-minded old witch.'

They were a full five minutes away from the manse and from Clarence Drive itself before either of them spoke. Walking past the large and gracious houses that lined Partickhill Road, Jean stopped dead in the middle of the broad pavement. 'What have I just done, Andy?'

He stopped too. She had left him standing in the lobby of the manse for five frantic minutes while she had stuffed her meagre belongings into the old red and blue carpet bag that had belonged to her mother. Carrying it in his right hand, Andrew used his left to pull Jean round to face him.

'Something you should have done a long time ago. You're well shot o' that place.'

She pulled her hand out his grip and backed away from him, sitting down abruptly on a low stone wall that bounded an overgrown garden. 'Have I not burned all of my boats?'

Andrew walked over to her, placing the carpet bag in front of the wall before he joined her on it. 'Ye're about to launch a whole new boat. I'll be crewing it wi' you.'

She looked at him, her eyes clouded. 'I've wanted to leave the manse for so long. Now that I've actually done it I'm a bit scared to be out in the big wide world all on my own.'

'You're no' on your own. You're wi' me.'

'And what are you going to do with me?'

'Take you to my mother, of course.' He planted a kiss on Jean's clammy forehead. 'She'll look after you.'

Accustomed to the busy and bustling manse, Jean was used to being in a house where lots of people talked. She'd never before been in a house where quite so many people talked all at the same time. Only Bella Logan was quiet, gazing at her son and this girl he had brought home with him out of tired and anxious eyes.

Picking up on some of the teasing comments flying like darting arrows around the overcrowded Logan home, one thing Jean soon learned was that she was the only girlfriend Andrew had never brought home.

She had a strong suspicion the Logan women thought that had been reluctance on her part to visit their undeniably humble house. She had a strong suspicion that misconception wasn't exactly winning her friends. Yet how – even if she could have got a word in edgeways – could she tell the women who clearly loved him as much as he loved them that he had been ashamed to show his girlfriend where he lived?

She wasn't a snob. She wasn't posh. She came from as poor a background as they did. She had only lived up the hill because she'd been working there. Despite all of that, she couldn't shake the feeling that the Logans – with the possible exception of young Chrissie, and just maybe Andrew's mother – soon had her down as a bit toffee-nosed. That didn't inhibit their curiosity about her one little bit. By seven o'clock on Sunday evening Jean was beginning to feel as if she'd told her life story twenty times over.

'Look,' an exasperated Andrew said at last, 'can you lot no' see that the lassie's had enough? C'mon, you and me'll go out for a wee walk, Jean.'

'Can I come?'

Andrew's face softened as he looked at Chrissie. 'Sorry, pet, no' tonight.'

'Och,' Jean said, smiling at the bright-eyed young girl. 'Can she not come with us?'

'No' tonight,' Andrew repeated, ruffling his youngest sister's hair. 'Jean and me have got things to discuss, Chrissie.'

'Like where she's gonnae sleep tomorrow,' put in Alice, his oldest sister. She rolled her eyes. 'Where she's gonnae sleep tonight, for that matter.'

'Aye. We havenae exactly got room for a lodger, Andy.' That was Agnes, the next oldest of the five sisters. It hadn't taken Jean long to pick her out as what Andrew had called the 'nippy sweetie' of the family.

'Don't pay any attention to them,' he said once he had led Jean down the stairs and out of the close.

'They're right, though. Your mother's worried about how she's going to fit me in too. She looks really anxious, Andy.'

'I know.'

'I'm an extra mouth to feed.'

'I know.'

'It's not fair to ask her and your sisters to squeeze up to fit me in. You don't have the room.'

'I know.'

'So if you know all of that,' Jean said wearily, 'do you know what we're going to do about it?'

'Och, aye,' he said, reaching for her hand as they turned the corner into Dumbarton Road. 'I know what we're gonnae do about it.'

'Any chance you might tell me?'

'If you ask nicely.'

'Andy,' Jean said, stopping and turning to face him, 'I'm really tired. Not to mention a bit upset and a bit confused. Not very sure what the future holds, either.'

He was instantly contrite. 'Sorry, Jean. But I think the answer's quite simple really. As of tomorrow you and me put on our glad rags and start going round the dance halls auditioning for jobs.'

Jean gulped. 'D'you think we're ready? I mean, you are. But am I?'

He placed both of his hands lightly on her shoulders. 'Of course you are. You're aye telling me to have faith in myself. Now I'm telling you to have faith in yourself.'

'And what about where I'm going to stay until we find a job?'

'Got any money?' he asked.

'About enough to pay for digs somewhere for a couple of months or so . . .' Her voice trailed off. They both knew what the next question was. He had to draw in a breath before he could ask it.

'Have you got enough money to pay for digs for me too? Maybe for half o' that time?'

Her eyes searched his face. 'You wouldn't like it if I did that.'

'I'd hate it,' he agreed, 'but it's the lesser o' two evils. I'm no' having you stuck in some boarding house on your own.'

'But I'd be taking you away from your family, Andy. What would they do without you?'

He shrugged. 'They'll miss me, I suppose. The same way that I'm gonnae miss them.'

'You're talking as though we're really going to do this.'

'We are really going to do this. And it's gonnae be better for my family in the end. I'll be able to give Ma some real money. No' the few shillings I get from the dole every week.'

'So,' Jean said, taking a deep breath to steady herself, 'are we going to go back now and tell them what we've got in mind?'

Andrew took her hand again. 'Aye. Let's do that.'

An avalanche of words hit them as soon as he had finished speaking. It seemed to Jean that every member of the Logan family had an opinion on the matter and wasn't loath to express it.

'I think Ma's got something she wants to ask,' Andrew said, cutting through the competing voices. Bella Logan looked up at her son.

'Is being a dancing partner a *respectable* sort of a job?'

He crouched down in front of her where she sat in a rocking chair by the big black-leaded range, took her hands in his and assured her that it was eminently respectable.

'There's all sorts of rules and regulations about it,' Jean contributed. Anxious to do her bit to ease the worried frown creasing his mother's forehead, she found her words being drowned out by Alice Logan.

'*Respectable?*' she spluttered. 'Dancing like a performing monkey for the delectation o' capitalist lackeys who're gonnae graciously deign to throw you a few coppers?'

142

'Give it a rest, Alice,' Andrew said drily as he rose to his feet again and propped himself against the wall next to the range. 'It's work. Well-paid work, at that.'

'How much does it pay, Andy?' Chrissie asked helpfully.

He folded his arms across his chest and lifted his chin in the direction of where Jean sat at the square table in the middle of the room. 'Tell them,' he said with an encouraging smile. 'You're the one who worked it all out.'

She knew he was deliberately bringing her into the conversation, doing his best to make her feel part of this noisy and opinionated family. She blushed furiously when the attention of every member of that family switched suddenly to her.

'We r-reckon we c-an m-ake nearly f-four pounds each,' she stuttered. 'Maybe even a b-bit m-more than that.'

'A week?' asked one of the Logan twins, her incredulity only too obvious.

'That cannae be right,' said Agnes Logan scornfully. 'Nobody's gonnae pay folk that much money just to dance!'

'It is right. Jean and me have looked into this.'

Agnes locked eyes with her brother. 'But the two o' youse have to get these wonderful jobs. You might be a good dancer but is she?' Seated to Jean's right, she had swivelled round in her chair so that she had her back to her. Jean couldn't help feeling that the posture she had chosen to adopt was no accident.

'Jean,' Andrew said, laying a slight but pointed stress on the name and giving his sister a very level look, 'happens to be an excellent dancer.'

'Well, I think it's a daft idea,' said Alice Logan, speaking in the tones of a woman who always knew her own mind and could rarely see that there might possibly be an alternative view to be taken on any subject. 'Apart from demeaning yourselves by doing it in the first place, there's bound to be loads o' folk after these jobs.'

'Nothing venture, nothing win,' Jean said quietly, daring to take advantage of the lull in the conversation that followed that comment.

'What about what Andy stands to lose?' Agnes demanded, at last and with obvious reluctance throwing a baleful glance over her shoulder at Jean. 'What about what we all stand to lose?'

'Like my dole money?' he enquired sarcastically. 'It's hardly a king's ransom, Agnes.'

'And he'll be earning an awful lot more than that,' Chrissie put in.

Agnes rounded on her youngest sister. 'What would you know about it, you wee nyaff? Do you no' understand that there's absolutely no guarantee o' him getting one o' these jobs?'

'Absolutely no chance o' it, mair like,' put in Alice.

'I think he'd have a good chance,' put in one of the twins, and the Logan girls were away again, going at it hammer and tongs. Despairing of them all, Jean momentarily closed her eyes. She was so tired, worn out by everything she'd been through today, exhausted by the strong emotions that had buffeted her over the last few hours.

'That lassie needs her bed,' someone said. Andrew's mother, she thought.

'Pity she hasnae got one here,' came the sour response. That was Agnes, the nippy sweetie.

'Enough!' roared Andrew, and Jean's eyes flew open. 'Jean and me have told you what we're gonnae do, and there's an end to it.' He hunkered down once more in front of his mother. 'I'm sorry, Ma,' he said, 'but I've got to do this. Gie it a try at least. If it works out it could make a big difference to all o' us.'

His sisters had shut up at last, all of them waiting to see what their mother would say. Bella Logan stretched out a hand and smoothed back the hair that had fallen forward over Andrew's brow. 'You've aye been a good son to me,' she said, 'and a good brother to the girls. Protected us from your father. Worked hard to support us all. You hate going to the Labour Exchange to collect your dole but you do it for us.'

'I've done my best, Ma,' Andrew managed, clearly moved.

'And now ye want to strike out on your own.' Bella Logan glanced across at Jean. 'Wi' your lassie.'

'Aye,' Andrew said softly. 'That's about the size o' it. But we'll be back often, Ma. And as soon as we start making any money I'll pass some o' it on to you.'

'You're a good lad,' his mother said, still smoothing the hair back from his forehead. She looked at all of her daughters in turn, daring them to say a word. 'And now we're all going to get away to our beds.' She stood up and walked across to where Jean sat at the table. 'Come on, pet,' she said gently, 'let's find you a place to sleep.'

Andrew caught her hand as she passed him. 'Things'll look better in the morning,' he murmured. 'You'll see.'

But the morning brought a thunderous knocking at the door, repeated until every occupant of the household was struggling sleepily up on to their elbows.

'Open up!' came a yell. 'Police!'

Hastily buttoning up the flies of his trousers, Andy went to the door. Having been squeezed in on a shake-down in the room where Mrs Logan and her two oldest daughters slept, Jean met him there.

'Andrew Logan?' came the voice of authority.

'Aye. I'm Andrew Logan.'

'You're lifted, lad. Finish dressing and then come with me.'

'You're arresting him?' Alice Logan put her hands on her hips and faced up to the policeman. 'I'll have you know ma brother's never been in trouble wi' the law in his life!'

'Well, he's in trouble now,' the police officer responded. 'Threatening behaviour. Insulting behaviour. Maybe breach o' the peace into the bargain.'

'Says who?' demanded Agnes as the other sisters gathered around their mother.

'Says the Reverend Ronald Fairbairn and his wife up on Clarence Drive,' said the policeman. 'They've made a complaint.'

Andrew was gone, clattering down the stairs with the policeman. Bella Logan stood for a moment in the doorway of her home, staring after her son. Then she turned, and seemed to crumple. Two of her daughters went forward to support her.

'The police at our door,' Bella moaned. 'The police at our door. We havenae had that since your father died.'

And Jean found herself alone in the tiny lobby, a battery of reproachful eyes trained upon her.

Chapter 14

THREE HOURS later, shortly before 11 a.m., Jean found herself sitting next to Andrew's formidable sister Alice on the hard wooden benches provided by the court for members of the public. Everybody else around them seemed also to be either a friend or relative of the people being tried before the stipendiary magistrate this Monday morning. Andrew himself was brought up at ten past eleven.

He looked pale and tired. With hardly time to get dressed before he'd been escorted away, he was badly in need of a shave and had obviously been able to do nothing more with his hair than smooth it down with his hands. Both that and the dark stubble shadowing his jaw made him look wild and unkempt but as his eyes ranged over the courtroom and found Jean and Alice he managed to throw them a smile.

As though he's encouraging us rather than the other way around, Jean thought. Her bottom lip and chin began to tremble in the way they always did when she was really upset.

'Don't you *dare* let him see you cry,' hissed Alice.

Jean pressed her fingers against her chin to steady it but it didn't matter anyway. The prisoner had already been curtly instructed to turn and face the magistrate. He peered down at

Andrew from his high bench, asking him for his full name, address and occupation. The voice that answered him wasn't loud but it seemed steady enough.

'The details of this case, please?' asked the stipendiary magistrate.

A uniformed policeman walked forward, flipped open his notebook and began reading aloud. 'At five p.m. yesterday evening, the duty sergeant at the Marine Police Station received a telephone call from the Reverend Ronald Fairbairn, minister of St Martin's Church of Scotland in Clarence Drive, Hyndland. The minister wished to report an altercation which had taken place in the manse. This altercation involved the prisoner. The prisoner used foul language towards Mrs Fairbairn, the minister's wife, and also threatened her with violence—'

Jean drew her breath in on a gasp. 'He didn't threaten her,' she shouted. 'He didn't!'

The magistrate looked up, gazing at her over the half-moon spectacles poised on the end of his nose. 'Who is this young woman?'

'Please, sir,' Jean said, only then realising that she had both flown to her feet and brought the proceedings of the court to a skidding halt, 'I'm Andrew Logan's girlfriend.'

Alice was tugging on Jean's skirt, trying to get her to sit down. Jean ignored her. 'I was there when this happened. I saw and heard everything. Andrew didn't threaten Mrs Fairbairn. He's not like that.'

The magistrate had a gold fountain pen in his right hand. He used it now to point at Jean. 'Who is that young woman?'

'I don't know, sir,' one of the court officials answered. 'I presume she's who she says she is. The prisoner's girl-friend.'

The magistrate looked at Jean again. 'Is that who you are?'

'Yes, sir,' Jean said. 'I was there—'

'Yes, yes,' the magistrate said testily. 'We all heard you. We also happen to have in front of us signed statements by other people who were there. To wit,' he went on, shifting the papers that lay before him, 'Miss Anne Reid, parlour maid at St Martin's, not to mention the Reverend Mr Fairbairn and his good lady. Both of whom, I need hardly add, can be considered the most reliable of witnesses. Whereas *the prisoner's girlfriend* is hardly likely to be the most unbiased of witnesses, is she? Sit down, young woman.'

The policeman who'd been reading from his notebook coughed. 'If you please, sir, I think I can supply some information about the young woman. If her name is Jean Dunlop, that is.'

The magistrate looked again in Jean's direction. 'Stand up,' he said.

Choking back an exasperated, 'You only just told me to sit down,' Jean rose again to her feet.

'Are you Jean Dunlop?'

'I am, sir. Yes.'

The magistrate turned again to the policeman who was giving evidence. 'You have information about Miss Dunlop?'

'Indeed, sir. She was present at the manse yesterday afternoon. She was being sacked when Logan intervened.'

'Being dismissed from her employment? What for?'

'Impertinence and disobedience, sir.'

'But that's not—'

'Be quiet, young woman. You're not helping your young man's case in any way.' It was neither that rebuke nor the insistent tugging at her skirt that made Jean sit down. It was the pleading look in Andrew's eyes.

The magistrate was once more peering down at him. 'Did you threaten Mrs Ronald Fairbairn with violence?'

'No.'

'She says you did.'

'All I did was walk towards her.'

'Did you use foul language towards her?'

'Oh, aye. She asked for that.'

That calm admission cost him a five-minute lecture from the magistrate. The tirade took in declining standards, lack of respect of youth for age and of the working classes for their betters, and the shocking nature of an offence that was compounded by such an equally shocking lack of remorse.

'Fifteen strokes of the birch,' the magistrate said at last. 'Sentence to be carried out at the end of the court's session today.'

Jean gasped, and turned to Alice Logan. 'They can't do that to him!'

'They can do what they bloody well like to him,' snapped the other girl. 'Pleased wi' yourself?'

With several hours to contemplate the prospect that lay ahead of him, Andrew had made up his mind that he would take his punishment like a man. Nor would he give those who administered it the satisfaction of hearing him cry out.

His first sight of the birching board made him swallow hard and bunch his hands into fists. Bolted upright to the wall of a room in the basement of the police station, it looked like a thin, hard and unforgiving piece of wood. Leather straps were fixed to it, three sets in all. He was still puzzling out the purpose of the small and grubby cushion halfway up the board when one of the two uniformed policemen in the room told him to strip off his jacket, shirt and vest and undo his belt and the fly of his trousers.

'Soon be over, lad,' he said, pulling down Andrew's loosened trousers to expose the small of his back and the top of his buttocks. 'Over here now. Forehead flat against the board.'

Allowing himself to be led forward, Andrew felt tears prickle behind his eyes, moved by the gruff sympathy. There was no vindictiveness here. The man was simply doing his duty.

'Arms up.' The brisk voice was quite cheerful. All in a day's work.

One set of leather manacles was buckled around Andrew's wrists, pinning his hands to the wall on either side of his head. The second set was for his knees, the third for his ankles. As he was fastened ever more securely to the board he felt the small cushion press against his belly. It must be designed to absorb some of the impact as you were slammed against the board. Just enough to stop you sustaining any internal injuries.

He glanced down and to his left. The birch had to be four feet long, the circumference of the bound twigs a good six inches. It stood upright in a bucket of brine. He could smell the salt. He could smell something else too: the stink of urine overlaid by the sickening aroma of disinfectant.

Andrew pressed his forehead harder against the board. It was warm. Some other poor bugger had stood here before him. Please God, he thought, I don't want to wet myself. *Please let me not wet myself . . .*

'Ready?'

He tensed, and felt a hand on his bare shoulder. 'Try no' to do that, laddie. It'll be the better for you if you dinna.'

He thought he'd prepared himself for the shock of the first stroke. He was wrong. It didn't feel like wood striking his bare skin. It felt like barbed wire. The shock of it brought Andrew's head snapping back and he forgot all about that determination not to cry out.

'Yell all ye like, laddie,' advised the policeman who'd positioned him on the board. 'We'll no' clype on ye.'

Reeling with pain, humiliation and sheer bloody anger at what was being done to him, Andrew once more placed his clammy brow against the board. *Don't tense up. It'll be the better for me if I dinna.*

Hard not to tense up when even your teeth were waiting for the next blow. Why was the other policeman taking so long to administer it? Just do it, Andrew thought viciously. Just fucking do it.

He felt hands on his back. Professional hands. 'No problem as yet. He's a strong enough specimen. I think you can proceed without hindrance, Sergeant. Let's say until the eighth stroke.'

At the seventh stroke Andrew felt the warm wetness of his own blood slide down his back, then the professional hands again. The doctor stated the obvious. 'You've broken the skin, Sergeant.'

'He's sentenced to fifteen strokes.'

'Keep going, then,' said the cool voice. 'But let me examine him between each one.'

Did they mean to be merciful? Andrew didn't know. What he did know was that the delay while the police surgeon peered at his back between each stroke only served to prolong the agony. He squeezed his eyes tightly shut and willed it all to be over. Jean, he thought, I'll think of Jean . . .

He was being washed down. With something that stung like hell. Andrew yelped as he felt the damp cloth pass over the welts that the birch had raised and wondered what the hell his back looked like. 'Make sure you keep it clean for the next wee while,' instructed the doctor. 'Salty water's a good antiseptic.'

The leather straps were unbuckled. 'Step away from the board now. You're free to go.' He was handed his shirt, vest and jacket. 'I doubt we'll be seeing you again in a hurry.'

He found himself in the next room, gazing at a wall of dazzling white tiles. The sun was streaming in through a small and high window. Andrew bit back tears of pain and rage. It was over now. He would not cry.

That resolution was tested to the limit as he dressed himself. His arms stiff and sore from the way they had been pinioned, he considered not bothering with his vest. He could stuff it in the pocket of his jacket. It might help absorb the blood, though. He put it on.

He kept having to stop, every movement agony, but at last he managed it. Heading for the pointing finger notice on the wall of the tiled room he found himself going through a small lobby and an open door. Blinking against the sunlight, he saw that he'd stepped out into a courtyard at the back of the police station. There were a few women standing around.

Jean was one of them. His sisters Alice and Agnes were there too. 'Come on, Andy,' Alice said, stepping forward to meet him. 'Let's get you home.'

'Yes,' Jean agreed. 'Can you walk all right, or do you need some help?'

Alice Logan rounded on her. 'You're no' coming back wi' us! It's you that's caused all o' this!' She turned her back on Jean, dismissing her. 'Gie me a hand wi' him, Agnes. If we don't get him away from here soon, folk'll know what's happened and Ma's gonnae die o' shame.'

Andrew briefly closed his eyes. When he spoke he sounded indescribably tired. 'Does Ma know yet?' he asked. 'What my sentence was, I mean?'

Jean saw Alice and Agnes exchange a furtive glance. 'We told her you'd got a fine. Thought it would be time enough to tell her the truth once we got you home. She thinks we're out at the pawn now, raising the money.'

'If I go off with Jean now, Ma doesn't need to know any different from that, does she?'

His sisters studied him for a long moment. 'You've aye been stubborn,' Alice said at last. 'Wait here. Me and Agnes'll go and fetch your girlfriend's bag. We'll pack one for you too.'

Chapter 15

J EAN OPENED her purse and extracted a note and a coin.
'Twelve-and-six a week. That's what you said, isn't it?'

'Don't you want to see the room first, dear?' The question
had been asked without much interest. Clearly this tarty-
looking woman who hadn't removed the cigarette from her
mouth during the entire conversation was only interested in
their money. She hadn't so much as glanced at her prospective
tenant's left hand to see if she was wearing a wedding ring.

'No, thank you,' Jean said crisply. 'May I have the key?'

'Jean.'

Both she and the landlady turned at the sound of Andrew's
voice. He was standing a few feet away from them in the big
square lobby of the boarding house and he looked terrible.
Pale and exhausted and completely at the end of his rope.

The wall against which he stood was covered in the most
hideous flowery wallpaper Jean had ever seen. Age and
cigarette smoke had rendered it even more repellent, turning
what had once presumably been huge pink roses into sludgy
green cabbages.

Andrew had his head tilted back against one of them,
carefully not allowing his back to come into contact with the
wall. Even without that pressure, the pain he must be feeling now was etched on his face. He didn't even have the

resources to utter the protest Jean knew he was on the brink of making.

'It's all right, Andy,' she said. 'Hang on for a wee minute.'

'What's up with him?' asked the landlady. Her eyes narrowed suspiciously 'He's not ill, is he? I'm not having him under my roof if he's got something catching.'

'He's not ill. He's just had a bit of a difficult day, that's all.' Jean took the key the landlady was brandishing at her and interrupted the recital of all the prohibitions in the middle of '. . . no noise after ten o'clock at night and absolutely no parties whatsoever—' 'Yes, yes. We'll be very quiet. What floor is our room on?'

It was on the top, of course, two precipitous flights up. When they reached the first landing, Jean took Andy's bag out of his hand for the umpteenth time that evening. He'd kept telling her that she couldn't carry both of them.

'Wait here. I'll take our things up and then come back down for you.'

'Jean, we need two rooms.'

'We can't afford two rooms. My total life savings amount to twelve pounds and we've got to spin that out for as long as possible. Besides, this is the sixth place we've tried and they've only got one double room free. It's three hours since you came out of the police station and you need to lie down before you fall down. Nobody knows us here anyway, so what does it matter?'

'As soon as I'm fit,' he muttered, 'we're going looking for work. As soon as we find work we're moving out. To two rooms somewhere else.'

'Aye,' Jean soothed. 'We'll do that. Of course we will. Wait here while I run up the next flight.'

She deposited the two bags in front of the door of their new abode without opening it before running back down to the landing where she'd left him. 'Put your arm about my shoulders.'

'Bossy wee thing, are ye no'?' He leaned heavily on her all the same as they made a tortuously slow ascent of the stairs. What little energy he had left was fading fast.

'It looks clean enough,' Jean said a few moments later, faintly surprised by that fact. Pulling the key out of the lock and kicking open the door with her foot, she helped Andrew into the room. 'Quite spacious too, and nice and light. That'll be the advantage of being on the top floor of a house on the top of a hill.' Her eyes swept the room. 'We've got a double bed and a sofa. D'you think you can sit down on the edge of the bed if I help you?'

Andrew grunted something she took to be assent. Once he was on the bed she slid out from under his arm and stood gazing down at him. He looked back up at her.

'Don't look so worried.'

'You'd look worried if you could see what I can see.'

He managed a smile. 'Death warmed up, is it?'

'The wreck of the *Hesperus*,' she agreed. 'If you're all right there for ten minutes, I'll run out for some supplies to that wee shop we passed on the way up the hill. I think it'll still be open. Or,' she asked with a faint blush, 'do you want me to help you get undressed and into bed straightaway?'

He gave her a very measured look. 'I'm taking the sofa, Jean. You're having the bed. Give me a minute and I'll get myself sorted out. I'll root around and see if there are any spare blankets.'

'You'll do no such thing! Anyway, you're going to have to lie on your front tonight. You'll be a lot more comfortable doing that on a bed than a sofa.'

'All right.'

Jean's spirits, low already, sank still further at that

157

uncharacteristically meek response. The pain must be bloody awful. She twitched back the counterpane on the bed. 'This looks pretty clean too. There's enough blankets for me to take a couple to the sofa. I'll be fine there.' Pulling back and straightening up, she found that she was still under scrutiny. Her voice grew gentler. 'How are you feeling?'

'I'll live. But I've had better days. Was that no' what you said to that wifie downstairs? "He's had a bit of a difficult day." That was good, Jean. I liked that.'

'Is your back really sore? Is that a really stupid question?'

'It's a really stupid question,' he agreed, his voice slurred with exhaustion. Jean put her hand to his forehead and tried to smooth out the frown that had settled between his brows.

'I'll get some aspirin while I'm out. Once you've rested up for a couple of days you'll be as right as rain.'

He fixed her with one of his glowers. 'We're no' staying here for more than tonight, Jean. We cannae both stay in the same room. Think about your reputation.'

'We've paid for the week. My reputation's already shot to hell anyway.'

Andrew groaned. 'Now you're swearing too. That's my fault, I expect. Being a bad influence on you.'

'You've been nothing but a good influence on me. You've got me out of St Martin's Manse. For which I shall always be eternally grateful. I'm only sorry for the price you had to pay.' Biting her lip, she moved towards him. 'Arms up.'

'Don't say that. That's what they said . . .' The mumbled words trailed off.

'I'm going to help you get undressed.'

'No, you're not.'

'You're not fit to do it yourself.'

'Aye, I am. Go and get those supplies you were talking about.'

By the time she came back he was in bed, lying on his front with the covers pulled up only as far as his waist. She tried not to gasp when she saw his back. Crisscrossed with a myriad of white welts, angry red lines and caked blood, it looked like nothing she had ever seen before.

Or maybe it looked like a lump of raw meat. A piece of beef that had been handled too much, slammed down on the butcher's marble slab far too many times. Jean's imagination presented her with a horribly vivid picture of what had really happened to turn his back into the mess it was now. He was looking up at her out of one eye.

'A pretty sight, is it?'

'It's not too bad,' she said quickly.

'Liar. Are you gonnae make me a cup o' tea?'

'I was going to heat up some soup.' Shaken by the graphic sight of what he had endured today, Jean's voice was shaky. 'There's a gas ring next to the fire. Should I maybe wash your back first?'

'Leave it alone tonight. And I'd like tea. Just tea.'

She made them both a cup, whitening and sweetening the brew with the condensed milk she'd bought at the local shop. Andrew leaned over the edge of the bed and drank half of his.

'Biscuit?' Jean queried, proffering the packet she'd bought.

He shook his head. 'Don't feel hungry.'

'I thought you'd be starving.'

'They fed us at dinner-time in there.' His mouth quirked. 'No' that I had much o' an appetite, knowing what was lying in wait for me, so to speak. How about you? Are you no' hungry?'

'I'm fine. I'll have a couple of biscuits. After that I'll turn out the light and we can both get a good night's sleep.'

A tinge of the old mischief crept into his face. 'Going to read me a bedtime story afore ye do that, Just Jean?'

'Certainly not,' she said, pretending to be stern with him. 'You need your sleep.'

'We're not staying here, Jean. It's no' right that we should be sharing a room.'

'Don't you trust me?' she asked, trying to hold on to the lighter mood.

'I don't trust myself.'

'I reckon my virtue is pretty safe tonight. What with you being temporarily incapacitated.'

'Temporarily is the word,' he said sleepily. 'I'll be fine tomorrow.'

'Of course you will.'

But he wasn't fine tomorrow. Jean awoke to find him feverish and bright-eyed, his skin pale and clammy and his cheeks too rosy. He was querulous and argumentative too.

'Let me go and ask the landlady where the local doctor is,' she said in the middle of the day, making the suggestion for the twentieth time.

'I don't need a doctor. There was a doctor there yesterday. Fat lot o' good he did me.'

Jean was forced to fall back on instinct. She made him drink as much water as she could get down him and she wiped his face, hands and arms with a damp cloth as often as he would let her. She was taking advantage of one of the fitful dozes into which he'd been falling all day to rub down his feet and legs – still not quite sure whether she should do the same for his back or not – when he woke up and caught her at it.

'What do you think you're doing, Jean Dunlop?'

'Shut up,' she said roughly, tired and upset and not at all sure she was doing the right thing. 'This is no time to be thinking about the proprieties. Is this not making you feel better?' she asked hopefully.

'That's not the point.'

'What is the point?'

'I cannae remember,' he mumbled, and promptly fell asleep again.

Jean woke with a start on Wednesday morning, pulling her blanket up around her shoulders in reaction to the chilliness of the room.

'Rise and shine,' said a cheerful voice. 'I've made us some tea.'

She sat up, blinking hard. Andrew was standing next to the sofa, smiling down at her. 'You're all right?'

'I'm fine.' He handed her one of the cups and saucers he held. 'Well, no' exactly fine. My back feels like something I'll no' say in front o' a lady and I'm walking about like a wee old woman wi' rheumatism but apart frae that I seem to be more or less back in the land o' the living. Shift,' he said, using his free hand to push her blanket-covered legs closer to the back of the sofa before lowering himself carefully down on to it.

Jean took a sip of her tea and surveyed him over the rim of the cup. 'I thought you were going to die on me yesterday.'

'Sorry about that. It's all a bit o' a blur. I do seem to recall that I was a wee bit tetchy with you.'

'A wee bit tetchy? That's the understatement of the century.'

He laughed. Then his amusement faded. 'I want to thank you, Jean.'

She shrugged. 'You were feverish. Not yourself.'

'I don't mean only for looking after me yesterday. I mean for trusting me enough to come away with me.'

'Och, Andy . . .' Jean said, her face troubled. 'It's me coming away with you that led to all of this. My fault that you were . . . that you had to go through what you went through on

Monday. I can understand why your sisters are so angry with me.'

'What happened on Monday was *not* your fault. Don't you dare say that.'

'But it was my fault—'

He extended his free hand and placed his fingers over her mouth. 'I'll be putting the blame where it belongs, Jean. On the minister and his wife. On that magistrate. It was a bit o' an extreme punishment for one wee curse,' he added bitterly, 'but it was absolutely, definitely and utterly not your fault. D'you hear me?'

She grabbed him by the wrist, tugging his hand away from her mouth. 'But—'

'No buts,' he said firmly. 'This subject is now closed. As I believe you pointed out the night before last, that twelve pounds o' yours won't last for ever. Time we were making plans. Give me a few days for my back to heal and we'll start applying for jobs.'

'But we'll stay here for the time being, Andy? Because we're short of money?'

'All right,' he said reluctantly. 'But we need to discuss the rules again.'

'Of course we will.' She gave him a shaky smile. 'Do you think you might be fit enough to go for a walk later on?'

They went that evening, coming down the last few yards of the hill into a Sauchiehall Street glittering with the lights of all of its picture palaces and dance halls.

'The Locarno,' Andrew said, beginning to name some of those. 'Green's Playhouse Ballroom. The Waldorf, of course. Lots of places for us to try.'

'It's like a fairyland,' Jean breathed. 'The shops are lovely too,' she added, gazing in awe-struck wonder at the frontages of Treron's and Daly's. She'd heard of the luxurious shops there were up in Glasgow. She'd never been inside any of them.

They walked along Sauchiehall Street until they came to the corner of Buchanan Street. Walking down it, they marvelled again at the lovely shops: MacDonald's and Copland & Lye's and Wylie and Lochhead's. Turning at the bottom of the street, they strolled halfway back up before going through an archway into Royal Exchange Square.

'Look at that,' Andrew said, reading the words off a gleaming brass plaque. ' "The Luxor. Exclusive dancing and dining in the heart of Glasgow." That place looks really posh.'

'It'll maybe not be our first port of call when we go looking for a job.'

'Maybe not,' he agreed. 'Hold my hand?'

A group of people, men and women, piled out of a car and headed for the door of the exclusive dancing and dining club. They were beautifully dressed, the men elegant in dark evening clothes, the women colourful in their lovely dresses and wraps.

'We can be part of this, Andy,' Jean said, looking up at him with shining eyes.

He cupped her face in his hands and pressed a gentle kiss on her mouth. 'You and me,' he said, 'are gonnae dance our way to the stars.'

Chapter 16

A LARGE FAT raindrop hit the pavement in front of Jean's feet. It was followed by half a dozen more.

'Oh, no,' she groaned, head snapping heavenwards. When she'd sneaked out of the boarding house to run down the hill to Sauchiehall Street, the day had been warm and sunny and the sky a brilliant blue. Its colour now was much more sinister in hue, and the plump white clouds that had so innocently decorated it ten minutes before had been replaced by scudding grey ones.

As more raindrops began to fall, their speed of arrival increasing with each one, Jean grabbed her change and the newspaper-wrapped parcel of tatties and carrots from the woman on the other side of the fruit and vegetable barrow.

'Best get under cover, hen,' the stall-holder advised. 'You're gonnae get soaked otherwise.'

'Tell me something I don't know,' muttered Jean as she turned away. She was both hatless and coatless. The weather during this first fortnight of July had been wonderfully sunny and she'd come out wearing only the red and white cotton print dress Andrew had insisted she buy when the heat wave had started.

It hadn't cost much – twelve-and-six at Arnot Simpson's in Argyle Street – but now Jean was wishing she hadn't succumbed to the temptation of having something cool to wear. Twelve-and-six would have paid for another week's rent at the boarding house.

As of this morning, she and Andrew had enough money left to pay the landlady for one more week and that was it. They could only manage that if they economised even further on their food.

Jean made a dash for the shelter of Daly's doorway. It was a mere few yards distant but by the time she dived in under the wrought-iron canopy the skirt of her dress was plastered against her thighs. With a small exclamation of disgust, she spared one hand to pull the sodden material loose. The other was clutching the precious parcel of vegetables. If she got it back to the boarding house without the newspaper disintegrating into papier-mâché it would be a minor miracle. What she and Andrew needed right now was a major one.

They had tried everywhere: all of the ballrooms in Sauchiehall Street and all of those further away from the city centre too, like The Albert and The Dennistoun Palais. Oh, they had tried every dance hall in Glasgow! Most of them had turned Jean and Andrew away without even a tryout. They had plenty of dancing partners and a waiting list as long as your arm into the bargain.

It didn't help that it was the summer and therefore hardly the peak of the dancing season. Raising their hopes, three or four of the halls had allowed them to audition. All had praised their dancing – before suggesting they come back in September or October. No *palais* was going to pay dancing partners over the summer if half the regular clientele was spending the summer on the Clyde Coast.

They'd started looking for other jobs last week. Andrew had headed for Anderston this morning, scouting out any possibilities there might be there. Jean had tried her third domestic registry yesterday. As she had predicted before she had climbed the stairs to the fifth storey of a building in Buchanan Street and sat in a queue for three-quarters of an hour, her lack of references had led to a disdainful dismissal.

Andrew had even steeled himself to go to the nearest Labour Exchange to sign on. He'd been too honest about his circumstances. When the clerk had discovered that he had voluntarily left his family home, he had turned him away without a penny.

Jean gazed morosely out at the rain. It was coming down in stair rods now, bouncing back up again before it splashed once more to earth. The gutters were running like rivers, carrying swirling torrents of rushing water down the slope of the street.

'The Venice of the North, wouldn't you say?'

Bestowing a mechanical little smile on the young woman who'd made the comment, Jean registered that the girl was as wet as herself and also wore only a simple cotton frock. Deceptively simple. It was beautifully cut, with a big white Puritan collar, the material much heavier than that of Jean's dress. It was wet, yes, but it was holding its shape. Quality always showed.

The girl must have money. Slump or no slump, there were still plenty of people in Glasgow who did. Like all those folk who were off holidaying somewhere down the Clyde and not frequenting the dance halls.

'Out of work?'

Jean turned instinctively towards the sympathy she could hear in that voice. 'I suppose I look it, do I?' she queried, her smile a lot more than rueful.

'I'm afraid so,' the girl responded. Her accent was quite posh. Jean wondered if she came from Bearsden or

Pollokshields or somewhere like that. 'What sort of a job are you after?'

'My boyfriend and I are looking for work as dancing partners.'

'And you're having no luck? Shame. You know,' she said carefully, giving Jean an assessing look, 'there really is no reason why an attractive young woman such as yourself should have to go hungry. Especially in a city which offers as many possibilities as this one does.'

Jean cast her a wary glance. 'Yes,' the girl said, 'I am talking about what you think I'm talking about. I'm by way of being in that line of business. Nothing sordid. I host little parties at my flat for some nice gentlemen whose wives don't understand them.'

Jean opened her mouth to say something. Nothing came out.

'I can't cope with all the work on my own so occasionally I do a little recruiting. Could I persuade you to let me put your name on my books?'

'I don't think it would be my cup of tea,' Jean managed, finding her voice at last.

'Pity. A girl like you could make a good living at it. Those nice gentlemen whose wives don't understand them can be very generous. With the right kind of gentleman the work can even be enjoyable.' She dug into her handbag and produced a small white business card. 'Take this in case you change your mind.'

As she disappeared into Daly's, Jean studied the card. A name, an address in the West End, and a telephone number. *The world is full of possibilities.* That was what Alison Dunlop had always said. Somehow Jean didn't think her mother had meant the particular possibility her daughter had just been offered.

If she could make it past the middle of the staircase she'd be fine. Home and dry. Catching a glimpse of herself in the tarnished mirror, which could in no way be described as gracing this shabby lobby, Jean stuck her tongue out at her own reflection.

Home and dripping wet, more like. She headed for the stairs, placing her foot on the first tread as stealthily as a cat picking its way along the top of a wall. The second tread was one of the two at the bottom end of the stairs that screeched like banshees with sore throats when you trod on them.

She'd wondered if the landlady had somehow managed to arrange for this to happen. The two creaky steps certainly helped alert her to the presence of one of her lodgers. Last week Jean had been subjected to an interrogation as to how much longer she and Andrew would be staying. If they were intending to leave, as much notice as possible would be appreciated. She had reminded Jean that terms were strictly cash only. No money, no room.

Jean made it safely to the top and set about chopping up her vegetables. When Andrew came in an hour later he looked tired, although his eyes lit up when he saw the pot bubbling on top of the gas ring on the floor next to the fire. 'Something smells nice.'

'Tattie soup.'

'You've made it yourself?'

'It's not exactly difficult,' Jean said, although she was actually rather proud of herself for having produced it. 'No luck today?'

'There is something. Although you probably wouldn't want to do it.'

'Try me. Sit down and I'll dish this up.'

'You know that dance hall in Argyle Street we thought was

a bit sleazy? They're putting on a dance marathon. Starting next Monday.'

Jean didn't say anything until she had set out soup plates and spoons for both of them. 'Going on till when?' she asked carefully.

'Midday on Friday. Four days and four hours. Or one hundred hours in total. They've got a big banner strung up outside advertising it like that.'

'What's the prize money?'

'There's no runner-up prizes. It's only for the outright winner. But it's twenty pounds, Jean.'

Jean ladled out the soup, thinking about what a difference twenty pounds could make to them. They had always vowed never to participate in a dance marathon, agreeing that they were humiliating and demeaning.

She thought about the girl she'd met in the doorway of Daly's. There were more ways of humiliating yourself than taking part in a dance marathon.

'Do you have to register beforehand?' she asked.

Chapter 17

H ER FEET were killing her, the pain so intense Jean was finding it hard to think about anything else. Her brain could find space for only one additional thought. However sore her feet were, she had to keep moving. Those two words echoed like a litany inside her head. *Keep moving. Keep moving. Keep moving.*

They had paid the rent for this week. Galling though that was when they weren't even going to be there for half of the seven days in question, it was the only way the landlady had agreed to hold the room open for them. If they weren't back by Friday afternoon with next week's rent in their hands she'd have no compunction about putting them out on to the street, bag and baggage.

The prospect of having no roof over her head struck terror into Jean's heart. She'd seen people who'd ended up on the street when their money had run out. Mainly men, but with a sprinkling of women too, you saw them queuing for hours at soup kitchens.

Each day they grew shabbier. Each day that worsening in their appearance made it even less likely that someone would give them a job. Each day the tiny spark of hope in their eyes was quenched. Until there was nothing left but resignation. This was to be their fate.

Four days and three nights into the dance marathon, Jean was feeling pretty resigned to her own fate, too tired to care much about anything: even the fact that she and Andrew had precisely four and sixpence left to their name. Maybe they'd both fall down dead of exhaustion before tomorrow afternoon anyway. Both of them lying in a crumpled heap on this dance floor. That would solve all of their problems in one fell swoop.

They'd signed up for the 'Grand One Hundred Hours' Dance Marathon' last Saturday afternoon. Along with one hundred and fifty other couples, they'd taken to the floor at 8 a.m. the following Monday. Apart from three hours' rest during the night and short meal breaks throughout the day, they'd been dancing ever since.

Not that you could really call it dancing any more. Few of those still sluggishly circling the floor this Thursday evening had much energy spare for fancy footwork. Whether the alternating bands struck up a tango, foxtrot, waltz or even the occasional charleston, the carefully executed steps of Tuesday and Wednesday had distilled down to little more than shuffling your feet in some sort of movement. *Keep moving. Keep moving. Keep moving.*

Squashed by her increasingly swollen feet, both of Jean's little toes were being pushed hard against the ones next to them, their nails digging into soft flesh. They'd drawn blood too. She could feel the warm stickiness of it inside her shoe.

'How are the feet?'

She gave Andrew a wan smile. 'Not too bad. How about you?'

'Not too bad.' The ghost of a smile curved his mouth. 'And we're both lying through our teeth. Think you can keep going?'

'Of course I can. Didn't someone tell us the Yanks have dance marathons that last for weeks? We can surely manage a few days.' She looked at him out of eyes dull with fatigue. 'Is this Thursday?'

'It is indeed.' He looked over her shoulder, towards the stage where the musicians played. A big clock had been placed there earlier today so that both dancers and spectators could count down the hours and minutes remaining.

'What time is it?'

'Time you got a watch.'

'I've got one. It seems to have stopped.'

Andrew's eyes came back to her face. 'Why d'you want to know the time anyway? Got a train to catch?'

'Nope. I'm working out how long we've got to go.'

'It's six o'clock. We've got eighteen hours to go. This time tomorrow night we'll be putting our feet up and counting our prize money.'

'This time tomorrow night I'll be in the Land of Nod.' Jean yawned. 'Oh, excuse me.' She put a hand up to cover her mouth, and yawned again.

'Lay your head on my shoulder,' Andrew suggested. 'I'll try and sort of carry you, let you take some of the weight off your poor wee feet.'

Jean shook the head in question, and made an effort to rouse herself. 'We'll be disqualified if we don't both keep both feet on the ground. It's a lot easier for the stewards to keep on eye on us now that so many folk have dropped out.'

Andrew checked out their fellow participants. 'Aye. Including us, there's only fourteen couples still up on the floor.'

The weak had gone to the wall early. A great swathe of those who had professed only to be doing this for a laugh had retired before midnight on the first night. Others, whose disappointed faces had shown with painful clarity what a difference winning twenty pounds would have made to them, had been unable to hold out against tiredness or aching feet.

Two or three girls had twisted or sprained their ankles. Several couples had been disqualified, either because one partner had tried to support the other or because they had momentarily stopped moving. Some folk had slunk away during one of the breaks, unable to take any more punishment. Or the shame of your desperation being watched by the sprinkling of people who sat at the tables set around the dance floor.

The spectators were an odd mixture. Some seemed to have wandered in from the street outside because they had half an hour to kill, curious to witness this odd new phenomenon of people dancing until they dropped. A reporter and photographer from the *Glasgow Evening Dispatch* had come in yesterday morning for the same reason.

A hopefully blurry picture of the whole group of dancers was one thing. The thought of Andrew's mother and sisters reading a detailed newspaper article was another. Nor could Jean have borne the idea of the Fairbairns reading about her doing this.

Anticipating that the dark-haired young female reporter would use all the tricks of her trade to persuade them to co-operate, she had prepared herself mentally to resist. The girl had simply looked into her face, patted her arm and wished her good luck. The unexpected kindness had moved Jean to tears.

A few of the onlookers were friends and relatives of the dancers, there to offer moral support. Other people came along to gawp. From the toss of his head, Jean guessed Andrew had spotted some of those now.

'Oh, golly gosh, Miss Dunlop. The posh folk are back. *Awfully* nice of them to drop by to see us.' Voice dripping with sarcasm, his faultless mimicry of an upper-class accent made him sound pretty posh himself.

'Probably want to see if any of us have dropped dead yet,' Jean mumbled. 'Is it the Bright Young Things?'

That was what they had christened the group of people who'd come in for the first time early on Tuesday evening. They weren't all young. Some looked to be in their late twenties, others a decade older. They were certainly bright, particularly the women. Their beautiful dresses stood out like the plumage of exotic birds against the beautifully cut dark evening clothes of their male companions.

Clearly on their way to a rather more elevated social engagement elsewhere, they had stayed for twenty minutes, gazing at the marathon dancers with unembarrassed fascination. They'd returned at midnight, repeating the pattern on Wednesday night too.

'Different clothes each night,' Jean said, looking over towards them. 'They must be rolling in it. How is it that the Depression has made so many folk poor, but other folk have still got money?'

'Because life's no' fair. Don't pay any attention to the Bright Young Things,' Andy added comfortingly. 'You'll have nice clothes one day. You'll have earned them too. I bet those so-called ladies over there have never done a hand's turn in their entire lives.'

He slid his right hand up Jean's back, passing over the damp and wrinkled fabric of her cheap cotton dress to curl his fingers around the nape of her neck. 'Yeuch,' he murmured, the softness of his voice belying the exclamation of disgust. 'You're all sweaty.'

'I should get my hair shingled if we're going to keep doing this.'

'Don't you dare.' His fingers tightened possessively. 'I love your hair just the way it is. Besides, we're no' going to keep doing this.'

She pushed herself back against his hand and looked at him. 'Aren't we?'

For a moment he said nothing. Then, awkwardly: 'I'm sorry you're having to go through all o' this.'

Jean sniffed back the tears. 'Stop apologising. You're having to go through it all too. It's not your fault that all those dance halls we've tried don't recognise talent, youth and beauty when they see it.' That was their own private joke, a defensive bolster against the disappointments they'd suffered over the past six weeks. 'Besides, at least they're feeding us here.'

'That's my girl.' He drew her head forward, planted a kiss on her forehead and returned his hand to her back. Jean became aware that they were being watched.

She turned her head. The Bright Young Things, of course. Who else? They were all staring across at her and Andrew. They had witnessed that intimate little moment. A flood of emotion assailed Jean. Shame. Humiliation. Anger. She lifted her chin and looked back defiantly at the people who got a kick out of seeing other people reach the end of their tether.

'It's no use.'

Both Jean and Andrew turned towards that voice. It wasn't raised, but there was something in it which drew attention: an edge and a rawness. The young man was standing a few feet away from them. Standing. Not moving.

'Oh!' Jean cried. 'Don't stop, you'll be disqualified! Start again quickly before any of the stewards notice.'

The boy threw her a glance.

'Please, Jim,' she pleaded. 'Don't stop now. There's less than twenty-four hours to go.'

It was odd. At the beginning of the marathon everyone had eyed everyone else up with barely concealed hostility. They were all potential rivals for the prize. Yet as the couples on the floor had grown fewer, a camaraderie had grown up

175

amongst those who remained. They were all on first-name terms now.

'Sorry, Jean. I can't do it.' Jim's attention swung back to his partner. He loosened his hold on her, and took a step back. He was tall and lanky, his wife, Annabel, much shorter than he was. That had looked funny on Monday. It didn't look funny now. 'I'm not going to let my wife do it either.'

Annabel gazed up at him, her eyes wide and filled with fear. 'But we need the money . . . especially with the baby coming.'

Jean's eyes went to Annabel's stomach. Now that she looked, she could see the faint bulge. The girl had kept that piece of information to herself.

'You need to sleep,' Jim said gruffly, reaching for his wife's hand. 'That's what you need.'

She slumped against him, and he scooped her up into his arms. She looked a light-enough burden but he stumbled as he began to walk off the floor. Andrew reached out a steadying hand to the young husband's shoulder.

'Careful.'

'I'm all right. Don't you stop. You'll have more chance now. The two of you are really good dancers, by the way. I noticed that at the beginning.' His mouth twisted bitterly. 'When this was still a dance hall and not a torture chamber.'

The eyes of the two young men met. Andrew gave Jim's arm a squeeze of support.

'I did everything I was supposed to do. Studied hard at school, got a good job and worked hard at it. I was told I had a promising future ahead of me. The company folded three months ago. Now there's no future. No future and no hope. They said things were going to get better this year. Have you noticed them getting better?' he demanded of Andrew. 'Have they got better for you?'

Jim laughed – a curiously light-hearted sound – before answering his own question. 'No, of course they haven't. You wouldn't be here otherwise, would you?'

Holding on to Jean with one hand while the two of them continued to move around the same tiny patch of floor, Andrew took his other hand from Jim's arm and thrust it into his trouser pocket. It came out holding half a crown. 'Take this,' he said gruffly. 'Buy yourselves fish suppers and go home and have a good night's sleep.'

Jim shook his head. 'I can't take your money.' Held fast against his chest, Annabel's eyes were closed. Whether she was asleep or not Jean couldn't tell. Perhaps she simply wanted to shut it all out.

'Take it,' Andrew repeated. 'We've some money left. Jean?'

She didn't hesitate. 'Please take the money, Jim. It's little enough.' She moved herself and Andrew towards the other couple. Awkwardly one-handed, she uncurled the fingers of one of Jim's own hands and put the coin into it. Over his shoulder she could see the Bright Young Things. Agog, she thought grimly. That's the word, isn't it? They're all agog.

Jim looked at Jean. His voice resonated with emotion. 'God bless you both—'

There were two stewards at his elbow, plus the dance hall manager. 'Can we carry her for you?'

Jim's arms tightened around his wife. 'No,' he snarled. 'You can get out of my fucking way.'

'Now, now,' the manager muttered reproachfully. 'We don't want that kind of language. There's no need for any unpleasantness.'

Jean and Andrew didn't speak for a while after Jim and Annabel had been ushered off. Not until she looked up at him and said, 'I'm glad you did that.'

'Even though we're now left wi' the princely sum of that florin you've got in your purse?'

She managed a smile. 'Like Jim said, we've more chance of winning now.'

'A thirteen to one chance,' Andrew agreed. He grimaced, 'Unlucky number.'

'Thirteen's always been a lucky number for me. Think of it as a baker's dozen if it makes you feel any better.'

Andrew groaned. 'Don't make me think about food. I'm that hungry I could eat a scabby dug.'

An hour later a supper of tea and fish-paste sandwiches was served to the contestants. Jean ate hers quickly before repairing to the ladies' room to check if her spare knickers had dried yet. The big solid radiators along the walls there were festooned with underwear. Her pants were still a little damp but she was uncomfortable enough down below to put them on anyway.

'A real shame about Jim and Annabel, isn't it?'

Running water into the basin to wash the underwear she'd taken off, Jean looked up into the mirror and met the eyes of one of the girls with whom she now felt as if she'd spent her entire life. 'I know,' she said sombrely. 'I don't know what they'll do now. They're really on their uppers.'

'Aren't we all?' said the girl. 'If my family hadn't disowned me for taking up with a Roman Catholic, I'd admit defeat and go back home.'

'*Did* they disown you?' Jean asked curiously, rubbing the soap over her knickers.

The other girl licked her fingertips and smoothed her eyebrows. 'More or less.'

'How come they agreed to the two of you getting married, then?'

178

'You don't actually *need* your parents' permission to get married.' The girl pulled a face at herself and Jean. 'It would have been nice to have had their consent, but you don't need it. Especially not if you do what Gerry and I did and go for a marriage by declaration.' She pulled another face. 'His old Irish mother's never got over the shame and disgrace of us doing that.'

'What is a marriage by declaration?'

'A very quick way of tying the knot. The two of you go in front of the sheriff, declare your wish to be married and there you are. Shackled for life.' She laughed. 'How about you and Andy? Got nobody to take you in?'

'I don't have any family. And things are a bit awkward with his. Which is all my fault,' she added glumly.

'It takes two to tango,' the other girl comforted. 'And it takes two to make an argument.'

'I suppose,' Jean said doubtfully. 'D'you and Gerry think you're going to make it through to the end of the marathon?'

'Can't afford not to, Jean. How about you?'

'Likewise.'

'Ach well,' the other girl said philosophically. 'What will be, will be.'

Chapter 18

NUMB WITH tiredness, her legs aching from her groin to the soles of her feet, Jean emerged, blinking like a pit pony, into the outside world. All thirteen of the baker's dozen had survived until the end of the marathon, the prize money divided up between them. 'All that effort,' one lad had muttered bitterly, 'and we end up with coppers.'

The camaraderie built up during the four days and four nights of the marathon had dissipated in that moment. The goodbyes had been muted and subdued, and no one had pushed the suggestion made earlier in the week that the group should meet up for a reunion sometime.

'We've enough to pay the rent for another two weeks, anyway,' Andrew said now. 'That's good.'

Jean didn't answer him. She hadn't the strength left for the pretence that something would turn up before those two weeks were up.

They gave the landlady her money and trudged upstairs to their room. When they got there both of them sank down on to the bed, perched back-to-back on either edge of it. Andrew yawned. 'Who's going to the bathroom first?'

The next thing Jean was aware of was a dazzling shaft of sunlight across her face. Startled, she snapped upright. 'What?'

The only answer she got to that was a gentle snoring.

Twisting round, she saw that Andrew was lying flat on his back beside her. Neither of them had managed to stay awake long enough even to take their shoes off.

Jean's legs felt as heavy as tree trunks. With difficulty, and the occasional suppressed gasp, she swung them over the side of the bed and bent forward to undo the straps of her shoes. The feet of her stockings were ripped and bloodstained, the marks brown and stale. She'd have to soak them for ages to get those out. The stockings might be past mending, anyway.

She straightened up again, checked that Andrew was still asleep and rocked her hips from one side to the other as she undid her suspenders. Rolling her stockings down her swollen legs was bearable. Trying to tug them free of the scabs and blisters on her feet was sheer bloody agony.

She took off her now useless wristwatch and stripped off her dress and underwear, bundling those up into a ball. Then she slipped on her dressing gown, opened and closed the door of their room as quietly as possible and made her painful way along the bathroom to the corridor.

She lay in the bath until the water was cool. She wasn't thinking about anything. She was lying in the bath, that was all. She didn't want to think about anything. Particularly not the future.

Stirring herself at last, Jean reached over the side of the tub to pick up her washing. Dropping her underwear into the water between her legs, she raised her arm to shake out her crumpled dress. Her fingers met on either side of something stiff. She put them into the little decorative breast pocket and pulled out the white business card she'd forgotten was there.

A name, an address and a telephone number. She studied them for a very long time.

★ ★ ★

181

Andrew was still asleep when she returned to the room but beginning to stir. Jean walked round to the foot of the bed. 'Shall I take your shoes off? I didn't want to do it before in case I woke you up.'

'Eh?' As he struggled up on to his elbows, his hair was all over the place. Under different circumstances, Jean might have found the picture he presented a comical one.

'Brace yourself. I'm about to ease your shoes off.'

'I'm no' sure the word *ease* had much to do wi' that manoeuvre,' he observed a gasping few seconds later.

'No,' Jean agreed. 'Your socks look as bad as my stockings did. Maybe it would be easier to soak them off in the bath.'

'No' a bad idea. It will also spare you the undoubtedly wonderful aroma my feet must be giving off.'

'Charming,' Jean said lightly. 'Go and have your bath, then. Maybe you should hang your suit up in there so the steam'll help take the creases out of it. Want to borrow my dressing gown for coming back?'

'What are you going to wear?'

'I'll find something.'

'We'll preserve your modesty in the usual way, then.' Suiting the action to the words, he gathered together what he needed and waited out in the corridor while Jean slid off the dressing gown and handed it round the corner of the door to him.

Preserving her modesty. Oh God. She was determined to go through with this all the same. It was either that or starve.

Sliding down naked under the sheet and blankets was an odd sensation. She'd never in her life gone to bed with no clothes on. Well, there was a first time for everything.

'That's better,' Andrew said cheerfully as he walked back into the room fifteen minutes later. 'Nothing like a bath to make a new man o' you.' Draping his towel over the back of one of the two upright chairs in the room, and depositing his shaving gear on the table in front of the window, he turned and saw where she was.

'Do you no' think you'd be better staying up for a while, Jean? The sooner we get back into the normal routine the better.'

She was sitting bolt upright in the bed, the covers tucked around her breasts. *Preserving her modesty.* She took a deep breath and allowed the sheets and blankets to slide down to her waist. Andrew froze.

Jean studied him as he stood there, so incongruously male in her pink cotton dressing gown. He was too broad for it to close on him, of course. Below it he was wearing the clean white vest and underpants he must have put on after his bath.

His eyes were on her breasts. She'd allowed him to see glimpses of them before, although never in broad, shining daylight. Living together in such close proximity to one another had brought about quite a loosening of the rules. Certain things were still taboo. An awful lot of things were still taboo. Or had been until now.

'Don't you want to?' she whispered.

'Of course I want to.' He coughed. 'But I thought we had agreed to wait. Until we can afford to get married.'

Jean heard the huskiness, knew what that thickening of his voice signified. How often had that sign accompanied her trying to restrain his urgent hands from travelling along routes that the rules forbade? She knew too what she would see if she allowed her own eyes to drop from his face. Lying together on the bed, kissing and touching, she'd been aware so many times of that physical change in him. It and what it implied had always scared her.

She couldn't afford to be scared now. She could tell he was fighting a battle with himself and his self-control. If her plan were to succeed she had to ensure that he lost that battle.

Flinging back the covers, she got out of bed and began walking towards him. She had to force herself to keep her arms by her sides, every instinct crying out to her to drape them modestly about her body.

As she approached him, Andrew let out a little moan. Jean's legs chose that precise moment to give way beneath her.

In the twinkling of an eye, the atmosphere changed. His arms were around her. Not in passion or desire. Not seeking his own gratification. Seeking only to support her. 'Come on,' he said roughly, 'you're going back to bed.'

'Come with me.'

He groaned, and buried his face in the hollow of her shoulder. 'Jean, you can barely walk!' He lifted his head and gave her a shaky smile. 'What's your hurry? We can take our time about this.'

'No, we can't,' she sobbed, and blurted out the story of the woman she'd met in Daly's doorway, the words pouring out in a passionate torrent. 'I could maybe do it just the once. She said the men are generous. But I don't want my first time to be with someone who's paying for it. I want my first time to be with you.'

Andrew had frozen again, his arms locked about her as he pulled her naked body close.

'I thought I could it without you knowing, tell you I'd got the money some other way. Only you would find out when we get married because you would discover that I wasn't a virgin. And I want the first man I ever do it with to be you. Not anybody else but you!' The torrent of words stopped as abruptly as it had started and Jean pulled herself out of his embrace, gazing up at him and waiting for him to speak.

'Put your dressing gown back on.' He shrugged it off his

own shoulders and swung it about hers. 'Do it up,' he instructed, his voice gruff, 'and I'll carry you back to the bed.'

When he got her there he lifted her legs up and into it before pulling the covers up over her. Jean was biting her lip as she looked up at him. 'Are you very angry with me?'

'I'm not angry with you.' He sat down on the edge of the bed and reached for her hand. 'But I want you to listen to what I'm going to say. Never in a million years would I let you do what you just suggested. Never in a million years. Do you hear me, Jean?'

'I hear you.' He was holding her hand so tightly her fingers were hurting. She wasn't about to tell him that.

'I'm the only man you're *ever* gonnae sleep with. The only one. That's important to me. Do you hear me, Jean?'

'I hear you.'

'Good. I've got one last thing to say. You will never, ever make this suggestion again. Do you hear me, Jean?'

'I hear you. But what are we going to do, Andy? About money, I mean.'

He lifted the hand he held and kissed it. 'I'll think of something.'

Keep moving. Keep moving. Keep moving.

Jean had lost track of time. This marathon seemed to have been going on for weeks rather than days. She was confused as to how that could be. You weren't allowed to dance on a Sunday, were you? Yet she had no recollection of a rest day punctuating any of these other interminable days.

Keep moving. Keep moving. Keep moving.

The spectators seemed to grow more ghoulish with each passing hour. It was no longer enough for them simply to watch you shuffling your feet around the same small patch of floor as you drew nearer and nearer to exhaustion. Now they were satisfied only if you danced towards it as fast as you could.

'Faster,' they called. 'Faster, faster, faster,' they shrieked. 'We want you to do it *faster!*'

Jean's head was against Andrew's shoulder. 'We're dancing as fast as we can, Andy,' she complained. 'Why don't we give up now? Walk away from it like Jim and Annabel did? Why don't we just go home, Andy?'

'Because we've no home to go to, Jean. That's why.'

His voice sounded funny. She raised her head to look up at him. She couldn't see his face properly. Wasn't even sure it was him she was dancing with. She was confused again. Who else would it be?

Keep moving. Keep moving. Keep moving.

Faster, faster, faster!

Jean was still peering up at Andrew, wondering why she couldn't make out his familiar features. Maybe they were being obscured by the smoke drifting across the floor from the cigarettes of the spectators. Unable to puzzle it all out, she lowered her head once more to his shoulder. And gasped.

She was stark naked. She had no clothes on, and all of these people were looking at her—

Jean woke up. It was morning again. Saturday morning. Subsiding back on to the pillows, she lay for a moment listening to the sounds floating up from the street below. A van chugged past. A woman scolded a child. Two men called a greeting to one another.

Jean tried an experimental moving of her legs and feet. They didn't feel too bad.

'Andy?' she queried, raising her head from the pillow. 'How are you feeling this morning?'

She was alone in the room. Perhaps he was in the bathroom along the corridor. Ten minutes later Jean decided to go and look. She sat up and lowered her feet gingerly to the floor. 'Oh,' she breathed as her soles made contact with the linoleum. She'd been right to be cautious. It still hurt.

'I must look like Charlie Chaplin,' she observed out loud to herself as she walked stiffly to the door of the room. By the time she'd made her way along the corridor, she was moving a bit more like a normal human being, although her search was fruitless. The bathroom door stood ajar, and there was no one inside.

Curling her hands around the banister, Jean leaned over and stood for a moment or two listening for any sounds floating up through the stairwell. Maybe Andy had taken their washing out to hang on the line in the back garden. She waited there for five minutes but he didn't appear.

He must have gone out. She returned to the room to investigate if there was anything in their paltry store cupboard she could offer him when he came back.

She found three rich tea biscuits, a little stale but probably eatable, some sugar and tea and a quarter-pint of sour milk she'd forgotten to leave out in a saucer in the back garden for one of the neighbourhood cats before she and Andrew had left for the marathon. Putting her nose to the top of the bottle, Jean removed it hastily. 'Yeuch,' she said softly. 'That's gone solid.'

She used the end of a wooden spoon to poke the lumps down the plug-hole of the sink in the corner and rinsed out the bottle. The thought of taking her tea without milk was horrible, but she needed something inside her, even if it was just hot liquid. She would nibble on one of the rich tea biscuits too and leave the other two for Andy. She lifted the packet of tea and saw what she hadn't seen before. A note left underneath it, weighted down by it so it wouldn't flutter away.

Jean stooped, letting out a little squeal of pain as the action compressed her lower legs against her upper ones. Straightening up again, she took the note to the table so she could read it by the brilliant sunshine streaming in through the window.

'Gone out for a wee while, Sleeping Beauty. Expect me back about four o'clock. Love, Andy.'

So he had done the impossible and thought of something.

Jean had never seen his handwriting before. He wrote a beautiful copperplate. She lifted the note and held it against her breast.

He was in the restaurant of Copland & Lye's in Buchanan Street, trying to look nonchalant. Which was quite difficult when his heart was hammering against his ribcage like a band crashing out a rumba.

He'd worn his suit. Wouldn't do to look like a working man. Not in a shop as posh as this one. Despite the steam treatment in the bathroom of the boarding house, he knew that his suit still looked a bit rumpled and crumpled. He thought he might manage to get away with that if he had the right attitude. Devil-may-care. With a bit of luck, the well-heeled ladies taking tea here this July afternoon would put him down as an eccentric artist or something.

He smiled at several of those ladies as he passed them, quite consciously exercising the charm he knew he possessed. It didn't take him long to find his quarry. An open handbag, sitting on the chair next to the one its owner was occupying. He looked again. There was a purse sitting at the top of the handbag, poking out from it. She must be getting ready to pay the waitress.

It was now or never. He approached the table, his arm casually by his side. Only his fingers moved. He had it. *He had it!*

He walked on, the purse safely in his jacket pocket.

'Just one moment,' said a voice from behind him.

Chapter 19

ANDREW TURNED. The woman was smiling at him. 'I hope you don't mind me pointing this out,' she said, 'but one of your shoelaces has come undone.'

He glanced down at his shoes. 'Why, so it has.' He looked up again, still speaking in his best pan-loaf. 'How kind of you to let me know.'

Relief flooded through him as he took in her appearance. He hadn't stolen from anybody who couldn't afford it. Everything about this woman screamed money, from the fur she wore around her shoulders, to her discreetly made-up face to her fashionable hat.

'Wouldn't want you to trip up.' Her voice was deep and mellow. There was a note in there that Andrew recognised. She was vamping him. Well, she wasn't *quite* old enough to be his mother . . . He returned her warm smile. Anything to distract her.

'I'll sort it out in a jiffy.'

'Best do it now,' said her companion. 'Easy to forget.'

He crouched down and forced himself to tie the shoelace properly, forced himself to act naturally. He had to suppress a squeak of pain. Adopting this position hurt like hell. Above his bowed head the two women were beginning to argue about whose turn it was to pay the bill. It had always annoyed him when women did that. It wasn't annoying him now. *Keep arguing, ladies. For the love of God, keep arguing!*

'Thanks again,' he said as he rose to his feet with an agility that belied how much they and his legs were hurting.

'Not at all.' Another seductive smile was bestowed on him. He walked away.

Try not to tense up. It'll be the better for me if I dinna. Any minute now. Any minute now. She's going to go to her handbag for her purse and she's going to find out it's not there. Any minute now she's going to stand up and let out a decidedly unladylike yell.

'Stop thief!'

It was so loud inside his head he almost heard it. 'My legs turned to jelly' – he'd heard people use the expression. He hadn't realised until now how accurate a description it really was.

There was a doorman. Shite, there were two o' the buggers. He wondered if it was only his guilty conscience that made him think they were looking at him a bit sideways. Were folk like yon allowed to stop you? What if they asked him to turn out his pockets?

With a huge effort of will, Andrew got his breathing under control. It was all in the attitude. Act like a toff and he might manage to pull this off.

One of the uniformed commissionaires held the door open for him. A blast of warm air hit, bringing inspiration with it. 'Bit of a heat wave we're having.'

'You're right there, sir.'

Breathless with tension, Andrew walked out into Buchanan Street. Any minute now he *would* hear that shout behind him: 'Stop thief! That man stole my purse!'

If I can make it past this next shop, he thought, if I can make it to the corner of Gordon Street . . .

Don't look back. Don't walk too fast. Try to look as if you don't have a care in the world.

He made it to the corner of Gordon Street. Once he had rounded that he walked along to Central Station, going up the broad stairs by the Union Street entrance and turning left to walk down the steps of the men's lavatories. He took one of the cubicles, closed the door behind him, sat down and brought out the purse. His haul exceeded his wildest expectations. There were fifty pounds in there.

For a moment he simply stared at the notes he held. Fifty pounds. *Fifty pounds!*

He stood up, slid the notes into his own skinny pocketbook and tipped the coins from the purse into the right-hand pocket of his jacket. He flushed the toilet and walked back up the stairs to the station concourse. He went out by the entrance at Gordon Street, dropping the purse itself into a waste bin before he got there.

He hadn't looked at anything in it other than the money. He didn't want to know anything about its owner. Didn't want to know if she carried photos of her husband or children. Didn't want to think of her as a person. Especially not as a person who was going to be shocked or distressed when she discovered that she'd been robbed.

He was a thief. And he didn't care.

Jean had dragged the room's two upright chairs to the window and was sitting on one with her feet up on the other when she heard his familiar step on the landing. She tried to get up and didn't make it, looking laughingly towards the door, which she'd left on the latch precisely because she'd suspected she might not be able to get to her feet too quickly.

'Have your legs seized up completely?' he asked as he came in.

'More or less. Och, but I'm so glad to see you. Where on earth have you been?'

'Out.' His smile counteracted the lack of information. 'Look what I've brought back with me.'

He was carrying a brown bag with a string handle, the sort you got from high-class grocery shops. Before Jean's bemused gaze, he lifted a series of boxes and packets out of it, announcing the contents of each one as he placed them on the table. 'Tea. Finest Ceylon. Milk. Best Ayrshire. Half a stone o' tatties. Ditto. One pound o' bacon. Best Belfast. One hand of bananas.' He smiled at her. 'Highly unlikely to be from Belfast or Ayrshire. Let's go for the Windward Islands. Some onions and carrots. From out o' the ground somewhere. And,' he continued, extracting a neat brown-paper parcel from the bag, 'one pound of mince from the butcher's. To go with the tatties. Or should that be the other way around? Last but most definitely not least, six Tunnock's Caramel Wafers to go with our afternoon tea now. Oh, and I got you a newspaper as well. I know how you like to keep up wi' current events.'

Jean was sitting forward in her chair, gazing in amazement at this bounty. 'But where did you . . .' She looked quickly up at him. 'Andy, you didn't . . .' She paused, clearly unwilling even to say the word that was so obviously in her head.

'I didn't steal them, Jean, no.' He took a deep breath and a step back from the table. He'd made his mind up about this on his way up the hill from Sauchiehall Street. She wasn't stupid and she wasn't going to fall for any stupid line he might try to spin her. 'I stole the money to buy them.' His voice was very dry. 'Decided it would be better to run one risk than a whole heap o' them.'

'You stole money,' Jean said, pronouncing each word slowly and carefully.

'Aye. I stole money.'

'From a shop?'

'From a woman in a shop.' He corrected himself. 'From a woman in a restaurant in a shop. Her handbag was lying open.'

Jean was gazing up at him, her face pale and her beautiful hazel eyes huge. Suddenly, emulating the event itself, he hunkered down at her feet. They both grimaced at the obvious pain the movement caused him. He reached for her hands. 'She was well-off, Jean. A well-off lady taking afternoon tea with her friend in the restaurant at Copland and Lye's. I didnae steal from some wee wifie trying to make ten shillings last out the week. This woman had fifty pounds in her purse, Jean. *Fifty pounds*. Just think how long that's going to keep us going.'

'But you *stole* it, Andy. It's not our money.'

'It is now.' He squeezed the hands he held. 'What was the alternative, Jean? Did you really want to do what you suggested last night?'

'I'd *hate* to do that. You know I would!'

As her eyes filled with tears he rose stumblingly to his feet, pulling Jean up with him. 'Don't cry,' he said, wrapping his arms about her. 'I've done it now.'

'But if they'd caught you . . .'

He said the words she hadn't been able to. 'I'd have got the birch again. At the very least.' She felt the shudder run through his body. 'You think that didnae occur to me before I did it?' He spared one hand to gently wipe her damp eyes. 'But they didn't catch me. And now we've got some money.'

'Even fifty pounds will run out eventually.'

'By which time we'll have jobs.'

'How will we manage that? We haven't had much luck so far.'

'We've been trying at the wrong time o' the year. What

we'll do is rest up for a week. Get over the marathon. Then we'll buy me a thirty-bob suit and you a couple o' pretty dresses and start all over again. But before we do any o' that we'll sit down and eat a good meal.' He dropped a kiss on the end of her nose. 'You cook the mince and I'll peel the tatties.'

She laughed when she laid their mince and tatties down and saw that he had put a candle in a saucer in the middle of the table. 'Very romantic. But it's not going to flicker very brightly when it's still so light outside.'

'I'm setting the scene,' he said, striking a match. 'There. That's it lit.' He put the box of matches on the shelf where it lived and swung back to the table. 'Sit down, Jean.'

'Aren't you sitting down too?' she asked as she took her seat.

'No. What I'm doing is this.'

She stared in amazement as he walked round the table and kneeled down in front of her. 'I thought it was sore when you did that.'

'It hurts like that word I don't use in front of ladies.'

'Apart from the occasional minister's wife?'

'She was no lady.'

'Why are you kneeling down?'

'Because this has to be done properly.'

'Done properly? What *are* you talking about?'

'Jean, could you do me the obligement of shutting up for a wee minute? There's something I want to ask you.'

She opened her mouth to issue a retort. She closed it again. The penny had finally dropped. He was down on one knee in front of her. Doing things properly.

'Miss Dunlop,' he said formally. 'I love you. Will you do me the honour of becoming my wife?'

Her eyes searched his face. Was he joking? No. Andrew Logan would never joke about something like this.

'This is crazy. We've no money.'

'We have now.'

'What'll we do when it runs out?'

'I told you, we'll have jobs by then. Say you'll marry me, Jean. For pity's sake. This floor's dead hard!'

Laughing, she flung her arms around his neck. 'Oh, yes,' she said. 'I'll marry you!'

Chapter 20

ANDREW'S FACE was set in lines of grim determination. 'You're having a ring, Jean. That's all there is to it.'

She blew out an exasperated breath. 'No, I am not. I'm not starting off my married life wearing a ring paid for from money—' Jean stopped herself, looking furtively about her at the people hurrying past them on Ingram Street as they walked away from the Sheriff Court this sunny Wednesday morning.

'You're having a ring.' Andrew glowered ferociously at her. 'I thought wives were supposed to obey their husbands.'

Jean raised one derisory eyebrow. 'Did you? Might I also point out that I've been your wife for precisely ten minutes?'

The glower disappeared. 'My wife,' he said. 'Mrs Logan. Do both o' those sound as nice to you as they do to me?'

'Mrs Logan?' Jean repeated with a little laugh. 'I suppose I am Mrs Logan now.'

'That's the way it usually works,' Andrew said smugly.

Jean frowned. 'What about the other Mrs Logan? And your sisters?'

'I'm sorry they couldn't be here to see me get married,' he said flatly.

'So you'll make it up with them?'

'Aye. But not today. Today you and me are going for a sail

doon the watter.' He pulled her arm through his. 'Don't bother arguing wi' me about that. I've already bought the tickets.'

So they took the train down to Craigendoran and walked from the railway station along the covered platform, which turned into a pier. The little boat waiting for them there carried mail and supplies to the people who lived in the coastal communities dotted around the Firth of Clyde, and the day trippers who wanted simply to enjoy the sunshine and fresh air and sea breezes.

'This is lovely,' Jean said, her face up to the sun. 'I could do this every day.'

Standing by the handrail, Andrew's arms wrapped snugly about Jean's waist and his chin resting on her shoulder, they were watching the boat cast off from the jetty at Kilcreggan. 'When we're rich we'll live somewhere like this. Wake up to a view o' the sea every morning. What about that big house over there?'

'Too big. Too many turrets. It looks as if it might be haunted.'

'I'd protect you from the ghaisties and ghoulies.'

'Thanks for the offer, but I'd prefer something like that.' As the boat moved back out into the Firth more of the village had become visible. Jean pointed to a house at one end of it. 'An overgrown cottage with a garden full of flowers.'

As they watched, two children and a small white terrier ran down the grassy sward in front of the white-harled cottage. The children tumbled over their wilkies and the dog ran round them, barking its heart out.

'And would we have some o' those sort o' flowers too?'

She twisted round in his arms so she could see his face. 'Would you like to?'

198

'I asked first.'

'Aye,' she said softly. 'I'd like to have children.'

'Good,' he said. 'So would I.'

'Dogs and cats too?'

'Hundreds of 'em. One to be a collie dug called Fly.'

She kissed him for remembering. 'But we'll not have children just yet, will we?'

'Not for a few years,' he agreed. 'Once we've had a career as famous dancers.'

'We could start a dancing school down here,' she said. 'Train the children up to help us.'

He smiled at her before closing his eyes and raising his face to the breeze. 'Wonderful air. So fresh and clean.'

'Mmm,' Jean said. 'They say you always sleep really well after a sail.'

Andrew opened his eyes again. 'I wasn't planning on sleeping very much at all tonight, Jean.' He laughed his wonderful laugh when his new wife turned scarlet.

It was a week after their wedding and he was lying on the bed with his hands behind his head, singing. He'd given her 'You're the Cream in my Coffee'. Now he was on to 'It Don't Mean a Thing if It Ain't Got That Swing'. He was doing half the instruments as well as the vocals on that one.

'Pleased with yourself?' Jean was sitting by the window, wrapped up in her pink dressing gown and watching some children playing in the street below.

Andrew stopped in the middle of being a rhythmic drum riff and rolled his head lazily towards her. 'I'm *very* pleased wi' myself.' The navy-blue eyes brimmed with devilment. 'I've had a most enjoyable and relaxing afternoon. Bring me my fags and make me a cup o' tea, wife.'

Jean gasped. 'What did your last servant die of?'

He grinned at her. 'I didnae think I'd get away wi' that. Although it would be in your interests to comply. Tea and tobacco always assist my thought processes.'

She adopted an expression of exaggerated interest. 'Is that what you're doing? I wondered what the noise was. It's obviously that long-disused and rusty machine, otherwise known as your brain, cranking back into life. Now I'm getting your winning smile,' she observed.

'Which you cannae resist.'

'Is that right?' She was returning that winning smile all the same. In this mood he was well-nigh irresistible. 'I shall deign to make you a cup of tea and bring you your cigarettes, Mr Logan. But I want you to know I'm only doing it because I love you.'

'That's all right then, Mrs Logan. Although I did already know that. Our activities over last week in general and this afternoon in particular had already given me a wee bit o' a clue that you don't exactly find me repulsive.'

Fighting a blush at a memory of those activities – some of them more than others – Jean filled the kettle and set it on the gas ring. 'Spill the beans,' she commanded, walking over to where Andrew's old suit was hanging and slipping her hand inside the jacket.

'Going through your old man's pockets already? That's a bad sign.'

'I'm looking for your gaspers.' She found them and his box of Swan Vestas and tossed them both over to him.

'Thanks,' he said, pulling himself up to a sitting position and patting the bed beside him. 'Come and join me and I'll let you have a puff on my cigarette.'

'Your generosity overwhelms me,' Jean muttered, getting up on to the bed she hadn't long vacated and kneeling beside him. He was still naked, the tangled sheet covering barely enough of him to spare his blushes. Or maybe hers. 'What's the big idea, then?'

'I have two. The first is that we need a better approach. The second is that we need to start at the top.'

'Elucidate.'

'That's easy for you to say.'

She put one hand on his leg and gave it a shake. 'You know fine well what that means.'

'Like to move your hand a bit further north?' he asked hopefully.

'No. Get on with telling me about your ideas.'

'Firstly,' he said, 'I don't think we should just turn up at places. I think we should submit a letter of application. That's where you come in. Something really well composed.'

Jean nodded thoughtfully. 'Selling ourselves, as it were.'

'Exactly. You'll tell them how good we are, how particularly good our choreographed tango is and what a good teacher I am. At the end of the letter you'll suggest we come in and audition for them at a mutually convenient time. Is that no' the phrase?'

'That's the phrase. But should we not suggest at a time to suit them?'

'That's too humble. Dancing partners have to be confident folk. Wouldn't you say?'

'I would,' Jean said, thinking about it. 'They have to encourage customers to want to dance with them. What you're saying is that it's our personalities we're selling almost as much as our dancing skills?'

'I knew I'd married a clever lassie.' He beamed at her. 'My other idea is that we start at the top. The clubs and more exclusive places. Like yon place we saw in Royal Exchange Square. What was it called again?'

'The Luxor. But, Andy, d'you really think there's the

remotest possibility of somewhere like that giving us a start?'

'About as much as a snowball's chance o' surviving hell,' he said cheerfully.

'So why bother?'

'Because it's all practice and it's all experience. If we start at the top, we'll be pitching what we do really high.'

'It makes sense,' Jean said slowly.

'Of course it does. We'll starting writing those letters tomorrow. Now,' he said, stubbing out what was left of his cigarette in the saucer, which served as his ashtray, on the floor beside the bed. 'Go and turn the gas off and then come here.'

'Come where?' she asked a moment later.

'Kneel over me. One knee on either side of me.'

'Why would I do that?' Jean asked innocently, although she was already straddling him. He placed his hands on her knees, pushing the cotton fronts of her dressing gown up the smooth skin of her thighs.

'So that I can do this,' he murmured. 'Did I tell you I went to the barber's again this morning?'

'Funny,' Jean murmured, 'you've been to the barber's twice this week but I don't think you've had your hair cut on either occasion. Do I take it you're ready and willing for me to have my wicked way with you yet again?'

He pretended to groan. 'Neither of us will be able to walk soon. Let alone dance.'

Chapter 21

'H ANG-ON-a-wee-minute!' The words came out in a
breathless rush.

Already turning left towards The Luxor, Jean wheeled
round to look at Andrew. What she saw had her hurrying
back towards him. 'What's the matter?' she asked anxiously.
'Are you not feeling well?'

He was standing with his left hand braced against the stone
wall of the huge archway through which they'd walked to get
here from Buchanan Street. The fingers of his right hand
were splayed out over his chest, and his head was bowed. He
looked as if he was studying something lying on the ground
at his feet.

He straightened up just as Jean reached him and took his
hand from the wall. 'I'm a wee bit nervous,' he explained with
a quick smile. 'Needed to catch my breath.'

'Och, Andy!' she said, relieved to know that was all it was:
and relieved to know he was nervous too. 'Go back a wee bit,
so the doormen at The Luxor can't see us.'

They retraced their steps, going back through the archway
into the lane that ran beside the bank. Jean glanced across
Buchanan Street to the clock that adorned the imposing
portico of the *Glasgow Evening Dispatch* building. 'Time and
tide wait for no man,' she read, tilting her head first to one

side and then the other so as to be able to read the inscription that ran round the clock-face. 'But we're ten minutes early. D'you want to have a cigarette to calm your nerves?'

'I'm fine now,' Andy said, 'but that's no' a bad idea. D'you want one?'

'Give me a couple of puffs of yours. That'll do me.'

He laughed when she coughed violently after the first of those puffs and immediately handed the cigarette back to him. 'You need more practice, Jean.'

She looked at him with anxious eyes. 'I think I need more practice dancing too, Andy. Have I not got an awful cheek to be auditioning for a job as a dancing partner?'

'You dance beautifully,' he said. 'And I've told you a hundred times that I wouldnae say that if I didnae mean it.'

'I'm not as good a dancer as you.'

'I'm a wee bit more experienced than you. That's all. And that's why we're going to The Luxor today. For both o' us to get some more experience. You know and I know that a place like that is highly unlikely to take on the likes o' us.'

'I'm surprised they even agreed to give us a tryout,' Jean agreed.

'I'm not surprised at all.' He used his thumb and the ring finger of his right hand to delicately pick a shred of tobacco off his tongue. 'Yon letter of application you composed was a masterpiece.'

Jean shrugged. 'Pity I can't dance as well as I can write.'

Andrew rolled his eyes in exasperation. 'Confidence,' he said crisply. 'We've got to have confidence in ourselves.' He spent the next few minutes smoking and giving Jean a pep talk. Once that was done and the cigarette end ground out under the toe of his well-polished shoe, he reached for Jean's hand. 'Come on. We want to be punctual.'

'A kiss for luck? Or do we not have time?'

'There's always time for a kiss.' He suited the action to the words before leading her back through the archway, slanting her across an appreciative glance as they emerged out of its shadow into the sunshine of Royal Exchange Square. 'You look lovely in that frock, by the way. Wasn't I right that you should go for the dark blue with the big splashy red flowers?'

Jean gave him a fond smile. 'You always think I look lovely.'

'You always do. That's why I always think it.'

Don't think about the big things. Concentrate on the details. Really look at them and think about them. It gives your brain less space to panic. That had been one of Andrew's pieces of advice. Following it, Jean fixed her eyes on the brass plaque beside the door, which proclaimed the establishment they were rapidly approaching to be:

The Luxor
Exclusive Dancing and Dining
in the Heart of the City
Members Only

She studied the building itself. In a city full of magnificent Victorian architecture, this one still managed to stand out. Its sandstone frontage was punctuated by tall and narrow windows. Like the brass plaque, they were dazzlingly clean. Each one was surrounded by a band of raised stone, decorated by carvings. Jean picked out a repeating pattern of shells, palm leaves and mysterious, unblinking eyes.

They must employ an army of window cleaners to keep those windows as bright as they were. Slump or no slump, Glasgow remained an industrial city. Many of the shipyards might now be lying idle but there were still iron foundries and locomotive works belching smoke and soot and dirt up into the sky day and night. Most of them were no distance from the city centre either.

'Funny, isn't it?' Jean mused aloud. 'On our way down here we walked past that restaurant at the top of Buchanan Street, where they dole out free soup at their side entrance. That's probably the only food some of the folk who go there get all day. Yet a few hundred yards away there are other folk who're rich enough to be able to afford to come to places like this.'

'Aye,' Andy said as they began to make their way up the wide marble steps. 'I bet they pay a fortune to be members o' a place like this.'

The club's entrance portico was as impressive as everything else about it. Framed by an even broader band of the same exotic stone carvings that surrounded the windows, it looked high enough to admit a giant. Huge burnished brass doors were pushed back, showing a white marble lobby and more wide marble steps inside the building.

'It looks like an Egyptian temple.'

'Probably why they decided to call it The Luxor, Jean.' He adopted a deep and mysterious voice. 'Shall we go inside and see if we can find our mummies? Break a leg,' he muttered in his more usual accent.

'You too.' They'd learned that expression from a chorus girl working at Green's Playhouse, who stayed in the boarding house.

'Members only. Sorry.' One of the doormen had stepped forward to bar their way.

His attitude wasn't exactly what you could have called welcoming, but Jean bestowed a dazzling smile on the man all the same. 'The name's Logan. We have an appointment.'

There was the faintest hint of a thaw in his manner. 'Can you show me a letter to that effect, miss?'

Jean dug in her handbag and produced it. Their interrogator

read it through, handed it back to her and pointed towards the interior of the building. 'Go right ahead, madam. The office is on the first floor. Up the grand staircase and to your right.'

'From "miss" to "madam" in ten seconds flat,' Jean murmured under her breath once they were safely at the top of the second flight of marble steps.

'Even for the hired help.' Andrew pulled a face. 'Or help hopeful of being hired.'

'I thought we didn't have any hopes of that.'

'You'd have to be mad not to *want* to work here,' he responded. Pivoting around on his heels the better to take in their surroundings, he had both awe and admiration in his voice. 'Would you look at this place?'

They were standing at the foot of what could only be the grand staircase the commissionaire had mentioned. Its dark wood was polished to a high sheen. 'Like a black mirror,' Jean murmured.

'Aye,' Andrew agreed, his eyes on the luxurious carpet, which ran up the middle of those gleaming treads. Decorated on both edges with a geometrically shaped black and red border, its main colour was a lush forest green. At the top of the central sweeping flight, the staircase curved off into two graceful wings.

Each of those led to a broad landing. Tilting her head back and gazing up, Jean saw that they ran right round the walls. Protected by curving wrought-iron balusters painted alternately in gleaming black and shining silver, the landings formed what she supposed you would call an indoor balcony.

Both on that balcony and in the lobby where she and Andrew stood were little bays and circular groupings of basketwork chairs, settees and low tables. The pale yellow curves and firm lines of the woven willow were softened and brightened by cushions and throws in red, green and leopard-skin print covers.

The seating arrangements were also interspersed with exotic greenery. The only plant inside the manse had been a large aspidistra, which had occupied its own tall table in the dead centre of the morning-room window. Jean had always felt a bit sorry for it, thinking of it as a lonely soldier permanently condemned to solitary sentry duty.

The plants inside The Luxor didn't look at all like that. For a start, there was a whole regiment of them. No, Jean thought, her eyes narrowing as she thought about it, regiment's not the right word at all. The foliage here was too abundant, too lush, too casually positioned . . .

She looked more closely, and saw that the positioning wasn't casual at all. Someone had gone to a great deal of trouble to place each plant where it would be shown to its best advantage.

As Jean watched, an elegant female hand holding a cigarette in an amber holder emerged from behind the shield of one of those plants and beckoned. Within seconds, a young fair-haired waiter was in front of the owner of that elegantly manicured hand, bending forward to hear whatever it was she was saying to him. Then he turned, and looked directly at Jean and Andrew.

He was very smart, a full-length and impeccably clean white linen apron fastened around his slim waist over what was clearly his uniform of white shirt, black trousers and matching waistcoat. Jean lip-read the first few words he said before he swung back round to the elegant lady: 'I don't know, madam, but . . .'

'*I don't know, madam, but I'll find out?*' Was that what he was saying? Obviously the lady was curious as to who they were. Jean was confident that she and Andrew looked as smart as they had been able to make themselves but she was under no illusions that they looked like members of The Luxor. They were too young, for a start.

Most of the people – mainly women – who were sitting around taking afternoon tea were middle-aged, the youngest in their thirties, the oldest in their fifties.

'It all seems very respectable,' Jean whispered to Andrew.

'Aye,' he agreed, speaking in similarly low tones. His lips twitched. 'Cannae really see many o' the old dears tripping the light fantastic, though, can you? It must be gey hard to dance wi' a walking stick.'

'Maybe there's a younger crowd in the evenings.'

'Maybe. Is someone playing a piano somewhere?'

Jean cocked her head and listened. Discreetly low though it was, the combined buzz of conversation was quite loud when it all joined together. Once she started listening for it, she could hear it. Somewhere out of sight, someone was playing a rather sedate version of 'Let's Do It'.

'Come on,' Andrew said, 'we'd better be getting up those stairs.'

'Yes,' Jean agreed. Placing her hand on the banister, she paused for a moment at the foot of the grand staircase, tilting her head back again to find the source of the light that flooded into the lobby. Invisible from the street outside, a glass cupola crowned the top of the building. 'It's beautiful,' she breathed. 'Really beautiful.'

'So glad you like it.' She whirled round, and was forced to adjust her gaze upwards. The man who had spoken was not only tall and powerfully built but also had that upright bearing that spoke of a life spent in the services. Definitely officer class, Jean thought, making that judgement not only on the basis of the voice and the accent but also on the instantly recognisable air of command.

'Mr Templeton?' she enquired, frowning a little. The reply to her letter of application had been signed by a Mrs Templeton. Perhaps she ran The Luxor with her husband.

The man threw his head back and laughed. Jean judged him to be somewhere in his mid-fifties but he had a fine head of thick brown hair and a luxuriant moustache, both of which were only lightly peppered with grey. He was obviously full of life in other ways too, deep brown eyes twinkling as he looked down at her. 'No, no, my dear,' he said now. 'I'm merely a club member.'

'Never *merely*, Colonel Harris. We value our members highly.'

Now Jean had to lower her gaze a little. The woman who had placed a small hand on the fine grey broadcloth of the older man's sleeve was short and dark. Fashionably dressed, if a little on the plump side, her face was wreathed in smiles. She took her hand from the colonel's jacket and extended it in greeting. 'I'm Gloria Templeton. You must be Jean and Andrew. You don't mind if I call you by your first names, do you?'

They shook hands and assured her that they didn't mind at all.

'I'm giving these two young people a try-out as dancing partners, Colonel Harris.'

'Well,' the colonel replied, 'I must say you both *look* the part. Most attractive. But The Luxor has very high standards to uphold. Can you dance?'

Andrew lifted his chin. 'We dance very well, Colonel Harris.'

The older man smiled at him. It was an open and friendly smile, and the encouragement it seemed to hold within it made Jean's spirits soar. At the same time, she was keenly aware that Mrs Templeton was standing back a little, observing how these two young applicants dealt with someone who was one of her club's most valued members.

Working at The Luxor obviously required other skills than the ability to dance well: a talent for getting on with people of a much higher social status than your own, for one. A new thought flashed through Jean's brain. If Mrs Templeton was going to so much trouble to assess their suitability, could there be a remote, wonderful and absolutely terrifying possibility that she possibly was willing to give them a start?

Jean took a mental deep breath. 'Why don't you put us to the test? In fact,' she continued, smiling up at him, 'perhaps you'd like me to dance with Andrew and then with you, Colonel Harris?'

He laughed again, wagging a finger at her in mock-admonishment. 'My dear young lady, you're being very naughty. Flattering an old crock. I doubt that I could keep up with you. I'm afraid that I dance abominably, which is why my wife enjoys her membership of The Luxor so much. It allows her to indulge to the full her passion for dancing, and in the arms of handsome young men who know exactly where to put their feet.' Once more he smiled at Andrew. 'As I'm sure you do, young man.'

'You underestimate yourself, Colonel.' Gloria Templeton rejoined the conversation at last. She laid a hand each on Jean and Andrew's shoulders. 'I'm going to give you two a try-out in the grand salon and I'm going to ask Colonel Harris to give us his opinion. He's really a very good judge. Go on through,' she said, turning to Jean and Andrew and indicating open double doors halfway up one side of the foyer, 'and have a word with the pianist. I'd like to see a foxtrot, a waltz and that tango you mentioned in your letter.'

'I do like to see a really good tango,' Colonel Harris said enthusiastically. 'Reminds me of my time in the Argentine.'

As breathless with excitement and nerves as Andrew had been earlier, Jean followed him through. 'A tango,' she said in a low voice. 'He likes to see a really good tango.'

'Which is exactly what we're going to give him,' Andrew replied as they walked through the double doors. 'Would you look at this?'

'This really is like an Egyptian tomb,' Jean breathed in response.

Between the tall and narrow windows that overlooked the square, hung scarlet banners in the heaviest cotton Jean had ever seen. Appliquéd onto them were huge hieroglyphs made out of black and white fabric. 'I wonder what the translation is.'

'Leave by this window if there's a fire,' Andrew answered flippantly. 'Have you seen what's behind you?'

Jean turned to look – and let out a shriek. Upright against the wall was a brightly painted sarcophagus of a mummy. Its partner stood on the other side of the entrance doors.

'I wonder if they're the real thing.'

Jean shuddered, and moved forward into the ballroom. 'I don't think I want to know. The pianist is looking our way.'

'Sprung floor,' Andrew observed as they hurried forward towards the stage where a white-painted baby grand piano stood next to seats for at least a dozen orchestral players.

'Nothing but the best in here,' Jean replied, taking in the dining alcoves, which bordered the edges of the room. Like the grand staircase out in the foyer, the round tables were in wood so dark and highly polished that they looked black. They were set into semi-circular banquettes richly upholstered in the same deep red as the curtains and wall hangings.

'Hello, there,' said the pianist. 'Please tell me you've come to save my sanity by allowing me to play something a bit more lively before I die of boredom.'

'I hope so,' Andrew said, introducing himself and Jean. 'Is this place a wee bit staid?'

'You might say so,' said the pianist, giving them his own name and dividing a friendly smile between the two of them. 'You'll forgive me if I don't shake hands.'

'Of course,' Andrew said. 'Can you talk and play at the same time? We need to discuss what music we're going to dance to.'

'No problem. What does La Templeton want to see from you?'

'A foxtrot, a waltz and a tango.'

'Are you doing them in that order?'

'Yes,' Jean said. 'The tango's our speciality.'

The pianist nodded approvingly at her. 'Working up to the big finish? Good thinking. Ah,' he said, as Andrew extracted a rolled-up piece of paper from his pocket and pushed off the rubber band that secured it, 'you've bought the sheet music for that.'

Andrew unrolled the paper scroll and rolled it back the opposite way to flatten it before showing it to the pianist.

'Fine,' said the young man, 'I know this one quite well. Any ideas for your other two dances?'

'We're happy to take suggestions,' Jean said.

'How about "Button Up Your Overcoat" for the foxtrot? Would that suit you?'

'That's perfect.' Jean beamed at the pianist. 'That's the song that was playing when Andrew and I first met.'

'Then I hope it'll bring you luck. Look out, here comes the firing squad. Break a leg, you two.'

Andy gave Jean a little smile, took her hand and led her out into the centre of the room. She moistened her lips and cast him a nervous glance. 'Are you thinking what I'm thinking?'

'That we might actually be in wi' a chance here?' He was very solemn as he looked back at her. 'Aye. I am.'

'Just the thought makes me feel as if I'm about to fall over my feet.'

'Pretend it's just you and me at the dance hall back in Partick. I've spotted the loveliest girl in the room and I've got my courage up to walk across the floor to her.'

'Did you need courage that night?'

'Tons o' it. Even from the other side o' the hall I could tell you were a superior sort o' a lassie. And me riffraff from the wrong side o' Dumbarton Road.'

A pair of hands clapped. 'Where are they?' muttered Jean, scanning the dining alcoves and finding them empty.

'Up on the balcony,' murmured Andrew.

Jean looked up. The colonel and Mrs Templeton were up there, plus half a dozen other people, men and women. Sitting on the basket chairs and settees that were obviously a feature of The Luxor, the group looked for all the world like passengers on a steamboat sailing down the Nile.

'Jean and Andrew,' Gloria Templeton called down, 'whenever you're ready, please.'

'Remember to smile,' Andrew murmured as they took hold of one another. 'And let's enjoy this for its own sake.'

That wasn't so hard as Jean had anticipated. The setting was perfect, the sprung floor felt wonderful beneath her feet and she was dancing with the man she loved: the man with whom she was going to spend the rest of her life. Once her back was to the watchers on the balcony, she murmured a soft, 'I love you, by the way.'

'Nice time to tell me. You'll put me off my stroke.'

But she hadn't. Those three little words that were still so special to them fired them both up, giving them an extra lightness and grace as they glided across the beautiful floor. It was almost possible for them to forget why they were here and how much was riding on their performance.

They finished exactly in time with the music. On impulse, Jean held out the floaty material of her dress and bobbed Andrew a curtsy. He responded by bending over her hand and kissing it. The men and women watching them broke into applause.

Their waltz provoked the same warm appreciation. When it came to the tango, the pianist surpassed himself. By the time the sensuous music with its pulsing and passionate beat and the story they were telling had reached their dramatic climaxes, Jean knew that she and Andrew had danced their best tango ever.

When they had finished there was a moment's silence. The applause that followed was loud and prolonged. Colonel Harris even put his fingers in his mouth and gave them an appreciative whistle. Jean grinned up at him.

Gloria Templeton leaned forward over the handrail of her own private ship. 'Come on up. My husband will meet you at the top of the stairs.'

Colonel Harris met them before they got there, on the stairs themselves. Looking endearingly boyish, he seized both their hands in turn and shook them vigorously. 'Marvellous tango! Absolutely marvellous! I've put in a good word for you!'

Hardly daring to look at Andrew as the colonel went on down the staircase, Jean found her hand being shaken again by a fair-haired man who introduced himself as Richard Templeton. 'Come on through,' he said with a smile, ushering them into a room that occupied the space between the foyer balcony and the one overlooking the grand salon.

The décor and colour scheme of what was obviously the Templetons' office was in keeping with the rest of The Luxor, only much simpler. A large black desk sat diagonally across one corner, a huge red sofa occupied one entire wall and a pair of basket chairs sat in front of the desk. Mr Templeton indicated that Jean and Andrew should take the basket chairs, and then he joined his wife behind the desk.

Here comes the firing squad – that's what the pianist had said. It did feel a bit like being in front of a firing squad, especially when Gloria and Richard Templeton started rattling out questions at them.

They quizzed them on their respective family backgrounds first. Jean answered as honestly as she could, although she managed to slide over the fact of her mother's death without actually mentioning that TB had been the cause of it.

The Templetons moved on to questions about previous employment; both of them seeming to listen with sympathy as Andrew explained how the economic slump had led to him being laid off from his job at the coal-yard. Worrying how she was going to explain leaving the manse, Jean found it all worked out much more easily that she'd anticipated.

'Well,' she began, when the Templetons turned expectantly from Andrew to her, 'I worked for the Reverend Ronald Fairbairn and his wife. As a maid in their house.'

Mrs Templeton was leaning forward over the desk so her husband could light a cigarette for her. She raised her head again without putting it to her lips. 'The Reverend Ronald Fairbairn? That name sounds familiar. Where is his church?'

'In Hyndland. St Martin's. You might have heard of him because you've seen his name in the newspapers. He writes a lot of articles.'

'Not the minister who's so against dancing?' Richard Templeton queried. 'That old killjoy who's always going on about how those of us who love to dance are all condemned to perdition? No wonder you left his employ. How long have you two children been married?'

Andrew blushed. 'Two weeks.'

'You're newlyweds!' breathed Gloria Templeton. 'How romantic!'

'You don't mind us being married?' Jean asked. 'I mean, you don't have a marriage bar, do you?'

It was Richard Templeton who answered her. 'Not as such. Although we prefer our patrons to remain in ignorance of such things. Some of them are a bit conventional, you see. Don't approve of married women working. Would you mind keeping that under your hats?'

Jean and Andrew looked at one another. 'I don't *suppose* so,' Andrew said.

'You do mind,' Richard Templeton said. 'And I can perfectly well understand why. But I'm afraid we'd have to insist. It'd be as well not to tell your fellow dancing partners either. People gossip.'

Your *fellow* dancing partners? Jean's heart began to pound with excitement. Mrs Templeton was looking at Andrew. 'The kissing of Jean's hand at the end of the foxtrot was a nice gesture. Think you could do it with a fat lady in her fifties who's spent the whole dance treading on your toes?'

Andy blinked. 'A-aye,' he stuttered. 'I suppose I could.'

'That's what would be required of you, you know,' Gloria Templeton said, a hint in her voice that a core of steel lay beneath the soft outward appearance. 'We wouldn't be paying you to dance with your wife. Apart from your demonstration dances, that is.'

'We know that being professional dancers is hard work,' Jean said quickly.

'It's bloody hard work,' Gloria said with some warmth. 'Sometimes literally. You'll get sore feet and backache and

217

blisters and cracked heels and you'll have to dance when you've got a cold and when you don't feel like it at all. And you,' she said, pointing her cigarette at Jean, 'will have to dance with some old devils who'll want to put their hands where they shouldn't. Think you can cope with that without offending them?'

Jean took a chance. 'So telling them to take their hauns aff ma boady wouldn't be acceptable, would it?'

'A sense of humour,' Richard Templeton said, laughing at the expression she had just used. 'I like that. Would you use humour to deal with those sorts of patrons?'

'Surely,' Andrew put in, 'a girl's best defence against those sort of men is to always act like a lady. As Jean always does.'

'Got it bad for her,' said Richard Templeton, 'haven't you?'

'There's nothing bad about the way I feel for Jean. It's all good.'

'True love and chivalry all wrapped up in one package,' Richard Templeton said. 'Nice to know both of those commodities still exist in these cynical, modern times. Although you might have to live by a slightly different set of rules at The Luxor. Wouldn't you say so, Gloria?'

His wife inclined her fashionably coiffured head. Then she regarded her husband with a question in her eyes. He nodded, but left it up to her to speak.

'Would I be right in thinking that neither of you has any evening clothes? That, in fact, the only dance clothes you own are the ones you're wearing now? And that you probably aren't staying in the most salubrious of accommodation at the moment?'

Heart thumping at what those questions seemed to imply, Jean sat up straighter in her chair. 'We've only got what you see us in. And yes,' she admitted, 'we'd really like to get out of the place where we're staying now.'

'It's not an option for you to live with Andrew's family?'

Andrew let out an odd little bark of laughter. 'To say that my mother's house is overcrowded might be a bit of an understatement, Mrs Templeton.'

'Not to mention the fact that Andrew's family don't like me very much,' Jean said.

'So we'd have to find you somewhere to stay,' said Gloria Templeton. 'I think I might know of a rather nice flat out at Anniesland which would suit you two down to the ground.'

'Would it have a very high rent?' Jean asked anxiously.

'About two guineas a week, I think.'

'Two guineas a week?' Andrew spluttered, 'I don't think we can afford that.'

'You haven't heard what we're going to pay you yet. Besides, we'll take care of all of your expenses for the moment.'

'We'll pay you back.'

'Damn' right you will. We're going to have to kit both of you out and that's not going to cost tuppence three-farthings. But we can wait for a while and then start taking a small amount out of your wages each week. Agreed, Richard?'

'Agreed, Gloria.'

The Templetons smiled at one another and then turned to Jean and Andrew.

'All right,' Gloria Templeton said, 'you're hired.'

Chapter 22

THEY WAITED until they had walked back through the archway and were once more out on Buchanan Street. Only then did they stop and turn to face one another. The slow smile was spreading across Andrew's face. 'Did I imagine all o' that? Or do I think I'm standing on Buchanan Street when I'm really in the middle o' a dream? One that's whatever the opposite o' a nightmare is?'

'If you are, I'm in the same one,' Jean said happily. 'Andy, we've got ourselves a job! A dancing job! At seven guineas a week! Each!'

He let out a wild whoop, grabbed her by the waist and lifted her right off her feet. A middle-aged man in a pinstriped business suit did a hasty side-step to avoid being struck by Jean's swinging legs.

'Sorry,' she said breathlessly as Andrew lowered her to the ground. 'We've been out of work for ages and we've just got a start. We're so happy!'

'That really is something to celebrate.' The pinstriped gentleman divided a smile between the two of them. 'Good luck to you both.'

Watching him stride off down the street, Jean let out the happiest of sighs. 'Oh, Andy, isn't this the best day there ever was?'

'It certainly is. We've got a job. A good job at a classy place. Plus an advance on our salary and a nice place to stay into the bargain. We can easily afford that rent out of fourteen guineas a week. There wasnae even any talk o' a trial period.'

He sounded as amazed as Jean felt. She tucked her hand into his. 'That's because we danced so well and we managed to converse with the colonel.'

'Huh,' he said, pretending to be annoyed as they set off up Buchanan Street. 'You flirted wi' him, you mean.'

'Old men like that.'

'Young men like it too. Any man wi' good red blood running through his veins likes that.' He squeezed her fingers. 'As long as it doesnae go any further than a wee bit o' flirting.'

'Would you be jealous?' she asked, delighted at the very thought.

'What d'you think?' he growled.

Laughing, Jean glanced over at the restaurant they had passed on the way down. 'Let's go in there for lunch.'

'Lunch?' he said. 'It's *lunch* now, is it?'

'Aye,' she said cheerfully. 'What d'you say?'

He said yes and they lingered over the meal, chattering excitedly about the future and their impressions of The Luxor and the Templetons.

'He's a lot posher than she is.'

'You think so?' Jean asked in surprise. 'I thought she seemed quite posh herself.'

'She's perfected it all,' Andrew said, 'the way she speaks and the way she looks. I think she's worked at it, though. And as for her starting out in life as a Gloria, well, I have my doubts.'

Jean laughed. 'You think she was a wee Aggie or a Betty?'

'Something like that.' He grinned, and gave her his own posh voice. 'I say, darling, would you care to finish this delicious meal with a few crackers and a slice or two of cheese?'

221

'I'll be glad to get out of this place,' Jean said as they returned to the boarding house half-an-hour later. 'Won't you?'

He turned his mouth down. 'Except that I've spent many a happy hour in this room. Especially over the last two weeks.'

'It'll be even better in a nice new place.' She glanced around. 'Don't suppose we'll be taking much there with us. I'd better clean out our rubbish.'

'Not much except old newspapers, is there?'

'Mainly those,' Jean agreed, lifting the small bundle of papers that had accumulated since they'd been able to afford to buy them again. She turned it over in her hand. 'I never even read that one you bought me that day after we'd finished the marathon.'

'No' much point reading it now,' he replied. 'All old news. Jean?'

For the newspaper he had bought her the day after they'd finished the marathon had flapped open, and she was staring fixedly at it.

'What's wrong, Jean?'

Her eyes had filled with tears. 'Look,' she managed, carrying the paper to the table and opening it out flat. 'Look.' She was pointing at the short article in the bottom right-hand corner of the page with a finger that wasn't steady.

' "Shocking double tragedy at Kelvinbridge",' Andrew read out, scanning the brief headline and the article itself. ' "Police alerted when neighbour smelled gas. Too late to save doomed pair. They were later named as James and Annabel—" ' He stopped reading in mid-sentence, his head snapping up. For a moment neither he nor Jean said anything.

At last she wiped her eyes. 'It wasn't a double tragedy, it was a triple one. Annabel was expecting a baby.'

'Aye. A poor wee bairn that never had a chance.' The blood

222

had drained from his face, leaving him pale and sombre. 'It was probably change from that half-crown I gave him that Jim put in the gas meter.'

Jean walked forward and put her arms about him. 'You couldn't have known what he was going to do. Probably he didn't even know. Not when he left the dance hall.'

'Poor bugger,' Andrew said. 'He must have seen it as the only way out.' His own eyes filled with tears. 'Oh, Jean! There but for the grace of God!'

She drew his head down on to her shoulder and they stood together for a while. Until he lifted it again and wiped his eyes with his hands as she had done earlier. 'So many folk don't have a chance,' he said, a determined edge to his voice. 'Now we do.'

'Yes. Now we do.'

'Let's make the most of it, Jean. Let's make the absolute most of it.'

Jean pushed open the door of the lift, darted out on to the sunny landing and burst in through the door of the flat. 'Andy! Where are you?'

'In the bathroom,' he called back. 'With you in a wee minute.'

'Hurry up!' she yelled. 'I'll be in the sitting room.' She ran through there and dumped the burdens she held on to the square beech table which stood in front of the window.

All of the furniture in their new home was pale in colour, as the décor in general was as light and as bright as the pleasant lawns and flowerbeds that surrounded these three low blocks of modern flats.

'A-a-ah,' Jean breathed as she uncurled her aching hands. 'That is *so* sore!'

There were red marks across her fingers, the skin raised by

the imprint of the corded string handles of boxes and bags. She'd only just made it into the flat without dropping them all over the landing. Who'd have thought a couple of hats and a few dresses could be so heavy? She hadn't carried them very far either, only from the taxi that had dropped her off on the pavement twenty-five yards away from the front door.

Gloria Templeton had seen Jean into the black cab, handing over the purchases she'd been carrying. Explaining that she had an appointment with an old friend for afternoon tea, she'd told Jean that she and Andrew should present themselves at The Luxor punctually at one o'clock the following day so they could be shown the ropes before the regular Wednesday afternoon *thé dansant* began.

Andrew had already started working. He'd been giving his first dance lesson today, an activity that, it had been explained, was much more likely to involve him than Jean. Among The Luxor's clientele, more women wanted to learn how to dance than men.

Realising that she'd laid two shoe boxes on the beech table, Jean swiftly transferred them to one of the matching chairs. 'Oh, hurry up, Andy!' she called again, going over to the door and shouting along the corridor.

She skipped back over to the table like a little girl, her eyes roaming over what lay on it. Even without knowing what was inside them, the bags and boxes looked exciting.

One was of glossy cream-coloured paper with the shop's name lettered on it in gold. Another was black, the writing done in silver. There were two hatboxes, one decorated in pink candy stripes, the other a pale powder blue with a dark blue trim. Jean decided to keep them all as a memento of the wonderful day she'd had: even the ones she wasn't going to need to store the gorgeous things they contained.

'Come *on*, Andy!' she yelled again.

'I'm coming, I'm coming,' he grumbled. 'Where's the fire?' He was walking along the corridor, drying his hair with a towel. 'I've been having a shower. Is that contraption in the bathroom no' the most wonderful invention known to man? Just what I needed after my first session in the dance studio.'

'How did that go?'

'Great. One lady told me she loved the way I spoke and that I wasnae to change it. So there. Stick that in your pipe and smoke it, Miss Up The Hill.' He pulled the towel from his damp locks and stopped dead in the doorway. 'Oh, Jean! Your hair!'

'I've had it cut,' she said unnecessarily. Trying not to laugh at the expression of horrified dismay on Andrew's face, she patted her crowning glory. Pulled up by its own natural wave, her hair extended now only to just below her ears, exposing the line of her neck. 'Don't you think it looks really nice, though?'

'Y-e-s,' he said as he walked forward, sounding as though he thought no such thing.

'It's very fashionable.'

'It's certainly that,' he agreed, dropping his towel over the back of a chair. He stirred the air. 'Turn around.'

Jean obeyed the instruction. 'What do you think of my new outfit?'

'Classy,' he said, taking in the black-and-white afternoon frock and matching short jacket. 'I like the bow at the neck. Very smart.'

'Oh, Andy,' Jean said, so excited she couldn't keep still, 'Mrs Templeton's bought me loads of nice things. There's two blouses and skirts for daywear – and two gorgeous wee hats to go with them – and two dresses suitable for the tea-dances and three evening dresses. There's a red one and a black one and this one. It's my favourite.' She opened the glossy cream-coloured bag and pulled out a dress that shimmered as the sun caught the sequins that smothered it. 'Midnight blue,' she said breathlessly. 'I've always wanted a midnight-blue evening dress. There's a wee bolero to go with it.' She held it against herself and waltzed over to the full-length mirror fixed to the wall by the door. 'Don't you think this is the most beautiful dress you've ever seen?'

'Almost as beautiful as the girl who's going to be wearing it.'

Jean smiled at his reflection in the mirror. 'So your first shot at the teaching went well?'

'It went great.'

'Were there other dancing partners there?'

'Three o' them.'

'What were they like with you?'

'Friendly enough. A bit wary, maybe.'

'I suppose we're all rivals for the work.'

'I suppose so,' he said, agreeing with her for the third time.

Jean allowed the dress to fall forward over her arm and turned to face him. 'What's the matter?'

'It's all this stuff,' he said, indicating the boxes on the table. 'The clothes that were bought for me yesterday too. I'm wondering how we're going to pay them back for all of it.'

'You know that: out of our pay. A little every week over a year. And they're not going to start taking it off until January. I think that's really good of them.'

He came forward and put his arms around her waist. 'They'll soon be making money out of us.'

'We'll soon be making money out of them. If any of the club members fancy dancing with us, that is.'

'When you wear that dress everyone will want to dance with you.' He kissed her on the cheek. 'Going to try on all your nice new things and give me a wee fashion parade?'

PART III

Chapter 23

January 1934

'HIYA, GORGEOUS.'

'Hello, handsome,' Jean said in return, meeting Andrew on the grand staircase. After three months at The Luxor, the sight of him in evening dress could still take her breath away. He looked so debonair, long-limbed and relaxed in the dark and sophisticated clothes as he ran nimbly down the forest-green carpet to join her. She herself was wearing the midnight-blue dress with the little bolero and all the glinting sequins. They must, she thought happily, make a handsome couple.

'Where are you off to?'

'The partners' dressing room. It's half-past eleven.'

'Time for you to transform yourself into Miss Nineteen Thirty-Four? Why don't I come up and help you?'

'Because the female dressing room is out of bounds to the male partners, that's why.'

'We're married, Jean,' he said in a ludicrously exaggerated stage whisper, turning and walking up the rest of the stairs with her.

'No one's supposed to know that, you numpty. Besides, won't one of your coterie of middle-aged admirers be languishing downstairs waiting for you?' Jean batted her discreetly mascaraed eyelashes at him. 'Several of them are probably going into a decline even as we speak.'

'Miaow, miaow,' he retorted amiably. 'Besides, you've got your own coterie of middle-aged admirers.'

After their first fortnight at The Luxor they had sat down one Sunday and worked out a new set of rules to deal with their new situation. They had agreed to allow one another a little gentle flirting with their respective admirers. That was more or less part of the job. There was, however, a line to be drawn and they solemnly agreed where that line was.

Small presents were acceptable. Large and expensive ones were to be gracefully declined, as were invitations to meet patrons outside of the club. Those rules were also The Luxor's, and both Jean and Andrew were more than happy to abide by them.

Andrew had been initially reluctant to accept even the small gifts. Jean had persuaded him. The mature ladies who became all girlish and giggly when they danced with him were lonely, she reasoned. They gave him silver cigarette cases and silk ties and boxes of manly striped handkerchiefs to express their gratitude and appreciation for his company and the pleasure his cheerful conversation gave them. It would be churlish and unkind to refuse them.

Jean herself was beginning to amass a collection of powder compacts and bottles of scent and lace-edged handkerchiefs far too delicate ever to use but where was the harm?

They both suspected that some of their new colleagues didn't adhere to any rules whatsoever, not even the ones imposed by the Templetons, and that flirtatious friendships begun on the dance floor sometimes ended up in entirely different places. Those were the choices other people made. If they wanted to jeopardise their positions at The Luxor, running the risk of instant dismissal, that was up to them.

'I wonder how many of those admirers of yours are going to drop dead of overexcitement when they see you in your Miss Nineteen Thirty-Four costume,' Andrew mused now.

Hogmanay of 1933 had fallen on a Sunday. As a dancing club, The Luxor could get round a lot of the rules that governed dance halls. Since dancing on the Sabbath wasn't one of them, the Templetons had decided to postpone the celebrations until the first full weekend of the New Year.

Jean cast Andrew a sideways glance as they walked through to the back of the building where the partners' dressing rooms were. 'You all right about my costume now?'

'I suppose I can stand the thought of other men ogling far too much of your legs as long as I know said legs are coming home with me.'

'You've changed your tune.' When he had first seen the dress she was about to change into he'd described its skirt as more akin to a pelmet than an item of clothing. He had further suggested that if the neckline were only a couple of inches lower she could call the damn' thing a belt and have done with it.

Nor had he been too happy about the costume Gloria Templeton had devised for Jean to wear when she and Andrew regularly performed their story tango as a demonstration dance.

'You do look like a streetwalker,' he grumbled when he first saw her in the short black skirt with the slit up the side, the tight red sweater and the black beret which Mrs Templeton had decreed he should rip off Jean's head as part of the routine. 'What's more, you look like a *French* streetwalker.'

Jean had managed to tease him out of that one by asking which he thought was worse, looking like a prostitute or looking French.

Once the two of them had gone through the half-height

wooden gate with 'Staff Only' lettered on it in gold paint, and turned the corner that took them out of sight of any club members having a drink up on the first floor, Jean slipped her hand through the crook of his arm. 'Where else would my legs be going? And where,' she demanded, as they reached the girls' dressing room and Andrew wrapped his fingers around the door knob, 'do you think you're going?'

'None o' the lassies are up here right now.' He pushed the door open and called out all the same. 'Anyone at home and are you decent if you are?'

When no answer was forthcoming, he ushered Jean into the dressing room. 'You'll get us both into trouble,' she complained. 'Just because the Templetons know that we're married to each other doesn't—'

He shut her up by the simple expedient of grabbing her waist with his two hands, yanking her towards him and placing his mouth over hers. Her own hands rising in initial protest, it took only seconds for Jean to capitulate, those same hands fluttering down on to his shoulders.

The evening clothes were too firm, too well-tailored, too much of a barrier. She slid her hands down and in under his open jacket. He moaned softly against her mouth and deepened the kiss.

'I needed that,' he murmured when it was finally over, laying his forehead against hers. 'I've hardly seen you all day.'

'So what's new?' Jean queried ruefully. 'We hardly see each other most days.'

'Sometimes I get fed up with it, that's all. I'll be dancing with some woman who's blethering on about nothing and has absolutely no sense of rhythm into the bargain and all I'll be thinking about is you. How light on your feet you are. How I'd really like to spend all my time dancing with you and only you. How much I love you.'

'I love you too. But I've only got fifteen minutes to get changed.' Jean patted him on the front of his starched shirt and pulled herself out of his embrace. 'Nobody would pay us to dance with each other. We're being paid handsomely to dance with other folk.'

'I know. I just miss you sometimes, that's all.'

'Miss me?' It seemed an odd thing to say. 'We live together. We have Sundays together.'

'Most of which we spend sleeping because we're so knackered after dancing all week.'

'We don't spend the *whole* day sleeping,' Jean murmured. 'As far as I can see, you seem to have plenty of energy left over for our normal Sunday afternoon activities.'

' "Our normal Sunday afternoon activities",' he repeated, rolling the words around his mouth. 'I really enjoy those, you know.'

'I'm well aware of that,' Jean said cautiously, not missing the dangerous glint in the inky-blue eyes.

'I don't suppose you'd fancy transferring some of those Sunday afternoon activities to Saturday night?'

She shoved him in the chest, half laughing and half horrified. 'No, I would not! Somebody might come in at any minute! Beside, I've only got ten minutes to get changed now.'

'Five minutes would do.'

'You underestimate yourself.'

He laughed. 'Let me help you undress at least.' His practised hands were already on the fastenings of the midnight-blue dress.

'Get lost,' Jean said cheerfully. 'Away back to your duties with the middle-aged ladies, you lounge lizard!'

'I demand my rights before I go! It's only fair when you're sending me out on to the battlefield!'

233

'Your rights?' Jean queried, her eyes widening.

'At least another kiss. One last kiss afore I go. Ye cannae send me back to the fray without the comfort o' your bonnie mou', lassie.'

'You been reading Robert Burns again?' She was laughing so hard she could hardly kiss him.

'You're happy, though?' she asked. 'Apart from us hardly seeing each other?'

He looked deep into her eyes, the long, slow smile spreading across his face. 'Right at this moment I couldn't be happier.'

She woke shortly before noon on Sunday to find him standing over her, wearing only his red and navy striped pyjama bottoms and a broad grin.

'Breakfast in bed,' he announced, placing a tray over her lap as she slid up into a sitting position.

Jean pushed the hair out of her eyes and surveyed the tray: tea and toast and scrambled eggs for two. 'This is nice.'

'Shift over a bit so that I can sit down. I'll lift the tray again while you move.'

They did that and he settled comfortably on the bed facing her, one leg crooked on it and the other dangling over the side. Jean glanced out of the window. They were still in January but the day looked crisp, sunny and inviting. 'Fancy a walk round Bingham's Pond later, or something?'

Andrew swallowed a mouthful of eggs. 'I prefer the "or something" option.'

'You usually do,' Jean murmured.

'You got any objections to that?'

'Not a one.'

'Didn't think you did,' he said smugly. 'Not very observant this morning, are you?'

'Is this a riddle?' Jean put her second piece of egg-covered toast in her mouth and chewed it ruminatively.

'No. All you have to do is look at what's lying in front of your saucer.'

She looked. It was a small red jewellery box. The sort that held a ring.

'Open it, then. I know you can only wear it on a Sunday,' he said as she flipped up the lid, 'but I'd really like you to do that.'

'Of course I will.' She placed the box in front of him and extended her left hand. 'Put it on my finger.'

Once he had obeyed that instruction he dipped his head and put his lips to the plain gold wedding band. 'I love you, Mrs Logan.'

'I love you, Mr Logan.' She held out her hand so the ring would catch the sunlight. 'I love my wedding ring too. It fits perfectly. How did you know what size to buy?' He gave her a pained look. 'How often have I held your hands? I know what size your fingers are. One more thing before we get on with our breakfast.'

Jean looked expectantly at him.

'It's Chrissie's birthday a fortnight from today.'

'And you'd like to give her a present? Take it yourself so you can see your mother and your other sisters too?' Jean's voice was carefully matter-of-fact. She wanted him to heal the breach with his family. Right from the very beginning she'd known how much his mother and his sisters meant to him. 'Will you go in the afternoon or the evening?'

'I thought we'd go in the afternoon, Jean.'

'We?'

He held her gaze. 'We.'

She could see the determination in the set of his mouth. She knew she had to try to dissuade him all the same. 'D'you not think it might be better for you to go on your own?'

He lifted his tea by the cup rather than the handle. 'Why would I go on my own, Jean? You're my wife. Part o' the family now.'

She looked doubtfully at him as he drank and replaced his cup in its saucer. 'I'm not so sure your mother and sisters are going to see it that way.'

'It's no' a matter of choice. You're a Logan now. You *are* part o' the family. Once they get to know you properly they'll be fine.' He smiled at her. 'Once they get to know you properly they'll love you as much as I do.'

'Andy . . .' She stopped, not sure how to word her conviction that all of the Logan women with the possible exception of wee Chrissie had no desire to have anything at all to do with their brother's wife. Jean's stomach lurched at the realisation that they didn't even know yet that she was his wife.

Andrew lifted the tray and swung it down on to the floor before sliding up the bed and taking hold of her hands. 'Let me explain something, Jean. I left Partick wi' my tail between my legs. After the birching, I mean.'

Held between his own, her fingers twitched nervously. She and Andrew never spoke about that event. Even hearing him say the word was shocking.

'I dare say Ma's found out about it now. And that she's had to put up wi' all the tongues that'll have been wagging about it.'

'I'm sorry if she has,' Jean said. 'Especially as what happened to you was my fault. Your sisters are never going to forgive me for that, you know.'

'What happened to me was *not* your fault.' He lifted their joined hands, emphasising the point. 'Not in any way. But that's no' what I'm trying to say. I left home more or less in disgrace. I want to go back there and show them that I've done well for myself. I want to go back there and show off my new wife. Come with me, Jean,' he said again. 'Please?'

She was unable to resist the plea in those inky-blue pools.

Ten minutes till the end of the lesson and she still hadn't betrayed by the slightest flicker of an eyelid that she had recognised him. When Gloria Templeton had brought her into the studio she had waited calmly for him to be introduced to her. The way women of her class did, knowing that almost everyone they met, man or woman, was bound to be their social inferior.

Andrew had the distinct impression that Mrs Edward – 'do call me Mona' – Forsyth liked what she saw. He always knew when women fancied him. She continued to show no signs of recognition. That was odd. They had spoken to one another that day, looked one another full in the face. She'd liked what she'd seen then too.

Seeing her for the first time without a hat, Andrew found that she had dark brown hair, very short and very chic. She was impeccably well groomed in every other way.

How could it be possible that she didn't remember him? After almost an hour spent in her company it was obvious that she was neither stupid nor scatter-brained. Mrs Edward Forsyth was as sharp as a tack. Not a great dancer, though.

She admitted as much, so good-humoured and self-deprecating that Andrew found himself warming to her.

'Am I a hopeless case?' she asked, laughing up at him.

'Not at all. I'm sure we'll be able to do something with you.'

'I do hope so. My husband keeps telling me how ashamed he is of my execrable footwork. That's why we have a membership here. So he can dance with the young ladies who know how to dance properly.'

'I thought you were a new member,' Andrew said politely.

'No, we've been off travelling for the past few months.' She smiled at him. 'Bet you wish we'd stayed away. I'm sure you've never taught anybody who's trod on your feet as much as I've done this afternoon.'

'Not at all,' he said, and found himself telling her a little about teaching Jean to dance. As soon as he'd done it he was aware of a twinge of guilt, suspecting that Jean herself wouldn't much like him sharing the story with anyone else.

'That's us, Mrs Forsyth,' he said pleasantly, glancing up at the clock on the studio wall. He was beginning to relax now, reassured that she really hadn't recognised him. 'I hope you've enjoyed your lesson.'

'I could enjoy a few more moments of your company if you were to walk me to my car, Andrew.' She tapped him lightly on the back of his hand. 'And I told you to call me Mona.'

'Against the rules, I'm afraid,' he responded, softening the refusal with a smile. He let out a long, low whistle of appreciation when he saw her car: a sleek red Alvis.

'Do you drive, Andrew?'

'Had a few shots on the lorry when I was working as a coal-man. I'd *love* to drive something like this, though,' he said, running an admiring hand along the gleaming paintwork.

'You worked as a coal-man? How fascinating.'

He laughed. 'It was hardly fascinating, Mrs Forsyth. Especially when I was paid off because the orders had fallen.'

'How awful for you. Were you out of work for a long time?'

'Long enough.'

Taking him so much by surprise he didn't have time even

to think about moving back, she stretched out one beautifully manicured hand and traced the line of his jaw with her fingertips. 'Poor boy. You must have been so very desperate that day we met in the restaurant at Copland and Lye's.'

Andrew coughed to clear a throat that was all at once as dry as the Sahara Desert. 'I thought you hadn't remembered me.'

'How could I forget a handsome young man like you?' she murmured. She took her hand from his face. 'Don't worry, Andrew. I have no intention of telling anyone what happened that day.' She laughed. 'As they say in the shockers, your secret is safe with me.'

She got into her lovely car and drove off, raising one hand in a wave as she pulled away from the kerb and turned the corner into Queen Street. Andrew stood staring at the junction long after Mona Forsyth had disappeared from view.

Chapter 24

'WHAT'S THE matter with your young man this evening?'

'Och,' Jean said, neatly executing a gliding side-step, 'Andrew's a bit under the weather, Colonel Harris. He got caught in that awful sleet we had last weekend and he's ended up with a bad cough. It's really irritating him.'

'And you too, eh?' The colonel smiled down at her. Jean had become a great favourite with him. She was fond of him too, and had been cock-a-hoop when she'd finally managed to persuade him up on to the dance floor. He wasn't a wonderful dancer but he wasn't nearly so bad as he had made out either. For a tall and solidly built man he was surprisingly light on his feet.

'A bit,' she admitted. 'It seems awful to be annoyed when somebody's not well, doesn't it?'

'Tell that to my wife,' said the colonel, allowing Jean to lead him rather than the other way round. 'She's never ill herself and she can't abide sickness in anyone else. If I have a cough she always threatens me with the Caligula treatment.'

'What's that?' Jean asked, interested as she always was to learn something new.

'Caligula was one of the emperors of Ancient Rome. When

his nephew had a cough which kept *him* awake, he gave orders for the nephew's head to be cut off.'

She laughed up at him. 'That seems a step too far!'

'It stopped the cough.'

'It stopped the nephew too,' Jean countered.

Colonel Harris smiled. 'I don't think Caligula was too concerned about that. We *are* talking about a man who married his sister and made his horse a member of the Roman Senate. I take it you'd much prefer young Andrew to keep his handsome head upon his handsome shoulders.'

'Was the sister the mother of the nephew?' Jean asked, dipping her head to conceal the blush that observation had provoked.

'That I don't know, Miss Curious.' The colonel gave her the sort of approving look a teacher might bestow upon a bright pupil. 'I'll look it up for you and tell you the next time we're in.'

'Will that be on Friday night as usual?'

'Saturday this week. We have guests for dinner on Friday. One would think one's social life would get less hectic after Christmas and New Year but that isn't how it's been for us. Although I expect Mrs Harris will be popping in and out as usual.'

Like many of its patrons, particularly the female ones, the colonel's lady used The Luxor not only as a dancing club but also as a base when she was in town, popping in and out for luncheon or afternoon tea. All of the dancing partners had to take their turn acting as hosts and hostesses, offering company and conversation to patrons of either sex who required those services.

An interested Jean had asked Gloria Templeton if that couldn't be construed as the 'sitting-out' that the City's regulations forbade. That was when Mrs Templeton had

241

pointed out that the regulations applied to dance halls. The Luxor was a club, an exclusive one open to members only, and was therefore exempt from many of the restrictions.

Nor did The Luxor go in for anything as common as dance tickets. Each dancing partner kept his or her own dance card. Issued with a fresh one for each session, Jean soon found this already had several names written in when she got it. It was explained to her how the system worked. The patrons had their favourite dancers and would often book them in advance.

Mrs Templeton kept a chart in her office in which she filled in all of the bookings. Jean always thought it looked as complicated as the hieroglyphs on the banners that decorated the walls.

Andrew and his current partner passed close by Jean and the colonel. Jean gave her young husband a swift smile. The one she received in return was pretty mechanical. The sleepless nights his cough had cost him weren't doing much for his mood.

Why he'd decided to walk through a miserably sleety afternoon when they were both now well able to afford a tram or a taxi was beyond her. Men. There was no fathoming them.

'What's worrying our little Miss Dunlop now?' teased her partner.

'Sorry,' Jean said, blinking as she snapped back to reality. 'Was I frowning?'

According to Gloria Templeton, that was one of the most heinous crimes in the book. The guests came in here to get away from the gloom and doom of the world outside, the Depression, and their own personal worries. They didn't want to hear about your worries either.

'I'm fine,' she told the colonel. 'Absolutely fine.'

A few hours later Jean climbed thankfully into a black cab. 'I'm whacked,' she said to Andrew. 'How about you?'

'I'm all right.'

She laid a sympathetic hand on his arm. 'Is your cough still bothering you? Why don't we ask the taxi driver to stop by the late-night chemist and get you some medicine?'

'I don't need any medicine. Horrible, syrupy concoctions. A cold has to run its course, Jean. Don't you know that?' He shook her hand off his arm.

Jean turned her head away and gazed out at the sleeping city. He's got the cough, she thought, but it's me who's just been subjected to the Caligula treatment.

'No' one of my better ideas.'

'Perhaps not,' Jean agreed. The reception his family had accorded her this blustery February afternoon had been barely civil. The air had crackled with tension and they had stayed no more than three-quarters of an hour.

Young Chrissie had done her level best to keep the conversation going. While it was clear that she really had been delighted with the parcel of books her brother and his wife had given her for her birthday, her thanks had been just a wee bit too prolonged and overenthusiastic. Jean had tried all the same to match that valiant effort. Under the cool gaze of Andrew's other sisters, that had been hard going.

Bella Logan had clearly been torn in several directions at once. She'd been overcome with emotion to find her son standing on her doorstep. He'd held out his arms and enveloped her in a long bear hug. It was only when Bella emerged from his embrace that she even noticed Jean, standing back to allow the reunion to take place.

The hurt that flashed across her face when she realised that the son she loved so dearly had married without telling her had made Jean want to cry. Her instinctive move forward to console the woman who was now her mother-in-law and tell her she'd have loved to have had her at the wedding had been checked by the arrival of Alice and Agnes Logan, clattering up the stairs of the tenement.

Now Jean was thinking wistfully that Andrew's mother might just have brought herself to welcome his bride if those two in particular hadn't been quite so hostile.

'You *should* have gone on your own.'

'You're my wife.' He repeated that as they walked along to the railway station to catch the train back to Anniesland. 'You're my wife.'

'That's the problem, as far as they're concerned.'

'I can understand them being hurt because we didn't invite them to the wedding. But that we werenae exactly on speaking terms at the time was more Alice and Agnes's fault than it was mine.'

'I don't think they see it that way,' Jean said, following him up the stairs to the station. 'They blame me for what happened to you and they always will. They also blame me for taking you away from them.'

'Well, they shouldn't. Ma understands why I had to go. So does Chrissie.'

'Maybe,' Jean said doggedly as they sat down on a bench to wait for the train. 'But the others don't. And we've really upset your mother by getting married without telling her. I'm not sure if she's ever going to be able to forgive me for that.'

'I want them all to like you.'

He looked so unhappy Jean heard herself saying something she didn't believe: 'They'll come round to me eventually.'

'They'll come round to you now or not at all. I gave

Ma some money today and I'll send her some more regularly but we'll not be visiting again in a hurry.'

Jean put her hand on his arm. 'Don't say that. I don't want to come between you and your family. You go and see them whenever you like.'

'I'm not going without you,' he said stubbornly.

'Yes, you are,' she coaxed. 'If you don't go they'll think it's me that's stopping you. That'll give them another excuse not to like me.'

Andrew looked at her, drew in a deep breath and slowly released it. 'All right,' he said. 'Maybe I'll go and see them again sometime. Maybe.'

'Here's the train,' Jean said. As they stood up and stepped forward to board it she thought wistfully that she had wanted the Logan girls to like her too. She'd have loved to have been accepted into Andrew's family but if that wasn't to be, it wasn't to be.

The week that followed was a difficult one. Although he seemed to have shaken off his cold, Andrew was in a prickly mood throughout it, moody and uncommunicative. Hurt and confused, and wondering if the sunny-tempered young man with whom she'd fallen in love was ever going to come back, Jean withdrew. She'd just have to leave him to come round in his own good time.

It didn't help that he was managing to hide his black mood from the patrons. He was quite the life and soul of the party at The Luxor, throwing himself into all of it with what seemed like boundless energy. It was like working with Dr Jekyll and living with Mr Hyde.

Padding through from the bedroom late next Sunday morning, Jean found him sitting at the kitchen table sipping coffee and nibbling on a piece of toast and already fully dressed, casual but smart in lightweight linen.

'Going somewhere?'

'Partick,' he said without looking up. 'I thought I'd spend the afternoon there today.'

'Oh,' Jean managed. 'Will you be home for tea?'

'I don't know. I might stay there for it.' He stood up abruptly. 'I think I'll just go now, Jean.'

'Oh,' she said again. 'All right.'

He had already left the kitchen. Seconds later, she heard the door of the flat close behind him and found herself staring fixedly at one half-drunk cup of coffee and one half-eaten slice of toast.

'Miss Dunlop? Jean, if I may?'

Jean had known who was coming up behind her before Mona Forsyth had so much as opened her mouth. She wore a very distinctive perfume, richly floral and rather heady.

Jean turned, the professional smile in place. 'How can I help you, Mrs Forsyth?'

'By calling me Mona, for a start.'

'You must know we're not allowed to call the patrons by their first names, Mrs Forsyth. We're only the hired help.' Jean regretted the brutal statement the instant it was out of her mouth, especially when she saw the pained look that crossed Mona Forsyth's lovely face.

'But, my dear,' she said, laying her beautifully manicured fingers lightly on Jean's forearm, 'you must know that we club members in no way think of you young people in those unkind terms. We like to think of you as our *friends*.'

Aye, Jean thought cynically, right. Do you think I came up the Clyde on a water biscuit with my leg held up for a funnel?

For one wild and delicious moment, she contemplated putting her hands on her hips and rattling out that question. She substituted a repeat of her earlier one.

'Can I tempt you to come and take afternoon tea with me?' Mona Forsyth asked.

'I'd be glad to,' Jean said politely.

The two of them sat down on a pair of the basketwork chairs in the lobby, a waiter instantly appearing at Mrs Forsyth's elbow.

'Earl Grey for two,' she said. 'And some scones and cakes and things.'

'I'd prefer Assam,' Jean said. Refusing afternoon tea hadn't been an option. Club members might couch their invitations as requests but the dancing partners taking their turn acting as hosts and hostesses had no choice about accepting. All the same, she was damned if she was going to drink a type of tea she didn't much care for.

A little smile played along Mrs Forsyth's mouth. 'You have an independent spirit, Miss Dunlop.'

Jean accepted a cigarette from the gold case being proffered across the low table. 'I'm afraid that's been forced on me, Mrs Forsyth. I've more or less had to make my own way through life.'

'Your parents are no longer with us?'

'My father was killed in the war,' Jean said simply. 'My mother died when I was fourteen.'

'You have no other relatives?'

'None.'

'But, my dear! How awful for you to be all alone in the world!'

Taken aback and a little embarrassed by the obvious depth of the older woman's sympathy, Jean wasn't quite sure how to respond.

'Then again,' Mona Forsyth said, 'I suppose you're not all alone. You have your Andrew.'

Jean's cigarette stopped halfway to her lips. Some of their

colleagues knew – or thought they knew – that she and Andrew were boyfriend and girlfriend. Because he'd been there the day they first came to The Luxor, Colonel Harris too thought that he knew that. None of the other patrons of The Luxor were supposed to have the merest inkling of relationships going on between any of the dancing partners.

'I like to observe people, my dear. I can tell how you and young Andrew feel about each other. May I say how much I envy you both?'

'You envy *us*?'

'You find that hard to believe?'

'Yes. Andrew and I only have what we earn here. You're obviously a wealthy lady.'

'Ah, but, Jean –' said Mona Forsyth, leaning across the table towards her – 'you will let me call you, Jean, won't you? – don't you know that money can't buy happiness?'

'It must make misery a sight more comfortable, though.'

Mona Forsyth laughed. 'You're very outspoken.'

'I'm sorry,' Jean said with an embarrassed shrug. 'My mother brought me up to tell the truth.'

'How sad for you that you lost her so early.'

'Not a week goes by that I don't think about her.' Jean's voice was very soft. 'And miss her.'

'I find it very moving to hear you say that. Edward and I have never been blessed with children. How I wish I could have given him—' Mrs Forsyth broke off. 'Here comes our tea.'

Here comes our tea. It was nothing more than an observation, the most prosaic of ones at that. Something about the way it had been said struck Jean to the quick. Raising his eyebrows in a silent greeting to her, the white-jacketed and aproned waiter laid out the tea things.

Once he had left, she looked across the table. 'I'm sorry.'

'Sorry?'

Haltingly, Jean expressed sympathy for Mrs Forsyth's childless state. The older woman took a handkerchief from her pocket and raised it to her mouth, holding it there for a moment. 'Thank you,' she said. 'People seem to see one as some sort of a social butterfly, flitting from one frivolous entertainment to the next. When all I've really wanted is to be a mother at home with her children. You've a kind heart, Miss Dunlop.'

'Oh,' Jean blurted out with sudden sympathy, 'do please call me by my first name!'

'Only if you'll let me serve you with one of these delicious-looking scones and you can tell me all about yourself.'

'I'm not sure there's much to tell.'

'I'm sure there is. Let's start with how you and Andrew met.'

To her considerable surprise, Jean found herself telling her some of the story. And waxing lyrical about the Reverend Ronald and Mrs Fairbairn and their rather blinkered outlook on life. Despite herself, she was flattered by the attention this sophisticated lady was paying to her.

'Do say that you and Andrew will come and lunch with me in Bearsden next Sunday.'

'That's very kind of you,' Jean said, almost meaning it. 'But it's against the rules. Against our own rules too.'

Mrs Forsyth leaned forwards. 'Your own rules? What are they?'

'Oh,' Jean said, putting one hand up to rub the back of her neck, 'when we first started going out together we laid down some guidelines for ourselves.'

'Do tell,' said Mrs Forsyth eagerly. Her eyes sparkled with interest.

Jean was still rubbing her neck and wishing she'd never

mentioned the flaming rules. 'They're all a bit personal,' she mumbled.

Mrs Forsyth turned her mouth down in a charming gesture. 'So you're not going to tell me? Spoilsport. But please come to lunch. I'll square that with the Templetons. We'll have some really interesting guests. Especially if you and Andrew come too.'

The charm was impossible to withstand.

Chapter 25

'S HE'S WHAT?'

'Invited us out to her house in Bearsden for Sunday lunch,' Jean said, her voice faltering in the face of the way Andrew was glowering at her.

'And you've said yes?'

'It was kind of hard to say no. She's very charming.'

'Oh, aye, she's that all right.'

'She said she would make it all right with the Templetons and I thought you might enjoy it. Something a wee bit different. Unless you're going to see your mother and your sisters again this Sunday.'

'What's that supposed to mean?'

'It's not supposed to mean anything,' Jean replied, guiltily aware that it had meant a great deal. Having encouraged him not to lose contact, she was trying not to feel too hurt that he had visited his family on the last four Sundays in succession. 'I thought you might enjoy seeing a big house in Bearsden. But if you've arranged to go to Partick—'

'I haven't arranged to go to Partick.'

'So you'll come to Bearsden?' She tried an apologetic smile. 'I think it might be quite hard to get out of it now.'

'I think it might be quite hard to get out of any of this, Jean.'

As he turned on his heel and left the sitting room, she stood staring after him. She jumped when he reappeared in the doorway, stripped down to his pyjama trousers.

'Are you not coming through to bed?'

Jean blinked. There had been nothing lover-like about that question, no invitation contained within it. 'I'll come now. I'm sorry about accepting that invitation. I'll tell Mrs Forsyth the next time I see her that we can't go.'

'Don't be so bloody stupid. Ye cannae do that. We'd be out on our ear for rudeness to one o' the club members.'

He's really upset, she thought, hearing the tell-tale sign of the acquired accent he used for The Luxor and its patrons slipping back to the way he more naturally spoke.

'I'm sorry,' she said again.

'Stop apologising,' he said gruffly. 'And come to bed.'

'I'll have my bath first.'

'Fine.' He padded off down the corridor and Jean was once more alone in the sitting room, blinking back tears.

She had a shower instead of a bath, her mind racing as she stood under the water. She had to do something about this, and she had to do it now: for both their sakes. She could stomp through to the bedroom and insist on having it out with him . . . or she could try a different tack.

They hadn't made love since the morning of that day they had gone together to Partick. That was something else Jean couldn't understand. Lovemaking was the glorious centre of their relationship, a passionate and joyful meeting of bodies and mouths and hands and minds. Before everything had started to go wrong Andrew had been trying to coax her into sometimes making the first move, telling her how exciting it would be for him if she did. She'd been too shy to do it. Until now.

He was still awake when she climbed into bed. She could

tell that from his breathing. Her nightdress left under her pillow, careful not to touch the scars on his back, Jean curled her arm about his waist. He was not only awake, he was tense. She could feel it.

Her hand was on his bare chest. She slid it slowly downwards, towards the waistband of his pyjama trousers: and found her fingers caught by his even as they trailed across the evidence that he was very wide-awake indeed.

'Don't.'

The shock of that refusal brought her snapping up, peering down at him. In the gloom of the bedroom it was hard to see the expression on his face. 'Don't?' she repeated stupidly.

Andrew lifted her hand off himself and gave it back to her. 'I'm tired, Jean,' he said gruffly. 'Go to sleep.'

'It's an experiment in living,' said the fashionable young man sitting on Jean's left-hand side. 'That's what we have to remember. Why, it's the most exciting thing to have happened in Europe since the days of the Romans!'

'I agree,' said the girl sitting opposite him at the long dining-table. 'The Germans have found a leader with the courage to impose order on society.'

'And sort out the Jews,' said the fashionable young man, adding darkly, 'high time somebody did.'

Jean cast him a doubtful look. 'But how can you blame one group of people—'

The girl on the other side of the table interrupted, the smile that curved her scarlet lips reminding Jean of the way a cat might contemplate a nice juicy mouse. 'Men do look so *divinely* handsome in uniform. Especially all of those blond-haired and blue-eyed types they have in Germany. Don't you agree?'

The question had been addressed to the rather precious-looking young man who sat next to her. 'Absolutely, darling. Why don't you and I motor over there this summer and take a gander at them for ourselves? After all,' he drawled, 'your mama must know that I'd be the ideal travelling companion for you. Your virtue would certainly be safe with me!'

Jean wasn't sorry when the laughter that comment provoked drew her neighbour's attention away from her.

'Scapegoat theory,' murmured a voice in her ear.

'I beg your pardon, Dr MacMillan?' The man on her right had been introduced to her at the start of the meal as a golfing friend of Mr Forsyth's who had a medical practice in Yoker. He was a little older than the other lunch guests.

'Scapegoat theory,' repeated the doctor. 'Goes right back to biblical times. Load the blame for all the evils of society on to one person or group – especially a group whose religion and way of life and even appearance makes them easily identifiable – and you've done several things. Shall I go on, young lady?' he asked. 'Not boring you?'

'Not boring me at all. Please do go on.'

He inclined his head in graceful acknowledgement of her encouragement and began counting out points on his fingers. 'One. You thereby create a common enemy. Two. You focus everyone else's attention on to this common enemy. Three. You draw everyone else's attention away from what you *don't* want them to see.'

'But it's not logical to think that one group of people can be responsible for everything that's wrong in a country.'

'Logic doesn't come into political movements as strong and as forceful as fascism. They grow and multiply on huge surges of emotion. In their wisdom, the Allies demanded punitive reparations from Germany at the end of the Great War. They also carried through policies in other areas which were deliberately designed to humiliate the Germans. With that marvellous quality known as hindsight some of us can now see that was a dangerous thing to do to a defeated nation. Add to that unhappy situation a gentleman like Mr Hitler and you find yourself with a very volatile mixture.'

'Because,' Jean said, listening attentively to what the doctor was saying, 'someone like him comes along and starts telling this defeated and humiliated and presumably deeply resentful nation that they're actually the most wonderful people on Earth?'

Dr MacMillan nodded again. 'The Master Race.'

'But they're only the Master Race if they keep themselves pure? Isn't Sir Oswald Mosley always going on about the Jews in this country?'

'Both Sir Oswald and Herr Hitler are very gifted orators,' the doctor agreed. His mouth curved into a cynical smile. 'Or rabble-rousers. Depending on your point of view and your politics.'

'It's like a pan of milk,' Jean said thoughtfully. 'Hitler – and Mussolini too, I suppose – are like the heat underneath it. If everyone else walks away and forgets about it, it'll all boil over and make a terrible mess.'

'Got a brain in that pretty head?'

She rested her elbow on the table, her chin on her hand and batted her eyelashes at him. He chuckled. 'Now you're playing the vamp to put me in my place for being such a patronising old fellow as to think beauty and brains can't possibly mix.'

'You haven't patronised me at all,' Jean protested. 'And you're hardly old.'

He laughed again. 'That's your profession talking, young lady. Don't think I don't know it.'

Uncomfortable with many of the opinions and attitudes being expressed around Mona and Edward Forsyth's table,

Jean talked to Dr MacMillan for the rest of the lunch. Finding temporary relief from her worries in a discussion that ranged across politics and history and books, she remained aware that Andrew was very quiet. If he was asked a direct question he answered it but not in any way that encouraged further conversation.

Mona Forsyth, presiding over one end of the table while her husband sat at the other, kept trying to tease him out of his black mood. Her efforts met with no success. Give up, Jean thought. Once he digs his heels in there's no budging him.

She wasn't surprised when he was the first one to break up the party. He did so without any of his usual polish. Refusing coffee from the parlour maid, he almost cannoned into the girl and her tall silver coffee pot when he rose abruptly to his feet. He muttered an apology and looked across the table at Jean. 'Time we were off.'

'Oooh,' said the precious young man, 'the caveman type.' He rolled his eyes at Jean. 'Aren't you the lucky girl?'

She had only just started her own coffee but she excused herself to the doctor and the other guests and walked round the table to join Andrew. By the time she got there Mona Forsyth was also on her feet.

'Won't the two of you stay a little longer?' she asked, laying one hand on Andrew's arm and the other on Jean's and moving them all away from the table. 'I so wanted to show you the garden, Jean. It really begins to come into its own again at this time of year.'

Since Andrew obviously wasn't going to say anything in response to that, Jean did the honours. 'I'd love to see your garden, Mrs Forsyth. But maybe another day.'

Her hostess turned her mouth down in that charmingly rueful gesture Jean had noticed before. 'Surely you can call me Mona here, my dear.'

All too aware of the brooding presence at her side, Jean managed a tight-lipped smile. 'I'd love to see your garden, Mona. But not today,' she repeated.

'I can't persuade you?'

'We have to go.'

'Why, Andrew,' said Mona Forsyth as both women turned towards him, 'Jean and I were beginning to think you'd joined a religious order and taken a vow of silence.'

He gave her a look that would have made a weaker woman flinch. 'We have to go,' he said again, and reached for Jean's hand. 'Goodbye, Mrs Forsyth. I'm afraid we won't be able to come back and look at your garden another day. In fact, I'm afraid we won't ever be able to come back.'

Mona arched her beautifully plucked eyebrows. 'My, my. We are fierce today, aren't we?'

Jean looked at her, at Andrew and back again to Mona. And all at once everything fell into place.

Running down the curved driveway of pink granite chips that led to the road, Jean flung herself through the ornate stone gateposts and round to the right. Andrew caught up with her and grabbed her arm.

'Not that way. There's a shortcut to Bearsden Cross down this lane.'

'You would know, I suppose!' she yelled, wheeling round to face him. 'You would know!'

'Yes,' he said tightly. 'I would know. But let's no' do this here. Not where they can see us from the house.'

'Where, then?' Jean demanded.

'There's a church off the lane. We'll go into the graveyard.' He led her past the church door and round the other side of the building. Halfway down, he backed himself up against the wall, tilted his head against it and closed his eyes.

'What's the matter with you?'

'Give me a moment,' he said. 'I just need to *breathe* for a bit.'

'You "just need to breathe for a bit"? What the hell does that mean?'

He opened his eyes again and looked at her. 'Jean . . .'

She cut him off. 'What really gets me is how stupid I've been. How naïve. I never suspected. Not for a single moment. Not till she said that to you back there. I really thought you'd been going to Partick these past few Sundays.'

'I wouldn't go to Partick without you, Jean. You must know that.'

'But you'd go to *her* house? I thought you loved me, Andy. I really thought you loved me.'

'I do love you!' he burst out. 'More than anything! And I *hate* Mona Forsyth. I hate her. But she likes me. And she's been paying me to like her back. Letting me drive her car. And giving me money.'

'Which you earn in her bed?'

'Aye. Which I earn in her bed. Know what she really likes, Jean? For me to be dead rough wi' her. She likes me to swear too, use the filthiest language you can think of. Words I would never in a million years use in front of you. She likes my back too.'

Staring at him in horror, hardly able to believe the foul words spilling out of his mouth, Jean repeated the last of those words. 'She likes your back?'

'The marks on it,' he said, suddenly sounding very weary. 'Hearing how they got there excites her.'

'You told her about that? Does she know that we're married too?'

'She got that out of me.'

'It makes no difference to her?'

258

'As far as she's concerned me being a married man and her knowing you only makes it more fun. That's what she's like.'

'What about her husband? Where was he while all of this was going on?'

'Playing golf.' Andrew's voice had grown very dry. 'Seemingly he plays a lot of golf.'

'So her asking us to lunch today was so you could both laugh at him and at me?'

'It's the sort of thing that amuses her,' he agreed. 'Underneath all the charm she's actually quite a vicious bitch.'

Jean stared at him, standing there against the mellow old stone of the church wall, telling her these awful things.

'Why, Andy?' she asked, her voice breaking. 'I don't understand why.'

'For the money, of course. There's no other reason I'd go to bed with her. You and me have had money off her before. Mind when I stole yon purse? It was her I stole it from.'

'She blackmailed you into doing this?'

'No. It was my choice. But it's over now. I cannae stand it any longer. No' even for the money.'

'That's what you were telling her when we left her house?'

'Aye. That's what I was telling her.'

'But we're both earning good money at The Luxor, Andy. If the Templetons find out what you've been doing, you'll be for the high jump. Me too, probably. If you couldn't give a damn about hurting me, you might at least have thought about that. How could you take such a risk with our jobs and our future?' Jean's voice rose in anguish. 'How could you? *How could you*?'

She was shaking now. He pushed himself off the wall of the church and came towards her. 'Don't touch me!' she yelled. 'I don't want you to touch me.'

His hands shot up. 'All right. But you have to keep listening to me. I've got something else to tell you.'

'I think you've told me enough,' Jean sobbed.

'I have to make you understand why I did it.'

'You already told me that!' She was flinging the words at him. 'You did it for the money! Money we don't need! How can you tell me you love me when you've done this awful, disgusting thing?'

'I love you more than anything! I love you more than life itself, Jean Logan!' Once more he reached for her. Once more she fended him off.

'Empty words!' she howled. 'They don't mean anything!'

'They mean everything! I slept wi' her *because* I love you so much! I had to force myself to do it!'

'You're not making any sense!'

'I'm making perfect sense! I need to leave you wi' as much money as possible!'

'Leave me? You going somewhere?'

He sucked in a breath as though it were a cup of water and he a man crawling across a desert. Then his eyes flickered to the gravestone on the other side of the path.

Bemused, Jean followed his gaze. Whoever lay underneath the stone had died in 1796.

'He was a wheelwright,' Andrew said, his voice as flat as a cracked bell. 'A real man doing real work. Like the men down at Clydebank will be when work starts on the Cunarder again after Easter. When they die it'll say what they were on their tombstones. "Riveter", "Cabinet Maker", "Fitter". Do you think they'll let you have "gigolo" carved on my tombstone?'

'You're havering,' Jean said harshly. 'What are you talking about your tombstone for?'

'I've been trying to outrun this thing.' He laid a hand on

his chest and smiled faintly. 'Which is entirely the wrong metaphor. Especially as it's beginning to catch up wi' me.'

Jean's brain began to run too, stumbling forward in a jumble of memories and thoughts. She recalled the coughs and colds that had plagued him throughout the winter just gone. She considered his moodiness, black depressions interspersed with periods of almost frantic gaiety.

She should have recognised all of it. Hadn't she encountered something very similar before, in someone else whom she had loved?

'Your handkerchiefs,' she said. It had been a standing joke between them that he received so many as gifts he could afford to throw the old ones out. Now she knew the real reason why he'd never given her any to put in the bundle for the laundry. The realisation brought a strange calmness with it. At least now she knew what was wrong.

'I would have thought a man who grew up in a household of women would have known how to get bloodstains out of cloth.'

Andrew drew in a calmer breath. 'Explaining to you why I was soaking them in cold water might have been a wee bit more difficult. Given the game away.'

She looked him straight in the eye. 'You've got TB, haven't you?'

Chapter 26

JEAN COULD never remember how they got home that day. They were standing in the cemetery and then they were in their own sitting room. At first they had both wept. That was over now.

'Lie down and put your head in my lap.'

They had often arranged themselves like this, her sitting at one end of the sofa and him lying with his legs stretched along it. Sometimes she read to him, often out of the poetry book he had given her for her eighteenth birthday.

Stroking the thick dark waves of his hair back from his forehead, Jean raised her own head and gazed out of the window. The outside world was bright and sunny.

On the other side of the window there would be people taking their babies for a walk in the pram or strolling through the park with their dogs, throwing sticks for them to chase. How odd it was that none of those people seemed to have realised that the world had stopped turning.

His head felt heavy and solid, his body still looked strong. As though he were as fit and as healthy as he'd always been. Only he wasn't.

Sometime when they hadn't been looking, this bloody disease had crept through his body's defences and mounted an assault on his lungs. Even as the two of them sat here together it was eating away at him. Working in the darkness where you couldn't see what it was up to. *The captain of all the men of death.* Jean's fingers twitched.

'What is it?'

'That cold you couldn't shake off,' she said, gazing down at his well-loved face. Why had she never noticed those blue shadows under his eyes? Or the unnatural flush that stained his pale cheeks? Because they hardly ever saw one another in daylight, she supposed, only under the artificial lights of The Luxor. 'The one you blamed on walking home through the sleet. It wasn't a cold at all, was it?'

'No,' he admitted. 'I hadn't walked home either. I'd taken the tram. I knew the cough had nothing to do with the weather. I'd been getting breathless too. Mind yon day we first came to The Luxor? That started then.'

Jean cast her mind back. 'Or maybe the day after you left Partick. When you were so feverish.' Anger flooded her. 'You probably had it then. When they did what they did to you.'

'They weren't to know. I didn't know myself. D'you think I'd have asked you to marry me if I'd thought there was anything wrong with me?'

'You told me you were nervous that day we came to The Luxor. I should have realised it was something more than that. You don't get nervous.'

'Don't I?' He gave her a smile so brave it threatened to break her heart.

'It's not going to defeat us, Andy,' she said in a voice that wasn't quite steady. 'We're going to fight this horrible thing.'

The smile was still in place. 'So determined. You almost make me believe there might be some hope.'

'Of course there's hope, Andy. Oh, why didn't you tell me earlier?'

'Because you'd been through all of this before with your

mother.' He bit his lip. 'Because I didn't know what I was going to do about it all.'

'You're going to a sanatorium. That's what you're going to do about it. As soon as possible.'

He sat up, swivelling round so he could take her hand. 'If I even go to see a doctor, the whole world'll know I've got TB. You know better than anybody what's likely to happen then. What *has* to happen then. No, don't say anything yet. Hear me out. D'you think you'll keep your job at The Luxor if they find out your husband's a consumptive? Do you, Jean?'

'What's your alternative plan?' she asked quietly. 'To let your health get worse and worse until you can't work any more? You've got to go for treatment.'

'But the march past,' he protested.

'I've got a plan that'll get us round that.'

Andrew's grim expression relaxed. 'The girl with the plan. I think this problem might defeat even you, sweetheart.'

'No, it won't.' She drew her fingertips around the line of his jaw. 'Are you very scared?'

'I'm bloody terrified. The worst bit o' it is leaving you.'

'You're not going anywhere. Only to a sanatorium.'

'You're asking me to break the law, child.'

'I'm asking you to help us,' Jean said passionately, willing the doctor whom she had met at the Forsyths' house to agree to her plea for anonymity. Remembering that his practice was in Yoker, she had looked him up in the telephone book and made an appointment to come and see him at the surgery attached to his house. Now she was begging him not to notify the appropriate authorities of Andrew's illness: the illness that the medical man had just confirmed.

'My husband's youngest sister will make sure the rest of the family sees its own doctor. You've examined me and given me a clean bill of health. Surely I would be the person most likely to have contracted the disease? I don't think we have to worry about anyone at our place of work.'

The doctor sighed, made a steeple of his fingers and studied Jean and Andrew over his desk. They sat very close together in two upright chairs and they were clutching one another's hands like two lost children.

'Please, Dr MacMillan,' Jean urged. 'If the people we work for at The Luxor find out about Andy they'll sack me too. I know they will. How can we afford for my husband to go to this sanatorium you think is so good if I'm not working?'

For, after an examination of Andrew that had left him solemn-faced, the doctor had held out one fragile spar of hope. A sanatorium near Nairn, on the dry and sunny northeast coast of Scotland, which had a reputation for three things: the strictness of its regime; the high proportion of its consumptive patients who were restored to full health; and its discretion.

It charged a pretty penny for all of those privileges, of course. It did, however, take in a small proportion of patients of limited means each year. At five guineas per week, those restricted rates were just affordable – if Jean kept her job at The Luxor.

'Please, Doctor,' she said again. 'You said yourself this place might be Andrew's only hope.'

'There are no guarantees,' Dr MacMillan said gravely. He looked at Andrew. 'You should have consulted a member of my profession some time ago, laddie.'

'Wasn't so easy, sir.'

'This sanatorium I'm talking about isn't going to be easy either. Its superintendent insists on complete isolation from the outside world. You won't be able to visit him at any time throughout the six months of the treatment, young Mrs Logan.'

Jean felt Andrew's fingers tighten on hers. She could tell that the prospect of being separated for so long cast him into as much despair as it did her. 'We'll be able to write to each other?'

'They allow a monthly exchange of letters. Yours will be read to make sure they contain nothing which might upset or overexcite the patient.'

Jean nodded. 'I can understand that. I can accept that.'

'And you, young man,' Dr MacMillan said, turning to address Andrew. 'You're going to find this hard-going. While you're at Seafield House you'll be told what to eat and how much to eat. You'll be told when to go to bed at night and when to get up in the morning. After an initial period of complete bed-rest, that is. No newspapers, no reading, no listening to the wireless. The medical superintendent at Seafield even bans smoking. Has a bit of a bee in his bonnet about it. His belief in the efficacy of fresh air is a more commonly held view in his particular speciality. You're going to spend much more time out of doors than you might think possible.'

'I can hardly wait,' Andrew said lightly. 'When do I go?'

'The sooner the better.' The doctor turned to Jean. 'How are you going to explain his absence to your employers? Isn't that going to be a little difficult?'

Jean lifted her chin. 'That's my problem.'

'So how *are* you going to explain my absence to our employers?' asked Andrew as they left the doctor's house at the top of Yoker Mill Road.

Jean cast him a nervous glance. 'You're not going to like this.'

'Try me.'

'I'm going to say that you and I have had a terrific quarrel and you've taken yourself down to the Pool and gone to sea.'

'You're dead right, Jean,' Andrew said as they made their way up towards the Forth and Clyde Canal and the bridge over it that would take them on to the Boulevard and then back along to Anniesland. 'I don't like it one little bit. What the hell are the Templetons going to say to that?'

'I've no idea. Let's not talk about it any more.' The subject she was about to broach was an even more difficult one. 'That money you got from . . . her,' she said, unwilling to allow Mona Forsyth's name to intrude into this conversation.

'What about it?'

'I think you should give it to your family.'

'All right,' Andrew said evenly. He slanted Jean across a wry smile as they walked over the wooden canal bridge. 'Expecting me to put up a fight on that one? That I'd want to use it to help pay for the sanatorium?'

'Not since you've obviously realised that it's going to be the last money you'll be sending your family for a while.'

'For a while,' he repeated as the two of them stepped down on to the opposite bank of the canal. He stopped, and turned to look at her. Another word hung in the air between them. *Ever.*

'We're not going to think like that, Andy,' Jean said firmly.

He pulled her to him for a moment. 'Of course we're not. Of course we're not, Jean.'

They were determinedly matter-of-fact over the next few days, packing a case and getting him organised to leave. Dr MacMillan had given them a leaflet issued by Seafield House Sanatorium, which listed what patients should bring and what they should leave at home.

On the Sunday night before Andrew left, they stood together looking out of the window of the flat.

'We're asking Chrissie to bear a heavy burden,' Jean said, expressing a thought that had been troubling her since she had come up with her plan. 'Keeping it to herself that you're ill, I mean.'

'I know,' Andrew said sombrely. 'But she is wise beyond her years. And you'll see her, won't you? Keep her up-to-date and tell her how I'm getting on?'

'Of course I will.'

He put his arm about her. 'You're going to be bearing a heavy burden too, Jean.'

She buried her face in his shoulder. 'I'm going to miss you so much!'

'Same goes for me,' he murmured into her hair. 'One last dance before I go?'

She pulled back and gazed up at him. 'Is that what you want to do?'

'Aye. Don't know that I've got the energy for our tango, though.'

'A waltz, then,' she said, and left him for a moment to put a record on the gramophone. She stooped to roll back the rug that covered the wooden floor. They had done this often on their free Sundays. No matter how much they danced during the week, they loved still to dance with one another. This waltz would be their last one for a long time.

The last waltz. Unbidden, the words slithered into Jean's head. They refused to go away again: as did the thought that she was already dancing with a ghost.

He found an empty compartment, booking his place next to the window by tossing the newspaper Jean had bought for him at the station bookstall on to the maroon cushions. As he hoisted his case up on to the overhead luggage rack, she thought how vital he looked today. A little thin, maybe, but not ill at all.

It was a bright and breezy April morning and none of this seemed real. Not his illness, not the fact that he was going away, not the reality of their impending separation.

They were together now. How could it be that in ten minutes' time this train would carry him away from her? Six months. An eternity. Jean blinked back tears and stared with ferocious concentration at the sunlit platform on the other side of the window of the compartment.

'It's a lovely day. You should have a nice run up.'

'Aye,' he agreed, folding his coat and stretching up to put it on top of his case.

'Oh,' Jean said, wondering why she hadn't noticed this on the taxi ride in from Anniesland, 'you're taking the navy-blue coat.' He'd acquired a much smarter one since they'd started working at The Luxor.

Fingers curled around the edge of the luggage rack, he turned and smiled at her. 'From all accounts I'm going to be more or less living outside. Wrapping up warm seems like a good idea. That coat's always kept me warm. Right from the first moment it was given to me. I got it as a present, you know. From the most beautiful girl in the world. Beautiful inside and out.'

For a moment they simply stood and looked at one another. Seconds later Jean's resolve to see him off without shedding a tear crumbled. 'Och, Andy! I'm going to miss you so much!'

He stepped towards her, his arms already opening.

'Are these seats taken?'

Jean heard him swear under his breath but the smile he turned on the middle-aged woman who had posed the question was bland and polite. The man who was presumably her husband appeared behind her at the door of the compartment, struggling under the weight of two large cases.

'Only the one by the window,' Andrew said, lifting his chin to indicate which seat he meant.

'Your young lady's not travelling with you?' asked the woman.

'My wife,' Andrew corrected. 'No, unfortunately she's not travelling with me.'

'Could you help my husband put our luggage up on the rack, young man?' There was a hint of exasperation in the woman's tone, as though Andrew should have offered help without having had to be asked.

'Be glad to,' Andrew said. He did it so swiftly he made everyone blink. After that he took Jean by the hand and pulled her out into the corridor. 'Before that wifie asks me to do something else,' he muttered, jumping out on to the platform and turning to offer Jean a hand down.

'Now you're breathless,' she scolded, seeing the quick rise and fall of his chest. 'You should have told her you're not fit to lift heavy cases. If she and her husband get off before you, tell her to get somebody else to help get them.'

'Shut up,' he said. 'I'm not wasting our last five minutes talking about things that don't matter. I'm not wasting our last five minutes talking about *anything*.'

He took her face between his two hands and placed his mouth over hers but he was still breathless. The kiss lasted only seconds before Jean pushed him away. 'Catch your breath,' she urged. 'You need to catch your breath.'

His shoulders were heaving. She placed her hand on his back and rubbed it slowly up and down, and soon he had straightened up again and was smiling at her. 'Probably shouldn't be kissing you anyway.'

'It's a bit late to be thinking of that.'

The guard blew his whistle.

'Get on the train! They're closing the doors!'

He was barely back on board before the porter was instructing Jean to 'Stand well clear, miss' before walking speedily along the platform to secure the remaining doors. Bang. Bang. Bang. The guard blew his whistle again.

Andrew lowered the window and leaned out. One last swift meeting of the lips. One last despairing look. 'I love you.'

Jean gave the words back to him. The train jerked and began to move. She plastered a smile on her face. It seemed important that what he should take away with him was a memory of her smiling at him.

She stood there until the train had completely vanished. She would wait until she couldn't hear it any more. She was straining her ears to do that when the engine at the next platform spluttered into life and blocked out the ever-fainter sound of the departing train. That was it, then. He was gone.

She made her way back down to the barrier, handing in her platform ticket to the railwayman who stood there. 'Cheer up,' he said. 'It might never happen.'

'It just has.'

She felt rotten when his cheerful face fell. 'Och, I'm sorry, pet. Anything I can do for you?'

She tried to come up with something so that he would feel better. 'A map,' she said. 'Is there a map that shows all the stations between here and Inverness?'

She stood and studied it, reading the names of the stations and the times the train arrived at each one, doing her best to commit the information to memory. After she'd done that she walked down the hill and sat for a while in George Square. It was too early to go to The Luxor and she didn't want to go

271

home. Without Andrew the flat would be nothing but an empty shell.

She sat in the square looking at the pigeons and the passers-by without seeing them at all. She sat there until her watch told her Andrew's train had reached Stirling. And then Perth. She was stiff by the time she stood up, deciding to take herself off for a cup of tea and something to eat. She had made a proper cooked breakfast this morning but neither of them had eaten very much of it.

Jean gave some consideration to going into a church to pray, but rejected the idea. She could do that as well out here in the fresh April morning.

Let him get better. Let him get rid of it completely. Oh, please, let him get better!

She wasn't entirely sure who she was praying to. God, maybe. Would He answer her prayer even if she didn't believe in Him? She tried Jesus and St Martin too. There was always the power of positive thinking. Bloody hell, she'd pray to every deity and philosophy of life there was if she thought it would help.

She got up and walked away, passing a newspaper kiosk. Glancing at the papers, she realised that today was her birthday. Neither she nor Andrew had remembered. 'I'm nineteen years old,' she said out loud.

A woman who'd just bought a newspaper gave her an odd look and pulled the little girl she held by the hand more closely in to her. Protecting her daughter from the madwoman talking to herself in the street.

Jean decided she might as well head for The Luxor now. The sooner she faced the music the better.

Chapter 27

'GONE? WHAT d'you mean, gone?'
'Gone to . . .' Her voice was husky, barely audible. She coughed to clear her throat. 'Gone to sea, Mr Templeton. His ship sailed this morning.' That was the first lie. How many more was she going to have to tell before this uncomfortable interview was over?

'Just like that?' demanded Richard Templeton. 'When did he sign on?'

'I don't know.' Her voice was quavering. Worrying about Andrew and his health, and feeling so lost and empty and alone without him, she was also realising that this story she'd concocted to explain his absence was as thin as tissue paper.

'We h-haven't been g-getting on very w-well l-lately,' she stuttered, clutching at any straw that might help convince her listeners that she was telling them the truth. Until he had told her about his illness, there had been occasions when it must have been obvious to someone as sharp-eyed as Gloria Templeton that all wasn't well between Jean and Andrew Logan. 'Not talking to each other very much.'

It was Richard Templeton who was in charge of the conversation at the moment. 'And now he's left you?'

'Yes.' Eyes downcast, Jean gazed at the hanky she held. It

was crumpled into a thousand tiny creases by the nervous working of her fingers.

'Do you think he'll come back?'

'I don't know. I hope so.' One truth in this tangle of lies.

'Did he sign on a coaster or was the ship going deep-sea?'

'Deep-sea. He said he'd be away for six months. When he comes home we're going to talk things over.' Oh God, this story was even thinner than tissue paper. It wasn't going to stand up, it really wasn't . . .

Richard Templeton threw himself down in one of the chairs behind the desk. 'Away for six months,' he repeated. 'Leaving us in the lurch. How am I to explain to our ladies that their new favourite has simply *gone off*? Honestly!'

Gloria Templeton stooped to place an arm about Jean's shoulders. 'Don't go on at her, Richard. Can't you see the girl's absolutely distraught?'

One more truth. She was absolutely distraught. 'I'm so sorry about this, Mrs Templeton, Mr Templeton,' Jean said. 'I'm really so very sorry!' Then she burst into tears.

'I'll ring down for some tea,' Gloria said soothingly. 'That's what you need. Best if you leave me to deal with this, Richard, I think.'

The tea arrived within minutes. Things always happened quickly at The Luxor. The club ran like a well-oiled machine.

Concentrate on the details. It gives your mind less space to panic.

Jean studied the black lacquered tray, which had been placed on the low table in front of her. The tea-set was vibrantly coloured. Painted in red and orange and cream and black, the design was of the sun rising behind a perfect little house, all soft and pretty and somehow all the more so because the shape of the crockery was so sharp and angular.

'Milk and sugar, dear?'

Jean nodded. Gloria poured milk into both of the cups

274

on the tray, picked up silver tongs and dropped two lumps of sugar into each of them and then added the tea. She stirred both cups vigorously and handed one to Jean. 'You'll feel much better once you've drunk this. Nothing like a nice cup of tea in times of trouble. Take a piece of shortbread to go with it,' she said, pushing the plate in Jean's direction.

Jean did feel a little better after she'd sipped her tea and nibbled on a petticoat tail. How daft was that? Or maybe it wasn't daft at all. The tea and sympathy was surely a sign that Gloria Templeton did believe her. She hoped it was also a sign that she wasn't going to sack her.

'I'm really sorry about Andy going off like this. But nobody but you and Mr Templeton knows that we're married, so I don't think it's going to cause a scandal or anything.'

'Of course it isn't,' Gloria said from where she now sat on the other side of the table. 'The rest of the staff and those very few patrons who knew that the two of you were close will assume a lover's tiff. More tea, dear?'

Encouraged by that response, Jean placed her cup and saucer on the table. 'No, thanks.' She slid forward on the chair, ready to stand up. 'I know I can't make up for Andy's absence. But I promise I'll work doubly hard from now on. I won't let you down.'

'Oh, Jean,' Gloria said, 'I know that. In fact, I'm absolutely confident that you won't let me down.'

'If there's nothing else I think I'd best be going downstairs and getting on with my work.'

'Don't go yet, Jean.'

Gloria rose to her feet and went to the high green filing cabinet, which sat in the corner behind her desk. Pulling open the middle drawer, she ran one finger along the top of the files. 'Lawson, Logan . . . Ah, here we are.'

Pushing the drawer of the filing cabinet shut, she came

forward and placed a buff folder on the table. Flipping it open, she turned over the pieces of paper it contained. Jean caught a fleeting glimpse of Andrew's beautiful handwriting. She had composed their letter of application to The Luxor but he had written it.

Gloria extracted two typewritten lists and placed them side-by-side in front of Jean. 'Have a read of these and tell me what they are.'

'Accounts,' Jean said, scanning down the two pages. 'Mainly for clothes for Andrew and me. When you kitted us out when we both came here.'

'Don't forget the cost of that very nice flat the two of you have been occupying for the past six months.' Gloria leaned over the table and pointed it out to her.

Jean's eyes widened as she glanced down at it. 'But we haven't been paying nearly that much rent for it!'

'Correct. The Luxor has been paying most of it. It's accumulated into quite a substantial sum.' Gloria leafed through the contents of the buff folder again and produced another sheet of paper. 'Add that to the clothes and the figures come out like this.'

Once more her finger indicated two columns, one for Jean and one for Andrew. The totals at the bottom of each one were for large sums of money.

'I don't understand,' Jean said, reading them and looking up again. 'I thought we were paying you back every week out of our wages.'

'Got anything in writing to that effect, Jean?' Gloria shook her beautifully waved head. 'I don't think so. The Luxor would be perfectly within its rights to demand that all of this money you owe us be paid back immediately. As of now.'

'I can't afford to do that!' Jean's voice was sharp with anxiety. 'Especially with Andrew having gone.'

'Taken all your savings, has he? Dear me.'

Andrew *had* taken all their savings but with Jean's complete blessing. That money was still only going to pay for a little more than half his stay at the sanatorium. She'd been counting on paying the rest out of what she could earn by herself over the next three months. 'You can't expect me to pay it all back in one go!'

'I think you'll find that we can expect exactly that. We might even choose to sack you and pursue you for the money. Put the matter in the hands of our solicitors. Or we could simply lay a charge against you, Jean. The bench takes a very dim view of young women who live wildly beyond their means. Especially ones who're so scandalously separated from their husbands.'

Jean stared up at her, horror-struck. She didn't know if she was guilty of any crime. All she knew was that her job was in jeopardy. If her job was in jeopardy so was Andrew's health.

'Of course,' Gloria said pleasantly, 'there is one way in which you could climb out of this hole you appear to have dug for yourself. A way for you to pay off your debt to The Luxor and earn yourself a little extra money into the bargain, dear. It's not exactly arduous work, either. I believe young Andrew was indulging in a little private enterprise in this area himself. I imagine that's what the two of you really fell out about. Well,' she went on, 'what's sauce for the goose is sauce for the gander. Or should that be the other way round in this case? I think that's how I'd see it.'

It was at that point Jean realised that she was indeed guilty of a crime: the crime of having been a stupid, trusting, naïve fool. She also realised that she knew exactly what Gloria Templeton was going to suggest as a means of her working off her debt to The Luxor.

Chapter 28

'I'M NOT asking you to stand on a street corner, Jean. And you'd be entertaining only a select group of our gentlemen. Several of them have already expressed an interest in entering into an arrangement with you. They all like to think they're having exclusive access, of course, so everything will be done very discreetly. Perhaps it's just as well that Andrew has taken himself off. I expect he might have been rather tiresome about allowing you to do this. A bit hypocritical, don't you think?'

Jean rose slowly to her feet. 'Why?' she asked.

Gloria blinked. 'Why what, dear?'

'Why do you do this?' Jean waved an unsteady hand in the direction of the glass doors that gave on to the balcony overlooking the grand salon. 'Don't you and Mr Templeton make enough money from The Luxor already?'

'Jean,' Gloria said reproachfully, 'you can never make enough money. Nobody can ever make enough money. Oh, and a word to the wise. Mr Templeton knows nothing about this little enterprise of mine and I'd like to keep it that way.'

Jean frowned. 'But you're the one who's really in charge here.'

'How astute of you to have realised that,' Gloria murmured. 'Unfortunately I was rather naïve when I married Mr

Templeton.' She laughed grimly. 'Also a little too grateful to him for having made an honest woman of me. We started out in business with the paltry sum settled on him by his parents. He persists in thinking that he owns the lion's share of what's been made out of that initial investment and our lawyers persist in agreeing with him. I'm inclined to think it's largely my business acumen which has made The Luxor what it is today. Part of that business acumen has to do with giving the customers what they want. Exactly what they want.'

She laughed again. 'And as you know, several of our members are men who wield considerable power and influence in this city. That's something The Luxor often finds very useful. When our various licences come up for renewal and so on. The fact that I also know what they like to get up to behind closed doors doesn't hurt in persuading them to plead our case either.' Gloria's voice was as smooth as silk. 'Not to mention my own case in terms of ownership of the club.'

Jean was listening to her. She was also edging her way towards the door out on to the first-floor landing. Gloria was smiling at her again. How was it that she had never noticed before how none of those smiles ever reached her eyes?

'There's money to be made here, Jean. Easy money, at that. You'll be able to pay off what you owe The Luxor in no time. After that all I take is a percentage of your earnings.'

'My earnings from selling myself?' Jean asked, unable to keep the revulsion out of her voice.

'You've been doing that for the past six months,' Gloria said briskly. 'Think all those men who choose you as their partner come here for the love of the dance? Think they all watch you in your slit skirt doing your tango for the love of the dance? Think again, Jean.'

Jean was almost at the door now. 'I won't do it,' she said quietly. 'Not in a million years.'

Gloria raised her eyebrows. 'No? What else are you going to do? Who's going to help you? I seem to remember you've got no relations at all and that Andrew's family don't like you very much. Think they'll take you in?'

'I won't do it,' Jean repeated as she opened the door of the office. 'I'm leaving now.'

'You'll be back,' Gloria said equably. 'You're a sensible girl. Once you've had time to think about it, you'll be back.'

Her lungs were bursting. Why did domestic registries always have to be on the top floors of buildings that didn't have any lifts? Jean stopped to catch her breath.

To catch her breath. Where would Andrew be now? She glanced at her watch. Way up in the Highlands. Almost at Inverness. He had to change trains there.

A girl a few years older than herself was coming down the stairs. Jean leaned back against the wide windowsill to let her pass, giving her a polite, automatic smile. She got a rather rueful one in return.

'I don't know whether to laugh or cry.'

'They found you a new position?' Jean hazarded. Why else would anybody climb these stairs?

'As a cook-general,' the girl said. 'Which basically means you do all of the cooking and all of the skivvying too. All this for my board and the princely sum of one pound ten shillings a week. I've got five years' experience and good references,' she said wearily. 'I hope you have better luck.'

Jean stayed perched on the windowsill, listening as the girl's shoes beat a tattoo on the stone stairs. Thirty bob a week for five years' experience and good references. Thirty bob a week.

A flicker of movement from the street far below caught the corner of her eye. Jean slid round on the smooth painted sill and looked down. There was a girl standing there. She was a blonde, like her, except that even from this height Jean could tell the colour had come out of a bottle.

The girl looked cheap and brassy. She pulled a packet of cigarettes out of the pocket of her summer dress and confirmed that impression. Well-brought-up young women didn't smoke in the street. As Jean watched, she saw her call out to a man who was walking towards her. Asking him for a light, presumably.

He gave it to her, cupping his hands over hers in the way people did to protect the flame of a match against the breeze. He held on to her hands for quite some time. A few words were exchanged before he took her arm and hurried her off up the street. They disappeared down a lane between two high buildings.

Jean took out her own cigarettes. She had her own silver case now and a matching lighter. One of her regular partners had given them to her as a gift. Or had he thought he'd been buying himself something more than dancing and a little conversation?

She lit up with hands that trembled slightly and thought long and hard. She thought about Andrew. She thought about his family. She thought about Jim and Annabel, the couple who had seen no other way out than to end it all. She thought about Gloria Templeton.

I'm not asking you to stand on a street corner.

Jean took a long pull on her cigarette.

When she walked back into The Luxor a quarter of an hour later, the afternoon was in full swing. The usual ladies were sitting in the basketwork chairs drinking tea and chatting and enjoying the atmosphere, and the piano music was playing in the background.

You'd have to be mad not to want to work in this place. That was what Andrew had said the day they had first come here.

All they had seen then was the grace and the charm, the beautiful furniture and décor, the sense of a place where people could take their ease, relax and unwind. Now Jean knew what lay beneath all of that. It was like sinking your teeth into a beautiful shiny apple and finding the inside was rotten: discoloured and full of the cloying sweetness of decay.

She climbed up the grand staircase, feeling as if she were an actress in some film, following a preordained set of movements, playing a part assigned to her. When she pushed open the door of the Templetons' office she found Gloria still there and still on her own, behind her desk, working on the roster. She leaned back in her chair and smiled at Jean.

'Come in, dear. And close the door behind you. It won't be so bad, you know,' she said once Jean had done that. 'You'll soon get used to it. Might even enjoy it.' She raised her eyebrows. 'With some of them, at any rate.'

Jean walked forward to stand in front of the big desk. 'I have some conditions.'

'Let's discuss those, then,' Gloria said, looking up at her with the customary pleasant expression on her face.

'I want copies of those accounts you showed me. For me to keep. Each month I want a private meeting with you to review them. So I know exactly how much I've paid off.'

'A businesslike approach.' Gloria nodded approvingly. 'I like that.'

'I also want a reference for when I leave. Which will be just as soon as I've paid you off. A glowing reference to whom it may concern. I'd like that now, please.'

'Oh, I don't think so, Jean. What would be my guarantee

282

that you wouldn't simply take this glowing reference off with you now, heading for some other dancing job in some other city?'

Jean drew in a breath. She could see Gloria's point of view. 'All right,' she said. 'But I want your solemn promise that you will give me that reference when I leave. In fact, I'd like you to have it prepared now and put in my file. Ready for when I go.'

'I'm perfectly happy to do that for you, dear,' Gloria said. 'Although I don't think you will go, you know. There have been other girls who've stood where you're standing now and said very similar things to me. Most of them are still here. It's easy money, you see. A girl can get used to that. Now,' she said briskly, pulling forward the roster, 'you seem to be free tomorrow afternoon. That gives us the chance to get organised.'

Chapter 29

THE BED dipped as he sat down on the edge of it. The bed dipped quite a lot. The senior partner at one of Glasgow's foremost legal practices was a well-built man.

Jean's eyes were closed. She'd had them closed from the beginning. She contemplated the wisdom of keeping them shut, pretending to be asleep, but she rejected that course almost immediately. Why on earth would she be asleep at half-past one in the afternoon? Just because you were in a bed that didn't mean you'd been sleeping. She opened her eyes.

The lawyer smiled down at her. He was dressed again, formal in his pinstriped suit. Smoothing the tumbled blonde waves back from her brow, he bent forward and pressed a kiss on Jean's clammy forehead. 'There now. That wasn't so bad, was it?'

She hoped he didn't expect an answer to that question. Especially when his next one was even worse. 'You were quite a scared little girl half-an-hour ago, weren't you?'

She dropped her eyes to his chest, studying the heavy gold chain of his pocket watch. It gleamed against the darkness of a waistcoat buttoned over a stomach whose expanse had to be the logical result of twenty years of good living. Twenty years during which she assumed this man had denied none of his appetites.

He was old enough to be her father. His wife was one of the mature ladies who had become all girlish and giggly when she danced with Andrew. Jean had always thought she and her husband were a really devoted couple.

He put his hand out to touch Jean's cheek, trailing his fingers down over her neck and shoulders. She had the sheet pulled up over her breasts but he tugged it down, exposing them to his view. 'Delicious,' he murmured. 'Quite delicious.' Jean's stomach heaved as he dipped his head and kissed each of them in turn.

He was still smiling when he straightened up again. 'I know we don't normally deal directly with The Luxor's young ladies but I've left a little extra on the table in the dining room. Thought you might go into town this afternoon and buy yourself a pretty little something as a souvenir of our first time together.'

He pretended to grimace. 'Perhaps you'll think of me when you do that. Toiling away over dusty old deeds and wills and conveyancing.' He kissed her again, on the lips this time, his moustache brushing against her upper lip. He tasted, as she now knew, how a man who liked Cuban cigars and fine whiskies did. 'I'll see myself out. Until the next time, little Jean.'

She heard him walk down the corridor of the flat and open and close the front door. Floating in from the landing outside, she heard the whine of the lift. She heard the clunk of it arriving, its door opening and closing and the sound of it descending once more to the ground floor. Only when she heard a motor car starting up and moving away from the kerb outside did Jean let out the breath she hadn't realised she'd been holding.

That was him gone back to his work. Back to his dusty old wills and deeds and conveyancing. For someone like him that would be the most discreet way of going about this, of course. His nice, plump, motherly wife would never know what he had fitted into his lunch hour today. Presumably he'd done that on a lot of days. Judging by that reference to 'The Luxor's young ladies'.

There now. That wasn't so bad, was it?

You were quite a scared little girl half-an-hour ago, weren't you?

Until the next time, little Jean.

He had wanted her to be a scared little girl. It had excited him. The nausea broke over her like a breaker on a stormy beach. She didn't quite make it to the bathroom in time.

Once she was sure she was finished she rose stiffly from where she'd been kneeling in front of the toilet and mopped up the mess she had made on her way there. After that she brushed her teeth so hard that her gums bled. When even that didn't make her mouth feel clean enough, she picked up the Listerine that Andrew had always liked to use and gargled with it.

Now it was time to deal with the foul stickiness between her legs. Last week Gloria Templeton had accompanied Jean to the consulting rooms of a doctor who was prepared to fit young women with a little device known as a Grafenberg ring. 'To protect you, dear,' Gloria had said brightly, 'and because gentlemen prefer things to be . . . well . . . *natural*.'

The horrible doctor, nothing at all like nice, kind Dr MacMillan, had put it much more crudely. 'No man likes to have to wear a mackintosh when he goes in here. Much more fun without one.'

She had flinched at his words, as she had flinched from his rough-and-ready handling of her. Now it seemed insignificant in comparison with how she had been handled today.

Stepping into the shower, Jean turned it on full blast and soaped herself vigorously all over. She remembered that she had to wash her hair too. The lawyer had kept touching it. She reached for the shampoo, which stood on the bathroom windowsill, and poured half the bottle over her head. It was going to take forever to rinse. That was all right. That was good. The longer she stood under this torrent of water the better.

She stood under it for ages. Even when all the suds from the shampoo and the soap had been rinsed away and the water was running clear over her feet she still didn't feel clean. She needed a bath.

She turned on the geyser and reached for the bath salts. Then she remembered that they had been a gift from Colonel Harris. That same Colonel Harris whom she had always liked and had always thought took a fatherly interest in her. She'd been told to expect him on Saturday afternoon.

Quite calmly, Jean opened the window, checked there were no dogs or cats or wee birds on the flowerbed below it and tossed the bottle of bath salts on to the soft earth between two rose bushes. She would use clean water and soap. Nothing else. She spotted the nailbrush lying between the taps of the bath.

She had raised welts on her breasts. That was good. Those angry red marks were wiping out the memory of a greedy mouth and hands. She came up on to her knees and began to scrub herself between the legs. Like a thin scarlet ribbon wafted by a summer's breeze, a strand of red floated up onto the surface of the water. She had drawn blood. She had rubbed so hard that she had drawn blood from herself. Jean stayed her busy hand.

There had been blood when Andrew had first made love to her. Quite a lot of blood. That had been only right and proper and expected. She had been a virgin and he had taken her virginity. That was why there had been blood.

Jean swished the nailbrush through the water to clean it and leaned forward to put it in its place between the bath taps. Andrew had taken nothing from her. She had given herself and her innocence to him, joyfully and willingly.

She hadn't given herself to the man who'd just left this flat. What had gone on here this afternoon had been a trade. She had something he wanted: sex, of course; her youth too, she supposed. What he had to offer her in return was quite simple: money.

Jean splashed herself between the legs and stood up. She stepped out of the bath and wrapped a towel around her body and twisted a smaller one about her wet hair. Then she padded barefoot through to the dining room to see what the lawyer's little extra amounted to.

It was sticking out of her handbag, lying open on the table. She never left it like that. He must have twisted open the clasp to slip it in. More discreet that way. More like a little present. He didn't want to believe this was a trade. He wanted to think she was doing this because she wanted to. Because she liked him.

Jean took the note between her thumb and forefinger and lifted it out of her bag. Five pounds. That was as much as he was paying Gloria for her. She was keeping back so much for what was owed to The Luxor and giving her thirty bob a time. Apparently that was the going rate in less elevated places anyway. According to Gloria that meant Jean wasn't losing out at all.

Buy yourself a pretty little something as a souvenir of our first time together. She smoothed the big banknote out on the table. The paper crackled in the silence of the flat. Five pounds. Obviously it was nothing to the lawyer, money he could easily afford to part with. *Buy yourself a pretty little something.*

The anger washed over Jean then as completely as the

earlier nausea. Anger at the man who was old enough to be her father trying to pretend that this was more than a sordid little arrangement. Anger at Gloria Templeton for backing her into this corner. Anger at herself for having been so naïve as not to see it coming. Anger at Andrew for leaving her to cope with this.

Anger at Andrew? That wasn't fair. Andrew was ill. Andrew might be going to die.

Andy might be going to die. It was the first time Jean had allowed herself to formulate that thought. Andy might be going to die.

She slid down one leg of the table until she was huddled at the foot of it, a tight little ball of panic and misery. She sobbed so hard she almost made herself sick again. In the end, what stopped her was that she was too just tired.

Wiping her eyes with the heels of her hands, she sat staring out into the lobby of the flat. A white envelope lay on the floor. The porter must have pushed it under the door while she'd been crying. She stood up and went to get it. It was postmarked Nairn and her name and address were typewritten on the envelope.

Her hands were shaking so much she could hardly open it. When she did and saw the familiar copperplate, she held it for a moment to her breast, breathing heavily with sheer relief. She had to wipe her eyes again before she could read what Andrew had written.

Dear Jean,
I'm only allowed to fill one side of this silly wee sheet of paper. I'm fine but dying of boredom. I've got one thing to say to you. I love you. I love you. I love you. Here comes Mussolini's sister to take my writing materials away already. I love you. I love you. I love you.

The nurse is at the foot of the bed now and she's glaring at me. I love you. I love you. I love you.

Andy

PS. I love you, I love you, I love y—

The last 'you' trailed away into a squiggly line of ink. Jean could visualise the scene; he playfully holding on to the sheet of paper while the nurse tugged it away and scolded him for overtiring himself.

Jean folded the letter and pressed it to her mouth. He had touched it. Now she was touching it too. It had probably been fumigated or disinfected or something but it was still a physical connection to him.

I'm fine but dying of boredom. Such a casual expression. Until you thought about it. But he wasn't going to die. She wasn't going to allow that to happen. The nurses and doctors at the sanatorium weren't going to allow that to happen. As long as she could afford to keep him there for the six months it was going to take him to get better.

Jean walked back into the sitting room and across to the table. She lifted the banknote the lawyer had left her, folded it neatly and slid it into the little pocket inside her handbag. Tomorrow she would use it to open a savings account at the Post Office.

She had to eat and she had to pay fares. Apart from when she came home from The Luxor in the wee small hours there would be no taxis from now on, though. Every last farthing she could spare was going into that savings account.

This money wasn't going to buy something pretty. This money was going to buy something beautiful. It was going to buy Andrew's health back. That was why she was doing this.

What did it matter who possessed her body? Just so long as they paid for the privilege. She would extract as much money as possible out of them. She would find out what they wanted and she would give it to them. If they wanted her to be a scared little girl that's what she would be. If they wanted something else they would get that from her too.

They would never have her heart. That belonged to Andrew. It always would belong to him. They would never have her mind or her spirit either. They belonged to herself. She would build a wall around that self, one that only one other person in the world would ever be allowed to breach.

He must never know what she had done, though. The price she was paying to buy back his health had to remain her own secret. Andrew must never know.

Chapter 30

'THE SUPERINTENDENT says we may now be cautiously optimistic,' Andrew had written. 'He seems even to be inclined to allow me to persuade him that I should give some dancing lessons for my fellow sufferers. Those of us who are regaining our health and strength are inclined to find time hangs rather heavily here.'

As Jean had discovered, when Andrew wrote a letter he tended to couch his news in rather formal turns of phrase. She knew her letters to him at Seafield House were scrutinised in case they contained anything upsetting or even exciting. She wondered if his letters to her were also read. Perhaps that was why he wrote them the way he did.

Not that such a consideration had stopped him writing the letter full of all those 'I love you's. She had kept all of his monthly letters but that one was the most precious of all. Or so she had thought until she had started reading this one.

'Cautiously optimistic'? Reading between the carefully composed lines, Jean allowed herself for the first time to believe the news was much better than that.

'The Superintendent does say that, despite my good progress, it would be advisable to think about where I'm going to live and how I'm going to earn my living when I'm discharged, although he doesn't rule out dancing as a profession. When I'm discharged,' he'd written again. 'Aren't they the most wonderful words you ever heard? I think, Jean,' she read on, 'that you and I might even begin to think about making plans for the future.'

A note of informality crept in, an echo of the Andy she knew and loved. 'Touch wood and all of that. Hopefully I shall have even better news when I write next month. Your very loving husband, Andrew Logan.'

' "When I'm discharged," ' Jean said out loud into the quietness of the flat. 'Those are wonderful words. "Those of us who are regaining our health and strength" are even more wonderful.'

She lifted Andrew's letter and kissed it as she always did after the first reading. He had graduated to being allowed to cover four sides of paper now. 'You're getting better,' she whispered. 'You're getting better.'

She folded the letter, replaced it in its envelope and returned it to the little quilted blue satin handkerchief bag in which she kept the others. Pulling open the shallow top drawer of the dressing-table at which she sat, she put the bag away. She closed the drawer and leaned forward, her elbows on the glass top that covered the dressing-table, and her chin propped on her fists.

His letters might be out of sight; they were never out of mind, as he was never out of mind. Jean studied her own reflection in the big central mirror of the dressing-table. Two slimmer mirrors were attached to it, the kind of which you could adjust the angle.

They were almost flat at the moment, allowing Jean to see not only herself but the bedroom behind her. At the beginning, in those first few nightmarish weeks, she had thought she hated this room. She had decided she would never sleep in it again, making up a bed for herself on the sofa in the sitting room.

She'd kept that up for the first month. One Sunday after a visit from Colonel Harris she had cried herself into hysterics and subsequently sunk into an exhausted sleep in the bedroom.

Waking a few hours later to the darkness of the evening, she had lain there and thought it all through. What she should remember about this room were the times she had spent here with Andrew. What happened in here these days was a means to an end. She shouldn't accord it any more significance than that. She changed the sheets a lot. That was her only proviso.

She'd had to grow a little wise about 'the little extra to buy something pretty' which all of the men now gave her. Occasionally she did buy some trinket, convincing each of them it was his money that had paid for it. She made sure the things she bought were cheap but not tawdry, good enough to sell or pawn before she left The Luxor so as to accumulate as much money as possible for the future.

'I'm going to be discharged soon too,' she told her reflection. 'Not long to go now.' Two weeks before, she'd had one of those private monthly meetings she'd insisted on with Gloria. The debt was now paid off in full. When Jean had said nothing about wanting to leave The Luxor, she'd seen from the look on Gloria's face that she thought she'd been right. Like those other girls, Jean too had succumbed to the lure of easy money. Let her think that. For a while.

Studying herself in the mirror, Jean wondered if she looked any different from the girl who had seen Andrew off at the railway station four and a half months before. She failed to come up with an answer to that question. Did she *feel* any different?

She was more cynical, definitely. Was there also a

knowingness about her, an air of world weariness? She couldn't make up her mind about that either.

Straightening up, she squared her shoulders and allowed herself to think about the future. Frustratingly, Andrew hadn't said what his ideas for that were. Jean knew enough about recovering consumptives to know what they should be. He would need a dry and sunny climate and a job that would allow him to spend plenty of time in the sunshine and the fresh air. She considered all sorts of permutations of how they might achieve that until his letter came the following month with an idea she hadn't considered.

There are a number of large and de luxe hotels in Nairn – did you know that Charlie Chaplin regularly spends time here? – and several of them employ dancing partners. I have a bit of an ace up my sleeve in this regard. The superintendent's brother is the owner of one of these establishments. It's called the Royal Cawdor Hotel. He's taken on people from the san in the past. The Royal Cawdor is right on the sea front so it would be a fine and healthy location. We could live in, as well. As long as he gets a medical certificate to say that my lungs are sound again, he's prepared to consider offering us both employment. Write back straight away, Jean, and let me know what you think of this idea. If it appeals to you, make sure you get a good reference from The Luxor before you leave. That shouldn't be difficult! It was great news that they gave you a raise in pay.

I've been saving this next bit of news as a surprise for you. The san is set in several acres of its own policies. There are three or four cottages dotted about these grounds and it's customary for patients who're being discharged to spend their last fortnight in one of them, one member of their family being welcome to join them.

The superintendent calls this a halfway house and says it eases the transition from having been in an institution to return to normal life. So will you join me, Jean, in our own wee cottage by the sea? You always wanted one of those, didn't you? (I'm sorry it's only for a fortnight but never mind. We'll enjoy ourselves anyway.) Will you come here and meet me as I walk out of the prison gates?

Jean's spirits soared when she read those lines and realised the implications of what he was telling her. She could walk out of her own prison gates two weeks earlier than expected too. 'A halfway house.' This little cottage would be that also for her, easing her transition back to normal life.

'Don't worry about my reference, Andy,' she murmured. 'I've got that all sorted out.'

'A reference?'

'Yes,' Jean said coolly. ' "To Whom It May Concern." Mrs Templeton and I have already discussed this. I'd like it as soon as possible, please. My train leaves in less than an hour.'

'Your train?' Richard Templeton spluttered. 'Your train to where?'

'I think that's my business.'

'You're leaving us? Just like that? Walking out on us?'

'Yes. Can I have that reference, please?'

Richard Templeton turned to his wife. 'Gloria, are you going to stand by and let her do this?'

'I'm not sure that I can stop her, Richard. Young Jean seems to have her mind made up.' Gloria Templeton said what she had said six months earlier. 'Leave me to deal with this, dear.' She waited until her husband had left the office, muttering darkly about the unreliability of young women as he went. Once the door had clicked shut behind him she walked forward and offered Jean a cigarette. 'What about your gentlemen friends?'

Jean accepted a light and put the cigarette to her lips. 'I'm sure you'll be able to arrange for them to find consolation elsewhere.'

Gloria Templeton studied her thoughtfully. 'You've hooked up with Andrew Logan again, haven't you?'

'I think that's my business too.'

'You're a fool,' Gloria said. 'You could make good money at this for quite a few years yet. You've got that bloom of innocence so many of them go for.'

Jean blew out some smoke rings. 'Really? How terribly fascinating.'

'As long as you don't display an attitude like the one you're demonstrating now,' Gloria said drily. 'You hardly look like Little Miss Innocent in that pose. Going to tell young Andrew what you've been up to over the past six months?'

Jean shot her a quick, sharp glance. 'My reference,' she said, stubbing out the barely smoked cigarette in the marble ashtray sitting on the sideboard next to which she was standing. 'I want my reference now.'

Gloria went to the filing cabinet behind the desk. Jean scanned down the sheet of paper with which she was presented, nodded and asked for an envelope. Once the reference was neatly folded and stowed away in her handbag she headed for the door. Gloria intercepted her as she reached it.

'I still think you're mad,' she said. 'But I hope there aren't any hard feelings.'

She was holding out her hand. Jean glanced down at it. No hard feelings? She could have said lots of things in reply to that. She chose to utter not one single word. Not even a goodbye.

She walked slowly down the grand staircase. The place was worth saying farewell to, if only in memory of the two babes-in-the-woods who had skipped in here so bright-eyed and hopeful a year before. Mona Forsyth was taking tea in the lobby. She must have realised that she was being watched. She looked up.

Smiles can hide so much – that's what Jean thought as she stood there with one hand on the banister looking down at Mona Forsyth. They can hide malice and breath-taking selfishness. Charm can be a carapace. Underneath the smooth and glossy shell a mean spirit can lurk: one that takes pleasure in inflicting pain and hurt; one that revels in destroying anything that's good or pure.

You didn't destroy us, Jean thought. Gloria Templeton and all the men who care only about satisfying their own lust didn't destroy us. He and I are going to be stronger than ever now. None of you have destroyed us, Mona.

Jean walked on down the staircase and into the fresh air of the outside world. Half an hour later her train pulled out of Glasgow heading for the north.

Chapter 31

HE WAS waiting for her at Inverness, not Nairn, standing on the platform scanning the windows of the train as it pulled in. So excited that she tripped twice on her way from the compartment to the end of the carriage, Jean stepped out of the train when Andrew's head was momentarily turned in the opposite direction. He turned it again, and saw her.

He strode up to her, laughing all over his face, arms flung wide. He was flexing his fingers too, beckoning her towards him. She dropped her mother's old carpet bag on the platform and went.

'Ouf!' he exclaimed as she flew into his arms.

'I'm sorry,' Jean said, pulling back. 'Have I made you breathless, Andy? I'm so sorry!'

'I'm only breathless in a good way. The excited way. Stop apologising and hurry up and kiss me.'

Neither of them said anything for a very long time after that, the kiss being followed by a prolonged hug. He released her only far enough for them to exchange another lingering kiss.

'You missed me, then?' he asked after they had kissed for the third time.

'I missed you,' she said, drinking in the sight of him. 'You look great.'

'You're a sight for sore eyes yourself, Mrs Logan.'

Jean was still gazing wonderingly at him. 'You look just like your old self.'

'I'm better than my old self.' He beamed at her. 'Fit as a fiddle and raring to go.'

'Should you be standing out in this cold, though?' she asked, a tinge of anxiety creeping into her voice. 'It's quite chilly up here compared to Glasgow . . . What have I said?'

For he had started to laugh. That old exuberant laugh, halfway between a guffaw and a chuckle. With no idea at all what was so funny, Jean found herself joining in. It was so wonderful to hear him laugh again. It was so wonderful to be with him again, simply breathing the same cold air as he was.

'What are we laughing at?' she asked when she was eventually capable of speech.

'They make us go out and about in all weathers at Seafield.' Andrew wiped his eyes and grinned at her. 'And none of the wards is heated. This is nothing,' he said, lifting one hand to indicate the draughty station around them. 'You must be getting cold, though, you poor wee frozen Glaswegian. We'll warm you up with something from the tea-room while we wait for the Nairn train. Let's go and retrieve your bag. It's looking a bit lonely up there.'

'Did the trunk arrive safely?'

He swung the carpet bag up with one hand and pulled her in close to himself with the other. 'They delivered it to our little Highland holiday home yesterday. You've lost weight, Jean.'

'I suppose I have.'

'Working too hard, I expect. Never mind, you can have a good rest over the next fortnight. What did the Templetons say about you leaving? Were they all right about it?'

'They were fine.'

300

'Are you all right about it?' he asked as they walked along the platform. 'Not going to miss The Luxor?'

'No,' Jean said carefully. 'I'm not going to miss it one little bit.' She paused for a moment in the open doorway of the station tea-room and looked at him. 'Right now I'm exactly where I want to be. Right now I'm with exactly who I want to be with.'

'That's good,' Andrew said, and bent forward to kiss her cheek.

'This is . . . *different*,' Jean said.

Andrew laughed as he took the key out of the door of the cottage. 'You were expecting a cosy wee place, weren't you? All frilly curtains and stuff? I must admit it looks a bit austere.'

Jean looked around her. Everything was spotlessly clean but the place was indeed a bit austere. On the floor there was only linoleum with no rug of any description in sight. There were plain blinds at the windows and no ornaments on the mantelpiece. Apart from an amber glass bowl on the table filled with fruit, the only decoration in the room was a framed photograph of a beach with waves breaking on it.

'There's some medical reason why it needs to be like this?'

'Aye. Easier to keep the germs at bay if there's as little as possible to trap them in. Easier to keep the place clean too. I'm afraid you're not allowed to smoke in here, either. You don't mind, do you?'

'I don't mind at all.'

He indicated the photograph. 'You can light up when we walk on the beach. That's allowed.'

'That's the local beach? I'm impressed.'

'There are lovely beaches along at Nairn too. I was graciously permitted to go there last week.'

'To see the manager of the hotel?'

301

'Aye,' he said again, a little smile beginning to curve his mouth.

Jean put her hands on her hips. 'Are you going to tell me or do I have to torture it out of you?'

'We start in a fortnight,' he said triumphantly.

'Living in?'

He nodded. 'We've got a wee sort of flatlet thingy, with its own balcony overlooking the beach. You'll be dancing five days a week and I'll be doing two.'

'To allow you to build up your stamina again?'

'Yes. The manager says I can help him in the office the other three days. Are you hungry, by the way?'

'Not for food.'

He came forward to stand in front of her. 'Hussy,' he murmured.

Jean drew in a quick little breath. 'Only with you.'

He raised one dark eyebrow. 'I'm very glad to hear it. Go back on your left foot.'

'You want to dance me there?' Jean asked. Her heart was thumping with anxiety, but she was already obeying the command.

'Thought it might add a wee touch o' finesse to the proceedings.' His footwork marrying in with hers, he backed her towards a door that presumably led to the cottage's bedroom. 'I'm afraid there might not be very much finesse in evidence once we get through there. No' this first time, anyway.'

'Is this a warning that it's going to be a bit rough?'

'I think I might not be able to help it being a bit rough. Comes of me having been deprived for such a long time. Is that all right with you?'

Jean coiled one hand around the back of his neck. Her voice was raw and husky. 'I want you to be rough. I want you to claim me back.'

'Claim you back? That's an odd way of putting it.'

'No, it's not. That's what I want. That's what I need.' She pulled his mouth down on hers.

'You look like a woman who's spent an interesting night.'

He was lying beside her, propped up on one elbow. Jean turned her head on the pillow and smiled at him. 'I ache all over. I've probably got bruises.'

His voice was a warm and amused murmur. 'Give me five minutes and I'll kiss each and every one of them better. Although I didn't hear you complaining last night. What I did hear was you expressing a certain amount of enjoyment in our nocturnal activities. Rather a lot of enjoyment, now I come to think about it. Good job we're on the outer edges of the grounds here. How embarrassing if the superintendent or any of the nurses had heard anything. And me a convalescent man, too.'

'There's nothing wrong with your health now,' Jean said happily. She felt elated this morning. She had worried and worried that somehow he would be able to tell. Studying his grinning face now, she knew that concern had been groundless. He searched for her hand under the bedclothes and lifted it to his mouth, the grin fading a little.

'Did you ever think I wouldn't get better, Jean?'

'I did think that. But don't let's talk about it. You *have* got better.'

'Thanks to you making sure that I came here.' He kissed her hand. 'I think I'm a very lucky man, Jean Logan.'

'I think I'm a very lucky woman. I *know* I'm a very lucky woman.'

'Then what are you greeting for?' he asked, using their entwined hands to brush away the tear that was sliding down her smooth cheek.

303

'Because I'm so happy,' she exclaimed, caught halfway between a sob and a laugh.

'Women are off their heads,' Andrew said cheerfully, kissing her hand again. He pulled it away from his mouth, a little frown creasing his forehead. 'Why are you not wearing your wedding ring?'

'Because I wanted you to put it back on my finger. It's in my handbag.' She leaned over the side of the bed and came up with the little red jewellery box. 'Here.'

'Is this to do with claiming you back as well?' he asked as he opened the box and took out the ring.

Jean nodded, and bit her lip.

'Are you crying again? Daftie,' he scolded softly as he slipped the gold band on to her finger. 'There. Now you're my wife again.'

She smiled at him through her tears. 'Aye. Now I'm your wife again.'

Chapter 32

April 1935

'WHAT ARE you doing?'

'Nothing,' she said, rising hurriedly from the small desk in front of the window and turning to face him. 'I was just leafing through the newspaper while I was waiting for you.'

'Lying wee bisom. You were only pretending to read that newspaper.' Standing by the bookcase full of the volumes Jean had borrowed from the hotel library, he narrowed his eyes at her. 'What did you hide underneath the paper as I came through the door?'

'Nothing,' she said again.

'If it's nothing, you won't mind me looking at it, will you?' He was too quick for her, sliding across the sitting room of their little flat and scooping up the newspaper and what lay beneath it.

'Don't!' She tried to snatch it all back from him.

Keeping her at bay with one hand, Andrew allowed the newspaper to fall to the floor and held on to the sheets of paper she'd been trying to conceal with the other. He scanned the topmost of the handwritten sheets, then looked up at her again, his blue eyes ablaze with interest. 'You've been writing a story! Can I read it through?'

'It's not finished yet.' This time she managed to grab the papers back from him. 'I'm still editing it.'

'What's it about?'

'It's a love story,' she said, blushing a little. 'What they call a boy-meets-girl story. A humorous one.'

Andrew folded his arms across his chest. He was casually dressed today, in cream-coloured flannel trousers and a matching short-sleeved and open-necked shirt. Knotted round his neck by its sleeves, a navy fisherman's jersey hung from his shoulders. The two of them were going off for a cycle ride today in honour of its being Jean's twentieth birthday.

He treated her to his winning smile. 'Have you used me as the model for the hero?'

'As a matter of fact, I have,' she said crisply. 'He's a right numpty. Can't see what's right in front of his nose. That the girl in the story is crazy about him.'

'The way you're crazy about me?'

'Modest, aren't you?' she said, turning away from him and neatening up the sheets of paper before slipping them into the top drawer of the desk. She'd no sooner closed it than she felt Andrew's arms come round her waist, his head dipping to press a soft kiss on the side of her neck.

'Does the heroine fall for him and ride off into the sunset with him?'

'Of course she does. This sort of story has to have a happy ending. That's what the readers like.'

'Ah-hah,' he said, moving her around in his arms so they were facing one another. 'The girl with the plan has obviously been doing her research.'

Jean coiled her own arms about his neck. Like him, she was dressed for their expedition, wearing a navy-blue divided skirt, a white blouse and a V-necked and sleeveless Fair Isle top. She'd pulled her hair back into a ponytail and tied it with a ribbon whose colour exactly matched that of her skirt.

'Well,' she said, 'with the hotel taking all the different magazines it does for the guests, it's been easy to read through them all and find out what kind of stories they like.'

'So once your story's finished you're going to send it off to one of the magazines whose readers like boy-meets-girl stories and see if they'll publish it?'

'That's the general idea.'

'You'll need a *nom de plume*.'

'You said that well.'

'Comes of spending so much time with Monsieur Bertrand.'

'*Vraiment?*' Jean said, having also picked up a smattering of French words and expressions from the manager of the hotel. Marcel Bertrand had taken a real shine to Andrew, and frequently expressed the opinion that he'd never had such an efficient assistant. He was always reluctant to spare him for his two days' dancing per week.

'As a matter of fact, I've already thought up a pen name.'

'Let's have it, then.'

'Joanna Colquhoun.'

'Sounds good. Your mother was a Colquhoun, wasn't she?'

'That's why I chose it. And I thought Jean maybe sounded a bit too plain and simple.'

'I think it's the loveliest name in the world,' Andrew said, and bent his head forward to kiss her.

'Staff lift or back stairs?' Jean asked as they stepped out into the attic corridor that housed the staff accommodation. Up under the eaves with the pigeons they might be, but the Royal Cawdor was built on the grand scale. Even this attic floor had plenty of headroom and large skylights allowed sunshine and light to flood into the passageway.

'The lift,' Andrew said. 'And you can go into the kitchens and fetch our packed lunches.'

'Don't tell me you're scared of Chef as well,' she teased as the lift descended through the four floors of the building.

'The man's a maniac,' Andrew said darkly. 'You're the only person in this place he doesn't shout at. Or threaten to throw his knives at.'

Jean laughed as they emerged from the lift. 'His bark's a lot worse than his bite.'

She went off down the service corridor to fetch their lunches and caught up with Andrew on the brick steps that gave access from the rear door of the hotel to its extensive gardens, sloping down in a lush green carpet towards the Moray Firth.

Tucked away in one corner of the grounds was an outhouse shielded by carefully tended shrubs and flowers, where a selection of bikes were kept for the use of guests and the hotel staff alike.

'So,' Andrew asked, 'where shall we head for today?' He pretended to groan. 'As if I didn't know.'

Jean threw him an arch look. 'You think Culloden's an interesting place too.'

'I'm not obsessed by it like you are,' he said, teasing out a ladies' bike from the collection and wheeling it over to her.

'Today is the anniversary of the battle.'

'And since it's also your birthday you were probably fated to take an interest in it and everything that goes with it.'

'So you don't really mind going there?'

'I don't mind,' he said, as he mounted his own bicycle. 'Even if it is nearly a thirty-mile round trip.'

'Good exercise,' Jean said. 'Think yourself lucky you weren't one of Bonnie Prince Charlie's men who had to *walk* to Nairn and back the night before the battle. That stupid night attack on the Duke of Cumberland's camp that came to nothing.'

'Marching on empty stomachs too,' Andrew said, knowing both facts because he'd been the chief recipient of the knowledge Jean had picked up through the extensive reading she'd done on this subject over the winter. 'Not a packed lunch between them,' he added flippantly, putting their own sustenance for the day into the leather bag fixed behind the saddle of his bike.

Jean sighed. 'Aye. By the time the men of the Jacobite army lined up on the field that day, they were already exhausted and starving.'

Andrew took one look at her sombre face and groaned again. 'Don't go all melancholic on me, Jean.'

When they reached Culloden two hours later, however, he looked pretty melancholic himself as he read out the inscription on the memorial cairn.

' "The Battle of Culloden Was Fought On This Moor 16ᵗʰ April 1746. The Graves Of The Gallant Highlanders Who Fought For Scotland and Prince Charlie Are Marked By The Names Of Their Clans." So why is the cairn on this particular spot?' he asked, glancing behind him towards the low grey stones that marked the burial places of the clansmen.

'Because this is where the fighting was at its fiercest.'

Jean raised her face to the cobalt blue of the sky. She was as much moved by the knowledge that she was standing where so many men had breathed their last as she had been when she and Andrew had made their first visit to the battlefield on a bright, sharp day in December of the previous year.

'It lasted less than an hour, you know. Less than an hour for the Cause to be lost. After that it was all over for the House of Stuart and Bonnie Prince Charlie's dream of wresting the British crown back from the House of Hanover. More importantly, it was the end of any hopes Scotland had of regaining her independence and also sounded the death knell for the clans and the Highland way of life. Of course,' she went on expansively, 'the Jacobites were completely worn out by the night march to Nairn and in the twenty-four hours before the battle each man had been given a ration of only one dry biscuit. It was terrible weather too. They say the sleet drove into the highlanders' faces as they charged——'

Something about the quality of the silence emanating from her listener brought her up short. She lowered her gaze from the sky above their heads. Arms folded across his light shirt, Andrew was standing with his head cocked to one side. His blue eyes held a gleam of unholy amusement, and the corners of his mouth were lifting.

'What are you looking at me like that for?' she demanded.

'Don't you recognise my intelligent sheepdog act? I'm hanging on your every word, Professor Logan.'

Jean's face fell. 'I was getting a bit carried away again, was I?'

'You were getting a bit carried away,' he confirmed. Unfolding his arms, he stepped forward, cupped her face between his hands and laughed softly. 'But I love you for it. You get so caught up in this. So involved in it all.'

She coiled the fingers of her own hands around his wrists. 'I can see them,' she told him earnestly. 'In my mind's eye. Old men and young men. Fathers and sons and brothers. Lots of them fighting on opposite sides from each other. The 'forty-five split families and friends and communities. What if your brother was fighting for Bonnie Prince Charlie and your lover was a redcoat? What if the two of them had been friends before the whole thing started?'

'Ever considered writing about this, Jean? The story of how all those old men and young men and fathers and sons and brothers found themselves standing on this moor back in April seventeen forty-six? The story of the women who were praying for them all to come home safely?'

'Other people have done it already. Done it really well, too.'

'That doesn't mean you couldn't bring something different to it. You're really interested in this. You really care about this.'

'It would have to be a book,' she said doubtfully. 'You couldn't do justice to something like this in a short story.'

'There's some law against you writing a book? Come on,' he said, taking his hands from her face. 'Like the poor old Jacobites, I'm starving. I need my lunch.'

Jean narrowed her eyes at him. 'We're not eating here.'

'Of course we're not. Do you think I have no soul, woman?'

'Where are we going, then?' she asked as she followed him to where they'd left the bikes lying on the grass.

'One of the hotel guests told me about this place called the Clava Cairns. It's only about a mile or so from here. More history, but a lot earlier than the Jacobites,' he said as they rode away from the memorial cairn and back to the crossroads through which they'd come from Nairn. 'We turn right here. Just before the Cumberland Stone.'

'What are these Clava Cairns?' Jean called forward to him.

Beginning to free-wheel down a short hill, he threw the answer back over his shoulder. 'Ancient burial chambers, I think.'

'About as cheerful as Culloden, then,' she muttered.

When they got there a few minutes later, however, she was forced to admit that the atmosphere was quite different from the sorrowful one they had left behind them at the battlefield. Wandering hand-in-hand through the circular cairns and investigating their surrounding stone circles they agreed that the place felt very peaceful.

'Welcoming,' Jean said. 'If there are any ghosts here they're quite happy for us to visit them.'

Andrew's stomach rumbled, and they both laughed. 'Do you think that's a message from the ghosts to tell us they've no objections to us having our picnic now?' he queried.

They sat under the sun-dappled branches of an ancient oak tree and ate, happy to be quiet for a while and soak up the unique atmosphere of the place. Jean had finished her packed lunch and was almost on the point of dozing off when Andrew suddenly stood up and strode over to the bikes. He came back carrying two packages.

'Happy Birthday. Open the bigger one first.'

She unwrapped a large pad of plain white paper. 'Och,' she cried, 'you knew fine well that I'd been writing!'

'Of course I did,' he said cheerfully. 'You've got too honest a face to be any good at keeping secrets, Jean. Open the second parcel now.'

It contained a pen: a beautiful fountain pain with a dark-blue barrel decorated in swirling curves and curlicues of silvery-coloured paint. 'It's lovely,' she said. 'Really lovely.'

'Glad you like it.' He sat down under the tree again. 'But it's a functional object too.'

'You want me to handsel it and the notebook now?'

'No time like the present for wetting the baby's head.'

'What should I write about?'

'You could put those people you were talking about where we are now. Those two friends fighting on opposite sides at Culloden. The girl who's the sister of the one and the sweetheart of the other. They must have known these cairns.'

'That's an idea,' Jean murmured. 'That is a very good idea.'

Andrew slid down so that he was stretched out full length on the grass beside her. 'While you're doing that I'll just close my eyes for a wee minute.'

312

A good forty-five of those wee minutes later he gave one final soft snore, stretched, opened his eyes and smiled up at her. 'Did I fall asleep?'

'You did,' Jean said, gazing fondly at him.

'Have you done some writing?'

For answer she held up the pad of paper so he could see it. 'Several pages.'

'Quite a lot of pages by the look of it. Are you happy with what you've written?'

'I'm already beginning to get to know these three characters,' she said thoughtfully.

'Good,' he said, coming up to a sitting position. 'I suppose we'd better make a move now.' Suiting the action to the words, he leaped to his feet and extended a hand to help her to hers. 'Why did we agree to do a performance of our tango tonight?'

Jean wasn't sure about that either. She'd had to be coaxed into doing the story tango again in the first place. The tale she had thought up in the days of her innocence of the girl begging her lover's forgiveness after her affair with another man now had too many uncomfortable parallels with real life.

Sometimes, when Andrew was throwing himself into the role, his eyes hurt, harsh and condemning, she really had to steel herself to meet his gaze. Once or twice she'd managed to convince herself that somehow he knew what had happened, that somehow or other she had been found out.

Then, still in character, he would forgive his faithless lover, those same inky-blue eyes softening and brimming over with the boundless love Jean knew that he felt for her. And she would be gripped all over again by shame and anger and sorrow and the sense of never being able to lay down the burden of the awful secret she was keeping from him.

There were days – especially when he said things like he'd said today about how honest she was – when it threatened to overwhelm her, when she longed to pour it all out, throw herself at his feet and beg his forgiveness in earnest. There were other days when she knew she never could do that. The knowledge of what she had done would break his heart.

Unfortunately, everyone seemed to love their tango, not only the hotel residents but also local people from Nairn and the surrounding area in search of an entertaining night out. Those non-resident patrons had kept the hotel ticking over very healthily during the winter months.

Although the mild and sunny climate of Nairn meant that its hotels did welcome resident guests all year round, Jean and Andrew had been warned to brace themselves for how busy things would become once Easter signalled the start of the season proper. So she completed her boy-meets-girl story, sent it off and tried not to think about it.

That proved easier than she had thought. Once the hotel began to fill up life distilled down into two major activities: working and sleeping. Until the unbelievably thrilling day in July when a copy of a well-known women's magazine was sent to her through the post.

Bumping into Andrew in the main entrance lobby of the hotel the day after the magazine was officially published, Jean posed a question. 'Don't we usually buy just two or three copies of that magazine for the main lounge?'

'Usually,' he said, grinning broadly at her.

'It seems to be strewn all over the place. You must have bought about six copies of it this week.'

'A dozen, actually.'

'I found it in that wee room the guests use to write their letters. And in the conservatory. There were three copies in the conservatory, actually. All left casually lying open at a story by someone called Joanna Colquhoun.'

Andrew laughed. 'I'm that proud o' you, Miss Colquhoun. If we weren't standing here within full view of a dozen guests, I'd give you a big kiss for being such a clever lassie.'

'I'm quite proud of myself,' Jean murmured. 'Getting published in a real magazine. One that people actually *read*.'

Andrew laughed again. 'They even paid you for it.'

'I know,' she said, opening her eyes wide. 'A whole five guineas. Imagine them paying me good money for my wee story.'

'They loved your wee story. They've asked you to send them any more you might write. Would you like to hear my wee story now?'

'Only if it's as good as mine.'

'It's good, all right.'

They were interrupted by Jean's name being called. Swinging round in response, she returned the wave and the smile being sent her way across the large and high-ceilinged entrance hall. The elderly gentleman sat in one of the tartan-covered wing armchairs that flanked the massive carved wooden mantelpiece, which was the focal point of the lobby. The fireplace itself was filled with the huge vase of fresh flowers that adorned it during the summer months.

'Should you go over and chat with your boyfriend?' Andrew murmured.

She responded in the same low tones. 'My boyfriend's a hundred and fifty if he's a day.'

'Hasn't stopped him tripping the light fantastic with you every evening for the past fortnight.'

'Would you grudge the poor old soul a little pleasure in his twilight years?'

315

'No,' Andrew said. 'Especially when I see his wife. Who, fortunately for us, is just entering stage left.'

'Keeps him in order, doesn't she?'

'Like you do with me.'

Jean accorded her partner and his wife one last wave before she turned back to Andrew. 'That'll be right. What's your wee story, then?'

'Perhaps we should go somewhere a little less public.'

'The back veranda?' she suggested. 'By the looks of the Firth it's quite stormy today. I suspect it's a bit chilly for any of the guests to have ventured out there.'

She was right. The three large French windows that gave access off the ballroom to the veranda were firmly closed, although not locked. Andrew turned the handle and opened one of them. 'Ouf!' he said, battling the wind. 'This is like being on a ship!'

'We'll get some shelter in the lee of the end wall,' Jean said, threading her way through the empty steamer chairs lined up neatly in a long line overlooking the Moray Firth. Waiting for Andrew to close the French windows and join her, she stood with her back to the mellow red bricks and gazed across the choppy water.

Low cliffs topped by green fields rose up from the northern shore of the Firth. Beyond them, smoky-blue in the distance, soared the more rugged hills and mountains of Sutherland and the Far North.

'Speak,' she commanded as Andrew walked up to her. He wasted no time in obeying her.

'You know how Monsieur Bertrand comes from Switzerland?'

'Lausanne, isn't it?' she said, digging her hand into the pocket of her red and white polka-dot dress for her cigarettes. When the wind blew her hair across her face she thought better of the idea. There was no way a match struck out

316

here was going to stay lit. 'Where is that exactly?'

'On Lake Geneva. He's had an offer to manage a hotel out there.' Andrew was unable to resist a short pause for effect. 'He wants to take me with him.'

'He's proposed to you?'

'Very funny. As a matter of fact he's offered me a job.'

Jean stared at him. 'When?'

'About ten minutes ago. He'd like me to be his official under-manager.'

'In Switzerland? Do you want to go?'

'I'd love to go. What do you think of the idea? The only problem is that there probably wouldn't be a job for you. But he's offering me good money and he says the accommodation for the two of us would be even nicer than it is here. What do you think, Jean?'

'I think it's a wonderful idea,' she breathed. She raised both hands to her head to hold back the hair being whipped forward by the wind. 'It would be great for your health too. All that clear mountain air.' She laughed. 'Even better than all the fresh air we get here.'

'That's what I thought. But I told Monsieur Bertrand I couldn't give him an answer until I'd discussed it with you. If you weren't working you'd have plenty of time to write.'

'When I wasn't learning French,' she said enthusiastically. 'We'd both have to do that.'

'Aye,' Andy said excitedly. 'Although he says this particular hotel always has lots of British guests too.' He took hold of her by her upper arms. 'You really fancy the idea, Jean?'

'I love the idea. Let's go and tell Monsieur Bertrand that we say *oui*. Let's go and tell him that right now!'

Andrew laughed, and kissed her. 'After you comb your hair, Jean.' He took her hand, and together they made a run for the French windows.

Chapter 33

SAFE AND secure in Andrew's arms as they lay in bed a few nights later, Jean gazed up at him. 'Are we really going to Switzerland, Andy? It seems like a dream. I keep thinking I'm going to wake up soon.'

'If you're having a dream I'm having it with you. But no, we're really going. On the sleeper from Inverness at the end of September. Then a month in London training at the company's hotel there.'

'Monsieur Bertrand's going on ahead of us?'

Andrew nodded. 'Will you be sad to leave this place?'

'A bit. We've had some good times here. I'm a bit worried I'm going to burst into tears and disgrace myself when we say cheerio to everybody.'

'So am I,' he said. 'And I have a suggestion to make. You know how we're doing a farewell performance of our tango on the evening that we leave?'

'Whose brilliant idea was that?'

'Mine. I like to think I've always had a flair for the dramatic. I bet there won't be a dry eye in the house.'

'Including our own?' Jean asked.

'Not if we avoid the send-off which I think is being planned for us, by slipping away as soon as we change after the tango.'

'Won't we hurt everybody's feelings if we do that?'

He shook his head. 'Not if we leave a farewell note somewhere prominent. You can deal with that. If we're not around to get embarrassed by it, you can say nice things about everybody. Well,' he amended, 'about everybody who deserves to have nice things said about them. Maybe you could even compose a farewell poem.'

'Maybe I could at that,' Jean said, already starting to think about it. 'It would be good to make it funny too.'

Taking care over it, she didn't complete the final version of the poem until the afternoon of the day they were due to leave. Taking it from her, Andrew sat at the table in the window painstakingly copying her verses out on to a large sheet of white card. Behind him, Jean moved around the room doing her final packing.

He finished writing it out at exactly the wrong moment. As he hooked his arm over the back of the chair, moving his fingers to free them up, he spotted what she had in her hand.

'I didn't know you had an account with the Post Office.'

'Didn't you?' she asked lightly, hoping he hadn't seen her take the passbook from behind the row of books where she had concealed it for almost a year.

She'd never been able to tell him about this account, having no idea how she could explain away the substantial amount of money that it contained. Once she had, as she hoped, made some more money from writing, she thought she might explain it away as earnings from that, put the funds into their common pot and help build up their combined savings.

'You know I didn't, Jean. Why did you feel you had to hide it from me?'

Her brain froze – and locked fast. She couldn't think of one innocent reason that would account for why she had kept the passbook out of his sight and never told him about the money. 'I was scared someone might come in and steal it,' she managed at last.

She'd come up with that excuse too late. Andrew held out his hand. 'Can I see how much is in it?'

She handed it over, hearing the astonishment in his voice as he read out the figures. 'How the *hell* did you manage to put this much money away?' He looked up at her, waiting for her answer, waiting for her to explain it to him.

She was feeling hot and cold all at the same time. She was feeling shivery. One thought penetrated the fog of panic. She had always known. She had always known that this day would come.

Chapter 34

He had been silent for so long Jean was beginning to wonder if he was ever going to speak. He was sitting on the floor in their room now, his back to the wall and his head and shoulders hunched forward so that she couldn't see his face.

'How many?' he asked at last.

'How many men?'

He nodded without looking up.

'About five or six.'

That brought his head up. '*About* five or six? Did you lose count, Jean?'

She had to moisten her lips before she could speak. 'Seven of them,' she said. 'Exactly seven of them.'

'One for each day o' the week?'

That made her flinch. 'It didn't happen every day. Not every day . . .'

'Who were they?'

Her lips were still dry. She licked them again. 'Andy . . . I'm not sure it's going to help you to know their names.'

'I'll be the judge o' that.' His eyes widened a little as she listed the names but he commented on only one of them. 'Colonel Harris,' he repeated flatly. 'Him that you flirted with the very first day we went to The Luxor.'

'I flirted with a lot of the patrons,' Jean said painfully. 'So did you.'

'Are you making some sort o' a point here?' Andrew asked, his chin rising.

'I don't understand what you mean.' She darted a nervous glance at him, wondering what was going on behind his eyes. Grown very dark, they were more black than blue.

'I mean, did you do this to get back at me for Mona Forsyth?'

'Get back at you for Mona Forsyth?' Jean repeated, stunned by the question. 'Do you think I did this because I *wanted* to? Andy, I was forced into this!'

'Gloria Templeton put a gun to your head, did she? Or did she hold a knife at your throat?'

Jean forced back tears at the icy sarcasm she heard in his voice. 'I'd have been out on the street if I hadn't done it.'

'You could have gone to my family for help.'

'Och, Andy! Your sisters would have slammed the door in my face, and you know it.'

'There must have been some other way.' His mouth set itself into stubborn lines.

'Not if we were going to keep you at the sanatorium.'

'Don't you dare put the blame on me for what you did,' he snapped, his voice raw and edgy. 'Don't you bloody dare!'

'You did do it with her,' Jean said painfully.

'I did it four times. And I'm a man.'

'What's that got to do with it?'

'You know what that's got to do wi' it. I also made a thief out o' myself to stop you from having to do it. I want the details.'

'The details?'

'What they did to you. What you did to them. I want every last detail.'

'Andy,' she protested. 'How is that going to help?'

'The details,' he said again. He pointed to the little sofa that stood against one wall of their sitting room. 'Sit down there and tell me.'

She delivered them in a flat and unemotional voice, answering every question he put to her. At one point he winced hard enough to make her stop and wait for him to speak.

'I've never managed to persuade you to do that for me.'

'It wasn't a case of being persuaded,' Jean said quietly. 'I didn't have any say in the matter. It was all about what they wanted to do.'

'You trying to tell me ye didnae enjoy any o' it?'

She wiped her eyes with her fingers. 'How can you even think that?'

His own darkened eyes fixed her as mercilessly as though he were pinning a live butterfly to a board. 'You trying to tell me none o' them made ye come?'

She drew in a great ragged gasp of a breath. 'Don't ask me that, Andy. Please don't ask me that—'

'That'll be a yes, then, will it?'

'It happened sometimes,' she said, her voice sunk to a whisper. 'I always felt worse when it did.'

'Say the words,' he demanded. 'Say, "Sometimes I came when I was being fucked by these men who were paying to fuck me. Sometimes I enjoyed myself when I was being fucked by these men who were paying to fuck me." '

No longer able to stanch the flow of tears, Jean shook her head slowly from side to side. 'I never enjoyed myself. Never ever. And I won't say those words. Don't you say them either. You've never used those words in front of me!'

'None o' them liked to use those words in front of you? Or wanted you to say them? Eh?'

Jean drew the back of her hand across her mouth and dropped her eyes. For a while neither of them said anything. He sat on the floor with his head in his hands and she sat on the edge of the sofa facing him. Her legs and feet were turned out awkwardly, like a gangly and gawky schoolgirl's.

She jumped when he rose to his feet and thrust his hands into his pockets. 'Here,' he said, depositing two handfuls of coins into her lap. He strode over to the desk, wrenching open its shallow drawer. From there he took out their little red and black cash-box. He turned the key to unlock it and scooped out the notes that were inside. They were also flung down into her lap.

She gazed up at him, not understanding what he was doing.

'I'm paying you, Jean,' he said. 'I must owe you a bundle. What is the going rate? A pound a time? Two pounds a time?' His voice was as hard and unforgiving as granite. 'A superior sort of a girl like you probably commands a higher price. And you'll know all the tricks of the trade now, eh? You must be due a small fortune from me.'

I want to die, she thought. *I want to die.*

'Andy,' she said brokenly, 'I'm so sorry . . .'

'Sorry?' he burst out. '*Sorry!* Dear God in Heaven, Jean! Sorry's what you say when you tread on somebody's foot!'

She rose to her feet, not sure if her legs were going to support her. 'I'll go down on my knees to you if that's what you want,' she sobbed. 'If that'll make you forgive me.'

She began to do it. He seized her by the elbows and stopped her. 'You can do that later on,' he hissed into her face.

'In the dance. In the dance I'll forgive you. In the dance,' he repeated.

'*I can't dance with you tonight!*'

'Oh yes, you can,' he said grimly. He threw her back down on the sofa, strode across the floor and yanked open the door. Before he went out into the corridor he jabbed one accusing finger at her. 'Be here when I get back.'

For a long time after he had left the room, Jean sat staring blindly into space. At some point she glanced at her wristwatch and saw that the time for them to perform their tango was drawing close. Rising to her feet as stiffly as though she were an old woman, she walked through to their bedroom, opened the door of the wardrobe and reached up for her costume.

She had brought it with her from The Luxor. The short black skirt, tight red sweater and matching beret had filled a space in the trunk she'd sent on ahead before leaving Glasgow. Andrew's costume was hanging next to hers.

His costume. Once the old and worn corduroy trousers and the striped blue and white collarless shirt had been his clothes. His working clothes.

She could remember him apologising for wearing them instead of his suit that first time he had come to the church hall. She could remember how much more solid he had looked in them, how much stronger and more masculine. When he had walked towards her in the kitchen of the hall that day, she had jumped, a little scared to find herself alone with him.

His eyes and his voice had softened at her reaction, and he had assured her that she was safe with him. He'd gone out of his way to put her at her ease, teasing her about her new high heels. *Sure you'll no' get dizzy up there?*

The black leather shoes with the narrow strap across the

325

instep, which she slipped on after she'd put on her costume, had really high heels. She had learned how to cope with that, learned how to dance in them. She had learned a lot of things.

Jean did her make-up, walked back through to the sitting room and looked at the money that lay on the sofa and the floor in front of it. She swung round to the desk and picked up the little cash-box. Lid open, it lay on its side, as he had discarded it.

She picked up the notes first, smoothing them out and putting them together before folding the small wad in half. She scooped up the coins and let them drop out of her funnelled hand into the cashbox. She closed it, locked it, tucked the key into the inside pocket of Andrew's travelling grip and wrapped the cash-box up in a soft shirt so the coins wouldn't rattle inside the bag. After she'd done that she sat down on the sofa again and waited for him to come back.

He arrived five minutes later, closing the door behind him and walking over towards their bedroom without even looking at her.

'Where did you go?' she asked. 'The beach?'

He didn't answer that, merely posed a curt question of his own. 'Are you ready to go downstairs now?'

'I'm ready.' She stood up, willing him to look at her. Dreading him looking at her.

He went into the bedroom. When he came back a few minutes later, dressed in the old clothes, he reached for the card with the poem written on it. 'Let's go, then.'

'Andy . . .'

His eyes were on her at last, roaming over her as she stood there gazing mutely back at him, her hazel eyes brimming with unshed tears.

326

'You always did look the part in that rig-out,' he said harshly, and stopped dead the words of supplication that were hovering on her lips.

They took the staff lift down to the ground floor. When they reached it he did as he'd always done, pulling back the metal mesh of the gate and allowing her to go out before him. She stepped out into the service corridor and turned to face him. 'Andy—' she said again.

'I don't want to talk to you.' Seizing her elbow with his free hand in a grip so strong it made her wince, he hustled her along the corridor to the ballroom. 'All I want is to get this over with.'

Had she hoped for a miracle: that the tale told in their dance would come true? Had she hoped that if she performed her steps with exquisite precision and strove to make her deportment and expression as perfect as they could be, fantasy would become reality? Knowing from the first bars of the music that he was matching her in giving their tango his all, had she hoped that he would forgive her for what she had really done?

If she'd had those hopes, she knew they'd been dashed to the ground long before the dance reached its climax. The applause of their audience rang in her ears, at once louder and more rapturous than ever before and somehow also coming from a very long way off.

Andrew's breath was warm on her face, but the inky-blue eyes locked with her own were cold and shuttered. Dark and opaque and as impenetrable as the sea in winter.

They travelled together to the railway station. 'Where should I go?' she asked him as the train to Inverness pulled in.

'I don't know where you should go. I have no idea where you should go. I don't care where you go.'

327

She was trembling, unable to believe that any of this was really happening. 'You don't ever want to see me again?'

'I wish I'd never met you.'

It couldn't have been worse if he had picked up a whip and struck her across the face with it. Yet despite those cruellest of words he brought his hand up to her face and brushed his fingertips across her cheek. 'Goodbye, Just Jean.'

'I did it for you,' she whispered. 'I did it for you.'

'I'd rather have died,' he said. 'I'd rather have died than have you turn yourself into a whore.'

'You on your own, young sir?'

When he nodded, the sleeping car attendant glanced down at his list. 'According to this there should be a Mr and a Mrs Logan travelling tonight.'

'There's been a change of plans,' he said wearily. 'Does it matter?'

'I don't suppose so. Although it would have been nice to have had more notice of any alteration. What time would you like your tea in the morning?'

'Whenever it suits you. I'm very tired. Can we close this door now?'

Once he was alone he stood for a moment resting his arms on the top bunk. Only this afternoon he'd been looking forward to this, wondering if it was possible to make love in a railway sleeping car. Knowing that he was going to try. Only this afternoon.

He turned and sat down heavily on the edge of the bottom bunk. So heavily that he banged the back of his head against the deep wooden edge of the top one. The stinging pain brought quick tears to his eyes.

'Och, Jean,' he said. '*Och, Jean!*'

As his voice wavered and cracked he bent forward, covered

his face with his hands and began to weep. He didn't notice
the train pulling out of the station, didn't feel it when it began
to gather speed. The racking sobs were shaking him from
head to foot.

Chapter 35

I T   M U S T   be nearly midnight. Sitting here on this beach, Jean had lost track of time. The moon was riding high, shining down on the dark waves in front of her like a searchlight. She was waiting for it to set.

She didn't know where she was. Yes, she did. The place was called Cullen. She'd come here because the woman in front of her at the booking office window at Nairn had bought a ticket to Cullen. It was as good a place as any.

I'd rather have died than have you turn yourself into a whore. I'd rather have died than have you turn yourself into a whore. I'd rather have died than have you turn yourself into a whore . . .

She'd walked down from the station carrying the old red and blue carpet bag that had been her mother's, along under the lee of the huge stone viaduct, past the cluster of houses on the shore. They called that the sea-town up here, the part of the village where the fishermen and their families lived.

A long sandy beach lay beyond it, stretching out away from a line made by three towering outcrops of gnarled and weathered rock. Glinting pink in the moonlight, they looked like the sails of a beached ship that had come to rest between the water's edge and the golf links.

Once the moon wasn't quite so bright Jean had decided that she was going to walk into the sea. At the moment she was speculating on whether she would end up in Norway or if the currents would carry her body up or down the coast. Perhaps she'd end up back at Nairn.

Maybe somebody walking their dog would find her on a beach further down the coast, part of the jetsam the sea tossed contemptuously back on to the land. She'd be in among the old logs and that seaweed that popped when you stood on it, and the detritus thrown overboard from passing ships.

In among the rubbish. Appropriate enough. That was where she belonged. She was a whore.

She studied the waves. One of the old salts down by the harbour in Nairn had told her some tale about every seventh wave being bigger than the ones which came before and after it. She began counting to see if that was true. In the end, she couldn't make up her mind whether it was or not.

Patterns, she supposed. People were always looking for patterns, something to help them make some sense and shape out of life. She stood up, leaving the carpet bag where it was, and walked down over the sand. The tide was coming in.

'Tears on the Incoming Tide'. That was the title of a story she'd once read. It had been a very sad story, all about a fisherman who fell in love with a seal-woman, one of the selkies. He'd hidden her sealskin so she couldn't go back to the sea but one day she found it. Even though the selkie loved the fisherman and the children she'd borne him, she couldn't resist the pull of her home in the sea.

Jean studied the waves in the moonlight and wondered if it was better to walk into them when the tide was coming in or when it was going out. Presumably the former would keep battering you against the shoreline. There were more clumps of rocks dotted along the edge of it. She'd be a right bloody mess after a battering against them.

331

Nobody would fancy her very much after that. Certainly not the men who had paid to sleep with her.

It would be a bit nasty for whoever found her, as well. An awful thought struck Jean. What if that person was a child, a wee boy or a girl running along the beach with their dog maybe? The dog would smell her, of course. Dogs had good noses. The child would come running eagerly up to see what their pet had uncovered and then find her.

Even if she hadn't been bashed against the rocks Jean couldn't see that anybody who had drowned would be a very pretty sight. This was something she hadn't thought of. She'd considered and rejected the idea of doing what Anna Karenina had done and flinging herself under a train. She'd decided it wasn't fair to make the train driver the instrument of your death.

She'd thought about renting a wee room somewhere and simply turning on the gas as Jim had done for himself and Annabel and their unborn child. That would be distressing for the landlady, not to mention the other lodgers. In the end she had come to the conclusion that drowning was the least offensive way of doing it.

She hadn't thought about the person who might find her body, though. She hadn't thought about that person being an impressionable child. If something like that happened to you when you were wee it was bound to affect you. It would probably affect you for the rest of your life.

Jean frowned. *The rest of your life.* She was measuring the rest of her life in minutes now. She tilted her head back and raised her face to the moon.

I'd rather have died than have you turn yourself into a whore.

I wish I'd never met you.

All she had to do now was take those few final steps and those burning, searing words would stop ricocheting around inside her head. All she had to do now was take those few final steps and the crushing pain and loneliness and desolation that had her in its grip would be gone.

I wish I'd never met you.

If he'd never met her, she would never have met him either. Where would she be now if she hadn't? Probably still skivvying at St Martin's Manse. It had been he who had got her out of there, after all.

Jean lowered her head to the waves. It wouldn't be long now before they were lapping over her feet. Should she take her shoes off?

While she was wondering about that it occurred to her that it wasn't strictly true to say it was Andrew who had got her out of St Martin's. Her own decision to ask him to teach her to dance in the church hall had set off the chain of events that had resulted in her leaving the place. She had made a choice, and that choice had inevitably led to consequences.

Life was full of consequences. You took one step and then another one and then another one and eventually you ended up somewhere you hadn't ever expected to find yourself. Backed into a corner at The Luxor, with only one way out. Standing on a beach at midnight, measuring the rest of your life in minutes.

Life wasn't like dancing. In a dance the steps did build up into a pattern. Learn how to follow that pattern and you'd bring yourself safely back to where you'd started from. Life was a lot more haphazard than that.

The water was lapping at Jean's toes. Any minute now her shoes were going to be ruined. The leather would never recover from a dousing in salt water.

Up in the sleeping town, a church bell began to ring out midnight.

The world is full of possibilities. That was what her mother had always said. At the moment there were only two possibilities open to Alison Dunlop's daughter. She could walk into the waves or she could step back from them. Choose the first possibility and the pain and anguish would end. Choose the first possibility and everything would end.

The world is full of possibilities.

He had taught her how to walk backwards without falling over. She did that now, retreating very slowly and deliberately to where she had left the old carpet bag. By the time the church bell tolled for the twelfth time, Jean had drawn back from the brink.

Chapter 36

INSTINCT GUIDED her. It led her off the beach, back beneath the looming stone of the enormous viaduct and up to the railway station and a long and cold wait for the first train of the morning heading for Aberdeen. By the late afternoon, two more wearisome train journeys later, Jean had crossed Scotland from north to south, from the East Coast to the West.

Catching her first glimpse of the Clyde after the train had rattled through Clydebank and Dalmuir and Bowling, she gazed out at the familiar landmarks. There was Dumbarton Rock and the castle that topped it. Then came Ardmore Point where the river widened and began to become the Firth of Clyde. On the other side of the water Port Glasgow and Greenock and Gourock sprawled along the water's edge. Shortly before they arrived at Helensburgh the train stopped at Craigendoran.

That was hard to bear. Gazing across at the pier from where the Clyde steamers left, it was impossible not to see Andrew and herself walking down there on their wedding day. Two summers ago, Jean thought, before mentally correcting herself. A lifetime ago.

Once the train had slid to a halt in front of the buffers at Helensburgh, she walked out of the station and down Sinclair

Street to the sea front. When she found herself stopping outside the Italian café on Clyde Street to which her mother had occasionally taken her as a treat on Saturday afternoons, she gave some serious consideration to the possibility that not only instinct but also Alison Dunlop's spirit was somehow leading her steps. There was a small card in the window: 'Room to Let'.

She pushed open the door of the café and found herself enveloped in warmth and noise and bustle. Cheerfully harassed, speaking that glorious mixture of Italian-accented Scots to her customers and rapid-fire Italian to whoever was in the back shop, Jean recognised the middle-aged woman behind the tall glass counter.

There was no reason why she should associate the pale young woman who stood in front of her with any of the hundreds of children to whom she'd served ice creams or fish teas over the years, and she didn't. She did agree to let Jean the room, apparently too busy to notice the oddness of a tenant who handed over the requested deposit and month's rent in advance without even asking to see the accommodation first.

It was above the café, a sparsely furnished but clean and high-ceilinged room with a window overlooking the esplanade. Jean lay down on top of the covers of the double bed, which stood in one corner of it, and slept the clock round.

Waking at seven the next morning, she realised with some surprise that she was ravenously hungry. Then she remembered that it was almost forty-eight hours since she had last eaten anything, not since she'd taken lunch with Andrew in the staff dining room at Nairn the day before yesterday. He'd been talking nineteen to the dozen, regaling their friends and fellow staff members with the details of the adventure on which young Mr and Mrs Logan were about to embark.

Struggling up on to her elbows, Jean surrendered herself to the grief, her sobs loud and ragged. She'd done it for him. Only for him. She'd had to force herself to do it, gritting her teeth so she could smile and pretend to like everything they had wanted to do to her and have her do to them in return. How *dare* he have accused her of having enjoyed it? Of having wanted to do it? *How dare he*?

'You did it too, Andy,' she whispered. 'You did it with Mona Forsyth. What would have happened to you or me if I hadn't done it? I'd have been out on the streets and you might have died.'

I'd rather have died than have you turn yourself into a whore.

Easy enough to say when he hadn't died. Easy enough to say when the terrible choice she had made had helped him to live.

'I hate you, Andrew Logan,' Jean cried. '*I hate you!*' She coiled her arms around her head, as though she were warding off a blow. 'And I wish I had never met *you*!'

Her flailing hands made contact with the bedstead. There was a clank as metal hit metal. She drew her left arm down, put her hand in front of her face and studied her wedding ring. Last night she had given her new landlady her maiden name but had forgotten to remove the ring. She hoped the woman had been too busy to notice.

The simple gold band had never been off her finger since Andrew had put it there the morning after their reunion at the sanatorium. Before that it had been on and off lots of times. She should have taken that as an omen. It had never been destined to stay on her finger.

She slid it off, weighing it for a moment in the palm of her hand. Then she lifted her hand and hurled the ring across the room. Once she heard it strike the wall and fall to the floor she swung her legs out over the edge of the bed. She would wash

337

and change and go downstairs to the café and find out if they served breakfast. Once she had some food inside her she was going for a walk. A very long walk.

She'd forgotten how steep Sinclair Street became as it climbed up out of the town. It was a good job all of that dancing had made her so fit.

After the road passed Helensburgh Upper railway station and shortly thereafter became Luss Road, the brae levelled out. Jean found herself passing the curling pond and then she was out in the country. The hills of the Highlands rose in the distance and in front of them soft and rolling countryside ran down in a patchwork of fields and moorland towards Loch Lomond.

It was another twenty minutes before she reached the end of the track that led to the farm where Jamie Colquhoun had spent his life working as a shepherd. Her grandparents' cottage, the one in which Jean had spent her girlhood, was halfway between here and the farm. It wasn't far away but the lie of the land meant that it wasn't visible from the main road.

She knew exactly how to get there from here all the same. The memories flooding her brain were intense, colourful and vivid. You went along the farm road until after the bend, climbed over a stile set into the dry stone dyke and walked over a jewel-bright sward of rough green grass dotted with daisies and buttercups to reach the cottage.

She could remember too that the low stone building stood above a trickling and peaty burn that you crossed by three stepping stones. Behind the house, and taller than it, stood a vast rhododendron bush and a line of Scots pines at whose feet waved a profusion of bluebells.

Gripped by nostalgia so strong that the pain was physical, Jean stood and wondered if she should head for the cottage.

338

While she was trying to make up her mind, she heard the chuntering of a car. As it turned into the farm road the middle-aged woman who was driving it raised a hand to Jean in greeting. Country folk. They always acknowledged anyone they saw on the road. Seconds later brakes squealed, the vehicle ground to a halt and the driver stepped out and looked back at her.

'It's never wee Jeannie Dunlop. Is it?'

How kind people could be. The farmer's wife insisted Jean join her and her husband at their midday meal. After that she walked with her to the cottage, introduced her to the current shepherd and his family, told her she was welcome to visit at any time and asked if she wouldn't give Jean a lift back to Helensburgh.

'Och, no,' Jean said. 'I don't want to put you to any trouble.'

'It's no trouble at all,' the woman said firmly, and in little more than ten minutes Jean found herself back down the hill. Reluctant to go inside out of the warm September air, she walked through Colquhoun Square, reacquainting herself with the town and thinking about the friendly enquiries that had been put to her this afternoon as to what she was now doing with herself.

She had responded with a heavily edited version of the truth, saying only that she'd been doing hotel work in Nairn but had decided to come home to the West Coast.

Pointing out that hotels locally were unlikely to be taking on staff now that the season was more or less over, the farmer's wife had mentioned that she had seen a card in the window of the local bookshop advertising for help. Would Jean maybe fancy that kind of work?

Following the directions the woman had given her, Jean walked through into West Princes Street and found the bookshop. The card was still in the window. She studied it for a moment.

The money she had in her Post Office account wouldn't last for ever. She was going to have to look for a job sooner or later. Now was as good a time as any. She supposed.

When the bell on the door pinged, a woman with a mass of auburn hair piled loosely on top of her head glanced over at Jean from behind a big table in dark wood, which obviously served as a counter. Another woman and a young girl were standing in front of the till, which sat on it.

'Be right with you,' said the woman on the business side of the till. 'Please feel free to browse.'

'Thank you,' Jean said, and skirted her way past a middle-aged man, who smiled a little absently at her before resuming his own browsing.

The shop was well laid out, with neatly hand-lettered notices indicating on which shelves different types of books were to be found. Jean scanned the titles in the history section, half listening to what was being said at the counter. The woman and the little girl were obviously mother and daughter and it was equally obvious from the friendly tone of the conversation that they were regular customers. The girl was buying two books with money she'd been given for her tenth birthday, excitedly sharing that information with the auburn-haired woman.

Once the purchase was completed she saw her customers out, closed the door behind them and walked over to Jean. 'She's a great reader, that wee one. It's nice to see. Now, can I help you? Or shall I leave you in peace?'

'It's about the job,' Jean said abruptly. 'Would it be yourself I would ask?'

'Indeed. My husband and I own and run this place. Are you interested in the position, Miss . . .?'

'Dunlop. And yes, I think I might be interested. Are you looking for someone with any particular kind of experience or qualifications?'

'Two main attributes are required for this job. The ability to get on with people and a love of books. Think you might fit the bill?'

'I love reading,' Jean said. 'And I've been doing a job where I've been working with people all of the time.'

'And that job was what exactly?'

'For the last year I've been employed as a professional dancing partner at the Royal Cawdor Hotel in Nairn.'

'Gosh, that sounds very glamorous! You don't think you might find working here quite dull by comparison?'

Jean shook her head. 'It wasn't always so glamorous.'

'Sore feet, I suppose,' the auburn-haired woman said sympathetically. 'And lots of people treading on them. That must have called for great tact and diplomacy on your part.'

'Oh, yes,' Jean said. 'You had to make sure the guests never felt uncomfortable about things like that.'

'Just as we insist that the customer is always right.' The auburn-haired woman grinned suddenly, making the freckles dance across her nose. 'Even when they're a pain in the neck. Although I'm glad to say we don't attract too many of that sort.' She stretched out her right arm, indicating an open doorway half-covered by a heavy red velvet curtain. 'Why don't you and I go through to the back shop and have some tea and I'll tell you what the job involves and what it pays and you can tell me a little more about yourself?'

'What if any customers come in?'

'We'll hear the bell on the door. That's what it's there for. And Mr MacLean over there knows to ring the bell on the table if he needs any assistance. Shall we go on through?'

Jean looked at her. 'Is there any chance you might just take me on trust? You could try me out for a few days and see if I suit. I'd be happy to work for nothing. You wouldn't have to pay me unless you decide to take me on.'

A strand of gleaming auburn hair had escaped from its pins. The woman tucked it away again and surveyed Jean thoughtfully.

'I could start right now if you like.' She gave an odd little laugh. 'I have no other calls on my time at the moment.'

The woman continued to study her. Jean bit her lip.

'I suppose it is asking too much. For you to take me on trust, I mean. You don't know me from Adam, after all. That was a silly thing to ask. I'm sorry,' she said, turning away to head for the door out into the street. 'I'm really very sorry for wasting your time.'

She already had the door open. The sounds of the outside world rushed into the peaceful atmosphere of the bookshop. A horse-drawn cart trundled by. Two seagulls wheeled overhead, squawking.

'Wait, Miss Dunlop. Hang on a wee minute!'

Jean felt the older woman take hold of the other end of the long door handle and push the door firmly shut.

'It's not asking too much. But you can start on Monday. And you'll not be working for nothing. A fair day's work for a fair day's pay, that's our motto.'

Jean lifted the back of her hand to her mouth and bent her head over it. The woman standing beside her didn't speak. All she did was lay one of her own hands on Jean's sleeve and wait for her to look up again.

'You're very kind,' Jean said at last. 'Thank you. You're sure you want to take me on?'

'I'm sure,' came the brisk response. 'As I'm sure that you're going to have a cup of tea with me before you leave. While we're drinking it we can talk books. Perhaps you could tell me which ones you've read over the past year. Would that be all right with you, Miss Dunlop?'

'That's fine by me, Mrs . . .?'

'McIntosh,' said the auburn-haired woman. She had a lovely voice, deep for a woman, and very mellow. 'But you can call me Avril. We're very informal here.'

Jean gazed into the warm and compassionate eyes. 'I'm Jean,' she said, and managed a shaky smile.

Chapter 37

'AND HOW are we this afternoon, my dear?'

Jean smiled at the woman. One of the shop's most faithful customers, she'd got to know her well over the last six months. The retired school teacher was a voracious reader, particularly fond of detective stories.

'I'm fine,' Jean told her now, taking the yellow-jacketed book that was being proffered to her where she stood at the till. 'You've decided on this one?'

'Have you read it?'

'I have. And I would thoroughly recommend it. It's a really good read and I don't think you'll be disappointed.'

'Then I'll have it. Put it in a bag for me, dear, would you?'

Once the bell on the door had signalled the woman's departure, Avril McIntosh finished putting an armful of new books out on the shelves and walked over to the counter to look approvingly at Jean. 'Another satisfied customer?'

'I hope so.'

'What happens if someone wants to buy a book you've read and haven't liked?' asked Avril.

'I try to be diplomatic. Although that can be hard sometimes,' Jean added, lips twitching ruefully as she indicated the book that was lying open beneath the counter.

Avril and Tom McIntosh were unusual employers and in

many ways unconventional people, sharing both the work of the bookshop and the upbringing of their small children. Their somewhat bohemian bent expressed itself also in the warm welcome they gave customers who spent as much time browsing as buying, and in their attitude to their young assistant reading whilst on duty. They actively encouraged her to do so.

'What's wrong with this one?' asked Avril, coming round behind the counter to peer at the dust jacket. 'I thought you liked historical novels.'

'I *love* historical novels. But this one's terrible. The characters are wooden, no self-respecting woman would ever fall for such a selfish and pompous hero and it's full of gadzookery into the bargain.'

Avril chuckled. It was she who had introduced Jean to the term. 'All "stap me vitals" and "forsooth" and "methinks"?' she queried. 'The way no real person ever spoke?'

'The way no real person ever acted, either,' Jean said in some disgust. 'I'm afraid I'm going to have to deliver the Dorothy Parker verdict on this one.'

'Let's have it, then,' Avril said, laughing again and holding out her hand palm upwards in invitation. The Dorothy Parker verdict was something else Jean had learned from her.

' "This is not a book to be tossed aside lightly," ' Jean obliged. ' "It should be thrown with great force". Honestly, sometimes you wonder why books ever get published!'

Avril folded her arms over the flowery pinafore that swept down over the impending latest addition to the McIntosh family. 'Well, Jean,' she said, 'maybe publishers don't get sent nearly enough good manuscripts for their consideration.'

Jean gave her employer a dirty look. 'Don't start that again.'

Having confessed some time before that she'd had one short story published in a women's magazine the previous summer, she was finding herself on the receiving end of considerable encouragement to pursue a writing career. Both Avril and Tom would be equally happy for her to write rather than read during those times when the shop was quiet.

'I've hardly got a writing career,' she had protested. 'One wee story published in one wee magazine.'

'Don't denigrate your achievement,' Tom McIntosh told her with uncharacteristic severity when she said that. 'Or your talent. How is it that a good–looking and intelligent girl like you has absolutely no confidence in herself?'

She could have told him: some of it at least. She knew she would have shocked both him and Avril if she had. They didn't even know that she was a married woman. They were good people. They had a liberal outlook on life and did their utmost neither to judge nor to condemn other people. Yet there was a naïvety about them. Or perhaps innocence was a kinder word.

Jean had lost her innocence, and she knew she was never going to be able to tell anybody how that had happened. She was condemned to keep the whole thing locked up inside herself, constantly reviewing the sequence of events that had led to her and Andrew parting. Sometimes she thought her head would burst with the pressure of it all.

She'd developed two strategies to help her cope. She lost herself in books, no sooner finishing one than she picked up another. When she wasn't doing that she walked, got out into the fresh air and moved, pushing herself until her body was exhausted.

There were times when neither of those tactics was successful in forcing her brain to shut itself down. There were dozens of nights when she trudged back to the room above the café and found sleep simply wouldn't come, when she lay there and found herself overwhelmed by the memories and emotions.

Shame. Sorrow. Anger. Sometimes she was so full of rage she could hardly breathe.

Admitting defeat at four o'clock on the Sunday morning following her twenty-first birthday, she got out of bed, trailing one of the blankets with her. She wrapped it around herself and sat huddled in one of the two armchairs that stood in front of the window, watching dawn break over the Firth.

There was a vicious wind blowing, whipping the waves up into angry peaks and troughs. Jean nursed the cup of tea she had made and thought what an ungrateful bitch she was. The McIntoshes were so kind to her. On her birthday they had given her a tea-party at their house with a cake and a present and everything.

'Very unsubtle,' Tom had laughed as she'd opened her parcel to find a ream of paper and a child's pencil case full of writing implements, 'but we're hoping you might take the hint!'

Jean had accepted the well-meaning gift with a grace and enthusiasm that had cost her dear. Tom and Avril weren't to know that it reminded her so painfully of another gift. Where was that, anyway?

Setting her tea on the green oil-cloth that covered the floor, Jean stood up and went to look for it. She found both the pad of paper and the beautiful pen Andrew had given her the year before in the old carpet bag. Having emptied out only what she needed from that, she had thrust it into the deepest recesses of the huge and spectacularly ugly wardrobe, which occupied half of one wall of her little bedsitting room last September and had never looked at it since.

She took both objects back to the armchair and leafed through the pages of the pad, finding the scene she'd written that day at the Clava Cairns and one or two more added in

347

snatched moments during last year's hectic summer at the hotel. She tore those pages off and laid them on the floor beside her rapidly cooling tea. After she'd done that she curled up in the armchair, pulled the blanket around herself again and began to write.

When she looked up again she blinked in surprise. The day outside her window was well advanced and had turned out bright and sunny. The wind had obviously died down and both sky and sea were blue. Soon the esplanade would be full of people strolling along, enjoying the sunshine and eating ice creams.

Jean laid paper and pen aside, yawned and stretched luxuriously. 'I could do with some sunshine myself,' she murmured. 'Maybe I'll treat myself to an ice cream too.'

Later that day, returning to her room after a leisurely walk along to Rhu, she read what she had written in the early morning. She had covered everything: from the moment she and Andrew had met in the *palais* in Partick until they had separated at the railway station at Nairn.

She cried a little, carried the writing pad and the pen to the big wardrobe and opened one of the half-width drawers in its base which held the handkerchief case in which she kept the letters he had sent her from the sanatorium. Her wedding ring was in there too. She'd walked around it for a week after she'd flung it across the room before deciding it was daft to leave it lying on the floor.

Once she had pushed the drawer firmly shut she crossed the room and stooped to retrieve the sheets of paper she'd torn from the writing pad: the start of her Jacobite book.

Her book. Jean's eyes narrowed as she read it through. Could she really take these few thousand words and develop them into a book? Real historical events with a thrilling story woven through them. Characters she could direct to do whatever she wanted them to do. She'd have the power to make everything work out all right in the end. Or at least how she wanted it to work out. The ends of her mouth lifted wryly. Unlike real life.

Writing a book was a daunting prospect. A challenging prospect. A thrilling prospect. Jean thought of one of the customers of the bookshop and the Chinese proverb he was so fond of quoting: 'The journey of a thousand miles begins with but a single step.'

She fetched the paper and pencil case the McIntoshes had given her, sat down at the square table in the middle of the room, pulled a fresh sheet from the top of the ream of paper and took out one of the pens. Centred at the top of the sheet she wrote two words: 'Chapter One'.

She laughed. It was a start.

Chapter 38

I T T O O K her two years, working during the evenings and on Sundays. Soon she was setting her alarm clock for 6 a.m. so she could also get some writing done in the morning before she went to work. She knew the McIntoshes would have been more than happy for her to work on her manuscript at the shop but she couldn't bring herself to admit to them or to anyone else that she was actually writing a book.

It belonged to her alone, as did the characters: although it wasn't long before she was chuckling at her own naïve belief that those same characters would do as she told them to. She quickly discovered that both the people she had researched and those she thought she had invented had a habit of saying and doing entirely unexpected things: things that brought the story alive.

'And what a story it is!' Avril McIntosh said admiringly when Jean finally summoned up the courage to ask her and Tom to read the manuscript.

'You liked it?' asked a furiously blushing Jean. 'You really liked it?'

Avril slapped the manuscript down on the counter and seized her hands. 'Liked it? I loved it! It's got everything: romance, friendships across the political divide, heroes and villains and lovers. Tom *adored* the sword-fights and battle scenes. So did I. It's wonderful, Jean.'

Avril pulled Jean over to the desk and sat her down in front of the shop's typewriter. 'Now you have to type it up. While you're doing that we'll all put our heads together and work out which publisher you should send it to.'

'Is that what we're going to do?' Jean asked in a very small voice, feeling a little weak with the excitement of it all.

'Most definitely,' Avril said, handing her the manuscript. 'Get typing, young lady.'

'How's it going?' Tom McIntosh asked a fortnight later, swinging round to talk to Jean after having completed a sale.

'Dead slow and stop,' she groaned as she looked up from the typewriter. 'Especially as I keep spotting passages which need more editing and refining.'

'But that's good, isn't it?' he queried. 'You're making the book as good as it possibly can be before you send it off.'

'That *is* good,' she agreed. 'I only wish I was able to hit the keys a little more efficiently. More quickly and with fewer mistakes. When the autumn comes and night school starts I'm going to enrol for a typing class. I think I might write the next one straight on to a typewriter. I could maybe buy myself a portable one.'

He smiled at her. 'So there's going to be a next book? Same historical period?'

'There are plenty more stories to tell about it,' she said enthusiastically. 'And there are characters who play a minor role in this book who seem to be trying to attract my attention to them already. I'm sorry,' she said, laughing up at him. 'Does that make me sound terribly fey, talking about my characters as though they're real people?'

'No,' he said with a decisive shake of his always unruly head, 'it makes you sound like a woman who's found her

351

métier. If your characters are real people to you that's how they're going to come across to the readers.'

'I hope so,' Jean replied. She wasn't at all convinced she would ever have readers other than the McIntoshes. Despite that, she'd been indulging for some time now in a very satisfying little daydream where Tom and Avril opened the first printed copy of her book to discover that she had dedicated it to them. A little shyly, she expressed her feelings out loud. 'I'm really grateful to both of you for everything you've done for me.'

Tom McIntosh waved his hand in airy dismissal. 'Think nothing of it. It's all self-interest really. When you're a best-selling author, Avril and I intend to bask in your reflected glory. "We helped her on her way, you know" – we'll be saying that to everybody and you'll think we're completely insufferable.'

'I'll never think that,' Jean said earnestly. 'And I appreciate a lot what you've done for me. I really do. You and Avril and the children and the bookshop and the customers and everyone encouraging me to write . . . Well, all of that has more or less saved my life.'

Tom's deep voice was very gentle. 'You'd been having a tough time of it before you found your way back to Helensburgh?'

'Did I cut such a tragic figure?' she asked ruefully.

'You're a much happier person now than you were when you first came to us. All that ailed you water under the bridge now?'

'Almost,' she said, smiling up at him and grateful all over again because he and Avril never pried or probed into her past. 'Shouldn't I relieve you at the till?'

'Nope.' He hoisted himself up on to the stool behind the counter and began turning over the pages of his *Glasgow*

Herald. 'Right at this moment we're not exactly overwhelmed with customers.'

'So what's happening in the world?' For some time now she'd been guiltily aware that she was much more caught up in the politics and crises of the eighteenth century than those of the twentieth.

'Europe's about to go up like a powder keg,' he said cheerfully. 'There's nothing you or I can do to sort that out, Jean. So get on with your typing.'

Four weeks later she had it done. Under the benign dictatorship of Avril and Tom, she parcelled up the typescript and sent it off to a publisher in Glasgow. After that she tried to pretend to herself, the McIntoshes and a large proportion of the regular customers of the bookshop that she wasn't lying in wait for the postie every morning.

Now that she had sent her characters off to seek their fortune, she was seized by an emotion it took her a few days to recognise. It was as if she had suffered a bereavement. All of those real and imagined people who'd been living and laughing and falling in love and fighting one another inside her head for the past two years had gone, and she missed them dreadfully.

For the next week or so, in a fruitless attempt to compensate for all of those hours they'd paid her to sit there typing her own book, Jean made it her business to wrest every last little task in the shop out of Avril and Tom's hands. Once she realised that this was driving them mad, she decided she had to force herself to relax and rejoin the real world. Although 'relax' wasn't a very good word to use.

Europe was in the grip of a crisis. Adolf Hitler wanted *Lebensraum*. Which, as Tom McIntosh put it, basically meant that he had a shopping list of the countries he wanted to bring within his new German Reich. Having the Sudetenland

– an area heavily populated by a long-established community of ethnic Germans – within its borders, Czechoslovakia appeared to be at the top of that list.

As the summer of 1938 gave way to autumn, the crisis deepened and intensified. It was pretty hard for anyone to relax when defensive trenches were being dug in public parks and on golf courses throughout the length and breadth of Britain; when the various emergency services and voluntary organisations began to rehearse their responses to the air raids everyone feared so much; when protective masks were issued to protect young and old from the even more feared gas attacks.

At the end of September the Prime Minister flew to Munich for the third in a series of talks aiming to resolve the situation. By the end of those discussions the German dictator had an agreement that he could incorporate the Sudetenland into Germany. It was supposed to be a compromise, a way of containing Hitler's territorial ambitions by giving him a little of what he wanted.

Two weeks after Neville Chamberlain flew back to Britain claiming to have secured 'peace in our time', Jean received a letter telling her that her book had been accepted.

Lunch in Glasgow with her publishers. What a wonderful phrase that was. She, wee Jeannie Dunlop, was having lunch in Glasgow with her publishers. She wished her mother and her grandparents were still alive. She knew they would have been proud of her. Jean thought wistfully that if things had worked out differently someone else would have been proud of her too.

After lunch she shook hands with her editor and smilingly announced her intention of walking to the railway station to catch the train back to Helensburgh. She went via Royal Exchange Square and The Luxor.

She stopped for a moment to study its elegant and sumptuous frontage. A well-dressed couple came out, a group of three ladies went in. Business as usual, by the looks of it.

There had been moments when Jean had dreamed of storming back in there, climbing to the very top of the grand staircase and yelling out a succinct but graphic description of the sleazy world that oozed beneath the layers of glamour and sophistication. She'd imagined herself naming names, shaming the men who took what they wanted from girls half their age while their wives remained in blissful ignorance.

Standing there reflecting on it all now, Jean found that the desire had faded. What was it that Tom McIntosh had asked her back at the start of the summer? 'All that ailed you water under the bridge now?'

Jean lifted her chin. Yes. It was all water under the bridge now. Or it would be if she took the final step. She walked past The Luxor and on into Queen Street. She had remembered that there was a lawyer's office just round the corner from the square.

She read the names on the brass plaque by the front door and didn't recognise any of them. Knowing that she was going to do this, she had known also that she didn't want to find herself sitting across a desk from anyone she had known in her previous life at The Luxor.

'May I ask what it's in connection with?' asked the receptionist in a discreetly low voice when Jean requested an appointment for the following week. 'It's helpful for the partners to know in advance.'

Jean didn't shout her answer but she didn't lower her voice either. 'It's in connection with a divorce,' she said firmly. 'I want to find out how I go about divorcing my husband.'

* * *

355

A letter from Scotland. A letter with a Glasgow postmark. The hotel's address was typewritten, though. Well, maybe she had bought herself a typewriter. Or maybe she had access to a machine wherever she was working now. The letter could be from her. Although the buff envelope was a large one. It felt pretty full too.

He'd never find out anything unless he opened it. Andrew took a deep breath, put his thumb under the flap and pulled.

Desertion. She wanted a divorce on the grounds of desertion. It should be a straightforward process as long as he didn't contest the action.

He read it all through once. Then, standing over the writing bureau in his own private sitting room, he let the papers fall from his fingers. From the desk he pulled out the umpteenth draft of the letter he'd been trying to write for the past three months.

He'd had no idea where to send it to, of course. He'd written to his wee sister Chrissie, just in case Jean had made any approach to his family. When that long shot failed to produce anything, the idea had begun to form in his head of commissioning a private detective in Glasgow who might be able to track her down, find out where she was living now.

He'd decided he had to write the letter first. He'd tried draft after draft, unable to get it right, unable even to work out what exactly it was that he wanted to say to her. While he'd been wrestling with himself, she had made her decision.

His eyes dropped to the letter from the lawyer. *Desertion.* He couldn't argue with that. He had deserted her: physically, mentally and emotionally.

Andrew studied his own draft letter for a moment. Then he tore it into four neat pieces, threw them on the fire and walked over to the window. He stood there, looking out at the beautiful blue lake, for a very long time.

Chapter 39

JEAN'S FIRST novel was published in the spring of 1939, to commercial success and a satisfying amount of critical acclaim. Well, apart from the two book reviewers whom she decided had probably had very unhappy childhoods. Tom McIntosh had a different interpretation to offer for one of those at least.

'Sour grapes,' he said briskly. 'The woman's a failed novelist herself. Take no notice, Jean.'

She accepted his advice. She also arranged with him and Avril that she would work part-time at the shop and went out and bought herself a shiny new Underwood typewriter so she could spend the rest of her week writing at home. That was new too – still on the front and overlooking the Firth, but much more spacious, with two bedrooms and two reception rooms, and a smart new kitchen and bathroom all behind her own private front door.

The night before she moved from the bedsit above the café she brought out the account she had written of her and Andrew's story. She didn't read it through again. Hadn't she learned very early on in life how dangerous it could be to revisit the past?

Even though it was the middle of summer she lit a fire in the grate and waited patiently until it was well established, glowing a bright orangey-red. Then she laid the pad on top of the coals and watched the paper curl and ignite.

Burned to a crisp.

Dead and buried.

Water under the bridge.

Jean lifted the poker and held it against the paper so that every last fragment of it would be consumed by the flames.

On a sunny Sunday morning at the beginning of September, Jean sat out on the grass in Avril and Tom's garden, keeping the children occupied and distracted while their parents listened to the Prime Minister broadcasting to the nation. How can they be going to start a war when the weather's so nice? That was the joke that was currently going the rounds.

She knew from the moment the McIntoshes stepped through the French windows that the nervous joking was over. Tom took his offspring for a wander down the long garden while Avril told her what Neville Chamberlain had said.

'So we're at war with Germany.'

'Incredible, isn't it?' Avril said sombrely. 'However much we all knew that it was coming.'

'How did Chamberlain finish up his speech?'

'Something about may God bless us all and may we defend the right. Oh,' Avril continued, frowning in concentration as she tried to remember the exact words, 'he also said that we would be fighting against "evil things. Brute force, bad faith, injustice, oppression and persecution." And he was sure that right would prevail.'

'Right will only prevail if we all put our shoulders to the wheel.'

'Jean?' came the anxious response.

She smiled at her friend. 'I've think I've just come to a momentous decision, Avril.'

'And what would that be?'

Her tone was light, almost flippant, but the determination that lay beneath it came through loud and clear. 'I've decided that my country needs me. I'm going to join up.'

PART IV

Chapter 40

January 1944

'FOR GOODNESS' sake,' Jean said to the girl sitting on the other side of her desk, 'have you no self-respect, Private?'

The young woman looked up at her through her eyelashes, ashamed and penitent, but still not entirely able to stop playing the vamp. Well, if she thought that the big eyes, quivering bottom lip and artfully tilted head were going to have any effect whatsoever on her exasperated welfare officer she had another think coming.

At the wrong end of a long day, Jean was in no mood to pull her punches. She'd had occasion to warn this girl before about her behaviour. Now that behaviour had led to its sordid, if logical, conclusion. She folded her arms and fixed this erring member of the ATS with a stern and unwavering gaze. 'Are you proud of the reputation you've earned for yourself in this camp?'

When no answer was forthcoming, Jean posed an even harsher question. 'You do know what they call girls like you, don't you?'

That provoked some sort of a response: a mumbled one.

'I didn't hear you,' Jean said crisply. 'Lift your head and speak up. And that's an order.' The steel that had entered her voice ensured that it was obeyed.

'Officers' groundsheets.'

'*Are* you proud of having earned that name?'

'No. But some of the officers are so charming. Especially the Americans and the Poles. In the heat of the moment you don't think about things like self-respect.' She'd said that last sentence in a way which implied Jean couldn't possibly know anything about the heat of the moment and the overwhelming emotions that went with it.

'That nasty little ailment you've contracted is going to last a lot longer than a moment.'

The sullen bravado cracked. 'I know!' the girl wailed. 'Oh, Captain Dunlop, there's no need for my parents to know anything, is there?'

As the tears welled up and spilled over, Jean stood up and walked round the desk. There was a time for severity and a time to offer a shoulder to cry on.

Twenty minutes later, she'd fed the miscreant hot sugary tea and biscuits and sent her on her way with instructions to get her kit together for immediate transfer to a military hospital twenty miles away. She'd also advised her to thank her lucky stars and Sir Alexander Fleming for the invention of penicillin and to consider being a bit more discerning in the future.

'Not that you'll pay a blind bit of notice,' Jean muttered to herself once the door had closed. 'You're away from home for the first time in your life, off the leash with too many healthy young men within flirting distance and the adrenaline's pumping through everyone's veins.'

Rolling her shoulders to relax the tension in them, she walked over to the window set high in one of the four square corner towers of this lovely Georgian mansion, which had been commandeered for the duration. Leaning her elbows on the high windowsill, she gazed out at the grounds. Once among the finest formal gardens in three counties, they now housed an assortment of hastily thrown-up buildings.

The house and the camp contained within them people engaged on a variety of tasks. One of the most visible and labour-intensive of those was the supply and fuel depot that serviced the military bases in the surrounding area.

The young women who took in, organised and reissued those supplies lived in the six utilitarian wooden huts Jean could see from the window. Next to the accommodation was a large and equally utilitarian vegetable patch. It had already been dug over so that the frost could get at the ground to help break it up in readiness for planting up as soon as the weather would permit. 'Dig for Victory' was a slogan that was taken very seriously in a camp housing several hundred young women with healthy appetites: appetites for all sorts of things.

'Human nature,' Jean murmured. 'It's only human nature. Who am I to be taking a high moral stance, anyway? Apart from the fact that it's my job, of course.'

That was the services for you: lots of square pegs in round holes. When she'd joined up back in 1939 she had expected that she might be drafted into the sort of job that required the ability to string a few words together in a vaguely coherent way. She'd rather fancied the black arts: those currently being practised by the Ministry of Information. Propaganda and counter-propaganda perhaps, or the delicate balancing act of the necessary censorship of a national press that valued its freedom above all other things.

In their wisdom, the powers that be decided she'd make an ideal welfare officer. 'My wife loves your writing,' said the bluff major who assigned her after she'd completed her basic training. 'Says you might be telling tales of the olden days but that it's obvious you really understand people and what makes them tick. God knows, we're going to need lots of sensible women like yourself to keep some of these silly little chits on the straight and narrow. We have a responsibility to their parents to send their dear little daughters home as innocent as when they left.'

'But I'm not a soft-centred person,' Jean protested, silently wondering if he also planned to sit on the beach like King Canute and command the tide to go back out. 'Quite a cynic, really.'

'Exactly what we need,' he'd countered. 'Compassion, common sense and strictness as and when required. But we'll keep mum about you being a writer, eh?' He tapped the side of his nose. 'Understand you include the occasional rather *racy* passage. Nothing wrong with that, of course. But it might undermine your authority all the same.'

Why, Jean had thought, because I try to write honestly about sex? Because my book's set in a bawdy age when men and women were more honest with themselves about their drives and desires? She'd kept that observation to herself, contenting herself with the knowledge that her soon-to-be-published second novel contained quite a few racy passages too.

She remained ruefully aware of the irony of her position as guardian of the morals of the young women of the ATS. Then again, they were choosing the paths they skipped so carelessly down. She hadn't exactly chosen the sort of life she'd led back at The Luxor.

During her various postings before she'd come to this camp she'd had three – well, what she would call them? Romances? Flirtatious friendships? Neither of those descriptions seemed to fit relationships she hadn't allowed to step over a very well-defined line, which hadn't lasted very long and which hadn't led to anything. She and the men involved had been ships that pass in the night, that was all.

Despite several offers, since she'd been posted to this camp in November of 1942 she'd resolutely refused to get involved with anyone in that way. She couldn't decide whether that was because she didn't want to run the risk of people gossiping about her or if she just couldn't be bothered to get involved again in the silly games men and women played.

Wondering what delights might be in store in the mess tonight, Jean extinguished the desk lamp and walked through to the main welfare office.

'Oh!' she said, startled to find herself confronted by a uniformed masculine back. 'You must be the new chaplain. We weren't expecting you till tomorrow.'

'The vagaries of rail travel in wartime,' laughed the fair-haired and broad-shouldered young man who turned to greet her, the dog collar he wore under his army jacket immediately confirming Jean's surmise as to his identity. 'Usually they get you in a week late. Sometimes they surprise you and do the opposite. I'm Peter Hilton. Captain Peter Hilton.'

'Jean Dunlop. Also a captain.' As her hand disappeared into his, she registered the fact that he was rather tall. He looked to be about the same age as herself, either in his late twenties or just into his thirties.

'A Scotch lass?' he queried, adding a further question when she nodded. 'Whereabouts in Scotland, exactly?'

'A place called Helensburgh. Ever heard of it?'

'No,' he admitted, his grin as broad as it was disarming. 'My knowledge of the geography of Scotland is pretty limited. I was hoping you might say Edinburgh or Glasgow or Aberdeen. I've a vague idea of where they all are.'

'Helensburgh's about thirty miles down the Clyde from Glasgow. A seaside town. Where are you from yourself?'

'A place called Newcastle. Ever heard of it?'

'Och, I've heard of Newcastle!'

'*Och*,' he said, 'I dinna think ye have, Captain Dunlop.'

'You know,' Jean said, folding her arms across her breasts, 'since I ventured south of the border I've been subjected to some truly diabolical attempts at a Scottish accent. That one takes the cake. While I'm at it, I should point out that although I'm a bit long in the tooth to be referred to as a "lass" if you must do it the correct term is "Scots" lass. "Scotch" refers only to broth and whisky.'

'You live and learn. But I'm a quick study. I won't make the same mistake again. Although I probably will continue to subject you to my truly diabolical attempt at a Scottish accent. I'm afraid I have a very juvenile sense of humour.'

Jean laughed, liking him. Her memories of the Reverend Ronald Fairbairn had always made her wary of men of the cloth, very much disinclined to give them the benefit of the doubt. This man seemed to be of a different stamp. 'Where is your Newcastle, then?'

'It's a tiny village in Suffolk. Blink and you'll miss it.'

'But you do,' she hazarded. 'Miss it, I mean?'

'Yes and no. My parents are gone now and I seldom go back there. Nowadays my heart lies in an equally tiny village in the Lake District. Oh dear, that sounds rather melodramatic, doesn't it?'

'Not at all,' Jean said, venturing another guess. 'Is that where your wife is?'

'My daughter. My wife was killed in the Liverpool Blitz.'

'Oh, I'm sorry. Had the Church sent you there?'

'I chose to go there. Glory be to God in the High Street and all that. Or perhaps I should say that God chose for me to go there. He has a plan for us all, you know.'

'That's the trouble with you parsons,' Jean said lightly. 'Sooner or later you always bring God into it. I've never had much time for Him myself. Don't tell me,' she said, seeing the new chaplain open his mouth to speak. 'He still has time for me.'

'Do you already know *all* of my best lines?'

'I just think that as you and I are going to be working together it might be as well to lay our cards on the table from the outset.'

Peter Hilton raised his hands in the manner of a man offering a peaceful surrender. 'Fair enough. I hope we can still be friends.'

'I hope so too,' Jean said. 'Would you like me to show you around now?'

He shook his head. 'I was only in for a quick shufti and you look like a woman who's had a long and tiring day. Is there a hostelry in the local village where I might buy you a cocktail?'

Jean's lips twitched. 'A cocktail might be stretching a point. Besides, I didn't think that people who wear their collars back to the front went in for alcohol.'

'You poor thing!' he exclaimed, holding the door open for her as they left the welfare office.

Startled by the vehemence of that statement, she looked up at him as she went out into the corridor. 'Why am I a poor thing?'

'Because that comment shows you must have been raised in a hellfire-and-brimstone Presbyterian household. We Anglicans are a little more relaxed about the pleasures of life.'

'Anglicans or Methodists or Catholics or Presbyterians,' Jean said drily, 'I could wish that a larger proportion of the females in this camp were more inclined to deny themselves some of those pleasures.'

'Want to talk about these troublesome females?'

'I'm sure you don't want to listen to my grumbles after you've come through a gruelling day's travelling.'

'Don't be so sure. Being a good listener *is* one of the tools of my trade.'

'There's not much to talk about. They're the girls we would call silly wee lassies in Scotland. Those who succumb to what might be termed self-inflicted illnesses.' Jean grimaced. 'Succumb being very much the operational word, these illnesses being inflicted with the all-too-willing co-operation of our dashing American and Polish allies.'

'It's a by-product of war, I'm afraid. You can't change human nature.'

She cast him a sideways glance. 'I was just thinking that myself. It's a very tolerant point of view coming from a man in your line of work.'

'You think so? What did you do in civvy street?'

'This and that.'

They were on the vast and high-ceilinged first-floor landing of the house now, heading for the main staircase. Peter Hilton stopped at the top of it, laid one hand on the black marble banister and turned to Jean with a ludicrously wide-eyed expression on his face. 'That is *the* classic evasive answer. Do I detect a woman of mystery here?'

Mystery woman, eh? Now you've condemned me to lie awake tonight wondering whether you're on the run after committing some heinous crime. Maybe you're wanted for murder. Or maybe you're an international jewel thief. Or possibly the agent of a foreign power plotting the downfall o' the government.

'What did I say?'

Jean blinked. 'Nothing. Let's go and get that cocktail. Or at least a warm glass of beer.'

As they threaded their way through the bustling and echoing ground-floor lobby of the house, Peter Hilton indicated a notice board covered in reminders about camp rules and regulations and one brightly coloured poster advertising a dance on the coming Saturday.

'All your own work?'

'The girl who does our typing did the posters. She has quite an artistic bent.'

'Does the house have a ballroom?'

'Yes, but it's full of desks and typewriters and teleprinters and people doing all sorts of mysterious and secret things. We'll be in the somewhat less salubrious surroundings of the rec hall, I'm afraid. Although why I'm encouraging fraternising between the sexes I don't know. They're more than capable of doing that all by themselves.'

'Might I invite you to fraternise with me? Come to the dance as my partner?'

She slanted him a look as they walked out of the building, down one side of the stone horseshoe staircase and on to the sea of white pebbles that surrounded the house like a moat. 'You're a very odd clergyman.'

'Maybe you have a very odd idea about what sort of a person a clergyman should be,' he countered.

'Thanks for the invitation but I don't dance. What *are* you doing?' For he had bent his long body forward and was subjecting her legs under their uniform skirt to exaggerated scrutiny.

'Looking for your tin leg. I must say your pins look perfectly fine to me.' His smile was much more man than clergy. 'More than fine.'

'I didn't say that I *couldn't* dance,' Jean said, a little flustered and annoyed with herself because of it. She never got flustered. 'I said that I *didn't* dance. There's a difference.'

'Never let those beautiful golden tresses down, Rapunzel?'

Jean's hand went to her hair, neatly curled up into a Victory

Roll. It was how she almost invariably wore it these days. 'Very seldom.'

'Maybe you're just a rotten dancer and don't want to show yourself up in front of the silly wee lassies.'

'I'll have you know that I can dance very well—' She caught herself on when she saw the triumphant smile on Peter Hilton's face. 'Which doesn't mean that I'm going to dance.'

'That's what you think,' he said smugly. 'You've thrown down the gauntlet to me now. I'll get you up on the dance floor on Saturday night or die in the attempt.'

Sitting down at the hideously over-cretonned dressing table in the cottage in the local village she shared with three other young female officers, Jean removed the pins from her hair, teased out her Victory Roll and picked up her hairbrush. Her hair was getting long again. She'd have to find the time to get it trimmed.

Funny that the new chaplain should have made that comment about her being a woman of mystery. Funny that it should have sent her whizzing back in time fast enough to make her dizzy.

It wasn't that she didn't think about Andrew sometimes, wondering where he was, what he was doing, whether he had married again. Now and again she worked out what age he would be. Right now he would have just turned thirty-three. Thirty-three to her twenty-eight.

She had no idea if he was still in Switzerland. It being a neutral country, he might be sitting the war out over there. Somehow Jean didn't think so. He too would have felt that his country needed him. It had occurred to her that he might have joined up and been killed but somehow she didn't think that either. She felt she would have known if that had happened . . . although she wasn't quite sure how she would have known.

Jean gazed at her reflection in the mirror of the dressing table. Funny how the new chaplain had set her off thinking about Andrew again.

Chapter 41

'WHERE DO you think you're going, young lady?'
'Home,' Jean said pleasantly, passing Peter Hilton in the doorway of the recreation hall. 'It's all well underway now and I have a date with a good book.'

'But we haven't had our dance yet. I'd have been here earlier, only I had a bit of an emergency.'

'An emergency?'

'A young woman going through an emotional crisis. She surprised herself by discovering that God could help. Through the medium of His and your humble servant here.'

'I'm very happy for all three of you. Would you excuse me, please?'

'No. It's my duty as a man not to let a lovely woman like you go to waste.' He glanced down the hall. 'For a bunch of enthusiastic amateurs the band's not half bad, don't you think?'

Before Jean had time to react, he'd taken hold of her and was dancing them back into the body of the hall.

'You know,' she said mildly, 'I could have sworn I told you that I don't dance.'

'Sssh. It wouldn't do for the lower orders to see their chaplain and their welfare officer engaged in an unseemly tussle in the middle of the dance floor.'

That argument had some validity, especially when it was

backed up by the reactions of the young women on the floor. Jean spotted the girl from Southampton whom she had helped through crippling homesickness and anxiety about the family she'd left behind to endure the bombers when she'd first arrived at the camp. Taking her hand out of her partner's long enough to give the thumbs-up signal, she called across the floor. 'Well done, Captain Dunlop! You dance really well!'

'See?' Peter Hilton said. 'Now they know you're human. Why would doing this undermine your authority in any way?'

'That's not why I don't dance.'

'What is the reason, then?'

'Does there have to be a reason?'

'Of course there does. Especially when someone's as good a dancer as you are. If a little tense at this precise moment. Relax,' he said. 'Nothing bad's going to happen to you.'

Jean gave a little start. That was the second time he'd come out with something that had reminded her of Andrew Logan.

'What did I say?'

'Nothing.'

'It must have been something to put that faraway look into your eye. What was it?'

'Anyone ever told you that you ask too many questions?'

'How can a man help being curious when he meets such an intriguing woman as you are?'

Jean gave him the look that had been known to make strong men blanch. It made Peter Hilton chuckle.

'I don't want anything from you, you know.'

'Don't you?'

'Ah-hah,' he said softly, 'a clue as to your past history. There's been a time in your life when you felt everyone wanted something from you. Am I right?'

'You ask too many questions,' she said again.

'Tell me all about yourself and I wouldn't need to.'

'Why don't we just shut up and dance?'

'Wonderful idea.'

She narrowed her eyes at him. 'You gave in awfully quickly there.'

'A good soldier always knows when to retreat.'

He made her wait through eight bars of music for the punch line. 'If you retreat, you can regroup your forces and fight another day.' He grinned down at her. 'And then win the battle.'

'Keep dreaming,' Jean said. The music stopped, the dancers applauded the band and she extracted herself from Peter Hilton's embrace. 'I'm going now. If you try to stop me there *will* be an undignified tussle in the middle of the dance floor. And before you ask, that's both a threat *and* a promise.'

'I can't persuade you to give me another dance?'

'No.'

'See you tomorrow then, Captain Dunlop,' he said cheerfully. 'Hope you enjoy reading that good book.'

She was actually coming to the end of writing that good book, confident now that the third of her Jacobite novels was going to be worthy of its two predecessors. She was well past the crippling panic she had discovered always struck her down halfway through. It invariably brought with it the absolute conviction that the book was so completely dire nobody in their right mind would ever want to read it.

She'd learned to deal with such crises of confidence by leafing through the two books she had published, deciding the writing wasn't half bad and considering the fact that both of them had sold well. Judging by the sales figures, people who had read book two were now going back to read book one. She must be doing something right.

As she walked down the driveway of the house on her way back to the village, her feet crunching over the white stone chips glowing in the moonlight, she was thinking about the scene she was about to work on. It was one of high emotion, the two central lovers in her story being finally reunited after the circumstances she and history had created had separated them.

She had already roughed it out. Now she was going back to do the real work, shaping and polishing and honing the words, crafting the scene so it could take its place with the others and help build up the whole thing into an atmospheric and satisfying story. It was a part of the process she particularly relished and she was looking forward to getting on with it.

She was aware all the same that part of her brain was thinking how much she had enjoyed that dance with Peter Hilton. She hadn't been up on a dance floor for years: not since the last awful occasion when she and Andrew had danced their story tango. Looking back now, she wondered how either of them had managed to get through it.

Since then she had made something of a fetish of not dancing. Now her decision to deny herself the pleasure of moving her body and her feet in time to the music seemed more than a little melodramatic. She was a mature woman now, beyond such empty gestures.

Jean let herself into the cottage, climbed the stairs to her bedroom and sat down with a sigh of satisfaction in front of her portable typewriter.

The following morning she walked through from the interview room to the main welfare office. 'Nobody seems to have any problems today. I'm casting around for something to do here.'

Peter was by himself in the main office, his chair propped back against the wall and his feet up on his desk. He was reading. Eyes flickering up to Jean, they went back down again almost immediately. 'Why don't you read one of those good books of yours? That's what I'm doing.'

Curious as any other book-lover to see what his definition of a good book was, Jean turned her head to read the title on the spine. The book in which he was apparently so engrossed was the first Joanna Colquhoun novel.

Chapter 42

'YOU SEEM to be enjoying that,' she said lightly.

He didn't lift his head. 'It's riveting. I started reading it before I went to bed last night and before I knew where I was it was two o'clock in the morning.'

Jean propped herself against the typist's unoccupied desk and folded her arms. 'I wouldn't have put you down as a reader of sweeping historical romances. If that's what that is,' she added hurriedly. 'Judging by the cover, I mean.'

'Maybe you don't know me well enough to know what I like.' He turned a page.

'Maybe I don't. Is it really any good?'

His eyes came up to her face. 'It's excellent. I thought I was taking a bit of a risk with it at first.'

'A risk?'

'Judging by the cover it's designed to appeal to women. Judging by the impossibly romantic way the hero is gazing into the heroine's eyes, I was anticipating gooey sentimentality. I'm rapidly discovering that there are romantic novels and romantic novels.'

'How very broad-minded of you,' Jean murmured. 'To even tackle a romantic novel, I mean.'

'I thought so.' He lowered his eyes again. Watching their movements, she saw him reach the bottom of one page and start at the top of the next. He had lovely eyelashes, several shades darker than his hair. They fringed rather nice brown eyes.

She unfolded her arms and pushed herself off the typist's desk. 'I think I'll go and clean out the cupboards in the interview room. See you later.' She had taken no more than two steps before Peter Hilton spoke.

'Don't you want to know why I'm enjoying this book so much?'

She turned, and surveyed him with a lofty air. 'Not particularly. But I suppose you're going to tell me anyway.'

'Not if you're not interested. That would be a waste of breath, wouldn't it?'

Jean heard herself grind her teeth. 'All right. Tell me why you're enjoying that book so much.'

He raised his head and looked her straight in the eye. 'Because it brings the past to life, it's peopled by complex and realistic characters with whom you can really sympathise and identify and it also has a wonderful sense of place and a page-turning plot. What more could any reader want?'

Jean opened her mouth to say something. She closed it again without uttering a word.

'I'll have to keep my eyes open for any other books this author might have written. My only problem in asking for them in a shop or a library is that I haven't the faintest idea of how to pronounce her surname.'

'It's *kuh-hoon*,' she said. 'That's how you pronounce it.'

Peter raised his fair eyebrows but said not a word. All he did was look at her. She looked right back at him. 'It's not an uncommon name in Scotland. Especially in and around Helensburgh.'

'Was it your mother's maiden name?'

Very slowly and very deliberately, Jean walked towards his

desk. When she reached it she placed the heels of her hands on its rounded edge and leaned forward. 'Who told you?'

'I have my sources. In very high places.' He pointed heavenwards. 'I'm not referring to the man upstairs. Well,' he amended cheerfully, 'the man who gave me this copy of your book *was* in an upstairs room at the time.'

She offered him a name, that of the major who'd decreed she would make an ideal welfare officer.

Peter grinned. 'Yes. He's my godfather. Are you writing a book at the moment?'

'I'm always writing a book. Even when I'm not.'

'Because you're always thinking up new stories and characters, you mean?'

'Yes. Although I really am writing a book just now. Trying to get it finished, as a matter of fact. Itching to get on with it.'

'I presume you're not doing it here because you don't want to be found out.' Making her jump, he brought his chair forward so that all four of its legs were once more on the floor. 'In which case I have a suggestion to make,' he went on, laying her book on the desk in front of him. When he folded down the top corner of the page he'd been on, Jean shrieked.

'Don't do that, you heathen! Have you no soul?'

His face lit up with laughter. 'Hardly a heathen, Jean. Not in my line of work. And I most certainly have a soul. It's going to reach out to yours now.'

She'd wheeled round to the box in which they kept the scrap paper. Neatly folding one small sheet of it, she handed it to him. 'Bookmark.'

'Thank you.' The brown eyes were sparkling.

'Unfold that corner. You've wounded my poor wee book doing that to it.'

'Yes, ma'am,' he said, saluting her. 'Want me to send it a written apology as well?'

'You could do worse.'

'Now that you've told me off good and proper *you* could do worse than put yourself on the other side of that door and get on with some writing.' He pointed towards the interview room. 'I'll be your watchdog if anyone comes in. Although there are some strings attached to my generous offer.'

'I thought there might be. If you want me to start attending your services on a Sunday morning I'm afraid I shall have to decline.'

'It's you that's the heathen,' he grumbled.

'I'm a free-thinker. There's a difference. Tell me what these strings are.'

'Only one string really. That you come out with me on Sunday afternoon. I thought we could go for a nice healthy hike somewhere. Say yes and I'll consider keeping my mouth shut about your true identity.'

'That's blackmail.'

'Got it in one, Captain Dunlop,' he said, laughing up at her. 'I'll call for you at two o'clock. Would that suit you?'

'I was planning to write on Sunday afternoon.'

'You can afford to take a couple of hours off if you get some of it done now.'

'Peter . . .'

'I'm not asking you to marry me, Jean. It's only a walk. Please say yes.'

Chapter 43

'ISN'T THE view beautiful from up here?'

'Wonderful,' Peter said, shading his eyes against the sun as he took in the landscape spread out at their feet. They had gone through the woods behind the village, wending their way to the top of a little hill and the clearing that crowned it. It had become one of their regular walks. Now that the days were lengthening and Jean had sent off her completed manuscript to the publisher they often came here for a stroll in the evenings.

'The village is such a pretty wee place.'

'Picture-book rural England,' Peter said as he took out his cigarettes.

'Complete with duck pond and village green,' Jean agreed, her eyes going to both of those features. She laughed. 'I *love* that duck pond!'

'You don't have duck ponds in Scotland?'

'Not to the same extent. Not like the English ones.'

'The scenery's a lot more rugged north of the border, I suppose. Does your wee heart yearn for the hills o' hame, lassie?'

Jean groaned, as she always did when he treated her to his truly diabolical Scottish accent. 'The Lake District must be pretty rugged too.'

'It's wonderful,' he said warmly. 'Majestic and grand and inspiring.'

'If its peaks aren't quite as high as the Scottish ones,' she teased.

'I still think you'd be impressed.'

'I'm sure I would. From the way you speak about it, it's obviously a very beautiful place.'

They had talked and talked over the past couple of months, their subject matter varied and wide-ranging. It had taken no time at all and very little coaxing to get Peter to pull the snapshots of his little daughter out of his wallet. Rosalind Hilton − Rosie for short − was quite obviously the apple of her father's eye.

A laughing moppet with a head of blonde corkscrew curls, the little girl was four years old and lived with her maternal grandparents. Peter's father-in-law was also a clergyman, vicar of the church near Keswick where Peter had started his own career as a curate. Susanna Lucas had been the vicar's daughter.

It had been love at first sight for the two of them, although they had both been shy of expressing it. Reading between the lines, Jean suspected that neither of them had had much experience with the opposite sex before they had met one another. It was Peter's promotion to vicar of his own parish in Liverpool two years on from his arrival at the church on the shores of Derwentwater that had impelled him and Susanna finally to declare their feelings to one another. They had married in 1938 and their daughter had been born a year later.

After Susanna became pregnant, Peter had insisted she went back to her father's parsonage. When the baby was a year old, she had insisted on returning regularly to Liverpool. Her place was by her husband's side. If he was running the risks in order to console and comfort his parishioners during some of the darkest days of Merseyside's history, she ought to be with him. She'd been in the church when it took a direct hit in the prolonged and merciless blitz of May 1941.

'And did you accept that as God's will?' Jean had asked quietly. 'You said you believed He had chosen Liverpool for you.'

'I was angry at Him,' Peter had replied. 'Furiously angry. How could He have been so cruel as to take Susanna away from me? I nearly lost my faith: and my reason. If it hadn't have been for my parents-in-law and Becky I think I would have gone mad.'

'Becky?' Jean had queried.

'Susanna's kid sister. She's a great girl. A wonderful aunt to Rosie.'

Jean had been a lot less forthcoming about her own history. She had told him that she had been married and was now divorced. About Andrew she had said practically nothing. She had spoken of her grandparents and her mother and of the four years she had spent with the Fairbairns.

Peter had expressed the opinion that both of them sounded absolutely frightful but he continued to challenge Jean on her atheism, as he did now. He stretched out one arm, drawing an arc in the air to indicate the wonderful view.

'How can you deny the hand of the Creator when you survey the beauties of Nature?'

'How can you continue to believe in Him when the world's in the state it is? When so many people are dying and suffering so terribly? If God existed, why would He allow that to happen?'

'Man has free will,' he said. 'It's man who's making the mess. And many people are finding solace and succour in God during these terrible times.'

'Lifeboat Christians,' Jean said firmly. 'We're on our own. We should have the courage to acknowledge that.'

'You're a hard woman. Cigarette?'

'Thanks. Do you think the tide really is turning now?' she asked. 'In the Allies' favour, I mean?'

He nodded. 'Most people seem to think the invasion of Europe will happen this year. We wouldn't even be contemplating such a massive undertaking if we weren't confident of success.'

'Morale's so important, isn't it? At the beginning,' she went on, frowning at the memory, 'when the Germans seemed unstoppable—'

'When we thought we were next, you mean?'

'Yes. Do you remember what the mood was like?'

'Fear,' Peter said, 'panic. Suspicion of anyone who looked or sounded like a foreigner. That was a terrible time.'

'I used to lie awake at night waiting for the church bells to ring and signal the invasion,' Jean said, shivering at the memory. 'Once or twice I even imagined that I heard them.'

'But they rang to celebrate the victory at El Alamein instead,' Peter said comfortingly. 'And after that we turned a corner.' He took a contemplative pull on his cigarette. 'Do you ever think about what you're going to do once it's all over?'

'Up till recently that's seemed like tempting fate,' Jean said honestly. 'Now I'm beginning to allow myself to think about going home to Helensburgh.'

'You miss the place?'

'More than I can say. Boy, am I looking forward to this leave I've got coming up!'

'Tell me something,' Peter said. 'Does your dislike of religion extend to all ministers, priests and vicars? Present company excepted, of course.'

She smiled at him. 'Why would you think that I make an exception for you?'

'Why do you always answer a question with a question?'

'Do I do that?'

He groaned. 'Pax, Jean. Let's declare a truce.'

'Are we at war with each other?'

He let out another groan. 'Answer the question I asked you.'

'To dislike all ministers, priests and vicars would be as dogmatic as I find an awful lot of them to be. I'm prepared to take folk as I find them. Even clergymen.'

'Good,' Peter said. 'In that case I have another question for you. You know how I also have been granted the un-imaginable boon of a week's leave at exactly the same time as you? How are our charges going to cope without us, by the way?'

'They can survive for a week,' Jean said callously. 'Stiff upper lips all round. *In extremis*, the local doctor and or his good lady – as he invariably refers to the poor woman – have agreed to step in if required.'

'You'll be going back up to Helensburgh, I take it.'

'Yes.'

'I'll be going to see Rosie.'

'Yes.'

'So,' he said, 'why don't we travel north together and you come to Derwentwater for a couple of days? If you ask me nicely I might even come up and see your beloved Helensburgh before we come back down here.'

'I'd love to meet Rosie,' Jean said lightly. 'But don't you think your parents-in-law would be a little put out if you brought a woman they don't know to the house where Susanna grew up?'

'They wouldn't be put out at all. They're not like that.' He put his cigarette to his lips. 'I'm not asking you to marry me, Jean.'

It was what he always said when she was reluctant to fall in with any of his suggestions. Being persuaded to go to a camp dance or out for a meal with him was one thing. Going to what was effectively his home was quite another.

'Why do you want me to come?'

'Because I want to show off my daughter?'

'Now you're answering a question with a question.'

'It's catching,' he said drily. 'Please come with me, Jean. You'd enjoy it, I'm sure you would. And the Lucases would love to meet you. They've always welcomed my friends.'

'That's what you and me are, is it?'

'I'd like to think so. Please come,' he said again. 'I'd like to show off the Lake District to you as well. After that you can show Helensburgh off to me. Go on,' he urged softly. 'Be a devil.'

Jean opened her mouth to say no. She heard some other woman saying yes.

Chapter 44

'I FEEL LIKE the girl in that book by Daphne du Maurier,' Jean said as they got off the bus and walked up the rhododendron-lined drive of the parsonage.

'The nameless heroine being taken to the hero's home for the first time?' Peter threw her a reassuring smile. 'Don't worry. There won't be any fearsome housekeeper waiting for you. The only staff they have now is the lady who obliges daily, and she's a dear. They're all dears. You'll love them and they'll love you.'

'You're a cock-eyed optimist, Peter Hilton— Oh,' she exclaimed as they rounded a bend in the drive, 'what a lovely house!'

'It is nice, isn't it? Stop here for a moment and take it all in. I really envy you seeing it for the first time.'

'It's Georgian?'

'Yes. Built some time in the 1790s, I think. Perfectly proportioned, don't you think?'

'It looks like a doll's house,' she said in delight. Her eyes travelled up to the first-floor windows of the house. Tall and exactly the right width to complement their height, they matched the ones on either side of the front door. 'Green *and* red ivy. The leaves are so shiny and glossy. Such a wonderful contrast with the paleness of the stone too.'

'I'm glad you like it. Wait till you see round the back. The garden slopes down to the lake. Watch out, here comes trouble!'

For the front door had been pulled open and two small shapes were rushing helter-skelter towards them. One was a yellow-coated dog of indeterminate parentage, its furiously wagging tail circling like a windmill's sails. The dog's young mistress launched herself at Peter, emitting a series of piercing yells.

Peter dropped his and Jean's canvas kitbags on to the stone chips of the drive and sank to one knee, opening his arms wide. Once he had caught his daughter he stood up and began swinging her round and round, taking her and himself off the drive and on to the lawn. 'Rosie, Rosie, Rosie!' he cried.

Clearly not wanting to be left out of this reunion, the dog ran round them in an ecstasy of joyful barking.

'Oh, Rosie!' Peter cried, and began planting noisy kisses all over the little girl's face. She giggled in delight. Over her shoulder, Jean could see that her father's eyes were glittering with unshed tears.

He caught her watching him. 'Sorry about this. It's the smell of her skin. Gets me every time.'

Jean placed a hand on his shoulder. 'Don't apologise. I think it's lovely. All the way up I've been worrying on your behalf that she might be shy of you after the long absence.'

'Shy? Not our Rosie.'

Jean turned and found herself on the receiving end of a smile from a woman in her fifties who could only be Susanna's mother and Rosie's grandmother. 'Mrs Lucas?' she asked, walking forward and holding out her hand.

'The very same. You must be Jean. Welcome to our home.'

'It's very good of you to have me here,' Jean replied as they shook hands.

'Not at all, my dear. Any friend of Peter's is a friend of ours. How are you, Peter dear?'

'All the better for seeing you, Charlotte,' Peter said, setting Rosie down and stepping forward to give his mother-in-law a hug and a kiss on the cheek. 'Did the boys get their leave? And where are Reverend James and Becky? Rosie, say hello to Daddy's friend Jean.'

'Hello, Daddy's friend Jean.'

Jean laughed, bent forward and held out her hand. 'Hello, Rosie. It's very nice to meet you. What's your doggie called?'

'Roger,' the little girl replied as she solemnly shook hands. 'Would you like to pat him?'

'I'd like that very much,' Jean said, crouching down beside dog and child and listening to Mrs Lucas answering Peter's question as to the whereabouts of the other members of the family.

'Simon and Matthew did get home. Isn't it wonderful that I've got you all here together at the same time? James is out and about in the parish. As usual,' she said with tolerant amusement, addressing that comment to Jean as she bobbed back to her feet. 'I'm afraid my husband loses track of time. I gave him strict instructions to be home for four o'clock but there's no sign of him yet. Becky's in the kitchen seeing to our afternoon tea. She's my daughter.'

'I know,' Jean said. 'Peter's told me all about you and your family.'

'Yet you still came to see us? You're a brave girl.'

Wishing Peter hadn't chosen that moment to set off at a run across the lawn with Rosie and Roger, Jean smiled a little hesitantly at her hostess. So far the welcome seemed friendly . . .

'You're wondering what I'm thinking,' Charlotte Lucas said.

Jean had always liked people who spoke their minds. 'I am wondering that,' she admitted. 'I'm also wondering if you really don't mind Peter bringing me to your home.'

'Should we mind?'

Jean looked her straight in the eye. 'No, I don't think you should. Peter and I are friends. No more and certainly no less.'

'Just good friends? Isn't that what they used to say in the gossip columns? Shortly before actresses and racing drivers announced their engagements to each other?'

'That doesn't apply to Peter and me at all.' Jean gave her fair head a decisive shake. 'I can assure you of that.'

'And you want everyone to know what's what right from the outset.' Charlotte Lucas's face relaxed into another smile. 'I think you and I are going to get along famously, Jean. Come on into the house and meet Becky and the boys.'

The noisy and rumbustious Lucas family took Jean to their hearts. Charlotte proved to be a wonderful mixture of plain-speaking and warmth. The vicar was avuncular and charmingly gallant.

'You'll visit us again, Captain Dunlop,' he said. 'Once the war's over and petrol's no longer rationed by the teaspoonful I shall take you to Ullswater and you can see where William Wordsworth wandered lonely as a cloud.'

'When all at once he saw that world-famous host of golden daffodils? I'd love to see the place where the inspiration came from. And please call me Jean.'

'You'll know about our area's Jacobite connections, Jean,' he said, wasting no time in taking her up on the invitation.

'I know about the Battle of Clifton Moor just south of Penrith.'

The vicar nodded. 'Where the Jacobite army turned on its

retreat back to Scotland and engaged the government troops.'

'Last battle fought on English soil, I believe.'

James Lucas nodded again. 'As Culloden is the last one in Scotland and therefore Britain in general. You'll also know about the Earl of Derwentwater?'

'His leave-taking of his wife before his execution for treason being immortalised in song as it is?'

'Indeed,' sighed James Lucas.' "Derwentwater's Farewell". A melancholic beauty of a lament. Do you know about the Finsthwaite Princess, though?'

'I don't believe I do. Who was she?'

The vicar leaned forward over the table as though he were letting Jean in on an ancient family secret. 'She's alleged to have been the natural daughter of Bonnie Prince Charlie, possibly by his lady love Clementine Walkinshaw. Her grave's in the village of Finsthwaite. That's on the western side of Windermere.'

'Really?' Jean said, her interest quickening. 'How fascinating. We know that Clementine bore him his only acknowledged child, Charlotte. There are tales of other children by other lovers but I've never read of any real evidence of one. Where exactly is this village?'

Peter laughed. 'Look out, Reverend James, she'll have her notebook out any moment now!'

The vicar divided a smile between the two of them and leaned over to pat Jean's hand. 'I wouldn't mind at all if you did, my dear.'

'Perhaps not at the dinner table,' Jean said, throwing an apologetic glance at her fellow diners and realising from the expressions on the faces turned towards her that they'd all been mightily amused by the conversation she and the vicar had just had. 'But I'd love to talk to you at greater length about this some other time, Reverend James.'

'Be careful, Jean,' said the parson's elder son, Simon. He and his younger brother, Matthew, the two of them home on leave from the Navy and the Royal Air Force respectively, had gone immediately on to first name terms with her. 'Getting Dad started on local history is like opening a floodgate.'

'Impertinent youth,' said his father affectionately, and the conversation became more general. The two Lucas boys vied to cap one another's tall tales of service life and flirted outrageously with Jean. Everyone spoke quite naturally about Susanna, telling fond and funny stories about her.

Jean's secret fear that Peter's daughter wouldn't like her was allayed on the very first night. When her bedtime came Rosie announced that she wanted Daddy and Daddy's friend Jean to tuck her in and read her a bedtime story. Jean was astonished by the strength of the pleasure that childish acceptance gave her.

Her only source of disquiet as the short visit neared its end was Becky Lucas. A pretty girl with glossy brown hair that curled on her shoulders, she tolerated with good humour the joshing and teasing her brothers and Peter meted out to her. It was obvious that he looked on her as a kid sister too.

It was equally obvious – at least to Jean and she suspected, also to Charlotte Lucas – that Becky was in love with Peter. It was equally obvious that the girl was deeply unhappy that he had brought another woman home with him. Over their few days at Derwentwater, Jean observed Rebecca Lucas. She liked what she saw. It couldn't be easy for her to have Jean here, yet she never failed to treat her with friendly, if slightly reserved, courtesy.

Jean sought Becky out on the day before she and Peter were due to head north, finding her in the parson's library. She was tidying up the chaotic muddle of papers strewn in collapsing towers across the top of her father's desk.

'He won't hit the roof when he comes back and discovers that you've done that?'

'He might well do,' Becky said, her mouth set in lines of do-or-die determination. 'But he won't be able to find anything on here soon. I'm taking advantage of his absence to get things sorted out. It'll make life easier for him in the end.'

'It keeps you busy,' Jean said. 'Being your father's secretary, I mean.'

'I enjoy it,' the girl said. 'It's not only about helping him, it's about helping all of the parishioners too.'

'So you think you're doing as much good here as you would have if you'd joined up?' Jean probed gently. 'I know Peter is very grateful to you for how you helped him after your sister died. That must have been difficult when you were grieving for her yourself.'

She shouldn't have said that. It wasn't her place to thank the girl for having helped Peter through his bereavement. Becky, however, answered with her usual quiet good manners.

'I'd have loved to have joined up. See the world and all that. I had to ask to be exempted. The house and the church take a lot of running. Mother can't do it all on her own.'

'No doubt you'll get your reward in heaven,' Jean said flippantly, thinking that this might be the moment to beat a strategic retreat. She was probably the last person in the world with whom this girl wanted to discuss her feelings for Peter.

'I get my reward here. It's satisfying work. I'm a member of the WVS too. So I am doing my bit for the war effort. You and Peter are heading off tomorrow?' Becky asked, her voice carefully casual.

'We're going to my home in Helensburgh. That's a little town down the Clyde from Glasgow.'

'I know where it is. When he wrote and told us about you I looked it up on the map.'

The eyes of the two young women met and locked.

'Becky,' Jean said gently, 'I'm no threat to you. Believe me.'

'That's not what I see.'

'What do you see?'

'The way he looks at you. He's dazzled by you.'

'Maybe,' Jean conceded after an awkward little pause. 'I certainly think I'm a bit of an exotic specimen as far as Peter's concerned. But he and I are friends, Becky. I really value his friendship, but that's exactly what it is. It doesn't go any further.'

'He's in love with you.'

Jean shook her head, denying that statement for all she was worth. 'He's not. And I'm certainly not in love with him.'

Something flashed in Becky's green eyes. 'You're not?'

'Absolutely not. Please forgive me if I'm intruding here, but has it ever occurred to you to tell Peter how you feel about him and see what his reaction is? It's obvious that he's extremely fond of you.'

The light that had flickered in the green eyes guttered out. 'I think he might even love me. But in the way a brother loves a sister. That's how he thinks of me. He doesn't even see me as a grown-up woman.'

'Maybe all he needs is to be made to see that you are a grown-up woman. To have that pointed out to him.'

'Please don't say anything to him!' Becky's hands flew up to her mouth as though she wanted to stop Jean's words and her own. 'I couldn't bear for him to know how I feel about him!'

'Of course I won't say anything. But you must know that he wouldn't laugh at you. Peter's the kindest man I've ever met.'

'That's the trouble,' Becky said, sounding completely miserable. 'He'd feel compassion for me. He'd feel *sorry* for me. Knowing that I loved him but he could never love me back in the same way would make him unhappy too. Losing Susanna almost destroyed him. I want him to be happy,' she said pathetically. 'I really do want him to get married again and be happy.'

'Well, he's not going to marry me,' Jean said briskly. 'Apart from the fact that I would loathe and detest the role of parson's wife, I don't even believe in God. I write books, a reprehensible profession in itself. As you may know, I'm also a divorcee. A vicar could never marry a divorcee. Correct me if I'm wrong, but I don't believe any Church will agree to conduct a marriage for any couple where one of the partners is divorced.'

Jean was growing a little exasperated with the path this conversation had taken. Why on earth she was even feeling the need to spell out the reasons why something she had never remotely contemplated couldn't happen she didn't know. She resorted once more to flippancy. 'And I'm a blonde divorcee into the bargain. That always seems to make it worse.'

'My father did a blessing a month ago,' Becky said stubbornly, 'for a couple where the man had been divorced. They went to the register office and came on here for a blessing. There was a terrific hoo-hah afterwards. The bishop hauled Dad over the coals but he still says he would do it again. If the divorced person had been the innocent party in their divorce, as this man was, Father would do the same thing for Peter. I know he would.'

Now Jean's growing irritation was warring with compassion for the girl standing in front of her. She'd obviously been worrying herself sick over this, tormenting herself with all of the possibilities, unlikely in the extreme though Jean knew them to be.

'Peter's a vicar himself, Becky,' she said, determined to knock this on the head once and for all. 'He'd have to leave the priesthood if he married a divorced woman. Don't you of all people know how important his calling is to him? It and his faith are central to his whole being. Sometimes it's hard to tell where he stops and where his faith in God begins.'

Becky's face lightened. 'You wouldn't ask him to give up the Church for you?'

Hadn't the girl been listening to anything she'd been saying? Obviously not. Holding on to her temper with some difficulty, Jean couched her answer in terms she hoped would give Becky the reassurance she needed. 'Of course I wouldn't,' she said firmly. 'Of course I wouldn't.'

'Your beloved Lake District reminds me of Glasgow.'

'How so?'

'They're both places that know how to put on *real* rain. Would you look at that out there? It's coming down in stair rods.'

They were standing in the shelter of the lych-gate of the church, returning from an early morning walk by the water while they waited for Rosie to wake up and have breakfast with her father before he and Jean headed north.

'The sky was a perfect blue when we left the parsonage,' Jean mused. 'It's a good job Charlotte insisted I take a waterproof with me. Although I reckon I must look a pretty sight in it. Particularly when it's topped by this very fetching sou'wester.'

'You do look a very pretty sight in it,' Peter said. 'I can vouch for that.'

She was laughing as she turned from her scrutiny of the

rain to look up at him. 'Peter, you idiot. I look as if I'm standing on the deck of Captain Ahab's whaler.'

'No, you don't,' he murmured. 'You look absolutely adorable.' Then he bent his head and kissed her.

Chapter 45

JEAN HAD taken a step back, and her hazel eyes were troubled as she gazed up at him. 'I wish you hadn't done that. Oh, Peter, I really wish you hadn't done that!'

'I've been wanting to do it for weeks. I want to do it again.' His own beautiful eyes were as soft as his voice. 'And again and again and again.'

Jean took another step back. 'This isn't right. This is something which can't go anywhere.'

'I love you, Jean.'

'No, you don't,' she said sharply.

'Don't tell me how I feel. Do you really think I didn't try to fight this?'

'I don't think you fought very hard.'

'I fought *bloody* hard!' he cried, startling them both with his vehemence. 'When I started having these sorts of feelings for you I tortured myself by thinking of all the reasons why I shouldn't be having them. I felt I was betraying Susanna's memory by even *thinking* of you that way.'

'You're also an ordained priest of the Church of England, Peter. I'm a divorced woman.'

He raised his fair brows. 'I hardly thought you would approve of the Church's stance on that issue.'

'I don't give a damn what any Church thinks about divorce or any other issue. But you do.'

'You're so sure of what I think?'

'I'm sure of what you believe. Of how much your faith and your Church matter to you. I'm not going to come between you and that.' Jean shook her head. 'I'm not worth it, Peter.'

'I think you are.'

Jean's voice had a raw edge to it. 'You really don't know the first thing about me.'

'I know that I love you, Jean.' He raised a hand, stopping the words of denial that were rising to her lips. 'I know that you're a good person.'

'A good person?' she repeated. 'I've got a sharp tongue and a cynical outlook on life. I don't suffer fools gladly.'

'You're certainly brutally honest,' he said. 'Although more with yourself than anybody else. You're also very funny and very kind. But you're not really so cynical as you like to think you are. Anyway, you know what Oscar Wilde said about that.'

'He said a lot of things.'

'One of which was that cynics are only bruised romantics.'

'I'm done with romance,' Jean said. 'That sort of thing's dead and buried, as far as I'm concerned. Water under the bridge. All in the past. That's where it's going to stay.'

'How can you say that when you write such wonderfully romantic books?'

'There's plenty of cynicism in them too.'

'Alongside so many other things,' Peter countered. 'So many other things which are also found in the extremely complex and attractive character and personality of the author of those books.'

She looked away from him, and when she spoke her voice was flat and dull. 'The rain's stopped. We'd better go back to the house so you can spend some time with Rosie before we leave.'

'This conversation isn't over, Jean.'

'Yes, it is,' she said, once more meeting his gaze. 'I'm not worth it, Peter. Not worth the sacrifice of so much that you hold so dear.'

'Stop telling me that you're not worth it. How can you say that about yourself?'

'Because it's true.' She plucked off the sou'wester and shook her head to free her hair from the feeling of constriction. 'If you knew about some of the things I've done in my life you would say it too. Are we going back to the parsonage now?'

'Not unless and until you tell me why you think you're not worth it.'

'Don't you know when to let go of something?' she asked, closing her eyes for a few seconds. 'You're like a terrier.'

'Tell me, Jean,' he said. 'Please tell me.'

'No!' She rounded on him. 'Leave it alone, Peter! Believe me, you really don't want to know!'

Now it was her who had startled him. Enough to make him go pale. 'I'm sorry,' he said. 'Please forgive me for upsetting you, Jean.'

'I'm not upset. Let's go back to the house. Rosie must be awake by now.'

'Do you still want me to come north with you?'

Already on her way out from under the lych-gate, she turned and surveyed him. 'Do you still want to come?'

'Very much so.'

'You understand you'll be coming as a friend visiting another friend? On that basis and only on that basis?'

'If that's the way you want it, Jean.'

'That's the way I want it. Come on. Time we were getting the day underway.'

'I can see why you miss this place, Jean. You have some view from the window here.'

'It's great, isn't it?' she agreed, coming through from the kitchen of the flat with a tray piled up with tea things. She'd bought fresh supplies on the short walk from the railway station. The grocer had greeted her like a long-lost daughter.

Placing the tray on her desk, she skirted round to join Peter where he stood between it and the big bay window.

'Tell me what I'm looking at?'

She began pointing everything out to him. 'If you go all the way along the promenade to the right you come to Rhu and the start of the Gare Loch. That's all a restricted area for the duration.'

'The navy's taken over up there?'

'Uh-huh. That promontory over there is the Rosneath peninsula.'

'Can I make out a village?'

'Two of 'em. Rosneath itself and Clynder to the north of it. There's also Kilcreggan and Coulport and a couple of other wee places but you can't see them from here. Keep coming round and you have the mouths of two more sea lochs: Loch Long and the Holy Loch. Come round again to what we call the Tail of the Bank, where the Clyde turns the corner into the open sea.'

'Seems to be a lot going on directly opposite. On what I presume is still the river.'

'Aye,' Jean said. 'Port Glasgow to the left, Gourock to the right and Greenock in the middle. Lots of troop ships steaming in and out of there these days. When the newspapers report something happening in "a northern port" they're quite often talking about Greenock.'

'When they don't mean Liverpool,' Peter countered. 'Looks

as if it was pretty industrial over there before the war started.'

'Aye,' she said again. 'There have always been shipyards at Port Glasgow and Greenock. What are you smiling at?'

'Your use of the word "aye",' he laughed, turning at last from his contemplation of the Firth of Clyde and watching as she went back round the desk to set out the tea things. 'Your accent has been growing progressively more Scottish ever since the train crossed the border, with every mile we advanced into fair Caledonia. I thought I was listening to a foreign language when you were chatting with the grocer.'

'You were.' Jean threw him a cautious smile. They had talked very little on the journey north, what was being left unsaid hanging heavily in the air between them. 'Have some tea.'

Peter took the cup and saucer from her and surveyed the desk. Her office-sized Underwood took pride of place. To its right sat a drum of pens and sharpened pencils. On the other side of the typewriter stood a three-tiered wire basket, currently empty apart from the small accumulation of mail, which Jean knew Avril McIntosh would have been stacking there on her weekly visits to check the flat.

Peter lifted his cup to his lips. 'This all looks fearsomely neat.'

'That's because there's no work going on here at the moment. Normally there's as big a guddle here as on the Reverend James's desk.'

'Given my knowledge of that piece of furniture I think I can then work out that "guddle" means a state of extreme mess and confusion. Where do you keep your typing paper?'

'The desk drawers. I've got reams and reams of it in there. Along with several gross of typewriter ribbons. I was panic-buying before the balloon went up.'

'Unable to contemplate the prospect of running out of the tools of your trade?'

'Exactly. I also collect notebooks as assiduously as a squirrel gathers nuts. One drawer's full of them.'

'Lined or unlined?'

'Always the latter.' Jean lifted her cup and took a sip of tea. 'One of the things which lends excitement to my otherwise dull life is the constant quest for notebooks with nice covers and blank pages. I feel less restricted by an unlined notebook.'

Peter set his cup and saucer carefully back down on the tray. 'And you don't like to have any restrictions on you, do you, Jean?' he asked in a deceptively mild tone of voice. 'No ties and no emotional attachments.'

'Leave it, Peter,' she said. 'Let it go. You don't understand what this is about.'

'No? Well, I do understand straight questions and straight answers. I've got one of the former for you now.' He coughed. 'Did you like it when I kissed you this morning?'

Jean took a sip of the tea she no longer wanted. 'Do you think that I liked it?'

'Your technique for keeping the world at bay isn't going to work, Jean.' Peter walked round the desk until he was standing directly in front of her. 'I think you did like it when I kissed you this morning. I'm thinking of doing it again. What have you got to say to that?'

Jean looked up at him. 'All right, Peter,' she said tightly. 'If that's what you want, let's do it. In fact, why don't we have an affair?' She waved an angry hand in a gesture that indicated their surroundings. 'Right here and right now. There's no reason why you have to sleep in the spare bedroom. It'll ruin our friendship, of course, but at least it'll get me out of your system.'

He had gone very still. '*Get you out of my system? Have an affair?* You think *that's* what I want? That goes against everything I believe in!' His hands shot out to grab her shoulders. 'How can you think that? And how can you think so little of yourself as to make me an offer like that? Have you no self-respect, Jean Dunlop?' His eyes blazed with anger. 'You're worth so much more than some tawdry *affair!*'

She struggled against his imprisoning arms. *Have you no self-respect?* How often had she asked that question herself, trying to get through to the girls who were selling themselves so cheaply?

'I've got plenty of self-respect!' she yelled. 'I had to fight for every damned ounce of it! Claw it all back after what happened to me!'

His hands relaxed. His stormy eyes softened. 'What did happen to you, Jean? Won't you tell me?'

For a moment they studied one another in silence. Then she gave an odd little laugh. 'Well, it'll nip all this in the bud, that's for sure. I think I need some fresh air though. Will you come for a walk along the esplanade with me?'

Chapter 46

'WHY WON'T you look at me, Jean?'

Arms folded defensively across her breasts, she was staring towards Rosneath and Clynder. She'd taken him almost to Rhu before he'd suggested that, judging by the signs, they were soon going to come up against the restricted area. Jean had led him on to a little grassy promontory that jutted out over the Firth. She'd spoken for a full fifteen minutes, telling him succinctly but comprehensively about herself, Andrew and The Luxor.

'I'm scared to look at you.'

'Why are you scared?'

'Because you're my friend. And I don't want to see my friend's eyes full of revulsion and disgust.'

'There's none of that, Jean.' He laid gentle hands on her shoulders and brought her round so that they were facing one another. 'See for yourself.'

Her eyes scoured his face. 'You may not be disgusted. You *are* shocked.'

'A little. Not so much as you might think. I know you think I'm a bit of an innocent but you can't minister to a flock in a big port like Liverpool and not see life. I do also sincerely believe that there but for the grace of God go each and every one of us.'

Sparks flashed in the depths of Jean's eyes. 'I didn't tell you what I've just told you because I want or need your forgiveness. Nor do I want or need your God's forgiveness. I don't acknowledge that I need that from anyone.'

'Except perhaps from yourself,' Peter said quietly.

'I forgave myself a long time ago. I did what I did because the alternative was to starve.'

'And for your Andrew maybe to die,' Peter said, removing his hands from her shoulders and offering her a cigarette. 'You sacrificed yourself because it was the only way you had any hope of saving him.'

'You can see that?'

'I can see that,' he said, giving them both a light.

'He couldn't.' Jean put her cigarette to her lips. 'He turned his back on me.'

'Maybe he's able to see it now. He must have been utterly distraught at the time. Devastated and destroyed by what you had told him.'

Jean blew some smoke heavenwards. 'Do you *have* to see his point of view as well as mine?'

'Occupational hazard of those of us who wear our collars back to front. Don't you see his point of view? Now that you've had some years to reflect on it all?'

'I suppose,' Jean said, lowering her cigarette. 'When we first met I was his bright and shining girl, pure and untouched. What I did tarnished me for ever in his eyes. *Sullied* me beyond redemption,' she added, unable to keep the bitterness out of her voice.

'The two of you never met afterwards to talk things over?'

'Never. I don't even know where he is now. I can't imagine he knows or cares where I am either.'

'You don't know that he doesn't care. You don't know that

he hasn't come to deeply regret his rejection of you and that sacrifice you made for him.'

'He didn't even attempt to contest the divorce.' The bitterness was still in her voice. She didn't want to hear that. She didn't want to feel that. She didn't want to acknowledge how much all of this still hurt. 'He could have written to me then, sent a letter via the lawyer. He chose not to.'

They stood smoking their cigarettes and gazing out over the water.

'How about you?' Peter asked at last.

'How about me what?'

'Do you still care for him? Do you still love him?'

'Don't ask me that, Peter.'

'Because I won't like the answer?'

'Because I don't know the answer,' Jean said slowly and with painful honesty. 'I don't know how I feel about him now. I don't know what my feelings are. I try not to think about them too much. There's very little point, is there?'

'Does that mean I might be in with a chance?'

The breeze blowing in off the water blew a strand of hair across her face. 'Peter,' she said, tucking it behind one ear, 'you must see that I'm the wrong woman for you. Especially after what I've just told you.'

'What you've just told me makes no difference to my feelings for you.'

She stared at him. 'You can't possibly mean that. What man could?'

'I wish you'd stop telling me what my own feelings are.' He tossed his cigarette away and opened his arms wide. 'Come here. Let me comfort you.'

She shook her head. 'I don't think that's a very good idea, Peter.'

'I'm not asking you to wave a white flag, Jean. There are no strings attached to this particular offer.'

'Aren't there strings attached to every offer? Isn't that how life works?'

'All I want is to offer you some comfort. It's here if you want it, Jean.'

'No strings?'

'Not a one. So long as you promise not to fight me.'

'I'm too tired to fight anyone,' she said, discarding her own cigarette and stepping into his arms. As they closed around her she thought how warm he felt. How strong and solid and reassuring. He raised one hand to cup the back of her head with his strong fingers. She'd come out without even a headscarf to cover her hair.

'What age were you when all of these things happened?'

'Nineteen. Twenty when Andy and I separated.'

'Just a kid,' he murmured, his hand smoothing her blonde waves.

'That feels nice,' she murmured into his chest.

'Does it? That's good. I don't suppose there's any chance of another kiss.'

'Not a good idea,' she said again. 'I'm really not the right woman for you, Peter.'

'I beg to differ. Although I can see I'm going to have my work cut out convincing you of that.'

Jean sighed. 'Can we please not talk about this now?'

'What would you like to do now?'

'Introduce you to some of my friends. Would that be all right?'

'Fine by me.'

'They'll be consumed with curiosity about you, of course.'

'We'll keep them guessing, then, shall we?' His hand was

still stroking her hair. 'But we'll stay here for another five minutes before you take me to meet them.'

'Why's that?'

'Because I like holding you in my arms. You wouldn't grudge me that, would you?'

'I wouldn't grudge you anything,' she said.

'I thought you were Scottish, Captain Dunlop. Not Irish.'

'Eh?' Holding the door open for her typist, Jean looked blankly at the young woman. Her arms were full, wrapped around a large bundle of cardboard files.

'The luck of the Irish,' the typist elaborated. 'That's what you and the padre must have. You managed to get away before all leave was cancelled. Memo came round yesterday.'

'All leave?' Peter asked. 'In this camp here, you mean?'

'Across the board. We all know what that means,' the girl added darkly, already heading off down the corridor with her burden. 'Some people shipped out yesterday, including those three you share your house with, Captain Dunlop. You'll be all on your own-ee-oh tonight. Letter on top of the pile of mail on your desk, Padre. I'm under orders to point it out to you and suggest you open it *toot sweet*.'

'I think we all know what my letter means too,' Peter muttered as he and Jean walked into the welfare office. She stood and watched him open it.

'*Do* we know what it means?' she asked anxiously.

He looked up. 'As we suspected. I've got my marching orders.'

'When do you go?'

He glanced down again at letter. 'Tomorrow morning, first thing. I'm to report with my kit to the front of the house at six a.m. sharp.'

'This'll be it, then.'

411

'This'll be it,' Peter agreed. He dropped the letter on to his desk and came round to where she sat perched on the edge of her own, taking both of her hands in his. 'I want to go, Jean. I want to be in the thick of it: where the people are who really need whatever comfort and solace I can offer them.'

'I know you do.' She gripped his hands. 'I know that's what you want.'

'So you won't worry about me?'

'I won't give you a second thought.' Her voice wobbled on the last word, and he squeezed the hands he held.

'I expect I shan't be at the very front of the front line, you know. I'll also be wearing a helmet with a cross on it. Place your trust in the former to protect me. As you know by now, I also have absolute faith in the latter.'

'I've never heard that shells and bullets are any respecters of persons.' She pulled a face. 'Or parsons.'

Peter released one of her hands and mimed a punch to her chin. 'That's the spirit. Keep joking, old girl,' he said in a plummy accent. 'You'll soon have me back in dear old Blighty.' He reverted to his own accent. 'I'm assuming you do want me back.'

'Oh, Peter, of course I want you back!'

She went into his arms, wrapping her own tightly around his waist. 'I'm going to miss you so much!'

'Good Lord,' he drawled, hooking a finger under her chin to bring her head up, 'Captain Cynical is even shedding a tear for me. I think I deserve a kiss as well. Don't you? I'd go so far as to suggest that you can't send me off to war without one. It's your duty as a daughter of Britannia.'

Overcome with emotion, Jean answered that without words. The kiss lasted, growing ever deeper and ever more passionate. When it was finally over Peter gripped her shoulders and looked intently at her. 'Jean?'

She said nothing, but she smiled a little shakily at h.
Without taking his eyes from her face, he dug deep into th
pocket of his uniform jacket and brought out a little green
velvet drawstring bag. 'I've carried this all the way up to
Scotland and back down again.'

'It's beautiful,' she breathed, gazed down at the ring he
dropped into his palm. Gold, with a row of five little garnets
along the top, it was obviously an antique.

'It belonged to my mother. And her mother before
that. In case you're wondering, it's not the one I gave
Susanna.'

Jean's eyes travelled from the ring to his face. 'What are you
saying, Peter?'

'I'm asking you to wait for me, Jean. I know you don't love
me but I'm hoping that you might learn to. Given time. Oh,
Jean, this time I am asking you to marry me!'

'But, Peter, you can't give up your vocation for me—'

He placed the tips of his fingers against her mouth to still
that protest. 'But me no buts. There are other ways in which I
could serve the Lord. As a schoolteacher perhaps. I don't
know. Let's cross that bridge when we come to it. Right now
all I want is your answer.'

His eyes shone with the strength of his feelings for her. He
loved her. He knew the worst there was to know about her
and he still loved her.

He was a good man, strong and solid and dependable: and
he loved her. He really did love her.

Shaking with emotion, Jean held out her left hand. After
Peter had placed the ring on her finger she stretched up and
kissed him. 'Your love for me is such a precious gift,' she
murmured against his ear. 'Will you allow me to give you a
gift? Tonight, before you go?'

'Yes,' he whispered. 'I will.'

413

* * *

They stood facing one another in her bedroom, the cottage empty apart from themselves. 'Shall I pull down the black-out blind?'

'The ordinary curtains. So there's still enough light for me to see you by.'

'All right,' she said, touched by the blush that had stained his cheeks when he had made that request. 'Why don't you take your jacket and tie off?' She threw him a mischievous glance. 'Somehow I'm very glad that you're wearing an ordinary collar today.'

'Will you let me do something?' he asked as she turned from closing the curtains.

'What do you want to do?'

'Unpin your hair. I know it's corny but I've been longing to do it.'

Jean laughed. 'It is corny. But I'll let you do it. Shall I sit at the dressing table?'

'I don't know if I even know how to do it,' he confessed as he followed her there.

She smiled at him in the mirror. 'Pat it and you'll feel where the pins are. My hair's wound over a roll made out of old stockings. Find the ends of the pins and pull.'

As her hair came down, Jean tugged the roll out of it and tossed it on to the dressing table. 'There,' she said, shaking her hair free. 'Satisfied?'

'No. I want to brush it. Would you mind?'

She handed him her hairbrush. 'I wouldn't mind.'

'You're liking this?' he asked a few minutes later. Jean opened her eyes. She had her head tilted back, surrendering herself to the pleasure as he smoothed her hair away from her brow, drawing the brush through the gleaming strands from their roots to their tips.

414

'I'm liking this. It feels wonderful. But do you not want to progress on to the next stage?'

Watching him in the mirror, she saw him clutch the hairbrush and swallow nervously. 'Yes. But I haven't really had much experience of this kind of thing.'

'Only ever with Susanna?'

He nodded. Jean stood up, and turned to face him. She took the hairbrush out of his hands and replaced it on the dressing table. 'Then I'm honoured. You don't have that feeling any more that you're being disloyal to her memory?'

Peter shook his head.

'You don't think that what we're about to do is a sin?'

He shook his head again. 'I should think that, shouldn't I? But how can anything which feels as beautiful and as natural as this be a sin?'

He'd already undone the top button of his shirt. Jean's fingers went to the next one down, her lips twisting wryly. 'Unfortunately, I do have some experience of this kind of thing.'

Peter gave her a heart-stopping grin. 'Are you telling me to lie back and think of England?'

Chapter 47

JEAN WOKE on the morning of 6 June 1944 to the news that D-Day had come at last. The invasion of Europe had begun. On that first day alone, one hundred and fifty thousand men crossed the Channel. This was the greatest sea-borne assault in military history.

Over two million Allied servicemen were to be involved in the struggle to push the Germans back. While fighting continued to rage in all the other theatres of war throughout the world, it took the men on the Western Front almost a year to fight their way through to victory.

Jean devoured every newspaper she could get hold of and listened to every news bulletin. In August she received a letter from Peter telling her that he was fit and well and carefully not telling her anything about the fighting going on around him. The few hastily written lines kept her going for months. They had to. His next letter didn't arrive until February of the following year.

'The end's in sight,' he wrote. 'I'm sure of it. With God's help we'll get there soon.'

They got there at the end of April 1945. When Japan capitulated at the beginning of September 1945 the bloody conflict that had ripped the world apart for six long years was finally over.

'I suppose we should all still be celebrating,' came Charlotte Lucas's voice over the telephone, 'especially now the war's properly over and people are beginning to be demobbed. I'm afraid I can't help thinking about all those families who won't be welcoming their sons and daughters home.'

'I feel like that, too,' Jean said, glad to know she wasn't the only person who occasionally felt out of step with the mood of a nation still breathing a prolonged series of huge sighs of relief.

'What's the feeling like where you are, my dear? Still exuberant or beginning to be a little muted?'

'Neither,' Jean said truthfully. 'There's practically nobody left at the camp now. Those few of us who are still here are winding up and clearing up. I've been told my discharge date will be December the fourteenth.'

'Have you heard from Peter? Do you know when he'll be coming home?'

'He's being discharged on exactly the same day I am,' Jean said after the briefest of pauses. 'He's still in Germany, of course, but he thinks the RAF will probably fly him home. He expects to be back in this country a couple of days after the fourteenth.'

'Well, then,' Charlotte Lucas said with the cheerfully brisk manner Jean remembered from her visit to the parsonage over a year before, 'he'll obviously want to see Rosie as soon as possible and he'll obviously want to see you as soon as possible. Why don't the two of you meet up here? You have to pass us on your way north anyway, my dear. We'd love to have you both for Christmas.'

Realising that she was hanging on to the receiver for grim death, Jean forced herself to relax her fingers and ask the question to which she wasn't really sure she wanted an answer. 'May I ask what Becky thinks of this idea?'

'It was she who suggested I phone you, Jean. She doesn't want you or Peter to feel that you yourself are in any way unwelcome here at the parsonage. Quite the reverse.'

There was another pause in the conversation. Charlotte filled it. 'We do know that the two of you got engaged before he left, Jean. He wrote and told us.'

'Do you disapprove?'

'I'd be less than honest if I didn't say we're all dismayed at the prospect of Peter leaving the priesthood. Which he will have to do if you and he get married.'

Plain speaking. I've always been in favour of plain speaking. Reminding herself of that fact, Jean coughed to clear her throat. 'I'm dismayed at the prospect of him leaving the priesthood too, Charlotte. But I made him a promise before he went off.'

'I know,' came the warm response. 'And you're not the sort of woman to go back on her promises. We all want him to be happy, don't we? He deserves it so much after what he's been through.'

Don't I deserve to be happy after what I've been through? Jean didn't express the thought out loud.

'We'd love you to stay for as long as you like. Spend Christmas with us.'

Jean had been wondering what was going to happen at Christmas. She was longing to go home to Helensburgh but knew that she needed to take the small person she mentioned next into the equation.

'Is Rosie already getting excited about Christmas?'

Charlotte laughed. 'She's as high as a kite. By the way, she was delighted with that present you sent her last Christmas. I hope you got her thank you letter.'

'I did,' Jean said. 'I'm sorry I didn't write back.'

'We're sorry you haven't kept in touch,' Charlotte said firmly.

'But you understand why?'

'You're a sensitive person, my dear. I'm sure you'll do the right thing. Whatever that turns out to be. It doesn't affect our fondness for you one little bit, you know. Now, do say you'll come.'

Jean came off the phone a few moments later, gently replaced the receiver and then shoved her chair back. 'Ohhhh!' she cried to the empty room. 'Why did I agree to that? Am I aff ma heid?'

She knew Charlotte Lucas's warmth was genuine. She knew the whole family – with the possible exception now of Becky – did like her. She suspected all the same that the Reverend and his wife were hoping they might be able to talk Peter out of a marriage that would force him to give up his vocation. What was it Charlotte had said?

I'd be less than honest if I didn't say we're all dismayed at the prospect of Peter leaving the priesthood. Which he will have to do if you and he get married.

If you and he get married. Not *when*. If.

'There's a Freudian slip if ever I heard one,' Jean muttered, getting up from her desk and wandering through to the interview room. 'And if you don't stop talking to yourself soon, Dunlop, you're going to need the services of one of Dr Freud's colleagues.'

She propped her elbows against the high windowsill, threaded her fingers through the hair she was now wearing in a shoulder-length pageboy cut and gazed out at the grounds. She was desperate to get away from the camp now. The hustle and bustle that had characterised it for so long was completely absent, casting a rather forlorn atmosphere over the place.

The war was over and Jean was profoundly grateful for that fact. It was still possible to regret that the sense of purpose that had bound everyone together for so long had already evaporated.

'You're getting morose,' she told herself. 'Not enough work to do, that's your problem.'

She should be using this time to get a head start on her next book but she couldn't seem to settle to it. She knew she wasn't going to be able to settle to anything until Peter came home and the two of them decided what they were going to do about the future. Those last few hours they had spent together had been so precious, so romantic. It hadn't been the time to discuss practicalities.

Now they were all rushing in on her. Was he prepared to give up his vocation for her? Was she prepared to let him make that sacrifice? Where would they live if they did get married? What were they going to do about Rosie?

The only home the little girl had ever known was the parsonage. There she was surrounded by people she loved and who loved her in return. It would be cruel to uproot her. It was a problem that naturally concerned her father. He had told Jean as much in his most recent letter. He ached to get to know his daughter again but wasn't sure where precisely he was going to do that.

If he and Jean did marry he was going to have to find some other way of earning a living. He had spoken of becoming a schoolteacher but whether he went back to university or college for further training or looked for a different kind of job there would be more opportunities in a big city than in a rural area.

In one of Jean's letters to him – all of them written into something of a void because she had no idea when if ever they would reach him – she had thrown out the suggestion that he come to Helensburgh, well within striking distance of Glasgow.

She knew only too well what was wrong with that idea. It would leave Peter facing an agonising dilemma. Did he pluck his daughter out of the only home she had ever known or did he condemn himself to being Rosie's father only at the weekends and during the school holidays?

Keswick was reachable within the day from Helensburgh. Just. Undertaking that journey on a regular basis would be exhausting, time-consuming and expensive. All the changing from train to train and finally on to the bus would be wearing too. Jean had wondered if they could buy a car and take turns at driving it – before he'd left, Peter had offered to teach her how – but the roads at both ends were narrow and slow-going. You'd no sooner have got there than you'd be turning to come back again.

Rosie was also in school now. She could certainly come to Helensburgh during the holidays but she was bound to be forging friendships with other youngsters. She might well be reluctant to leave her wee friends for too long.

'Which leaves me moving to Keswick,' Jean said aloud, the guddle her thoughts were in making her forget her earlier resolution to stop talking to herself. 'If Peter can find himself a job there. If not, it would be Liverpool or Manchester or Carlisle. Somewhere which the parsonage is at least reachable from.'

She was sure she could make a life and home for herself and Peter and Rosie in any of these places. As a writer, it didn't matter where she lived. In theory. In practice Jean knew that it did. She loved Helensburgh. It had bustle and movement and shops and people when she wanted those things, and long walks by the sea and up into the hills behind the town when she didn't.

She liked Keswick. It had bustle and movement and shops and people too, and it was set in magnificent and inspiring scenery. The craggy grandeur of the Lake District spoke to something in Jean's soul. But it wasn't home. Helensburgh was.

She ached to go home. She'd been away for so long. I want to be able to see the Clyde from my window, she thought. That's what I want.

She wanted Peter too. She had missed him terribly. Every day of this long separation she had felt the lack of his sense of humour, his keen intelligence . . . and his love for her. She hadn't expected ever to be loved like that again. That it came from a man who knew all about her past made it all the more precious.

She was beginning to dream about having a family with him, giving Rosie some brothers and sisters. She had always wanted to have children, envying the happy family life enjoyed by people like Avril and Tom McIntosh. It was becoming a real longing now, a yearning to build something good, solid and true. She could have that with Peter. She knew it was what he wanted too.

'How are you enjoying your freedom, my dear Jean? Are you elated or does it all feel a little strange, even confusing?'

Jean smiled at James Lucas across his dinner table. 'How did you guess? For six years I had to go where I was sent and do the work assigned to me. Sometimes I felt really hemmed in by all of that. But freedom poses its own challenges.'

'Because you have to start making your own decisions,' contributed Matthew Lucas. 'In the services they're all made for you.'

'Exactly,' Jean said, lifting her glass and taking a sip of the wonderfully lush red wine the vicar had produced from his small cellar in honour of her arrival. 'I wondered if people like you, who were in the front-line and facing danger on a daily basis, might feel differently. Often thought I should just count my blessings because I was safe.'

'I'm extremely glad to be safe again,' replied the vicar's son, waving his fork in the air. 'But we do all have loads of decisions to make now. That's quite a daunting prospect too.'

His older brother, Simon, grinned at Jean. 'Right now, I think the most daunting prospect is who's going to be allocated the last scrapings of this delicious pudding Ma's managed to whip up out of nothing.'

Everyone laughed, but Jean hadn't missed the look which Charlotte and James Lucas had exchanged. Their younger son was right. There were loads of decisions to be made and it was quite a daunting prospect.

Sitting on the opposite side of the table from her, Becky Lucas all at once came out with an odd little exclamation, almost immediately stifled. The next thing Jean knew, a pair of strong-fingered hands were covering her eyes.

'Guess who?' asked a well-loved voice.

'Good job Rosie had already gone to bed when you made your dramatic entrance into the dining room last night,' Jean said the next morning as she walked to the lake with Peter. 'You wouldn't have stood a chance of tiptoeing in unannounced if it had been her who had spotted you in the doorway rather than Becky.'

'I know,' he laughed. 'My eardrums are still recovering from the welcome my delicately raised little daughter gave me this morning. To think I was worried that she'd see me as some sort of stranger rather than her daddy.'

'I understand it's largely Becky's doing that she doesn't. Apparently it's usually her who puts Rosie to bed and she always makes sure she kisses your photograph before she goes to sleep. And everyone here talks about you to Rosie.'

'She's a great kid,' Peter said. 'Becky, I mean.'

'You know, Peter,' Jean said carefully, 'Becky's not really a kid any more. She's twenty-two. I'd been through quite a lot by the time I was that age.'

'I still think of Becky as a kid. Take my hand now that we're out of sight of the house?'

They were both being scrupulously careful to avoid embarrassing their hosts with any overt displays of affection. There had been a snatched kiss on the upstairs landing shortly before the Lucas household had turned in for the night. Apart from the bear hugs all round when Peter had appeared, the physical contact between him and Jean had been extremely limited.

This afternoon was the first time the two of them had been alone together since he had got back. Charlotte Lucas had orchestrated that, saying a firm 'no' to Rosie when she had wanted to go along too. She had also reassured Rosie's doubtful father that the child would get over her disappointment within minutes of him and Jean leaving the parsonage.

'You and Rosie have all the time in the world now!' she'd told him brightly. 'Days and weeks and months when you can get to know each other again!'

'This is where I first kissed you,' Peter said dreamily as they strolled towards the lych-gate.

'Was there any point to that statement?' Jean murmured.

'Oh, yes,' he said, and proceeded to demonstrate exactly what his point was.

'That's better,' he said some time later. 'Don't you think that's better?'

'Mmm,' Jean said, her voice muffled by the way they stood.

Her arms wrapped about his middle, she had her head against his shoulder, tucked in under his chin. He was home and he was safe and he was unhurt and he was holding her tight. What more could she want?

'I like the way you're wearing your hair.'

'Thought you might. That's why I had it styled this way.'

'You did it for me? That's nice.' He pulled back far enough to kiss her brow before drawing her back into his embrace.

'Thought we were going for a walk along the lake.'

'We can see it from here. Where's your hurry? As Charlotte said, we've got all the time in the world now.'

'Peter . . .' Jean said against his chest, 'I don't know if that's really the case. Do you not think some decisions are going to have to be made fairly soon?'

'There's no great rush, is there? It's so nice to be able to relax.'

She opened her mouth to speak again and thought better of it. He was entitled to relax. He must be tired after everything he had been through in the past year. He must be exhausted. 'Do you want to talk about any of it?'

'Not yet. Is that all right?'

'Perfectly all right. Let's go down to the lake now. You don't need to speak at all if you don't want to. We can simply enjoy the beauties of Nature.'

It was an hour later before they strolled back up from the shore and found themselves once more passing under the lych-gate.

'Sunday tomorrow,' Peter said, as they took the path through the graveyard and approached the main door of the church.

'You'll be going to the service to give thanks for your deliverance?' Jean said awkwardly, feeling that something was required but not quite knowing what that something

425

was. This was one area of his life she couldn't share with him.

'I've done that already,' he said matter-of-factly. 'I spent some time in the church before breakfast this morning. But yes, of course I'll be going tomorrow.'

She knew what was coming next. She willed him to receive the silent message she was transmitting. *Don't ask me. Please don't ask me.*

'I can't, Peter,' she said when her attempt at telepathy fell flat on its face. 'I can't come to church with you and the family tomorrow morning.'

'Get the words right, Jean,' he said mildly. 'What you mean is that you *won't* come to church tomorrow. You don't think you could bring yourself to do it even as a politeness to your hosts?'

'Are you trying to convert me?' she asked, striving to keep her voice light. 'Because I should warn you right now that it's not going to work. I was finished with God a long time ago.'

'He's not finished with you. He'll never be finished with you.'

She stopped, making him stop too. 'Peter, if you keep this up we're going to fall out. I know my own mind.'

'OK, OK,' he said, raising his hands in a gesture of surrender, 'but you don't blame me for trying, do you? Give me a smile. You look too solemn.

'That's better,' he said when she responded. 'One more kiss before we go back in and have to behave ourselves?'

'Now you're pushing your luck.'

'Oh, I don't think so,' he murmured. 'Come here, ma bonnie wee lassie.'

Jean groaned happily, and went into his arms.

★ ★ ★

'Can't persuade you to come with us, Jean?'

'No, thanks,' she said, looking up from the magazine that lay open in her lap. James Lucas appeared to impose no restrictions on anybody's reading matter on a Sunday. 'I'll hold the fort here,' Jean told his wife now. 'Keep an eye on the roast and set the table for lunch.'

'You're a dear,' Charlotte Lucas said. 'See you later, then.'

Jean kicked her shoes off, curled her legs up beside her on the sofa and bent her head over the magazine. There must be at least one article in here that would hold her attention . . .

Somebody coughed.

'I thought everybody had gone to church,' she said as she looked up.

'Everybody but you,' said Becky. 'He'd be so happy if you came, you know.'

Jean closed the magazine and laid it aside. 'I take it we're not talking about your father.'

'You know we're talking about Peter.'

'He and I have to sort this out between ourselves, Becky,' Jean said carefully. 'I don't mean to be rude but I'm afraid it's not something I'm prepared to discuss with anyone else. I simply don't feel the need to explain myself or my views.'

'It would mean so much to Peter if you were to open your heart to God.'

'I'm not prepared to discuss this with you, Becky,' Jean said, feeling the familiar irritation at the assumptions Christians always made. Where did they get that certainty from that their God even existed and was constantly watching over them and everybody else? 'Don't you think you should go over to the church now? You'll be late.'

'I love him,' Becky said abruptly. 'Do you?'

Jean drew in a quick breath. 'That's a very personal question.'

Her interrogator ignored that startled protest in favour of spelling out the very personal question. 'Do-you-love-him?'

Jean looked up at the girl from the depths of the sofa and couldn't think what the answer to that question was.

'Last time you were here you told me you didn't love Peter.'

'I believe I told you that I was extremely fond of him. My feelings on that point haven't changed. If anything, they've deepened.'

'But do you love him? As a woman should love the man she's intending to marry? Do you think he loves you?'

'Yes. I think he does.'

'That's enough for you? Aren't you in danger of settling for second best?'

Aren't you? If I give him up and he turns to you for comfort? Jean bit back that retort. It was too cruel. 'The days when I dreamed of a fairy-tale romance are long gone, Becky. When you're a bit older you might understand that.'

'Don't patronise me.'

So there's some steel here, Jean thought, studying the determined set of Becky's mouth. Then again, didn't I recognise that when I first met this girl?

'I'm sorry,' she said, meaning it. 'I apologise. But I was only trying to speak the truth.'

'Which is? As you see it, that is?'

'I believe Peter and I could be very happy together. Respecting the differences which undoubtedly exist between us. Respecting one another's points of view.'

'Faith in God is a bit more than a point of view.'

'Not in my book.'

'I think that's my point.'

'I think it's mine too,' Jean said. She ran a hand through her hair. 'Becky, why did you suggest to your mother that she invite me here for Christmas if this is how you feel? Were you doing your Christian duty or something?'

She hadn't meant that to come out sounding both so bitter and so flippant. She might have had a bellyful of people doing their Christian duty by her when she'd been a girl at the manse but that didn't stop her from recognising that the Lucases were Christians of a different sort. They both felt and demonstrated loving kindness for their fellow human beings. As Becky Lucas did now.

'Jean,' she said earnestly, 'if Peter and you decide to get married I'll do my best to be your friend.'

Jean tried a smile. 'There's a *but* in there somewhere.'

'Several of them.'

'Shall I list them, then?' She counted them off on her fingers. 'Peter having to leave the priesthood. Me being unable to support him even as a member of the Church. What's going to happen about Rosie.'

'All of those. But I think the really big question is whether or not you really love Peter enough for his sacrifice to be worth it. Peter deserves to *be* loved,' Becky said passionately, 'not just to be the one who does the loving. Can I ask you to think about that, Jean? I'd better get over to the church now.'

Jean sat for a long time after the younger girl had left, the discarded magazine lying forgotten at her side.

Can I ask you to think about that, Jean?

She was thinking about a lot of things, turning them over in her mind.

She was thinking about Peter. She was thinking about Becky Lucas. Becky Lucas who loved Peter Hilton so much that she was prepared to extend the hand of friendship to the woman who had stepped between her and the man she loved. Becky's love for Peter must be as deep as the ocean, the sort of

429

love that was willing to make sacrifices and never count the cost of those sacrifices.

Jean had experienced that sort of love. From both sides. She had been loved, and she had been the one doing the loving.

She was so far inside her own thoughts she remembered she was supposed to be keeping an eye on lunch only when the smell of roasting meat began to drift through from the kitchen.

'A walk?' Peter queried that evening as he came back downstairs after reading Rosie her bedtime story. 'In the dark?'

'It's a mild night.'

'And you want to scare yourself by walking round the graveyard? Come on, then.'

She waited until they had reached the lych-gate. 'Peter, I think I should go home tomorrow. Leave you to follow on when you're ready.'

'But we've arranged that the two of us are heading north next week,' he protested. 'So I can spend New Year with you in Scotland. You've promised me parties and festivities,' he said, a smile in his voice.

'You can still have them. I'm going on ahead, that's all. It'll give me a chance to get the sheets aired and all that sort of thing.'

He laid a hand on her shoulder. 'And the real reason you want to leave, Jean?'

Her eyes had grown accustomed to the dark now. She could see his face quite clearly. 'I feel a bit surplus to requirements here,' she said awkwardly. 'You're all family and I'm not.'

'Of course you are,' he protested, bending forward and kissing her. 'You'll soon be properly family. And you can't spend Christmas on your own.'

'Why not? That's exactly what I'd like to do. I miss my home, Peter. I've been away from it a long time and I want to go home.'

His eyebrows went up. 'Would this have anything to do with me having been closeted in Reverend James's study for an hour this afternoon?'

'No. And I don't blame him for trying to talk you out of marrying me, either. If I were in his shoes I'd be doing exactly the same thing.'

'He wouldn't do that.'

'No,' she sighed, 'I don't suppose he would. Although I presume he's been encouraging you to give the problem over to God and let Him sort it out. That is how you Christians operate, isn't it?'

Peter gathered her into his arms. 'All I know right now is that I love you and that I don't want you to leave. Please stay.'

'I need to go home, Peter. I need to get away from here.'

'Here's a compromise. What would you say to you and me and Rosie going into Keswick tomorrow? We'll make an afternoon of it, do some Christmas shopping and have tea at one of the hotels.'

'All right,' Jean said reluctantly. 'All right.'

' "Under New . . ." ' Rosie had succeeded in reading the first two words of the banner draped above the doorway of the hotel but the third one had foxed her.

' "Management," ' her father supplied, beaming with pride at this evidence that his daughter could now read. ' "Under New Management," Rosie. It means they've got a new person in charge of the hotel. Usually means that the place is looking up.'

'Don't be silly, Daddy. How can a place look up? It's not a person.'

After a carefully straight-faced Peter had explained that conundrum to his daughter, the three of them walked through the lobby to the reception desk. 'When I first came here,' Peter said, 'this was *the* hotel in Keswick. Nice to see it being spruced up again.'

One of the two young women behind the desk looked up as they approached.

'I phoned this morning to book a table for afternoon tea. Party of three, name of Hilton.'

'They have the reservation book through in the restaurant, sir,' the girl said. 'If you'd care to make your way through . . .' She pointed across the lobby. 'Those double doors over there.'

'I must just go and powder my nose,' he said, throwing Jean a grin. 'Will you wait here for me, my girls?'

The sound of hammering caught Jean's attention. 'Not in the dining room, I hope?' she asked, swinging back round to look at the receptionist.

'Next door to it,' the girl said apologetically. 'We're completely renovating the ballroom so you'll have to excuse us a little noise. We do try to keep it down over mealtimes but we're rushing to finish it in time for the grand opening on Christmas Eve. Not everything will be ready but the floor's in. The boss says that's the most important thing.'

'He's absolutely right. Have you put in a sprung floor?'

'I have to admit that I don't know,' the girl confessed. 'But here comes the man himself. He'll be able to answer that question for you. Oh, someone's just waylaid him.'

Jean heard the laugh before she turned to look in the direction the receptionist had indicated. It was a wonderful sound, halfway between a guffaw and a chuckle.

The man who had made it had his back to her, talking animatedly with another man, one hand clapping his shoulder in appreciation of whatever the joke had been. His hair was very thick, very wavy and very black. As black as a raven's wing. Wasn't that the expression?

He gave the other man a final pat on the shoulder and wheeled round. And Jean found herself face to face with a ghost.

Chapter 48

'JEAN?' NARROWING his eyes, Andrew walked forward. 'Is it really you, Jean?'

'Last time I looked.' She'd thrown the glib answer out like a shield, an instinctive gesture of protection. Completely bemused, she watched him walk towards her. He was smiling, and she thought he meant to shake her hand. She took a firmer hold of Rosie's shoulders with both of hers.

'You're here because you got my letter?'

'What letter?'

'The one I sent you a month ago. Via your publishers. Thought they would know where to find you.'

'They don't know I'm here. They'll have sent it to—' She caught herself on. 'To my home in Scotland.'

An insistent little hand was tugging at her skirt. 'In a minute, Rosie,' Jean said absently.

'I need to go to the bathroom. I need to go to the bathroom *now*!'

Andrew looked down. Then he beckoned to one of the girls behind the reception desk. 'Kindly accompany this young lady to the appropriate facilities. Don't worry, Jean,' he said as the two of them stood and watched Rosie trotting happily off with the girl, 'the ladies' room is just over there. She'll hardly be out of your sight.' He swung back to look at her. 'She is yours, I take it?'

'No. She's the daughter of a friend. What on earth are you doing in Keswick?' That question had come out wrong. She sounded as if she was accusing him of a crime. Guilty of being in the Lake District without a licence.

'I might ask you the same thing, Jean,' he said mildly. 'Since you asked first, I'll tell you. I'm the manager and proud new owner of this hotel. You?'

'I have friends who live nearby.'

'The wee lassie's parents?' Andrew's eyes went to her left hand and rested briefly on the soft gleam of old gold and antique garnets before rising to her face. 'You haven't married again?'

'No. You?' She didn't know why she'd asked him that. It was nothing to do with her if he'd married again. She couldn't care less whether he'd married again or not.

'No,' he said. 'I haven't.'

'What's this letter you're talking about?' Not very sure why she had asked him that either, she felt a hand settle on her shoulder.

'What have you done with my daughter, Jean? And are you going to introduce me to your friend?'

She was in a dream. Or maybe a nightmare. 'Andrew, this is Peter Hilton. Peter, meet Andrew Logan.'

Peter's startled little gasp ruffled the smooth fall of her hair. He proved his membership of the nation that had spent several centuries perfecting the art of the stiff upper lip all the same. Leaning past Jean, he offered his hand and a smile. 'Jean's former husband? I'm hoping to be her future one.'

Andrew's eyes travelled from Peter's face to Jean's and back again. 'Congratulations. When's the happy day?'

'We haven't had time to make the arrangements yet,' Jean said sharply. 'Peter's only just got home—'

'— and Jean wasn't very far ahead of me,' he put in, his hand squeezing her shoulder.

Telling me to relax, she thought, and he's perfectly right. I'll be cool, calm and collected. I'll be polite and friendly and civilised. And there's no reason on earth why I have to justify anything to Andrew Logan.

'You've both been serving in the forces?'

Peter nodded. 'Jean as a welfare office in the ATS and myself as a chaplain with the army.'

Andrew raised his eyebrows. 'You're a clergyman?'

'I'm afraid so,' Peter said with a warm and easy laugh. 'Look, I'm not sure what the proper etiquette is – especially with you being in charge here – but would you like to join us for tea? You two must have a lot of catching up to do.'

Jean was resolutely avoiding Andrew's gaze. She was only too well aware that the inky-blue eyes were on her face. She could feel them.

A look as strong as touch, she thought, and found herself travelling back to the last time he had touched her. It had been that awful night on the railway station platform at Nairn. He had reached out his hand and brushed her cheek with his fingertips. *Good-bye, Just Jean*. That's what he had said. *Good-bye, Just Jean* . . .

'What?' she said, suddenly aware that Rosie was back from the toilet and that the two men who'd been standing behind and in front of her had changed position and were now both gazing quizzically at her. 'Mr Logan asked you a question, Jean,' Peter said.

She was forced to meet those eyes at last. At least he didn't make her pretend that she'd heard whatever the question was that he had put to her. 'I was asking how you would feel about me taking your fiancé up on his invitation to join you for tea, Jean.'

Don't ask me how I feel about that. I don't bloody know. That was what she wanted to say. She seemed to have been struck dumb. The silence lengthened.

'Perhaps it's not such a good idea. In any case, I have someone coming in to see me at half-past four.' Andrew took a step back. 'Enjoy your afternoon tea.'

'How much do we owe you?' asked Peter half-an-hour later. He sounded rather subdued. The tea and scones had been delicious, their surroundings pleasant and the service excellent. Only the youngest member of their party had seemed to appreciate any of it.

'Nothing, sir,' said the neat waitress. 'It's on the house. Orders from the top.'

Jean made a strange little noise. Peter sent her a warning look across the table. 'Don't make a fuss about it, Jean.'

'I don't want our bill written off,' she said. 'I don't want that!'

Clearly nonplussed, the waitress looked first at her and then back at Peter. 'It's all right,' he assured the girl as he put his wallet away. 'Please give Mr Logan our thanks.'

Twenty minutes later they were sitting side-by-side on the bus, being shaken about by the enthralling combination of the picturesque roads of the Lake District and a vehicle that had spent far too many years driving over them.

'Please don't subject me to the silent treatment, Jean. That's not going to get us anywhere.'

She turned from her contemplation of trees and fields and dry-stone walls snaking their way up hills and fells, and gazed at him across Rosie's head. Held securely in her father's arms, she was fast asleep, worn out by the excitement of her day. 'Isn't it?'

'I think you and he need to talk, Jean. It was obviously a

437

huge shock for both of you meeting up again like that.'

She tilted her head against the cool glass of the window. 'It was a shock. But he and I have nothing to talk about.'

'Look,' Peter said, concern in his beautiful brown eyes, 'I'm not exactly delighted that he's appeared out of the blue like this either. Nor am I exactly delighted that he's living and working in Keswick. But we can't pretend that he's not here.'

'Can't we?' Jean asked, a tiny smile playing about her mouth.

Peter mimed a punch to her shoulder. 'No. If there's anything unresolved between the two of you I'd like to know about it.'

'There's nothing unresolved between Andrew Logan and me,' she said. 'Come on. This is our stop.'

There had been no appointment at half-past four, nobody coming in to see him. The lie had sprung easily enough to his lips when he had looked at her pale and strained face and seen how much she hated the thought of even sitting down and drinking a cup of tea with him. Could he blame her for that?

Andrew sat at the desk in his private office, his elbows on its hard wooden surface and his fingers threaded through his hair. No, he couldn't. He couldn't blame Jean for anything.

He'd intended to stay where he was until he could be sure that she had left the hotel. He was still there at six o'clock when his sister pushed open the door to his office. Chrissie Logan snapped on the overhead light.

'Why are you sitting here in the dark?' she asked cheerfully. The expression on her face changed when her brother looked up at her, blinking in reaction to the sudden illumination.

'Andy?' she queried, walking forward to the desk. 'Are you all right?'

'No,' he said flatly. 'I'm not all right.'

'What's wrong?'

'The awful bloody mess I've made of my life. That's what's wrong, Chrissie.'

Christine Logan rocked back on her heels and folded her arms across her chest. 'Most folk would think you've made a spectacular success of your life, Andy. Especially if they knew where you started off from . . . Ah,' she said. 'You've heard from Jean, haven't you?'

The phone on her brother's desk rang. Christine leaned over, picked it up and answered it. 'I'm afraid he's rather busy at the moment. May I take your name and number and ask him to call you back?' She lifted a pen from the blotter in front of Andrew and began to write on the small white pad next to it. 'Peter Hilton,' she said, repeating the name as she wrote it down.

Deep in Andrew's eyes, a little gleam of light flared. 'I'll take the call, Chrissie,' he said, his hand already reaching for the receiver. 'I'll take the call.'

Chapter 49

'YOU'VE WHAT?'

'Phoned him and asked him to come out here tomorrow afternoon. Charlotte won't mind.'

Jean stared at him. 'Did it occur to you that I might?'

'I never thought you were a coward, Jean.'

'Not wanting to see him makes me a coward?' she asked, stung by the comment. 'I've already told you, Peter. He and I have nothing to discuss. I'm surprised he's even agreed to come out to the parsonage.'

Peter raised his fair brows. 'I'm not. Didn't I overhear him saying something about a letter? Why else would he have written one if he didn't feel the need to speak to you?'

Keep moving. Keep moving. Keep moving.

Jean had lost track of time. This marathon seemed to have been going on for days rather than weeks. She was confused as to how that could be. You weren't allowed to dance on a Sunday, were you? Yet she had no recollection of a rest day punctuating any of these other interminable days.

Keep moving. Keep moving. Keep moving.

The spectators seemed to grow more ghoulish with each passing hour. It was no longer enough for them simply to watch you shuffling your feet around the same small patch of floor as you drew nearer and nearer to exhaustion. Now they were satisfied only if you danced towards it as fast as you could.

'Faster,' they called. 'Faster, faster, faster,' they shrieked. 'We want you to do it *faster*!'

Jean's head was against Andrew's shoulder. 'We're dancing as fast as we can, Andy,' she complained. 'Why don't we give up now? Walk away from it like Jim and Annabel did? Why don't we just go home, Andy?'

'Because we've no home to go to, Jean. That's why.'

His voice sounded funny. She raised her head to look up at him. She couldn't see his face properly. Wasn't even sure it was him she was dancing with. She was confused again. Who else would it be?

Keep moving. Keep moving. Keep moving.

Faster, faster, faster!

Jean was still peering up at Andrew, wondering why she couldn't make out his familiar features. Maybe they were being obscured by the smoke drifting across the floor from the cigarettes of the spectators. Unable to puzzle it all out, she lowered her head once more to his shoulder. And gasped.

She was stark naked. She had no clothes on, and all of these people were looking at her—

Jean woke with a start. When she realised where she was, she subsided back on to her pillows. Just that old dream about the dance marathon. No prizes for guessing why it had chosen now to swim back up from her subconscious.

It didn't mean anything. She wasn't prepared to let it mean anything. She'd be restrained when he called this afternoon, make polite conversation with him. She would resist any inclination he might have for revisiting the past. Either separately or together, there was no point in either of them going there.

As Charlotte and Becky served tea to everyone, the atmosphere was at first rather formal, even a little stiff. Having one divorced person under their roof had obviously been a new experience for the Lucases. Having two – especially when the second one was divorced from the first and was, as far as they were concerned, the guilty party – was clearly a situation for which they weren't quite sure of the etiquette required.

They were, all the same, their usual hospitable selves. Doing their Christian duty by welcoming two sinners into the fold. As Jean watched the Lucas women she thought how stunned and shocked they would be if they knew the real reason why she and Andrew had separated. That story would test their Christian charity to its very limits.

She chided herself for her cynicism. Whatever hopes the Lucases were nursing for Becky and Peter and about keeping him in the Church, she knew they genuinely thought they were helping her by welcoming the man they thought was her erring ex-husband into their home like this.

All Jean wanted was for the visit to be over. Her thoughts were racing, trying to work out how she could avoid being manoeuvred into having a private conversation with him. Despite her preoccupation, she soon realised the tension in the room had relaxed. She had to admit that was in no small measure due to Andrew's warm personality. He was a little quieter than she remembered him being but the charm was still there. The smile flashed as easily as ever.

He was as handsome as he'd ever been too. Maturity had only enhanced his dark good looks, especially when they were complemented by the understated elegance of his clothes. Even in his poverty-stricken youth he'd always had a certain polish. Now he had a real air about him. His black suit was beautifully tailored, cufflinks glinted at his wrists and the striped tie knotted at the throat of a dazzlingly white shirt was made of silk. The sophistication of the outward shell did nothing to conceal the powerful masculinity of the man beneath it.

'You've taken on new staff, Mr Logan?' asked the Reverend, continuing a conversation about the refurbishment of the hotel.

'We're going to need them,' Andrew said warmly. 'We're aiming to bring the place back up to the quality and standard it was famous for before the war.'

'We?' Jean asked before she could stop herself.

'My sister Christine is working with me,' he told her, looking over to where she sat on the window seat of the room. 'You remember her, don't you?'

'Of course I remember Chrissie.' She hoped her voice hadn't sounded too sharp. 'Did she ever manage to go on and study languages?'

'Oh, yes. She's fluent in both German and French.'

'Like yourself, Mr Logan?' Charlotte Lucas suggested. 'I understand that you spent several years in Switzerland. Are you a linguist too? Such a wonderful talent to have.'

'I've always been a good mimic. It helps when you're trying to pick up a language. Especially in a country like Switzerland, which has four official languages and at least twenty-four different dialects. I learned French when I worked in Lausanne, German in Klosters and Zurich, and Italian when I was in Ascona.'

'That's on Lake Maggiore, isn't it?' asked the parson. 'A beautiful part of the world. I remember visiting it in my youth.'

'I suppose all of Switzerland is beautiful,' said Becky Lucas. A shy smile accompanied that observation. He's hard to resist, Jean thought. The charm and the looks, the sense that when he's talking to you he's concentrating on you and you alone . . .

'Much of it's spectacular,' he agreed, smiling back at Becky. 'When the mist isn't rolling down from the mountains and scraping the road.'

'We know all about that here!'

'I have heard the Lakes referred to as the English Switzerland,' Andrew observed once the laughter provoked by that comment from Matt Lucas had faded away. 'Personally I find the place has its own unique charm.'

'You're planning on settling down here, Mr Logan?'

That was Charlotte again, making a little more than polite conversation. Jean wondered if everyone in the room was aware of that fact.

'I may do,' Andrew said pleasantly. 'I may not. It depends how things work out.'

'You're hoping to expand your empire?' asked James Lucas.

'If we make a go of it in Keswick, yes. I'm already half looking for another hotel in Scotland. Probably somewhere on the Clyde Coast.'

Do you have to? Isn't it enough that I'm going to have to put up with you being here? Jean caught herself on. What did it matter to her what he did or where he lived? It didn't matter one iota. He could make a Monopoly board out of the Clyde Coast for all she cared. Cover it with bloody hotels. The vicar moved the conversation back to Switzerland, musing aloud about that country's neutrality during the recent conflict.

'Switzerland's always neutral,' Andrew said. 'Supposedly.'

The Reverend's sharp brain picked up on that cryptic comment. 'A hotbed of intrigue?' he suggested. 'Place for all the spies to meet up with each other?'

444

'I wouldn't know about that,' Andrew said awkwardly. 'I didn't spend much time there during the war.'

Oh, Jean thought, you're wishing Reverend James hadn't asked you that. And you're wishing you hadn't answered it the way you did. Maybe you're not quite so suave and relaxed as you'd have us all believe.

'The ability to speak several languages must be a very useful skill,' Peter said, his eyes narrowing thoughtfully. 'I should imagine that's even more true in wartime.'

The winning smile. That's what they were all getting now. Jean remembered it well. 'Not if you've got a terrible Swiss accent in all of those languages.'

'But a good mimic can presumably acquire any other accent he chooses. Pass himself off as a native wherever he happens to find himself. Like Occupied France, for example.'

Andrew shrugged. His attempt at nonchalant dismissal of the subject failed. Everyone in the room was suddenly alert, the Lucas boys in particular surveying him with a dawning respect in their eyes.

Her cause was lost. Now they were all going to make sure he got to speak to her alone.

'They seem very nice people.'

'They are very nice people. We go this way now,' she said, directing him to the path that ran round the side of the house and through the graveyard to the lych-gate.

'Given your personal history, I was a wee bit surprised to find you associating with the clergy. Especially getting yourself engaged to a minister.'

'A vicar,' she corrected. 'They don't call them ministers down here. How are your mother and your other sisters?' she went on, determinedly polite. 'Are they all well?'

445

'Fine,' he said. 'Apart from Chrissie, all of the girls are married now. Busy with their own families and their own lives. My mother's enjoying being a grandmother.'

'You have nieces and nephews?' she responded, wondering if she was imagining a hidden message in what he had just said. Too busy with their own lives to think of trying to interfere in his? What did she care?

'Lots of nieces and nephews,' he said cheerfully. 'I know them largely through letters and snapshots at the moment but I'm hoping to remedy that in due course. How did you and Peter Hilton meet?'

It was a reasonable enough question, the sort you asked when you were making polite conversation with someone you didn't know very well. 'He came as chaplain to the camp where I was stationed. He joined up after Rosie's mother was killed in the Liverpool Blitz.'

'How sad. He must have been devastated.'

'The Lucases pulled him through. And his faith, of course. Peter's faith is very important to him.'

'But presumably he won't be able to go back to being a vicar. If he marries you he'll be drummed out of the Church. Won't he?'

'That would be the situation as we understand it, yes.' Her voice was clipped. She swallowed hard to relax the tension that had seized hold of her throat. 'If we go through the lych-gate here we'll come down to the lake.'

'That's quite a big decision for him to make, then. You too, of course.'

'Yes,' Jean said as they left the grass and crunched down on to the shingle. 'It's a very big decision.'

'May I ask if it's made yet?'

She stopped dead. 'Can you please say what it is you've got to say and then go?'

Andrew pushed back his jacket fronts, shoved his hands in his trouser pockets and regarded her thoughtfully. 'You look as if you're bracing yourself, Jean.'

She folded her arms across her breasts. 'Why would I be doing that?'

'Because you're anticipating a blow. Oh, not a physical one. I never sank quite that low, did I? Although it might be argued that what I did to you was much worse.'

The breeze was rippling the surface of the lake, making patterns in it. Patterns. Steps. Choices. Consequences. Jean couldn't believe the strength of the anger surging up inside her.

'Do you really think there's anything to be gained by raking over old coals?' Her voice and her throat had tightened again. 'Sheer coincidence has flung us together again. That's all.'

He took his hands out of his pockets. 'It's no coincidence. You've forgotten about my letter. I was coming back to look for you anyway.'

'Why?' she asked. 'So you could tell me you've decided to graciously forgive me for turning myself into a whore?'

Andrew drew in a sharp breath. 'I said some terrible things to you that day. You can't imagine how many times I've wanted to travel back in time and unsay them.'

'A pointless exercise, I would have thought. Given that time travel's an impossibility. As is calling back words which have been said. Once they're out there they can't be taken back. Or forgotten.'

He sent her a look from under his black brows. 'I've read all of your books.'

'That's nice,' she said tightly. 'Although I fail to see what your reading habits have to do with whatever it is that we're discussing here.'

'I thought I recognised a bit of me in one of the characters in the second book.'

'Maybe you were flattering yourself.'

'I don't mean one of your heroes,' he said quietly. 'I mean the villain of the piece in your second novel. The son of the house who charms the servant lassie and then goes off and leaves her pregnant and alone. Abandoning her to her fate. That scene where she walks into the sea and drowns herself and her unborn child is so powerful. I cried when I read that scene, Jean. I cried.'

'Bully for you.' Too angry to keep still, she walked away from him, her movements jerky as she marched over the stones to stand at the water's edge. He followed her, trying to see the expression on her face. She turned her head away so that he couldn't.

'That scene was so vivid, Jean. Did it come from personal experience?'

'I'm a writer,' she snapped. 'I tell lies for a living.'

'I need to know, Jean.' He laid a hand on her arm. 'Dammit, I have a right to know! I've been torturing myself about this ever since I read that passage.'

That brought her head snapping round. 'You need to know? *You have a right to know?*' Her eyes blazed like angry coals. 'You have no right to know anything about me, Andrew Logan! You gave that right up more than ten years ago! Your choice, not mine! And take your hand off my arm! Take your hand off my arm right now!'

He ignored that. 'Have you told Peter Hilton about yourself?'

'Told him what about myself?' she demanded.

'You know what I'm talking about, Jean. Have you told him about your past?'

She opened her eyes wide, doing her damnedest to

substitute sarcasm for the terrifying rage that was beginning to consume her. '*Told him about my past.* Now, there's a phrase to conjure with. You make me sound like Mata Hari.'

'*Have* you told him?'

'That's none of your bloody business, Andy,' she yelled, that version of his name dragged out of her by the strength of her emotions. 'But if you must know, yes! He knows everything there is to know about all of that and he still loves me. Satisfied?'

He took his hand from her arm and stepped back.

'Go away,' she said. '*Please* go away.'

'I can't leave you when you're so upset—'

'Why not?' she howled. 'You did it before!'

He took a moment. When he finally spoke his voice was very flat. 'I'll send Peter Hilton down to you, shall I?'

'Do what you damn well like,' she muttered, and turned her back on him.

By the time Peter came running down to the shore a few moments later, Jean's anger was burning out of control. 'Do you know what he asked me?' she demanded. 'Do you know what he had the unmitigated gall to ask me?'

'Jean,' Peter said urgently, his hands going to her flailing arms. 'Calm down. He's gone now.'

'I told him to go. I don't want ever to see him again. I wish I'd never met him in the first place. That's what he said to me, you know. The night he left me he told me he wished he'd never met me. And now he has the sheer bloody *effrontery* to come wandering back looking for forgiveness or to *deign* to forgive me or to apologise for how he treated me or something. Just so he can feel better about himself. Who the hell does he think he is? Who the hell does Andrew bloody Logan think—'

'Jean,' Peter said again, taking a firmer grip of her arms. 'It's all right. It's all right. He's gone now and I'm here. I'm here with you.' He shook her. He did it hard enough to startle her into silence and to focus her attention on him. He sandwiched her two hands between the two of his. 'Jean,' he said, 'if you allow me to do it, I'll always be with you. I vote we stop shillyshallying and get on with it. Why don't we get married in the New Year? As soon as we can arrange it?'

She didn't hesitate. 'Oh, yes, let's do that, Peter! I really want to do that!'

He swept her up into his arms and hugged her as though both their lives depended on it.

'I've had an idea,' she said. 'Something that might help.'

'Tell me,' he said gently. They were sitting in the lee of the grassy bank above the little beach, his arm around her shoulders.

'I married in a civil ceremony. The Church doesn't acknowledge those, does it?'

'I wouldn't go that far,' Peter demurred. 'I've never much cared for the Church's attitude towards civil ceremonies myself.'

'My point is that maybe some other vicars might consider I never actually was married in the first place. Not in the eyes of God, as it were.'

Peter frowned. 'I don't know about that, Jean. Surely you don't think you weren't properly married?'

'I'm not talking about what I think. I'm considering the possibility that my first marriage having been a civil ceremony might give Reverend James enough leeway to feel able to give us a blessing after a register office ceremony.'

The warm arm around her shoulders stiffened. 'You'd do that for me?'

'I'd do that for you,' Jean replied, patting his jumper-clad chest. He caught her hand and held it.

'I love you.'

Jean looked deep into his eyes. 'And I love you.'

'No you don't.'

'Don't tell me what my feelings are,' she said mildly. 'I love you.'

'Prove it,' he said and bent his fair head once more towards her own.

Chapter 50

J EAN WOKE early on Christmas Eve. Fumbling for the switch of the bedside light, she discovered that it was only ten to five. She turned the light off again and sank back on to her pillows, staring up into the darkness of the room and thinking that today and tomorrow were going to be a bit of an ordeal for everybody. Particularly Becky Lucas.

Peter had at first suggested he and Jean get married in Helensburgh and then return to Derwentwater, presenting the parsonage and its occupants with a *fait accompli*. He'd realised himself as soon as the words were out of his mouth that such a course of action would be impossible: both inconsiderate and deeply hurtful to the Lucases.

'And what about Rosie?' Jean had asked. 'She's got to be a flower girl at her Daddy's wedding. You can't cheat her out of that.'

'I want her to be there,' he'd said. 'Of course I want her to be there. It's just all going to be a bit awkward if we get married from here, that's all.'

Jean tucked her hands behind her head and reflected that *awkward* didn't begin to cover it. She had tried to persuade Peter to delay breaking the news of their intended marriage until after Christmas was over. He was determined to make a formal announcement at dinner tonight. She couldn't budge him on that point.

She wondered if he fully realised what a bombshell he was going to be dropping. He knew the vicar and Charlotte Lucas would be upset because it would mean the end of his church career. He didn't seem to have the faintest idea of how Becky Lucas felt about him. What a thing to do to the girl.

Peter deserves to be loved, not just to be the one who does the loving. That's what Becky had said. Would it be enough for Becky to be the one doing the loving? Hoping, given time, that the love she gave would one day be given back to her?

Was it enough to be the one being loved?

She found Peter in the church an hour and a half later. It was still dark outside but he'd switched on enough lights to cast a soft illumination over the interior of the building.

When she'd been in the ATS Jean had occasionally found herself obliged to attend a religious service but it was a long time since she had voluntarily entered a place of worship. She was surprised by the sense of peace she felt as she walked across the flagstones of this simple and beautiful Lakeland church. She was glad she was able to acknowledge that, glad she could accept how much strength some people drew from the faith that this place represented.

Peter was down at the front, kneeling in prayer. He heard her footsteps, rose to his feet and turned to watch her coming towards him.

'Ah,' he said. 'Do you want to tell me here or outside?'

'Oh, Peter,' she said, 'how did you know what I was going to say?'

'Because I know you better than you'd like to think anyone knows you. Because I knew this was going to happen from the moment I saw you with Andrew Logan in the hotel.

Because I knew this was going to happen when I saw how angry you were with him yesterday.'

Jean shook her head. 'Meeting him again might have helped me make up my mind about this. But I'm not going back to him.' She raised her eyebrows. 'Can't imagine he wants me to, anyway.'

'I don't think you know what he wants. Seems to me you didn't give the poor chap much chance to tell you what he wants.'

'You don't know what he wants, either.'

'Someone does.' Peter pointed heavenwards. 'I've been here praying to Him on behalf of all of us. You, me and Andrew Logan.'

A tear rolled down Jean's cheek. 'You're such a good man, Peter. Far too good for me. And I did want to tell you here. This is where you belong.'

'You don't think you and Andrew Logan belong together?'

'We did once. But too much water has flowed under that bridge. Far too much water.'

'You've decided all the same that you're not prepared to settle for second best?'

'And that I don't want you to settle for second best.'

He came forward and kissed her very gently on the lips. 'I hereby release you from our engagement.'

'Peter, I feel awful about this . . .'

'Don't. For all you know I might be a tiny bit relieved.'

'Are you?'

'Not yet,' he said. 'Can we stay friends?'

'I'd like that. I'd really like that. I do love you, you know.'

'As a friend,' he sighed. 'I do know that. I suppose I've always known that.' He lifted her hands and kissed them in turn. 'But I allowed myself to hope. And I can't bring myself to regret any of it. Our love affair was as beautiful as you are.'

Jean was barely able to speak. 'We will stay friends,' she managed.

'Of course we will. You'll visit Rosie and me and we'll visit you. When she's all grown up she'll ask me how she came to have a Scottish Auntie Jean.'

'I'd love it if she thought of me that way.'

He pressed his lips to her forehead and stepped back. He had kissed her mouth, her hands and her brow. Taking his farewell of her as her lover. 'Then that's how we'll do it.'

'You'll stay in the Church?'

'You think some luckless congregation might be able to find a use for me?'

'They would be a very *lucky* congregation,' Jean said firmly. She glanced down at the ring that sat on the third finger of her left hand and tugged it off. 'I should give you this back.'

Peter plucked it from her fingers and dropped it back into her palm. 'Keep it as a memento of those heady days when you nearly lost your heart to a peddler of opium to the masses.'

'But it belonged to your mother.'

He folded her fingers over it. 'She'd have liked you. Keep her ring. One day you'll have a daughter. When she's all grown up you can tell her the story and give my mother's ring to her. I'd like that.'

'I hope your mother left you another ring.'

'Why?'

All of the love and affection and friendship that she felt for him shone in her eyes as she looked up at him. 'Because you'll need it for the girl you're going to fall in love with who'll love you back as much as you deserve.'

'Don't think she exists, Jean,' Peter said with a wry smile. 'After Susanna I never expected to find anybody else. It took the upheaval of a world war for me to find you.'

She bent forward and kissed him on the cheek. A friend's kiss. 'Maybe she's closer to home than you think.'

And, she thought silently, since she's already proved that she's willing to fight for you, perhaps it won't be too long until you notice that she's there.

Jean pulled her key out of the lock, dropped her luggage in the lobby and walked through to the front room, her footsteps echoing in the empty flat. When she reached the bay window in front of her desk, she stood for a few moments simply drinking in the view. Murky and sleety night though it was, she had the Clyde outside her window. She was home at last.

She turned, heading for the kitchen and a cup of tea to revive her after what had been a miserable journey. Put there by Avril McIntosh as usual, her mail was in the topmost wire basket. Two envelopes down she found the letter that had been redirected to her from her publishers. Only her name had survived the thick black strokes of the pen that had blocked out their address.

He'd chosen to address her by her *nom de plume*. It was written in the copperplate hand he obviously hadn't lost over the years: 'Miss Joanna Colquhoun'.

She stared at it for a moment. Then she lifted it out of the basket, walked quickly over to the fireplace and threw it into the empty grate. Where were the matches? She needed the matches.

She couldn't find them. They were neither on the mantelpiece nor in any of the kitchen drawers. Surely she hadn't run out of them last time she'd been home and forgotten to buy more? She was an organised person. She never forgot about things like that. She walked back through to the front room, carefully avoiding looking in the grate.

At the bay window again, she stood biting the tip of her

thumb and gazing out at the weather. It hadn't improved any in the last ten minutes. The wind had risen, whipping the Firth of Clyde up into galloping white horses. You'd have to be off your head to go back out in that. Jean threw her coat back on, clattered down the stairs to the street and plunged into the gloom.

Ten minutes later she was crouching in front of the grate ready to put a match to the letter. Something stopped her. This was cowardice. She had to read it first. That would round off this story once and for all.

Dear Jean,

I dare say you will be surprised to hear from me after all these years. I hope you are well. I have read and enjoyed all of your books and am sending this letter via your publishers, trusting they will forward it to wherever you are living now. I note from the short biography on the dust jackets of your books that your home is near Glasgow.

I am myself heading north shortly and should be most grateful if you would consider meeting me. Perhaps I could take you out to lunch.

Best wishes,
Andrew Logan

How polite he was. How formal. '. . . and should be most grateful if you would consider meeting me. Perhaps I could take you out to lunch. Best wishes, Andrew Logan'.

She remembered that from the letters he'd written to her all those years ago from the sanatorium. Those letters had contained something else, though. They had contained words of love. Lots and lots of words of love.

She wasn't going to do this. She absolutely wasn't going to

do this. So why, she thought, am I walking through to my bedroom and opening the top drawer of the dressing table? She brought out a quilted satin handkerchief case. She stared at it for a moment before carrying it through to the front room.

She had just lifted the pen, the letters and the wedding ring out of it when her doorbell rang.

Chapter 51

'I THOUGHT YOU had the grand opening of a ballroom to go to.'

'Chrissie's dealing with that. Any chance you might let me in?'

'Why would I do that?'

'Ten minutes,' he said. 'Ten minutes of your time.'

She looked at him. Then she swung the door open. 'Up the stairs.'

He stood in her front room, the sleet on his bare head and shoulders sparkling and twinkling as it melted. She recognised his coat. 'Why are you wearing that old thing?'

'Because it's warm,' he said, patting the navy-blue wool. 'This coat's seen me through some tight corners and chilly nights, I can tell you. I was bloody glad of it between Carlisle and Glasgow. The train was like an igloo.' He swallowed hard. 'Maybe I was also hoping that it might remind you of our shared past.'

'I don't choose to revisit the past,' Jean said tersely. 'I've never seen the point of that particular activity. How did you know where to find me?'

'Peter Hilton gave me your address.' The ghost of a smile played about Andrew's mouth. 'Subjected me to a bit of an interrogation first, mind. He's a good man, Jean. A fine man.'

There was a lump in her throat. She had walked away from that good man. Walked away from that fine man who loved her. And all because of the man who was standing in front of her now. Because she had found herself unable to settle for anything less than the love the two of them had known in that long-lost shared past.

'When did you see Peter?'

'He came to the hotel after he'd seen you on to the train. We bumped into each other on the front steps. I was on my way back to the parsonage.'

'Why were you going there?' She had just remembered that the pen, the letters and the wedding ring were lying on her desk. She moved over to stand in front of them, concealing them from view.

'Because I have three things I want to say to you. Three things I *need* to say to you. What's on the desk that you're trying to hide?'

Jean stepped aside. She wouldn't have put it past him to bodily move her out of the way if she didn't. She watched as he trailed his fingers across the letters and the pen, lingering on the wedding ring. 'I should have thought that a woman who chooses never to revisit the past would have disposed of all of these long ago.'

'I threw the ring across a room once.'

'But you picked it up again?'

'I wouldn't read too much into that. It was making the place untidy, that was all.'

He looked up, and their eyes met. 'I know that I failed you,' he said.

Jean shrugged. 'Maybe it was life that failed both of us. I couldn't help doing what I did and you couldn't help reacting the way you did. You had me up on a pedestal. Unless you're made of stone it's never a very sustainable position.'

'Especially when people make it their business to pull you off it.'

'I stepped off it. I chose to step off it, Andy.'

'You *had* no choices, Jean. Neither of us did. We two were like Hansel and Gretel lost in the forest. We didn't know it but the big, bad wolves were circling our poor wee flickering campfire looking for the first sign of weakness and the vultures were wheeling overhead with exactly the same aim in mind. Did you break off your engagement to Peter Hilton because you think he'll be happier with that girl at the parsonage?'

'You think I'm that noble?'

'You've been known to make sacrifices for the people you love.'

'And those people have been known to fling them back in my face,' she said, and took pleasure in seeing him flinch.

'This isn't an excuse, Jean. I know there is no excuse. But I was young and foolish and immature. And hurt,' he added, his voice not quite steady. 'So terribly, terribly hurt. Lashing out like a wounded animal because of it. Not seeing how viciously my blows were landing.'

'They were landing on me,' she said sadly. 'It was me who was lying there bleeding. And you stepped over me and walked away.'

He took a deep breath. 'Is it too late to ask your forgiveness for that, Jean?'

'It's far too late. And completely irrelevant to the people we both are now. You don't know me any more. I don't know you.' Her voice was flat and dull. 'If you hurry you'll catch the last train back up to Glasgow.'

'Is that what you want me to do?'

'Yes. That's what I want you to do.'

She heard him close the door and go down the stairs. She heard the street door close behind him. She heard his footsteps

461

on the pavement outside. She heard them stop and wondered if he was looking up at the window, hoping to see her beckoning him back. She waited, and heard the footsteps start up again.

She stared at the floor and calculated when he would be turning the corner into Sinclair Street and walking up to the railway station. It was no distance. In five minutes' time he'd be on the train. In eight minutes' time it would be carrying him out of her life. That was what she wanted. Wasn't it?

Jean continued to stare at the floor for another few seconds. Until it happened. Until the trumpets sounded and the walls she had built around her heart came tumbling down. She didn't hang round to watch the dust rising as the stones crashed to the ground.

Panting with exertion and the terror of having lost her balance on a patch of ice and nearly fallen flat on her face on to the pavement, Jean flung into the station. The train to Glasgow was swaying out from the end of the platform. She watched until the red lamps on the back of the last carriage were the merest pinpoints of light in the distance.

That was it, then. She was too late. She fastened the corded frog fastenings of her coat against the chill of the night and dug into its pocket for her cigarettes.

The voice came from behind her.

'Just Jean?'

Chapter 52

WHIRLING ROUND in a swirl of blond hair and black coat, she saw him nod in the direction of the departed train. 'I'm not on it.'

She tapped out a cigarette and placed it between her lips. 'So I see.'

'You shouldn't smoke those things, you know. Filthy habit.'

Jean took the unlit cigarette from her mouth and thrust it into one pocket of her coat and the packet it had come out of into the other. Not because she was following his recommendation. So he wouldn't be able to see how much her hands were shaking. She mimicked his own apparently casual tone of voice. 'How many times do I have to tell you to go away before you'll do it?'

'Always at least one more time. I was coming back to your flat now, as a matter of fact. Planning to go down on my knees to you if I had to. Gluttons for punishment, us faithless lovers.'

'I thought that was my role.'

'Weren't you listening to anything I said? You kept faith with me, Jean. It was me who broke it with you. You never let me tell you those three things.'

'Tell me them now.'

'I love you. I've never stopped loving you. If I had any doubts about that they evaporated the moment I turned round the day before yesterday and saw you standing there in the foyer of the hotel.'

'Oh,' she said. 'What's the third thing you want to tell me?'

'That I want us to start again.'

'Oh,' she said again, and thought about how she had felt when she had turned round in response to that so well-remembered laugh and seen him standing in the foyer of the hotel. And of how she had felt when he had touched her arm as they stood on the shores of Derwentwater.

'I'm not entirely sure if you think it's good news or bad news that I'm not on the train. Could you maybe see your way clear to giving me a wee clue about that, Jean?'

Out of sight in her pockets, she curled her fingers into fists. 'If it was bad news would I have come running in here like something out of the Ride of the Valkyries?'

'That's what I was hoping,' Andrew said. 'Although as far as I'm concerned, the ball's still in your court.'

'Can't you make deductions based on my behaviour?'

He adjusted his stance, extending one leg a little to the side. He looked very graceful. Like the dancer he was. 'You find it so hard to tell me what you're thinking?'

'I find it hard to tell anyone what I'm thinking. I'm afraid life has taught me that giving other people any information about myself gives them too much power over me.'

'You used to be such a trusting girl,' he said lightly.

Jean transferred her gaze to a seagull the size of a small dog standing looking for all the world as if it had just seen somebody off on the Glasgow train.

'Too trusting. And I'm not that girl any more. As you're not that boy you once were. We don't know each other any more. Not as we are now.'

'Then we'll get to know each other. I expect it'll be a fascinating voyage of discovery.'

464

'It might not always be a very calm one. I'm still angry with you. For all I know you're still angry with me.'

'I don't know about that. But if we travel through some storms and squalls so much the better. Life won't get boring.'

'I'm scared,' she said. 'Really, really scared.'

'I know,' he said gently. 'But you don't have to be. I love you.'

Jean stopped studying the seagull. 'I can't say the words yet.'

'I know that too. I'm going to have to earn them.'

'You really think it would be easy to take up where we left off?'

'Not always. It would be no fun if it were.'

'Fun?' She said the word as though she had no idea what it meant.

Andrew's face softened. 'You look tired, Jean.'

'I am tired. I'd like . . .' She stopped, and he looked curiously at her.

'What would you like?'

'Peace,' she said. 'And fun. Fun would be good too. I'm not too old to have some fun, am I?'

'You're thirty. A slip of a girl still.' He cocked his head to one side. 'You look like a beautiful Russian princess in that black coat. Especially with your hair all windblown as it is now. Beautiful inside and out,' he added, his voice as soft as velvet. 'As you always were.'

'I can't undo the experiences I've had, Andy. They're always going to be there.'

'Of course they are. They've helped make you the woman you are today. I've had a fair few experiences of my own since we last met, not all of which I'm proud of. But they've helped make me who I am today.'

'You really think we could make a go of it?'

'As long as you can forgive me. *Can* you do that, Jean?'

She looked at him, saw the hunger in his face and the hope in his blue, blue eyes. Then she looked up. 'Where's the music coming from?'

He lifted his head too, and listened. 'There must be some flats across the road from the station. If whoever that is keeps playing the music as loud as it must be inside the building they're going to be in trouble with their neighbours.'

'If I'm not mistaken they're treating the folks through the wall to a little number by the late, great Mr Miller and his boys.'

' "Pennsylvania Six-Five-Thousand", to be precise. You like the Glenn Miller sound?'

'I love it. You?'

'Fantastic,' he said. 'So lush and full.'

'Ever danced to it?'

'Now and again.'

'Do the old steps still work or do you *have* to do something like the jitterbug?'

'The old steps are fine if you adapt them. Fit them into the right framework.'

'Take the best from the old and build on it?'

'That would seem to be the soundest plan. Of course, if a couple were going to partner each other again after a long gap they would have to work at it. Build up trust between themselves. It might, as you've pointed out, be a long and rocky road. But I'm willing to take the first steps along it if you are.'

'I have the casting vote?'

'You have to meet me halfway. So I know you really want to do it.' Now his voice was husky. 'So I know you really do forgive me.'

466

She walked forward and extended her hand to him. 'Are you dancing?'

The old, slow-burning smile began to spread across his face. 'Are you asking?'

'I'm asking,' she said, her own mouth beginning to shape itself into a cautious curve.

Andrew stepped forward. 'Then I'm definitely dancing.'

'Good,' she said. 'Because I'd feel a right eejit staunin' here if you were gonnae turn me doon.'

There was a catch in his voice. 'I'd not make that mistake a second time!'

'Well, then,' she said. 'Shall we dance?'

'Give me what's in your pockets.'

He took what she handed him, stepped over to a waste bin and dropped it all in. 'You've smoked your last cigarette.'

'Is that right?' She scowled at him. 'Who made that decision?'

'Me. When I kiss you I want to taste woman, not tobacco.'

'What makes you think I'm going to let you kiss me?'

'Oh, I'm hoping I might be able to cajole you into it. It is my birthday in a week's time. Maybe I'll get a wee kiss for that.'

'You planning on sticking around that long?'

'I'm planning on sticking around for as long as you'll let me.'

'What about the hotel?'

'I'm happy to leave it in Chrissie's capable hands. Time I was looking for that one up here anyway. Maybe you'll agree to come back down with me to Keswick now and again.'

'Maybe I will.' With a little shiver of excitement and anticipation, she felt his fingers close about her own and his right hand come to rest halfway up her back. The champagne feeling. The feeling she'd only ever had with him.

'Tonight's Christmas Eve.'

'It was Christmas Eve when we first met. A lot of years ago.'

'Thirteen of them,' Jean said. 'Unlucky for some.'

He cocked one black eyebrow. 'Don't you know that thirteen is a lucky number? Think of it as a baker's dozen if it makes you feel better. Music's stopped.'

'We'd better hope whoever it is puts on another record. All of this might take quite a long time, Andy.'

'That's all right. My intention is to court you in the old-fashioned way.'

'What would that entail?'

'Boxes of chocoates. Posies of flowers. Walks in the country. Strolls along the bonnie banks of Loch Lomond and trips to the Braes o' Balquhidder to pull the wild mountain thyme. A little hand-holding. That sort of thing.'

'I think I can cope with that. Although I should warn you that I'm a bit prickly these days. Not always terribly gracious.'

'I think I can cope with that. I'll be doing my utmost to earn the occasional kind word, anyway. Ah, here we go. Another number coming up.' He laughed. 'Know the title of this one?'

' "At Last",' she said.

'Seems appropriate. Ready?'

They were in each other's arms and it was as though they'd never been out of them. She felt Andrew take his weight on to his right foot, the signal to her that he was going to move off on his left. 'Go,' he said.

Jean stepped back on her right foot and they were away. Under the gaze of the bemused seagull, and moving together in perfectly matched rhythm and harmony, the two of them began to dance.

The Bird Flies High

Maggie Craig

Glasgow, 1920s. Grinding poverty and violence are an everyday part of Josie Collins' life. Her mother's death has left her alone with an abusive stepfather, struggling to bring up her younger brother and sister. Sadly, the children are taken away and only Josie's secret ambition – to become a reporter on one of Glasgow's newspapers – provides any hope for the future. Geographically it's not a big move but socially it's a million miles away.

Disaster strikes when Josie is sixteen. A tragic love affair leaves her alone and pregnant. Forced to give up her baby, Josie starts a new life under a different name. With renewed determination, she eventually achieves her dream, even enjoying a close friendship with a male colleague. But, although Josie finally begins to enjoy her new happiness, she also realises that she must come to terms with her own past, even if it threatens to destroy everything she's worked so hard to build.

Praise for Maggie Craig's sagas:

'Craig seems to fully inhabit her fictional world in a manner reminiscent of Daphne du Maurier and provides a sensorial feast for the reader' *Scotsman*

'Few writers evoke the senses quite so strongly' *Scots Magazine*

'Maggie Craig, one of the most promising writers of romantic fiction, has all the answers in this spellbinding new book' *Middlesbrough Evening Gazette*

0 7472 6392 2

headline

A Star To Steer By

Maggie Craig

1920s. When her father dies, Ellie Douglas has little option but to go into service. Her position takes her out of the life of Frank Rafferty – childhood friend and now a member of one of Glasgow's notorious gangs – and into the world of Evander Tait – son, heir and black sheep of the Tait household.

These two men dominate Ellie's entire life. No one approves of her friendship with Evander and the bond she shares with Frank is misunderstood by everyone. Both relationships, for very different reasons, threaten to tear her apart. She must make the right choices, but will she be strong enough?

Passionate, spellbinding, packed with emotional highs and lows, Maggie's sagas have won her the hearts of many fans and have been well received:

'Maggie Craig knows her Glasgow and, more importantly, knows how to share that with her readers' *Scots Magazine*

'One of the most promising writers of romantic fiction, has all the answers in this spellbinding new book' *Middlesbrough Evening Gazette*

'Craig seems to fully inhabit her fictional world in a manner reminiscent of Daphne du Maurier and provides a sensorial feast for the reader' *Scotsman*

'[A] heart-warming story' *Peterborough Evening Telegraph*

0 7472 6526 7

headline

Now you can buy any of these other bestselling
Headline books from your bookshop
or *direct from the publisher*.

FREE P&P AND UK DELIVERY
(Overseas and Ireland £3.50 per book)

When the Lights Come On Again	Maggie Craig	£6.99
A Star to Steer By	Maggie Craig	£5.99
A Woman Scorned	Wendy Robertson	£5.99
The Loveday Honour	Kate Tremayne	£5.99
Second Chance of Sunshine	Pamela Evans	£5.99
Every Time You Say Goodbye	June Tate	£5.99
Return to Jarrow	Janet MacLeod Trotter	£6.99
A Mother's Love	Lyn Andrews	£6.99
Keep the Home Fires Burning	Anne Baker	£5.99
The Most Precious Thing	Rita Bradshaw	£6.99
The Girl from Number 22	Joan Jonker	£6.99
No Going Back	Lynda Page	£6.99
Pride and Joy	Dee Williams	£6.99

TO ORDER SIMPLY CALL THIS NUMBER
01235 400 414

or visit our website: www.madaboutbooks.com

Prices and availability subject to change without notice.